Praise for the acclaimed Rai-kirah saga

continued . . .

D0424055

SON OF AVONAR

Book One of
The Bridge of D'Arnath

CAROL BERG

A ROC BOOK

ROC
Published by New American Library, a division of
Penguin Group (USA) Inc., 375 Hudson Street,
New York, New York 10014, U.S.A.
Penguin Books Ltd, 80 Strand,
London WC2R 0RL, England
Penguin Books Australia Ltd, 250 Camberwell Road,
Camberwell, Victoria 3124, Australia
Penguin Books Canada Ltd, 10 Alcorn Avenue,
Toronto, Ontario, Canada M4V 3B2
Penguin Books (N.Z.) Ltd, Cnr Rosedale and Airborne Roads,
Albany, Auckland 1310, New Zealand

Penguin Books Ltd, Registered Offices:
80 Strand, London WC2R 0RL, England

First published by Roc, an imprint of New American Library,
a division of Penguin Group (USA) Inc.

First Printing, February 2004
10 9 8 7 6 5

Copyright © Carol Berg, 2004
All rights reserved

Cover art by Matt Stawicki

 REGISTERED TRADEMARK—MARCA REGISTRADA

Printed in the United States of America

PUBLISHER'S NOTE
This is a work of fiction. Names, characters, places, and incidents either are the product of the author's imagination or are used fictitiously, and any resemblance to actual persons, living or dead, business establishments, events, or locales is entirely coincidental.

BOOKS ARE AVAILABLE AT QUANTITY DISCOUNTS WHEN USED TO PROMOTE PRODUCTS OR SERVICES. FOR INFORMATION PLEASE WRITE TO PREMIUM MARKETING DIVISION, PENGUIN GROUP (USA) INC., 375 HUDSON STREET, NEW YORK, NEW YORK 10014.

For teachers, the overlooked heroes and heroines who illuminate and nurture young minds, who inculcate our values and teach self discipline, who shore up our freedoms, remind us of the lessons of history, and ensure the future of the arts. For a few in particular—Elizabeth Paar and Carol Roehl, Jane Conway, Marcia Stefan, Sister Francesca, Sister Anselma, Robert Patten, David Minter, Katherine Brown—and many others at OLV and Nolan and Rice, who inspired, who shared their devotion to art and literature, or who just flat expected their students to do the difficult, the boring, and the necessary in the name of learning.

CHAPTER 1

Midsummer's Day—Year 14 in the reign of King Evard

The dawn wind teased at my old red shawl as I scrambled up the last steep pitch of the crescent-shaped headland the villagers called *Rif Paltarre*—(Poacher's Ridge. A brisk walk to the eastern edge and I seated myself on a throne of rock as if I were a Leiran duchess attending a midsummer fete. But whereas my girlhood friends might celebrate the longest day of the year by watching jugglers, fire-eaters, and tittering ladies stepping through the spiritless mimicry they called "rustic dances," I beheld color and shape being born from a vast and silent wilderness of gray.

Stretching west for two hundred leagues, stood the snow-capped peaks of the Dorian Wall, their brilliant rose brightening to eye-searing white. To the north swelled the ocean of dark green forest. To the east the ground fell away gently in a stone-bordered patchwork of meadows and farmland to the bronze ripples of the Dun River and the haze-shrouded village of Dunfarrie squatting on its banks. It was a splendid desolation.

As the light grew, I stuffed my water flask into the cloth bag hanging from my belt, snugged the rags I'd wrapped about my hands, and took up the true business of the day—hunting dye plants to barter in the village. The first lesson I'd learned on coming to Dunfarrie, when I had scarcely known that food grew in the ground, much less that it must be coddled and coaxed and worried over, was that those whose bellies are pinched by hunger know nothing of holidays.

In early afternoon, back aching, hands dirty and sore

despite the rags, I abandoned the glare and blustering wind of the heights for a shady clearing of pine trees and oak scrub. I ate a few dried figs, hard and half turned to sugar, and refilled my water flask at the stream that mumbled through the weedy clearing, trying to decide whether to return to the ridge top to dig another bundle of scabwort roots or head down to the cottage and the uncountable tasks that needed doing before sunset.

A spider skittered across the scuffed leather of my boot. A jay screeched. Beyond the stream, something large rustled the bracken—one of Evard's deer, no doubt. No predators, human or beast, frequented the wooded hills behind Jonah's cottage. Nor did enemy soldiers. Leire's current battles were being waged in faraway Iskeran. Nor did sorcerous enchantments lurk in the wild forest, threatening to corrupt the soul. As the priests and people of the Four Realms had demanded for four hundred and fifty years, the dark arts and those who practiced them had been exterminated.

I lifted my head. The rustling came louder, closer, and now accompanied by a muted, rhythmic pounding. Running footsteps . . . human . . . that halted somewhere in the trees to my right. "Who's there?" I called out, scrambling to my feet.

As if from nowhere and everywhere sounded the blast of a horn, the clamor of a hunt sweeping through the forest on three sides: racing hoofbeats, jangling harness, a shouted command not ten paces from where I stood. The runner was closer than that.

"Stay away from me," I said softly, trying to look everywhere at once, "or I'll scream and let them know you're here."

A branch snapped. I whirled about, but saw nothing. Backing slowly away from the hunt toward the downhill side of the clearing, my hand moved slowly toward my slit pocket where I could reach the knife sheath hidden under my skirt. But whatever I thought to do with my pitiful weapon was left undone. A muscular arm reached from behind and wrapped itself about my neck, while another grabbed my waist, crushing my elbow into my ribs. I fought to keep my footing as my assailant dragged me downstream through the water and into a dense tangle of cedar, pine, and juniper. Twigs and sharp, dry underbranches caught in my hair, slapped and stung my face.

My captor's arm was fiercely sunburned, the skin scratched and abraded. The heart pressed so close to my back was thudding ferociously, and his sweat soaked the back of my tunic. He stank of unwashed terror.

I slammed my unrestrained elbow into his belly, tore at his arms, stomped my boot somewhere in the region of his foot, and flailed at his flank—discovering to my surprise that he seemed to be entirely unclothed. When I reached over my head to claw at his eyes, he used my own right arm to bat away my left and tightened his hold on my throat.

The pursuit careened through the woodland, the riders so close, I could almost smell the leather harness and feel the cool steel of their blades. Yet even if I could have mustered a shout or a scream, I wouldn't have done so. I had no illusions that those giving chase were more benevolent than my captor. Such was the state of the vile world. I just wanted to get loose, to get out from between pursuers and pursued. A bizarre struggle . . . both of us wordless, desperate.

My chest hurt. Feebly, I tried jamming my fingers between my windpipe and his arm, but he trapped both my wrists in one broad hand and pinned them to my breast. But just as the black spots before my eyes started swirling together, he shifted backward a few wobbling steps, jolting to a stop as if he'd backed into a tree. My knees buckled and left me sagging against his arm, and either the change of position or some release on his part allowed me to gulp a bucketful of air.

The day fell unnaturally quiet. The noisy pursuit had passed us by, but the more ordinary sounds—the bawling of crows, the rustle of rabbits scrabbling through dead leaves—had not yet resumed. Only the faint mumble of the stream accompanied my captor's breathing. While his chest heaved with harsh, shuddering gasps, painfully muffled, I dangled from his grip like a scrawny chicken waiting to have its neck wrung. *Filthy bastard.* I knew how desperate men were likely to release pent-up fear and anger when a vulnerable woman was within their reach, and I was having none of that. The slight quiver beneath his flesh hinted at weakness, and the sweaty hand that held my two wrists was trembling. One chance, perhaps . . .

I wrenched my hands from his grasp, clawed at his arm, and tried to duck my head under it. But weakness is a relative thing. With devastating speed, and strength that came near cracking my spine, the man growled and spun me about, grabbed my wrists again, and slammed my back against the bole of an oak, his other hand clamped about my throat.

He was big—tall and broad in the chest and shoulder. His face was a blur of white, red, and brown: fair hair, blood, sun, dirt, terror . . . no . . . fury, not terror. . . . I assumed I was going to die before I could see him with any clarity. But all at once, as if wrenched by an unseen hand, he snatched his hands away and staggered backward.

I took a full, satisfying, sight-clearing breath, and willed bone back into my knees. The naked young man—indeed he wore not a stitch—stood motionless. His limbs and torso were powerfully muscled and threaded with bloody scratches, his pale hair unkempt, and his eyes a startling blue, the deep, rich color of lapis, fixed on my face as if he had never seen a human person before.

Trying to hold his eyes engaged, I slid sideways a finger's breadth. My skirt snagged briefly on the tree. Another step. Then I felt nothing behind me. I spun on my heel and bolted.

Damn and blast! Two steps and I was sprawled on the forest floor, my mouth full of dirt and pine needles, my chin stinging. I scrabbled forward, trying to get my treacherous feet under me, half turning backward, expecting to see his hands reaching for me again. But the man had not moved a step. Instead he had extended his hands palms up, as if dedicating a sword at the temple of Annadis. Ripping my skirt loose from the brambles, I lurched to my feet and backed away, then turned and darted a bit more carefully down the hill. One last glance over my shoulder showed him take a single step in my direction, sway drunkenly, and crumple earthward. I didn't stay to watch him hit.

*   *   *

By the time I reached the lower boundary of the forested hills, neither feet nor pulse were racing any longer, but my thoughts lingered back on the ridge. Those unbelievably blue eyes might have been the single spot of color in a painting rendered entirely in shades of gray. He hadn't the look of any poacher I'd seen locked in the Dunfarrie pillory. Desperate, but without the ravenous derangement of a starving peasant. Skilled at violence, but lacking the reckless competence of the professional thief. He hadn't broken my neck.

The stream pooled in a weed-choked depression at the edge of the trees before meandering sluggishly across the dry meadow. Shooing away a cloud of gnats, I dropped to my knees by the pool and doused my face and neck, wincing as the cool water stung my scraped chin and the skin left raw and bruised by his wide hands. I didn't care what else he was. He was a brute. I'd wager that all of them were brutes—villain and hunters together.

Mumbling oaths like a common soldier, I straightened my skirt and yanked at my shift, which had gotten uncomfortably twisted beneath my shapeless tunic. As if my clothes weren't threadbare enough, I'd have to pull out my cursed needle to repair the rips. Drying my hands on my skirt, I set out across the meadow toward the squat, sod-roofed shack that was my home and the weedy garden that kept me living.

After a few hot hours of work, the immediate annoyances of turnip beetles and wire-like threadweed had pushed the incident to the back of my mind. The threats of persistent drought and harsh Leiran winters hung over my head like a heavy-handed schoolmaster, requiring me to work as hard as I could manage from dawn to dusk every day of the year. The work occupied only back, shoulders, and hands, though; my intellect was as dull as the flat, unvarying landscape east of the river. As I yanked at the stringy weeds choking my tender plants, I kept a wary eye on the ring of trees that bounded the meadow, but the morning's misadventure soon took on the quality of an uncomfortable dream . . . until the hunting party arrived.

In late afternoon, five horsemen came galloping across

the meadow from the direction of the village path. I kept at my work. No use in running. No use in wishing for a weapon more serious than my scratched dagger, still solidly and discreetly fixed to my thigh under my skirt. I didn't even look up when the dust of their arrival settled on the turnip leaves, and the massive presence of five snorting, overheated horses surrounded me. We take small victories where we can.

"I don't get many visitors," I said, yanking a snarl of threadweed from the dry soil.

"Isolation does not suit you, my lady."

My eyes shot upward to the trim, dark-haired man who urged his mount into the middle of the garden and halted right in front of me. "Darzid!" I searched deep for the proper expressions of contempt, of wounding, of hatred, furious that words of sufficient pith and clarity would not come at my beck. Captain Darzid—my brother's right hand, his chief aide, his lieutenant in all things despicable.

He jerked his head at the cottage. "After all these years, my first visit to your charming little refuge, and, sadly, I've no time to dally." As ever, amusement glinted in eyes as cold and sharp as black diamonds; the smile that creased his tanned, trim-bearded face held no more warmth. "I'll have to return for a tour another day."

"Are you here to exhibit your wit, Captain? Or perhaps to demonstrate your skill at confronting dangerous women? I'm sorry no infants are available to slaughter, or you could display your inimitable courage. But then, you didn't bring Tomas to show you how it's done, did you?"

Darzid's smile only broadened as he waved his companions toward the cottage and the solitary copse of willows and alders clustered about a muddy spring two hundred paces away. Two soldiers dismounted and entered the house; two rode for the copse. "Your brother is otherwise occupied today. He'll be as surprised as I to learn that this hunt has led me past your doorstep." His long thin hands—the grotesque scarring on the palms the result of some long-ago battle, he'd once told me—stroked the neck of his restless stallion. "Ah, lady, when will you realize that your battles are lost and your grievances long forgotten? These men don't even know who you are. Our search has nothing to do with you."

Returning my attention to my work, I shifted down the row and yanked on a spike-leafed thistle as if it were Darzid's honeyed tongue. "So who is it you seek? Has some peasant failed to tithe his full measure to our king?"

"Only a horse thief, the ungrateful servant of a friend of Duke Tomas. Your brother owes the lord a favor and has sent me to chase down the rascal. He seems to have vanished hereabouts. You've not seen him—a tall man, so I understand, young, fair-haired, a bit unsteady of temper?" Darzid's words were cool, unruffled, mocking, revealing nothing of his true purpose, but then, I would have expected flames to shoot from his mouth before I would have expected truth. Yet, in the pause as he awaited my response, I felt something more—a pressure, an intensity I had never noted in all the eighteen years I had known this meticulous soldier who hovered in detached deviltry about the bastions of power. I glanced up. He was leaning toward me from the saddle, all smiles vanished for that moment, his very posture trying to squeeze an answer from me. Darzid *cared* about this matter. It could be no simple thief he was hunting.

"I've seen no thieves today save you, Captain. And as soon as you leave, I'll drink fish oil to rinse the taint from my mouth and burn dung to cover the stench." Childish taunting, not worthy of my training in scholarly debate. But words helped diffuse the pressure of his scrutiny.

As I turned back to my work, the four soldiers returned with negative reports. Three more riders remained half hidden under the eaves of the forest. They hadn't expected much trouble from me, I supposed. I shuddered when I noticed the three—an inexplicable reaction, for the day was warm and soldiers had no power to frighten me.

Darzid nudged his mount to the edge of the garden and paused, speaking to my back. "So, a wasted venture. Good day, Lady Seriana. Behave yourself. Have you a message for your brother?"

I plucked off three beetles that had left the soft green leaves looking like ragged lacework, squashed them between finger and thumb, and flicked them into the dry grass beyond the garden.

Darzid snorted and spoke a clipped command. The five men spurred their horses, rejoined their fellows waiting at the edge of the trees, and disappeared down the forest path toward Dunfarrie.

For an hour I worked. Dug weeds. Hauled buckets of water from the pool to dribble on the beans and turnips. Salvaged what vines and plants I could from the horses' trampling and threw the ruined ones onto the waste heap. Refused to think of anything beyond the task of the moment.

The sun sagged westward. I stared at the ax waiting beside a pile of logs I had dragged from the forest on a wooden sledge roped to my shoulders. Then I ripped the grimy, blood-streaked rags from my hands, threw them on the ground, and strode back across the meadow, past the pool, and up the hill into the wood.

CHAPTER 2

The long body sprawled face down across the muddy stream bank. I sat on a stump just inside the circular clearing and watched him for a while. A squirrel screeched and nagged at me from an oak limb. Finches and sparrows rose in a twittering cloud beyond the stream, then settled back down on the very branches they had just deserted. High in the forest roof, the leaves shifted in a breeze that could not penetrate the stillness below. No sounds of horses or hunters intruded.

What was I thinking? Mysteries and desperate men were no concern of mine. I had reaped the bitter harvest of my fascination with mystery long ago. And this ruffian had come near strangling me. I should leave him to his own reward.

Yet I had never been accustomed to taking good advice, even my own, and so instead of retracing my path to the valley, I stepped warily across the stream and nudged the body with my boot, rolling him onto his back. His only injuries seemed to be the wicked sunburn, the network of angry scratches, and one slightly deeper gash on his chest. He was dirty. Fair-haired. A strong face, the square jaw unshaven, rather than bearded. He could be little more than twenty, and his big frame was well proportioned— exceptionally well—with nothing to be ashamed of if he ran about unclothed very often. How had he come to be in such a state? Nothing simple, I guessed. Nothing safe. Darzid was hunting him.

I scooped a handful of water from the stream and dribbled it on his cracked lips. They moved ever so slightly. "Thirsty, are you?" I gave him a little more, then pulled the red shawl from my shoulders and covered him. Some country-bred men thought you had to marry them if you saw them naked—another of the uncountable stupidities abroad in the world. I stepped out of arm's reach, watching. Waiting. Maybe he would sit up, say "Sorry, damnable mistake," and run away.

Every passing moment set my teeth more on edge. Pursuers who chased a man out of his clothes were unlikely to leave off. Two times I started down the path. Two times I came back, railing at myself for stupidity. Shadows stretched well across the glade. I detected no untoward sound or movement, but felt a creeping sensation up my back. The air smelled of something that was not hot pine needles or dry forest earth, something as out of place in this woodland as perfume, but far less pleasant: the odor of hot wind across old stone, bearing the unhearable residue of screams and the tainted smokes of unholy fires . . .

I shook off my foolish imaginings. Though tall for a woman and stronger than I'd ever been in my five and thirty years, I was not strong enough to carry a well-grown man down to the cottage. I crouched over him, and this time, instead of dribbling the chilly water on his lips, I threw it in his face. Gasping and spluttering, he opened his startling eyes—the deep, clear hue of midsummer evening.

"Who are you?" I said.

He squinted and blinked his sun-scalded eyes, fixing them on my face as he had earlier.

"What does Darzid want with you?"

He edged backward, struggling to sit up without coming any closer. As he moved, he seemed to notice his condition of undress and the now-ineffective red shawl. Though he quickly yanked the shawl onto his lap, he did not seem embarrassed. Nor even as he shook off his stupor did he offer any apology. Rather he raised his chin and continued to stare. Still without a word.

"I just want to know what's happened to you," I said. "I don't care what you've done or what you did to me. I understand that kind of fear." Fear of the things men do to each other out of greed and ignorance and jealousy. Fear that cripples your life and makes you lash out, not just at strangers, but at those you love. I had once killed a man out of fear.

Keeping the shawl well in place and one eye on me, the young man bent over the stream, cupped his hand, and drank long and deeply. Well, at least he wasn't an idiot.

When he sat up again, wiping his mouth on his scratched arm, I tried again. "You're a long way from anywhere. Where did you come from?"

He shook his head slightly, but the cock of his head and the blank look of his eyes told me that it was not a negative answer, but only that he didn't understand the question.

"Are you not from Leire, then? Valleor, perhaps?" I dredged up what I could of the language of the fair northern race, but either my pronunciation was too rusty or my guess was wrong. "Kerotea?" I had been no expert linguist all those years ago, but not incompetent either. Yet neither my Kerotean nor my smattering of Avatoir, the language of Iskeran, elicited anything but a negative shrug.

"Well, you say something, then. That's all I remember." I pointed to my lips and to him, inviting him to put out a bit of effort to join the conversation.

He tried. He closed his eyes, concentrated, and worked his lips. Soon his fists were clenched and his whole body straining, until he clasped his hands to his head as if it might burst with the effort. But he produced only guttural growls and croaks. In the end, roaring and red-faced, he snatched a rock from the stream and hurled it into the trees, then another and another until, flushed and shaking, he sank back onto his heels and wrapped his arms tightly about his head.

I wanted to leave him there. People made their own choices, and in the ordinary event, I would let them reap their own consequences as I had done. But I would abandon no one to the mercy of Evard or Darzid or Tomas, whichever of the bastards wanted him. No one. Ever.

Calling myself an incomparable fool, I invited him to follow me, using gestures to augment my words. "I've food in the valley. We'll find you some clothes, and you can sleep for a while." His only response was to grope awkwardly for the shawl, trying to hold it about himself, looking furious and utterly humiliated.

"Then you may rot in your own prideful stink." I didn't look back after starting down the path, having every confidence that he would follow just because I would so much rather he wouldn't. He followed.

I didn't particularly want a stranger inside the cottage, certainly not one who had already left bruises on my skin. So I was well content when the young man sat on the splintered pine bench outside my door, leaned his head against the wall, and closed his eyes as if he had no better destination. I kept my attention on the forest boundary, and my ears open, halfway expecting Darzid and his riders to burst into view at any moment. But no one came, and the young man himself seemed little concerned about whatever had driven him to his sorry state.

I had no man's clothes that might fit him, but went inside, rummaged through Anne's trunk, and came up with a sheet, yellowed and many times mended. I cut a hole in the middle and trimmed a piece of hempen rope to the right length, then took it out to him and showed him what I planned. He picked at the sheet for a moment, then threw it on the ground, his lip curled in disgust, as if I'd offered him dung for breakfast.

"I've nothing finer, my Lord Particular," I said. Then I threw the wadded sheet back at him. "But you'll not ruin Anne's shawl either. Go naked if you will." I yanked the red shawl from his lap and went back inside, slamming the door behind me.

Before I could decide what to do next, he kicked the door open and stepped inside. A formidable presence in the single cramped room. He was not wearing the sheet. Shoving the chairs out of his way, he rumpled the blankets on my bed, examined the dishes and stores I kept on the open shelves by the hearth, and picked through the box of spoons on the table, tossing them onto the floor in disgust when he failed to find whatever he was hunting.

He knelt beside the chest I'd pulled out from the wall and rummaged through it, strewing the meager contents on the floor: the blue dress Anne had put on when the old couple took their vegetables to market, my winter cloak, salvaged from a barge wreck on the river, three spare blankets, the finely sewn collars Anne had embroidered in youthful dreams of meeting a gentleman, but had never worn. Instead of a gentleman, she had married a sweet-spoken Vallorean lad stubborn enough to think he could grow his sustenance on this rocky meadow and avoid the humiliation of binding his body, soul, and future to the land of a Leiran noble. As if his suspicions were confirmed, the young man held up Jonah's slouched wool cap and gestured about the room, clearly asking where was its owner.

"Dead," I said, trying to show him with my hands. "Both of them dead long ago. They were old and they died." I stood by the door and pointed outside, meeting his hard gaze so he could not mistake my meaning. "How dare you touch their things . . . my things? Get out."

He surveyed the mess he'd made, then tossed the cap on the floor and walked out. I sagged against the cottage wall. Stupid to bring him here. No matter who was chasing him, no matter how much hate was in me, bringing him to the cottage was stupid.

I had just closed the chest again with everything refolded, when a shadow darkened the still open doorway. My guest stood just outside looking resentful, but draped in a halfway respectable tunic, his long legs sticking out from underneath the sheet's frayed hem. I stepped to the door and looked him up and down. In truth, the garment looked ridiculous, but it would do as long as the wind was not too high.

"It's a good thing it's summer," I said. He cocked his

head and frowned. I fanned myself, pointed to my own light clothing and his skimpy outfit, and raised my eyebrows. *That* he understood, and just for a moment there blossomed on his face a smile of such unrestrained good humor and unexpected sweetness that it almost took my breath. Earth and sky . . . he could charm a penny from a beggar with such a smile.

Unfortunately his fair humor disappeared as quickly as it had come. He scowled and rubbed his belly with unmistakable meaning.

From a basket hanging in the corner I extricated a hunk of dry bread, the last of a loaf I'd bought from the village baker. Pulling off the cloth wrapping, I stuffed the bread in the man's hand and waved toward the meadow. "All right. You won't starve. Now go."

He glared at me sourly from the doorway as I set out a leek and a turnip—the rest of my food ration for the day— and filled a pot from my water jug. Before I could hang the pot over the fire, he had thrown the hunk of bread on the floor and was striding across the meadow.

For one moment I leaned heavily on my table, vowing never again to yield to rebellious impulse. When I began peeling the fibrous outer leaves from the leek, my hands were trembling.

But my hopes that my brutish visitor had decided to seek food and fortune elsewhere were quashed when, after crouching at the edge of the trees for something near half an hour, he headed back toward the house. He walked through my door as if it were his own. Onto the table in front of me he threw a rabbit, neck broken, already gutted and skinned, evidently by the bloody shard of rock in his hand.

Though sorely disappointed at his return, I acknowledged the offering with a nod. I threw another leek and another turnip into the pot, along with the rabbit. I was not averse to fresh meat.

While the savory steam rose from the pot, he stood at the doorway watching everything I did. Retrieving a bone needle and a sad-looking length of cotton from a rolled canvas packet, I set about repairing the rip in my skirt, an immensely practical garment that Anne had helped me make years before—fashioned like a lady's riding togs with the modest, unremarkable appearance of an ordinary skirt, but split discreetly down the middle like wide-legged trousers. After a while he retreated a few steps, sitting cross-legged on the trampled grass where he could still see inside my door. I resisted the temptation to close the door, remembering the force he'd used earlier to kick it open.

His incessant stare, my sore fingers, and the crude stitches down the side of my one decent garment did nothing for my temper. When the meat had cooked long enough, I shoved a filled bowl into his hand and indicated he should remain outside to eat. His disdain did not extend to my ever-mediocre cooking. His bowl was empty in moments, and he gestured for more. I set the pot outside the door and went back to my own dinner. Before I could finish my first serving, soaking up the broth with the bread he had discarded, my visitor had emptied the pot.

He lay back on his elbows, watching as I cleaned up the mess, carried in wood to refill the woodbox, and mixed dough to make hearthbread for the next day. As the evening cooled he wrapped his arms tightly about his bare legs, and whenever his eyelids drooped, he would jerk his head upright.

When my work was finished, I washed my face and hands in the last of the hot water. Then, as was my habit, I wrapped a blanket about my shoulders and sat on the bench outside my door to watch the day come to its end. Pious Leirans believed that twilight was a sacred time, when Annadis the Swordsman, the god of fire and earth and sunlight, handed off his watch to his twin brother Jerrat the Navigator, the god of sea and storm, moon and stars. Many years had passed since I had had any use for pious Leirans or their warrior gods, yet I still observed the ritual, using the time to keep the days from blurring one into the other. On this evening a good-sized oak limb lay on the bench beside me.

When my visitor unfolded his long legs and looked about as if to decide what to do with himself, I waved him away from the cottage. "Don't think you're going to sleep anywhere close."

He eyed my blanket, my crude cudgel, and the cottage

door, which I had deliberately shut when I came out. But I didn't flinch. As he stood up and walked slowly toward the alder copse, I muttered a good riddance. After a few steps, though, he turned and gave me a half-bow, little more than a nod of the head, but graceful and well meant . . . and immensely revealing. The man was no peasant poacher. No poverty-dulled laborer. No thieving servant.

As he turned his back again, I called after him. "Your name. I need to have something to call you." I pointed to myself and said, "Seri." Then I pointed to him and shook my head in question.

He nodded seriously and worried at it for a few moments. Then he faced away from the cottage into the lingering dusk, pointing into the deep blue sky above the ridge. Slowly he waved his finger back and forth as if searching for something, until the quiet evening was pierced by the harsh cry of an aeren—a gray falcon. The young man gestured and nodded so there was no mistake.

"Aeren?" I said. He didn't agree or disagree, but only shrugged his shoulders tiredly and trudged across the grass to the copse. He lay down on the thick turf under the alders and was still.

A breeze rustled the dry grass. The plaintive whistle of a meadowlark echoed off the ridge. The stream burbled softly. But as the light faded across the meadow, my gaze moved from the unmoving form under the alders to the hoofprints left by Darzid's men, and my blood stayed cold. Karon had believed that enough beauty gathered in the soul might bury the knowledge of the evils of the world. I had never accepted his premise. Evil was too strong, too pervasive, too seductive.

Why had I asked the stranger's name? I didn't want to know anything about him. And when the longest day of the year was done, I went inside to bed, thinking that if there was any luck to be had, I would wake in the morning to find him gone.

CHAPTER 3

I dreamed of the fire again that night. After ten years, one would think such pain might fade into the dismal landscape of my life. Yet once more I saw Evard's banners whipped by the cold wind, bright red against the steel-blue sky. I heard again the jeering of the wild-eyed crowds that surged against the line of guards surrounding the pyre, and the stake, and the one bound there, maintaining as he could the last shreds of dignity and reason.

Where was justice? Time blurs so much of worth, so much of learning unused, so many of the daily pleasures that shape a life, too small to make grand memories. Why would it not erase the image of Karon's mutilated face: the ragged sockets where they had burned out his eyes, the battered mouth where they had cut out the tongue that had whispered words of love and healing? Should not mercy dim his last avowal of joy and life, given just before he withdrew from what relief and comfort I could give him? After ten years I should not hear, again and again, his agonized cry as the flames consumed his sweet body. Dead was dead.

But as much as I tried, I could not silence that cry. In the day, yes, as I worked at the business of survival, but I had never learned to command my dreams. I had vowed on the shields of my ancestors never to weep again. Yet was it any wonder that weakness threatened to betray my resolve upon waking from such a dream?

I had permitted no tears on that day or for many days after. The dream forced me to relive that, too—the two months they kept me confined in the palace with no companion save the mute serving sister, Maddy, and the doomed babe that grew within me. Even Tomas did not come to me in that time. My brother did not want my shaven head or bulging belly to stand witness against him for what he had done or what he planned to do. They could not kill Karon's child before it was born. The spirit might seek a new host, they said. They wanted to be sure.

Only Darzid had ever shown his face at my door, but it was not for me he came. Always he sat by the brazier, clad simply and impeccably in black and red, propping one boot on the iron hod. "Tell me of sorcerers, Seri. Who was your husband? What did he tell you of his people?" Always probing, always questioning, his unrelenting curiosity picking at my pain as the horror of what had happened settled into grim history, and the horror of what was to come took appalling shape in my ever-naïve head.

I had begged Darzid's help, promised him gold and power, love and loyalty if he would but smuggle me out of my palace prison before my son was born. But he brushed away my pleading just as he flicked off ash that settled on his shining boot, and always he returned to his questions. "Tell me of the sorcerer, Seri. Something happened when he died. Something changed in the world, and I must understand it."

Eventually I had stopped begging. Stopped talking. Stopped listening. Eventually Darzid had stopped coming, and eventually arrived the day that I willed my labor to stop, the day I struggled to hold the babe within me yet a few more moments, for I knew I would never hold him in my arms. Nature had its way, and I was left empty; the law had its way, and my son's life was cut short by my brother's knife. The physician, his head and throat wrapped in a black turban so that his cold face hovered above me like some cruel moon, had commanded the serving woman to take the child to Tomas. I wasn't even allowed to see my son until Darzid, sober and impersonally curious like an alchemist observing the turmoil he had wrought in his glass, brought him back to me—the tiny boy, pale, motionless, washed clean and laid in a basket, perfect but for the angry red slit that crossed his fragile neck. Then they took him away and burned him, too, and proclaimed the last sorcerer gone from the earth.

Why had they bothered to wash him? I had never understood that.

Once all was done as the law prescribed, they left me
alone in that cold room. Ten years it had been since that
last day, and still the dream made it real. . . .

Year 4 in the reign of King Evard

All was silent. The sprawling, squat-towered palace at Montevial, home to more than a thousand nobles, courtiers,
servants, and soldiers, as well as the Leiran king, might
have been abandoned. No sidelong whispers outside my
door. No thumping boots or rattling weapons as the guards
were changed. No clatter of dishes in the hallway or jangle
of harness from the bleak courtyard far below my small
window. Even mute Maddy, who had been my companion
for every day of my imprisonment and who had coaxed me
gently through the wretched birthing, had vanished.

I rose from the sodden bed, shivering from the sweat still
drying on my skin. The murder had been swiftly accomplished; Tomas had been waiting in the next room, so Darzid had told me. I found a discarded towel and cleaned
myself as best I could, tying rags between my legs to catch
the birthing blood. Then I pulled Maddy's spare tunic from
the plain chest beneath the window, wrapped it over my
stained shift, and tied it closed.

The door was no longer locked. Karon's babe had been
the prisoner, not Karon's wife. They planned to send me
to Tomas's keep, the home of my childhood, to live in
penitence and subservience to my brother and his pouting
seventeen-year-old wife. But even with nothing left for
which to fight, I was not ready to submit to that particular death.

Nothing was left to take with me. Every shred of clothing, every trinket, every paper and book and picture had
been burned. The gold locket with the bits of dried rose
petal inside, my wedding ring. The bastards had taken
everything—*No, don't think. Just walk.* The time for pain
and hatred and grief would come after I was away. And so
I walked out of the room and out of the palace and out of
my life.

Strange to find it mid-afternoon. Time had been suspended for so many months, the passing of days marked only by my changing body. For all those days I had existed in the unyielding, unvarying embrace of death, yet out here in the palace gardens, bitter winter had been replaced by damp spring. Life had continued for the hundred gardeners trimming the hundreds of trees beside the carriage road on which I walked. Crocuses were already drooping, and the showier blooms of daffodils and anemones fluttered brightly in the damp breeze.

Two horsemen raced by, then pulled up short and turned back toward me as I approached the first ring wall. Tomas and Darzid. "Seri, you damned fool, where do you think you're going?" Tomas, speaking in his best lord-of-the-manor style.

I kept walking. The two wheeled their mounts and placed themselves in front of me again, blocking the entire roadway. "I spoke to you, Seri. It can't be healthy for you to be out so soon."

Words broke through my vowed silence, as molten lava bursts the volcano's rocky cap. "And when have you ever concerned yourself with me or my health?"

My brother was not even a whole year older than me — as near twins as could be, so our nursemaids had always said—but the warm droplets trickling down my leg reminded me of the ageless gulf between us. My hands ached for a throwing dagger or my bow and a poisoned arrow.

"I won't see my sister die among the rabble like some whore who whelped in an alley."

"Then you'll have to carry me, brother, and risk bloodying your fine breeches. The blood will match that on your hands, and it will never wash away." I walked into the gardens beyond the first wall, hoping to get past the outer gates before I collapsed. My knees were trembling. *Vengeance is the right of blood kin, even against blood kin. Blood for blood.* Vengeance was my duty.

"Seri, come back here!"

Tomas ordered Darzid to follow me, while he himself fetched servants and a litter. So the captain trailed behind as I walked through the outer gates into the teeming mid-afternoon business of Montevial. Everything blurred to-

gether: smells of horses and new-baked bread, rushing figures of tradesmen, liveried messengers, and matrons in
fluttering cap-ribbons, the clattering of cart wheels, and the
shouts of drovers trying to clear a way through the muddy,
crowded streets. How could the matter of one dark winter
make such commonplace activity so utterly alien?

"Move along, wench. Are you struck dumb?"

Darzid observed from his black horse, unruffled as the
constable poked at me with his stick. Once I had considered
Darzid my friend, but I had come to believe that he would
have watched me burn alongside Karon with this same un-
emotional curiosity.

I wobbled against a barrow piled with apples before
heading down a sloping lane into the mobbed market of
the capital city, vaguely aware of apples bouncing all over
the street, a startled horse, and a careening hay wagon.
Someone in the street behind me cursed and cracked a
whip. But I could no longer bring the angry rider's name
into my throbbing head. Concentrating was so difficult. . . .

As I walked past booths hung with lengths of fabric, coils
of rope, and tin pots strung together, mats covered with
raw, staring fish, wagons of fruits and hay, and pens of
squawking chickens, thickening clouds devoured the sun. I
shivered in the sudden chill. Halfway down a lane of food
vendors, a hunchbacked old man doled out soup to anyone
with a copper coin and a mug. I felt hollow. Empty. But
when the old man held out his ladle to me, I shook my
head. "I've no money, goodman. Nothing to offer you.
Nothing." And then the world spun and fell out from
under me. . . .

Scents of damp canvas and mildew intruded on my chaotic dreams. A scratchy blanket was tucked under my chin,
and the surface under my back was hard and uneven. As I
dragged my eyelids open to murky light, my neck was bent
awkwardly, and a warm metal cup, quivering slightly and
giving off the scent of warmed wine, was pressed to my
lips. A few tart drops made their way to my tongue. A few
more dribbled down my chin.

"Poor girl," said a voice from the dimness, a cracked,
leathery voice of uncertain timbre.

"Who could she be, dearie? She don't have the look of a street wench, for all she's dressed so plain." This second speaker was surely an aged man.

"Nawp. No street wench. Look at the hands." Two warm, rough hands chafed my fingers. I was so cold. "It's a lady's hands. What're we to do with her, Jonah?"

"Can't just leave her, can we? She's just—" The old man's words quavered and broke off.

"Just the age would be our Jenny." So the sighing one was a woman. "Let's keep her for the night. Don't look as if she'll care this is no fine house, nor even that she might not wake up where she went to sleep."

"Aye, then. We'll be on our way."

While I drifted between sleep and waking, the bed on which I lay began to move, rocking and jogging over cobbled streets. The old woman stroked my hair and my hands, and crooned to me gently, while rain plopped softly on the canvas roof.

"How did you discover it, my dear?"

"She was shivering so, and terrible pale. I thought she was fevered. But when she held her tits just so and wept in her sleep for the pain of them, I knew. It's been less than a day, and she's lost a river of blood, and I don't know if it's been too much or no. If we'd left her in the market, she'd be dead for sure. 'Twas a good deed you did, old man."

"Ah. This adds a worry though. Fine ladies don't dress in working garb and take a stroll through the market after they've dropped a babe, live or dead. There's trouble here someways. We'd best get her afoot as soon as can be, and put some leagues in between us."

A hand gouged my aching abdomen, forcing me to cry out as I stumbled out of sleep.

"There, there, child. We must knead your belly a bit to stop the bleeding. You'll do better in a day or three." The hand pressed and squeezed again, then took my own hand and forced me to do it, too. "Feel your womb harden. That's the way it must be."

A worried face hovered above me in the dust-flecked light. Unlike that of the turbaned physician, this face was connected to a body—a small and wiry woman with broken teeth. Her gray curls were tied up in a red scarf, and her face was gently weathered.

"Here, my man Jonah's bringing summat to perk you up." A flap at the end of the wagon flopped open to let in soggy sunlight and the hunchbacked soup-maker from the market. The old man had wispy white hair and soft brown eyes that seemed to embrace the old woman when he looked at her.

"Thank—"

The old couple shushed me with a spoonful of soup. While they fed me, they gabbled about everything: business in the market, good prospects for the coming season, too much rain for the early crops. "We're headed south for Dunfarrie. It's planting time. If you've a place we can leave you on the way . . . friends who'll care for you?"

I shook my head. All our friends were dead. Like the books and the pictures, the few who had shared Karon's secret had been destroyed. He had been forced to hear them die, one by one: Martin, Julia, Tanager, Tennice, everyone he cared about. It had almost undone him. His tormentors told him he wasn't to know my fate, and they would taunt him with a different cruel story every day. But they never knew he could read my thoughts, or speak to me without words, or bury himself in my love so deeply that what they did to his body didn't matter. Until the end—until the fire.

"I didn't mean to cause you more grief," said the old woman in distress. "We'll take you with us until you can see your way, little girl. Old Jonah and Anne will have you up, if for nothing but to get away from our foolish prattle."

"Vengeance is my right," I said. "My duty . . ." But not on that night.

The old woman gathered me in her arms and rocked me softly, for at last weakness overwhelmed me, and I wept until there could have been no tears left in the world.

But I would never weep again. I was a Leiran warrior's daughter, and by the shields of my ancestors, I would not weep.

CHAPTER 4

When I woke, I was startled to find Aeren's face an arm's length from my own. He sat on the floor cross-legged, peering at me quizzically, his finger poised to touch my cheeks. I sat up abruptly, and he jerked his hand away.

"Keep your paws to yourself," I said, straightening my shift and running my fingers through my tangled hair, wishing he would point his eyes in some other direction, wishing I knew some way to banish dreams.

Aeren knitted his brow at my words, as if working at it hard enough would make the syllables fall together in a way that made sense.

Was it was worth the trouble to keep talking to the man? Could the sheer number of my words somehow alleviate his lack of understanding? I grimaced at him. "How am I to get rid of you? I'd hoped you were just another bad dream."

He tried his best to speak, but again produced nothing beyond hoarse croaking. As his attempts grew more desperate—and remained fruitless—his knuckles turned white and his face scarlet.

"Calm yourself. Like as not you've had a blow to the head and it's unsettled you." I tried to mime the words. Ineptly, as it appeared. He waved a hand as if to clear the air of my foolishness, while kicking savagely at a chair that toppled onto my woodbox, scattering twigs and limbs all over the floor and leaving my lone glass lamp in danger of tumbling off a shelf.

"Get out of here!" I said, pointing at the door. "Go and introduce yourself to Darzid."

He didn't go, of course, but I swore I would not attempt

to communicate again. I ignored him and went about my morning's work, stepping over his long legs when I needed to, controlling the temptation to drop an iron kettle on his head.

When I peeled my flat round of bread from the iron plate in the hearth, I expected him to pounce on it. But he remained seated on the floor, his back against my bed. He dug the heel of his hand into his temple, squeezing his eyes shut as if the bright sunlight that streamed through the door pained them.

"Are you ill?" Dismayed at the thought, I broke my vow of silence. "Curse you forever if you've brought fever here."

Whether or not he understood my clownish gestures, he shook his head as if to clear it, got to his feet, and stumbled out the door into the sunny morning. Before I could even wish him good riddance, he crumpled to the dirt. I hurried to his side, experiencing a perfectly idiotic wave of guilt, as if by wishing him away so fervently, I was somehow responsible for his collapse. Moments earlier, I had been wishing him dead.

"What's wrong with you?" I said, tapping his cheek when I could get no response. He still didn't move. But when I shook his left shoulder, his eyes flew open, and he cried out with bloodless lips, almost rising up off the ground. "All right, all right. Let's get you inside."

Once I had dragged and wrestled him onto the bed, I pulled aside the makeshift tunic. The mark on his shoulder that I remembered as a mere scratch was now swollen purple, hot, hard, and seeping a foul-smelling black fluid. I'd never seen anything like it. Dredging up what I knew of such matters, I scalded my knife and lanced the wound, trying to get as much of the vile fluid out of it as I could. Aeren almost bit through his lip as I worked. "I've got to do this," I said, grabbing a dry cloth to blot his brow. "You've gotten something nasty in it."

As I applied a stone-root poultice to Aeren's shoulder, he drifted off to sleep, leaving me awash in memory. How not? I even found myself whispering, *J'den encour*. The words meant *heal swiftly* in the language of the J'Ettanne. Unfortunately, the words had no efficacy coming from me.

Have you learned nothing, stupid woman? I threw down my towels and left the man to his fevered moaning, busying myself by splitting and stacking wood, filling the woodbox, hauling in extra water, pouring water on the garden, anything to stop thinking. Flour and water, salt and millet went into a bowl for more hearthbread. I threw the rabbit bones and two shriveled carrots in a pot of water on the hearth to make broth. Starving the bastard would not get him out of 'my bed. I needed him away from the valley. What if Darzid decided to make another sweep?

Aeren awoke near sunset, somewhat surprised to find himself in my bed and mostly undressed again. He watched silently as I made willowbark tea, mixing it with yarrow and a spoonful of wine to ease his pain and fever.

"Don't get any ideas," I said, deliberately and obviously holding the steaming cup above his bare torso and discreetly covered nether parts before putting it to his lips. He made no move to take the cup as he drank. "You've done yourself no service, running through the underbrush as you did." Setting the cup aside, I changed the dressing on his shoulder. Not long after I finished, his fever shot skyward again, and he slipped back into restless sleep. I sat up with him most of that night, applying cold cloths to his face and body, dribbling willowbark tea down his throat, and cursing myself for a fool.

The next morning, when I woke from an uncomfortable few hours on the floor, Aeren was sitting up, his eyes fixed so intently on my face that I could almost feel their heat on my skin. Sitting on the side of the bed, I removed the bandages and was astonished to see the horrid wound well on its way to healing, only a bit red and slightly tender. Youth has distinct advantages when it comes to recuperation. "So, you're better this morning," I said. Fires of Annadis, why did he stare so?

Once I had renewed the dressing and tied up the bandage again, I busied myself about the cottage, trying to break the lock of his gaze while tidying up the remnants of my herbs and pots.

After a wobbly visit outdoors—I did not even consider following him out—he seated himself at the table. With one hand he gestured at his stomach and his mouth, while with the other he pointed accusingly at the idle pots beside the hearth. Though sorely tempted to grant such rudeness the empty reward it deserved, I threw onions, cheese, and my last five eggs into a skillet on the fire. He'd been none too well fed when I'd found him; after his fever, he must be weak as an infant, and I wanted him to put leagues between us today. "Sorry, I'm not adept at bludgeoning rabbits. You'll have to do with what I've got."

I was convinced of his recuperative powers when I saw what he ate that morning: an entire round of hearthbread and every bite of my eggs. No encouragement to moderation had any effect on him, and when he emptied his bowl, he banged it down on the table in front of me, pointing a reproachful finger at its desolation. When I refused to cook anything more, he ate all the wild plums from the basket on the table and used his spoon to break off great slabs of cheese. Before I could get it wrapped up and stowed back in the stone-lined hole in the bank behind the cottage, he had eaten a quarter of the pale yellow wheel that I had planned to last until autumn.

Astonishingly, Aeren was pacing the floor by midday, restless with inactivity, not fever. I shoved a pail into his hand. "Fetch some water and I'll heat it, so you can wash before you go." But either he didn't understand my gestures or didn't want to understand. He dropped the pail at my feet, retrieved the dwindling cheese yet again from my crude larder, and sprawled on the woven rug beside the hearth to eat more of it. Grinding my teeth, I fetched water from the stream for my own washing, seriously considering whether it was enough to drown the brute. When I returned to the house, he was rummaging through my things again, just as he had on the first day.

"Get out of there," I said, slamming the lid of the clothes chest. Only quick reflexes saved his fingers from being crushed. "What are you looking for?"

With precise and insistent gestures, he demanded a sword.

When I made it clear I had nothing of the sort, he stomped away angrily and sat sulking by the pail of water, dabbling his hand in it and watching the dirt swirl around his hand as he rubbed two dirty fingers together. "That's mine," I said, moving the pail away from him and setting another log on the fire. "I'm no serving maid or bath-girl. You're quite well enough to take care of yourself, and you smell like a stable." I held my nose to illustrate my point.

He looked me in the eye and kicked over the pail, spilling the water all over my floor.

"As you wish. I've no time for spoiled children."

I began to sort the burdock, scabwort, sparrow-tongue, and bristling spur nettle that I would trade for eggs and butter in the village, purposely ignoring Aeren and the mess he had made; I would not give him the satisfaction of watching me clean it up. A childish response to match his childish behavior. But the hostility in his gaze told me that his anger was anything but childish. The swelling in my throat was only now subsiding, and the slightest touch reminded me of the bruises that remained. Whyever had I brought him here? *Never again. Never.*

When the plants were clean and bundled, I snatched up my sewing things and a shift that needed mending and moved out to the bench outside the door. The sun beat softly on my face, and the rasp of bees in the clover was the only disturbance on the hot, still morning. Aeren followed me out, slouching in the shadow of the doorway for a while. Then, abruptly, he strode to the center of the meadow and began to wave his hands about in jerking motions, like a scarecrow come to life. Soon he was whirling and thrusting, bending and kicking, rolling onto the ground, and then picking himself up again.

Dropping my work in my lap, I watched in fascination, certain he'd gone mad.

But gradually his movements lost their insistent frenzy and became more fluid, and I at last recognized their patterns: lunge, spin, slash, parry . . . Swordplay: graceful, powerful, masterful. Whoever was chasing him had better make sure the man never got his hands on a sword. I glanced uneasily about the boundaries of the meadow. Who was he? Why was Darzid after him?

The display ended abruptly when Aeren stumbled over a rock and fell to the grass. Bent over his knees, chest heaving, he slammed his fist to the earth, then dragged himself to his feet, trudged back up the path, and flopped wearily to the ground in front of the cottage. Without favoring me with so much as a glance, he began tracing his finger in the dirt, drawing a rough geometric pattern of lines, curves, and arrows or cross-marks with a crude beast to each side.

I twisted my head to see from the proper angle. Something about the arrangement of it whispered at me of familiarity. "What is it?" I said, tipping my head at the drawing.

He ignored me.

But the exercise gave me a thought. I sat down beside Aeren and began drawing in the dirt myself. "This is the house." I pointed to my picture and to the real one. He nodded, frowning. "This is the ridge." I marked on my map the place where I'd found him, the trail to the village, the river, the bridge, and the road. He waited for more. "Isn't any of this familiar? Where do you come from?" I added more features. "Montevial is to the north," I said. "King Evard's royal city."

He just shook his head and looked blank. Then he began drawing a map of his own, adding roads, towers, mountains, then furiously erasing and changing them. It was no geography I recognized.

How was I ever to get him gone if he couldn't tell me where he was going or where he'd been? We needed words. So I began to call out objects around the cottage and to name the things I drew. He learned incredibly fast. When I quizzed him, saying *door* or *sky* or *sword* and having him point to the object or the picture of it, he always got it right. He was either deceiving me that he didn't understand Leiran or his ranked among the quickest minds I'd ever known.

I tried writing words, but he couldn't read them. I tried to think of a way for him to tell who he was or who were his people, but he could not. I pointed to myself and to my house, then tried to find out where on his drawing was his dwelling, but he shook his head angrily and kicked dirt over his attempts. Perhaps he had been banished or disinherited. I tried drawing the devices of prominent noble houses, but he recognized none of them. And then I drew Evard's royal dragon ensign, but it evoked neither fear nor loathing nor any sense of familiarity, and I began to wonder if he had lost his memory along with his voice. After an hour of this his lips were thin and hard, his nostrils flared, and his knuckles white. I went back to teaching him words, and he liked that better. Unfortunately, though he didn't seem particularly happy, he didn't look in the least inclined to leave.

By midday I'd had enough, so I packed up my knife and my bundled plants and started down the track toward the village. Aeren wanted to come with me, but I waved him away. I could just imagine the uproar if I took a half-naked stranger into Dunfarrie.

"They'll arrest you. Put you in the pillory to wait for those who were hunting you, and all of this will be for nothing. If you want to leave, then by all means go, but take a different way at least." I'm not sure what my gestures communicated. He pouted like a spoiled child. Maybe he would be gone by the time I came back.

The path from my cottage entered Dunfarrie behind Gareth Crowley's pigsties. Crowley's hovel and its collapsing fence poked up from his muddy barnyard, all of it sprawled across the foot of the hill as if a particularly nasty avalanche had buried a respectable dwelling. I circled wide and came to the dirt road that meandered past the sorely overgrown statues of Annadis and Jerrat—no priest from any temple could be bothered to come and tend so small a shrine as Dunfarrie's—and through the jumble of tired wood-frame houses and shops to the Dun Bridge. The afternoon was still and warm, the stench of barnyard filth hanging over the stifling village.

The few people I passed hurried by with averted eyes or touched their fingers to their brows without speaking. The villagers tolerated me and my unsavory past out of respect for Anne and Jonah, but they kept a wary distance. I was well content to do the same. Life was difficult enough without moping over other people's hardships.

Jacopo, of course, was different. If it hadn't been for Jacopo, Jonah's younger brother, I could never have survived in the valley after Anne and Jonah died. He had no family of his own, and he came up every few days to help me cut firewood or work the garden, or to make soap or candles. He had taught me to snare rabbits and squirrels, and to make jack, the thin, tough strips of smoked meat that would keep forever. Every fall he helped me make the cottage tight against the coming cold. Jaco was all of my family and all of my friends together.

Eyed suspiciously by a bronze rooster, I picked my way through a cramped chicken yard to the back stoop of a tidy, sod-roofed house, where I traded my bundled dye plants to Mag the weaver for ten eggs and a fist-sized lump of butter wrapped in a rag. Jaco's shop was not as tidy as Mag's house. The outside had not been whitewashed since King Gevron's father ruled Leire, and the dirt- and soot-grimed window allowed little daylight inside. I pushed open the door and three cats made a break for freedom across my feet. "Jacopo, are you here?".

Jacopo had taken up shopkeeping after thirty years wandering the world as a sailor. An Isker saber had slashed the muscles of one leg, leaving it too stiff for scrambling in a ship's rigging, so he had made his way home to Dunfarrie. Out of this dusty room he sold all manner of things: old boots, clothes, anchors, rusty lanterns, cracked bowls, farm implements. Anything he could find or trade for, he would set in his shop, and someone would want it eventually.

"What're you up to in town this day, girl? It's not your usual." Jacopo emerged from the back room carrying a crate of rusty nails. He was very much like Jonah, wispy white hair and kind brown eyes. Though no taller than I, he had broad shoulders and a barrel chest, and the hands that gripped the heavy crate were wide, with short, powerful fingers. He set down the crate, then wiped his forehead with a rag. "Summer's on us today, for sure."

"Jaco, we need to talk. Privately."

"Not a soul in town to hear, I'd wager. Everyone's gone out to Augusto's. With the eviction tomorrow, everyone thinks either to help him move out or to steal whatever they can get their hands on. After the flogging, Augusto can't move fast enough to keep up with his children, much less his belongings."

I drew a pair of rickety stools close together where we could see the shop door. Jacopo pulled a wadded leather pouch from the pocket of his worn blue sailor's coat, extracted a pipe, and filled it from a battered tin.

"Yesterday a stranger showed up on the ridge. . . ."

When I was done, the pipe remained unlit. "And he can't speak at all?"

"Not a syllable. But he's not accustomed to it nor to rough living or having to do for himself. I can't seem to convince him to leave. So what am I to do with him?"

"Give him over to Graeme Rowan. That's the only way to stay clear of trouble."

I shook my head. "Darzid's surely spoken with Rowan. Our upright sheriff would turn Aeren over straightaway. I won't do it."

"But if he's a thief—"

"We've no evidence this man has broken any law, and whatever his crime, I've doubts he can remember it. He's not even sure of his name."

"Perhaps he's not the one the captain's hunting. Likely he's just a fellow wrecked himself on the Snags and wandered up the ridge. I've seen many a body with the clothes washed right off them after getting caught up at the Snags, though mostly they were dead."

"I won't believe that. It's too much of a coincidence."

"What if I was to trot down to the docks and have a smoke with Graeme, see what he knows?"

"You won't mention Aeren or me?"

"I'll be as clever as a boy when there's work to be done."

"I'll watch the shop." I had to offer, though I thoroughly disliked the task.

"Right then. Have a look through my bins and see if there's aught to dress the fellow in. I'll be back in a bit."

I delved into the three great wooden clothes bins. That the contents of the bins were entirely dead people's clothes didn't bother me. Dead was dead. The former owners weren't going to come back and haunt those who found some use for their breeches. I came up with gray underdrawers, a long tunic of russet, some worn and greasy loose breeches of brown kersey with a drawstring to hold them up, and canvas leggings. Aeren was clearly unused to going barefoot. His feet were soft, battered by the stones and sticks of the forest path, and the lack of calluses told me he was accustomed to boots that fit, not these hobnailed monstrosities the rest of us wore that weighed like oak and were no more yielding. The only thing Jacopo's bins provided were sandals that looked as if they'd been chewed by a goat.

I had watched the shop for Jacopo on other occasions. I wasn't much good at it. Jacopo could talk to a customer for an hour about nothing, and before you knew it, a woman who had come in search of a spoon would leave with two crocks, a bowl, three shirts, and a ladle. I rarely managed to get past "Good day." Fortunately, only two people came into the shop while Jacopo was out.

Mary Fetterling, a bony woman of indeterminate age, brought in a tidy bundle of clothes: a thin summer cloak, a boy's stiff jacket, some stirrup-footed leggings, and a pair of patched and baggy farmer's trousers. Her graying hair flew about her head in distracted tangles, and her eyes darted from here to there, never fixing on anything. "I've Tim's things. He won't be needin' them no more. And I could use a penny." Tim was the last of Mary's four sons, one of thousands of Leiran conscripts dead from Evard's determination to conquer the desert kingdom of Iskeran, the only one of the Four Realms not under Leiran rule. Mary's husband had been lost in King Gevron's campaign against Valleor, and her other three boys in Evard's conquest of Kerotea.

I had grown up with soldiers, but they were men hired by my father to defend his house and support his obligations to his king, not conscripts. Conscripts were necessary in a war—I understood that—but at the least they deserved good officers and reasoned strategies. And for a family to lose all of its sons . . .

"Jaco isn't here, but I'm sure he'd give at least two coppers." The clothes weren't worth so much, but Jacopo had taught me his ways.

The woman dipped her head. "Thank you, ma'am. A fella that was with him come to tell me of him. It's been nigh on two years that it happened, and I didn't hear of it till this week. But I wasn't surprised. A mother knows. Tim was my youngest. He would always come—"

"I'm sorry about your boy." Useless words. Not worth the effort to voice them. But I didn't want to hear of her sorrows. I swatted at a fly buzzing about my face.

"They say he died brave," she said. "Blessed Annadis will remember his name." She clutched her pennies and went on her way. Neither my words nor Jaco's coppers would keep her fed for long. And I'd seen no evidence that having either of the disinterested Holy Twins remember a dead soldier's name benefited his family in the least. Mary would end up harnessing herself to a plow on some noble's leasehold east of Dunfarrie and pull until she dropped dead from it. I hated working the shop.

An hour later, a ragged boy barged through the door carrying a wad of dingy rags, shouts of "Run, Donkey" following him. Underneath a scraggly mop of honey-brown hair and thirteen years' accumulation of dirt were a thin freckled face and ears that seemed too large for his scrawny frame. One of his legs was shorter than the other, and he loped through the village with an off-kilter gait that left one expecting him to crash into the nearest obstacle at any moment. Paulo was his name. Almost everyone in Dunfarrie called him Donkey.

The boy pulled up short when he saw me, and he quickly stuffed his bundle behind his back. "Where's Jaco?"

"Out. Do you have something for him?"

"Nope. Nothin'." He ducked his head, touched his forehead, and backed toward the door.

"Come, what's in your hand? You know I work the shop when Jacopo's away."

"Nope. I'll wait."

"Wait for what?" Jacopo stepped through the doorway, pipe smoke curling about his head.

The boy looked from Jaco to me, hesitating.

"I think Paulo has a treasure for you, Jaco."

"What've you got, boy? Out with it. I've no time to dally."

With a sideways glance at me, the boy unfolded the filthy cloth. Between the stained folds lay a silver dagger half again the length of Paulo's hand. The guard was a simple, elegant curve, and both guard and hilt were densely filled with intricate engraving that glittered as it caught the light.

Jacopo voiced our mutual astonishment. "Where in perdition did you come up with such a thing?"

"Found it, Jaco. Honest. Left on the ground. Nobody about." The boy held it well out of my reach. "Didn't steal it. I promise."

"Not saying you did." Jaco stroked the gleaming blade. "Just trying to figure out where such a fine thing might have come from."

I thought I might understand the boy's anxiety. The villagers were well aware of my origins. "You needn't fret, Paulo. I've not owned anything so fine for a number of years." Ten, to be precise. "Here, let me see if I can recognize the markings."

The boy allowed me to move in a little closer, but kept his thin hand firmly on the knife. A beautiful weapon. Wickedly sharp. I examined the engraving, and the day lurched off in a new direction. "Where did you find it, Paulo? Where exactly?"

Jacopo peeked over the boy's head and waggled his eyebrows at me in question.

"On the ridge up to the head of Poacher's Creek." Paulo glanced suspiciously from Jaco to me. "It's a fine thing. If you can't pay, I might try Sheriff. He needs a good one." The boy was studiously diffident. "Or someone as comes downriver might want it. No hurry."

I still had Jacopo's eye and shook my head ever so slightly.

Jacopo turned the dagger over in his hands. "Well, I suppose you could take it to Graeme and he might buy it, but then he might well take it without paying, as maybe it was evidence or something lost as someone will want. All I could give for it would be a silver penny."

"Three!" Glorious avarice burst through the boy's hangdog manner.

"Two, and not a copper more."

Paulo's eyes gleamed. "Done!" In moments the boy was trotting down the road, carrying more money than he could ever have thought to see in his life.

"Now what is it you find so almighty fascinating about this little bit of wickedness, young lady? It's cost me dear."

I pointed to the engraved device on its hilt. "This is the mark Aeren was trying to draw in the dirt." His version had been crude, but it was unmistakable: a rectangular shield with two rampant lions supporting a curved arch. Not arrows or crosses, but two starbursts sat atop the arch and a third underneath it. I didn't mention the nagging familiarity that still refused to resolve itself. "The knife might help us trace him, or perhaps there's another clue at the spring."

"Hmm. Or it might belong to the other odd fellow what's been hanging about. . . ."

"Another one? Tell me!"

Jacopo rolled the dagger in a cleaner rag. "Found Graeme havin' a pint at the Heron. He was low about Barti Gesso's thievin' Mistress Jennai's flour. Barti did it no question, but he's got seven little ones to feed and his hold's got the blight. Mistress Jennai wants half the flesh off Barti's back, and Graeme's got to do it, so—"

"Spare me the sheriff's moral dilemmas, Jaco. With two floggings and an eviction within three days, I don't think I can muster any sympathy for him."

Sheriffs were constable, judge, and hangman in most Leiran towns and villages. They were charged to enforce the king's law, to support the king's whims, and to prevent interference with the conscript gangs, tax collectors, and quartermasters who ensured the unending supplies of lives, money, food, and horses for the king's wars. But such duties had been acquired only in the past century. The badge sewn on a sheriff's coat was scarlet, fashioned in the shape of a flaming sword, for the office had been created to enforce the extermination laws—to root out sorcerers in every corner of the realm and burn them.

"You're still hard on Graeme, Seri. He's a fair man and does his job well. I've known him since he was a boy."

"I won't argue it again. So what else did he say?"

"He talked of the king's men come riding through yesterday looking for the missing servant. They told him no more'n they told you. But then he said another fellow come through here a few days ago, an odd one, dressed as a nob from Kerotea, but his look was not such as would fit his clothes. Said the man was telling how his groom run off with a prize horse, and he was offering a reward for either the groom or the beast."

"Aeren is no—"

"Now just haul in your jib. Graeme believes the man wasn't looking for no horse, neither. The fellow couldn't even describe the horse other than it was big and white.

Right odd, Graeme said. For certain, he was no king's man.
This Kerotean is staying down to Grenatte, and he wants
Graeme to let him know right off if there's any word of
the horse or the groom, but not tell anyone else that might
be asking. Says the groom is tall, light-haired, about twenty
and some years, fair in the face, but with a testy temper.
The boy's not quite right in the head, he says. Might be
talkin' wild."

"He's lying. If I'd not seen Aeren's hands or feet, perhaps, or noted his manner. Or if I'd not learned how
intelligent he is, I might have believed it. But he's no
groom, and he's not incompetent." No groom practiced
the kind of martial exercises Aeren had been doing that
morning. The more I thought of the whole matter, the
odder it was.

"It's a mystery, for sure. Graeme says he plans to look
into it. And after hearing all this and knowing this little
trinket is involved"—Jaco tapped the bundle on his hand—
"I don't know but what we'd best get you out of it as quick
as we may."

"I'm not getting involved in *anyone's* problems. I'm
going to give Aeren the clothes and send him off to Montevial. Could I take the dagger back with me?" Seeing Aer-
en's reaction to it might be interesting.

"Surely. But I think I'll come along with it and get a
look at your new friend myself."

I hefted the bundle of clothes, Tim Fetterling's gray
cloak, and my bag of eggs and butter, while Jacopo found
an unused knife sheath, bundled it with the knife, and
grabbed his walking stick. We strolled in quiet companionship past the clay statues of the Twins, glaring from their
unkempt shrine, across the fields, and up the trail into the
woods. The shadows were already lengthening.

My breath stopped when I glimpsed the still form
sprawled on the grass under the eaves of the forest. Stars
of night, was he dead? I sped across the meadow and
dropped to my knees beside the body, but I had scarcely
noted that Aeren was only sleeping when I found myself
face down with my arms pinned painfully behind my back,
my nose in the dirt, and not a breath left in my lungs.

"A blight on your thick head," I said, gasping. "It's only me and a friend."

At my first word, Aeren released me. By the time I had dragged myself to my knees and reassured myself that neither arms nor neck were broken, he stood ten paces away from me, taut, wary, and watching Jacopo limp across the meadow.

"Demons! The rascal didn't hurt you?" said Jacopo, no longer leaning on the sturdy length of hickory, but gripping one end of it fiercely.

I crept across the grass and leaned my back against a tree, rubbing my shoulder and neck and brushing the leaves and dirt from my skirt. "Easy, Jaco. I'm fine. Just a second layer of bruises."

"He's been trained to fight," said Jacopo, glowering at the young man. "No doubt of that. Quick and smooth. Strong, too, I'll be bound. What's he done to you, little girl?" Jacopo bent over to take a look at my neck.

"Ouch!" The old sailor was a ham-handed nursemaid.

Before Jacopo could apologize, Aeren grabbed his collar and shoved the old man away so forcefully that Jaco crashed into the dead lower branches of a pine tree. When the young man dropped to his knees beside me and reached for my neck, I flinched. To my surprise, his fingers brushed my skin quite gently. His brow was creased, as if he couldn't understand how the marks had come about.

"I'll live," I said, trying to calm the situation before he got more agitated. "We startled you."

His frown deepened, and he moved in closer, his bulk pressing me against the tree as he tugged at the tie that would loosen the gathered neck of my shift.

"Get away from me." With an ungentle hand to his chest, I managed to squirm out from between him and the tree. But he removed my hand and moved closer again, yanking the cloth down to bare my throat. With a stiff forearm I knocked his hand aside, while with the other hand, I reached through my pocket, drew my knife, and pointed it at his belly. I knew where to hurt a man, and I knew how to talk to a brute, whether he spoke the same language or not. "Get. Away. From. Me."

Face a deep scarlet, he let go of my clothes. Then, baring

his teeth, he grabbed my forearm and twisted it until the knife dropped to the ground. For a moment I thought he might break my wrist or snatch up the weapon and turn it on me. But instead, he pushed me to the ground, stood up, and walked away.

Jacopo gave me a hand up, stood close by my shoulder, and raised his stick to Aeren's back. "May the good god Jerrat drown you, you filthy devil—"

"Wait, Jaco." No point in letting things get out of hand. I retrieved my dagger and sheathed it. "Aeren"—I repeated his name several times and waited until he turned around again to lay my hand on Jacopo's shoulder—"this is my friend Jacopo from Dunfarrie. Jaco, this is . . . Lord Aeren of somewhere." Jaco was busy mopping his forehead with a kerchief, and his grudging bow was less than gentlemanly.

Aeren ignored both Jacopo and my introduction. With a sour expression, he gestured to his stomach and his mouth and pointed to the cottage.

"I've better things to do, you wretched beast. Time to fend for yourself a bit." I rummaged amid the eggs and butter in my pack and pulled out a well-bruised wild plum, left from my morning on Poacher's Ridge. I threw the plum at Aeren. Hard.

He caught it in one hand, deftly enough to prevent the soft fruit from splattering on him. As he bit into it, one corner of his mouth twitched. *Smug little bastard.*

I tossed the clothes bundle at his feet. Once he had finished the plum and flipped the stem into the trees, he squatted down beside the pile and, one by one, lifted the items by the tip of one finger. He examined each carefully, then gave me such a look of scornful disbelief that, despite all my annoyance, I could do nothing but burst out laughing. It seemed like a century since I had laughed, and finding myself doing so at an unpleasant brute of a man who had come near throttling me twice within a week was strange indeed. Aeren flushed, snatched the bundle of clothes, and disappeared into the trees.

"If ever I've seen a spoiled lordling, it has to be this one," I said, wiping my eyes with my sleeve. "Did you see his nose turn up? I've nursed him until I'm exhausted and full of splinters from sleeping on the floor, I've fed him half my food stocks, so that I'll be doing well to have a meal next week, and here he sits in Anne's old sheet and disdains something a hundred times better. I just don't think he's some common riverman, wrecked on the Snags."

"Mmm. No half-wit groom, neither." Jacopo fingered his own knife and did not laugh with me. "He's a killer, Seri. I've seen no man with such moves who wasn't, whether lowborn or high. I don't like the way he looks at you."

I clasped my hands about my knees and leaned back against the tree. "On that we are in complete agreement."

A short time later Aeren emerged from the woods dressed in Jacopo's gifts. He picked at the rough cloth uncomfortably, like a small boy dressed in his first stiff-collared suit.

"I sympathize," I said. "I can't say I prefer kersey or russet to silk."

"Do you think he understands what you say?" said Jacopo, as Aeren snatched my pack and rummaged through it, dropping it with an annoyed grunt when he found nothing of interest. Raking me with a glare, the young man strode across the field toward the cottage.

"Most likely not, but I'm less likely to take an ax to him if I say what I think." If he had broken my eggs, I was going to kill him.

"He looks older than you said."

Aeren soon returned, tearing at a hunk of the chewy hearthbread as a hunting dog tears at a doe. He did look more like mid- to late twenties than early. I had always considered myself a keen observer of such things. Perhaps it was his illness had changed him or the afternoon sunlight, revealing what forest shadows, soft mornings, and lamplight had hidden.

"Show him the dagger, Jaco."

"I'm thinking that might not be clever."

"As you said, a knife is no more dangerous than his hands. If he's of a mind to make away with us, then he needs no knife to do it. But somehow . . ." Twice in the past hour I'd seen his rage surge. Twice I had seen it quelled. Perhaps I was getting cocky.

Jacopo tossed the bundle on the ground in between us

and nudged the coverings open with his stick. Aeren picked
up the weapon and ran his fingers slowly over its shining
length, examining it curiously, especially the device on the
hilt. His expression exhibited no sign of recognition. The
knife's heft and balance were pleasing to him, though, and
he snatched up the sheath and fastened it to his cloth belt.
I didn't particularly like the idea, but wasn't going to argue.
I wasn't afraid of him. I hadn't been afraid for ten years.
What could anyone do to hurt me?

"Come on," I said, scrambling to my feet, "let's take a
look at where Paulo found the knife. Maybe Aeren got in
a fight there . . . got whacked on the head or something.
Whatever happened, seeing the place might force him to
remember where he came from or where he was going. I
want him gone by nightfall."

The angle of the sun was steep as the three of us set out
on the trail to the spring. Through the trees we glimpsed
the grassy hillsides brushed with gold. I showed Jaco where
I'd first encountered Aeren, and where the hunters had
ridden through, and I tried to get Aeren to show us which
way he had come down the hill. He was unsure, but as we
wandered up higher, beyond the boundary of the trees, his
steps slowed. His eyes darted about, the lines of his face
drawn tight, his fists clenching and unclenching.

"A little farther," I said, pointing up the hill.

A cool, rock-lined grotto taller than a man split the side
of the hill near the ridgetop. At the base of the smooth
boulders was the spring. The clear, blue-green pool spilled
over moss-covered stones into the stream that carved its
way down the sunny hillside into the dark line of the trees.

Jacopo and I searched the soft ground for tracks or any
sign that something unusual had gone on in the place. The
only thing I found was a rusty ladle thrown into the pool,
probably the offering of some drought-blighted farmer hoping to appease a local water spirit. Despite the priests' best
efforts to stamp out all remnants of any gods but Annadis
and Jerrat, a few stubborn, desperate people persisted in
their desperate superstitions.

After a fruitless half-hour, I flopped down on a rock in
the shade, discouraged. "There's nothing here." Why did I
care? Perhaps he was exactly the thief Darzid claimed.

Jacopo sagged onto the rock beside me, mopping his brow. "It would help if I knew what we were looking for."

"Enough is enough, Jaco. We'll give him some food, point him toward Montevial, and let him take his chances. He's certainly not defenseless, and if he sells the knife, he can keep himself far better than you or me."

Aeren wandered about the hillside restlessly, frustration shadowing his handsome features. He had drawn the silver dagger, and every few steps he would stop and glare at it, until at last, with an explosive croak that was the only expletive he could manage, he threw it at the boulder that sheltered the pool. His face did not change expression when the dagger embedded itself to the hilt in the smooth and unbroken rock face, heeding its impenetrable solidity no more than if it had been a loaf of bread.

"Demons of the deep!" Jacopo jerked backward as if struck in the head.

I thought my heart had stopped. Every nerve in my body quivered with the charge that lingered in the air. Enchantment . . . It was like the fleeting embrace of lightning, or the kiss of fire's breath on frozen flesh, or a moment's memory of passion that stands every hair on its end, flushing the skin with exotic sensation. Ten years since I'd felt the like—almost fifteen since the first time, the day I discovered that the man I loved was a sorcerer.

CHAPTER 5

Evard. To consider how infatuated I had been with him still revolted me. Oh, he was handsome enough: tall, with shoulders as sturdy as a fortress tower, fair hair that drooped over one of his gray eyes as if in invitation to share a wicked jest, graceful hands that were always warm and never unsure. What Leiran girl of sixteen would not have been swept off her feet by such a dashing young duke, conqueror of an enemy's city at twenty?

My brother Tomas was already a swordsman of wide reputation, and he had attracted Evard's notice while serving in his regiment during the subjugation of Valleor. It was on the brilliant summer day of Evard's triumphant return to Montevial, as I stood with my father on our townhouse balcony watching the victorious legions ride by, that I first fell under Evard's shadow. Life shifted when he looked at me. The first change in a year of changes . . .

Year 26 in the reign of King Gevron

"Look, Papa, there's Tomas, at the front of the troop! Next to the dark-haired adjutant just behind Duke Evard. Doesn't he look fine?"

My father squinted into the noonday, holding up one hand against the glare from the whitewashed houses and their new glass windows across the wide street. He rarely came out of his library anymore. He'd not been the same man since my mother had died of fever when I was nine. I hoped that seeing the proud legions, hearing the drums of their marching, and feeling the glory of Tomas so favored would inspire him to his horse and arms again. He was not too old to ride in service to Leire, not yet forty, and his forearms still bulged with muscle. But only my firm hold on his arm kept him from retreating into the dim room behind the balcony door. "Quite fine. Now let me loose, girl. Both flask and cup are empty." Even at noonday, he reeked of his wine.

Still holding my father's arm, I tossed the yellow and purple garlands the servants had brought from the market that morning. I came near letting loose a most unmaidenly yell at Tomas, afraid his manly bearing might prevent his looking up at us as the Third Legion of Leire rode through the cheering crowds of servants, boys, and shopkeepers, and the maidens of marriageable age being thrust into the warriors' path. But just as the purple-robed priests carried the guide-staffs topped with the Swordsman's rising sun and the Navigator's crescent moon past the stoop before our own, Tomas leaned forward, laid his hand on his commander's sleeve, and pointed up at our balcony.

Duke Evard tossed back his fair hair and fixed his attention on my face, and I felt my color rise as if I'd actually yelled out a soldier's lewd blessing or dropped straw on Tomas's head as I might have done in teasing one short year ago. I dropped my father's arm and gripped the rail of the balcony. To my breathless astonishment, the duke pulled out of the ranks and waved his troops on forward while he positioned his mount just beneath me, stood on his saddle, and reached for our iron trellis that was thick with the dark green leaves and orange blossoms of trumpet vines. As agile as an Isker acrobat, Duke Evard shinnied up the trellis and over the rail until he stood on the balcony beside me. Bowing gallantly from the waist, he presented me with a bouquet of white lilies some admirer had thrust into his hands.

Cheeks burning, I accepted the flowers and was scarcely halfway through my curtsy when he scrambled over the rail again. To a laughing roar from the crowd and his troops, he leaped into the saddle and spurred his charger forward, retaking his position at the front. Neither he nor Tomas looked back.

Evard claimed he was my slave from that moment. It did not occur to me at the time that the daughter of the oldest house in the kingdom would make an excellent match for one with royal ambition. And neither Evard nor Tomas nor any Leiran ever mentioned that his bloody victory had exterminated the entire population of the lovely, refined Vallorean city he had conquered. Years went by before I learned that part of the story.

My father died when I was eighteen. His passing was a mercy in so many ways, both for him—a great man before his grieving decline—and for me. Though Papa was only forty-one, the tally of noble deeds we had the priests engrave upon his memorial stele in Annadis's temple comforted us that the Holy Twins would not forget him or our family when telling stories of earthly heroes. And I could not be betrothed in the year of mourning.

During that year I learned a great deal about Evard. He spent much of his time with Tomas at Comigor Keep, our musty holding on the northern downs, sparring in the fencing yard and making himself at home in our grand old library, drinking my father's brandy and talking of those who would stand between him and the throne when King Gevron died. I had listened to men's politics since nursery days, more than ever since my mother's death. And so there came a time when my curiosity prodded me to question Evard's certainties.

Year 28 in the reign of King Gevron

"But Evard," I said on one evening, "doesn't the law say that when only nieces and nephews are left, it's the children of the king's eldest sibling that will inherit?"

"Don't trouble yourself, my duchess," he said. "When the time comes, there will be no one but me. I have information, you see. My aide Darzid—a truly valuable addition to my staff—has discovered that Vennick has troubles with his estates. I do believe the good earl has failed to pay his levies for ever so many years, and, in fact, evidence will come to light that he has unlawfully diverted the taxes of his vassals . . . to his own purposes." He widened his eyes in shock, then he and Tomas burst into laughter that I didn't quite understand. I didn't quite approve of it, either.

"And my cousin Frederic. Have you heard the rumors?

It's being said he's a bastard, that my Aunt Catherine was never legally married to Colburn. Why, the whole brood could be turned out onto the streets if a witness was ever to be found to the matter. Dear Aunt Catherine, who would ever have picked her for a common whore? I couldn't bear to see her made to do public penance, though. The thought of her shaven head nauseates me!"

"You can't be serious! Lady Catherine?" My mind stretched yet again into unfamiliar realms.

"And I don't think Martin is a serious contender. He has very strange friends."

Martin, Earl of Gault, was one of my favorite people in the world. He was about forty-five and, like all Leiran men, had been a soldier. He now held a powerful position at court. A distant cousin of my mother, he was a wise, cultured, and witty man. On my seventeenth birthday, Martin had issued me an invitation to join him and some guests for a few days at his estate, assuring my father that I would be properly chaperoned. He hosted these "salons" for three days in the first week of every month, inviting a variety of fascinating and unusual people, and providing his guests with charades and plays, jugglers and mimes, word games, puzzles, and lively debates about anything and everything. Martin thought no one too young to participate if the person could make good conversation, which he defined as anything beyond fashion, horses, and the war of the moment.

I had spent my childhood with horses and dogs, playing at war with Tomas, listening to my father and his friends talk of battles and conquest, politics and managing estates. I was sure that every intelligent person in Leire believed the same as they on every matter of importance. But every day spent in the stimulating company at Windham advanced my education a whole level. There I began to learn of history, art, philosophy, and music, to question the certainties of politics and piety, and to experience the pleasures of sharp wit and well-considered disagreement.

I thought Martin would make a marvelous king, but I never said so to Evard or Tomas or even to Darzid, Evard's charming, cynical aide who began accompanying Evard to

Comigor that summer and quickly became my favorite dinner companion. Tomas disdained Martin, saying that anyone who would dress himself up as a beggar for a Long Night entertainment had too little dignity to be a sovereign. When I told Martin of my brother's comment, he said, "It does me good to dress as a beggar now and then. Gives me wondrous understanding of my tenants and my soldiers, having to do without boots in the cold." Though he tossed it off lightly, I knew that he meant what he said.

It was at Windham, Martin's sprawling country house, that I met Julia, countess of Helton, a brilliant and elegant young widow. Julia was the first woman I had ever known who could hold her own in serious conversation with men. From the first evening of our acquaintance, I wanted to be like her. Fortunately, Julia's rank made her a chaperone of impeccable credentials, for my father—and later, my brother—would never have allowed me to continue in such liberal company without.

Julia and Martin were passionately in love. They could not marry because Julia's dead husband's powerful family refused their consent. Martin would have had her as his mistress in an instant, but as he was third in line to the throne, Julia would not permit him to compromise his reputation. Certain influential Leirans required behavior in their kings-to-be that they did not require in their kings, she told me. Though I never saw them so much as touch hands, their intimacy was such that on occasion I felt like a crass intruder just watching one offer the other a glass of wine.

Resident in Martin's household were two brothers, Tennice and Tanager, second and third sons of a minor baron who had too little property to share among his children. Only military service or the priesthood were considered suitable occupations for landless noblemen. The baron, unwilling for his sons to reap the scorn reserved for men who would choose temple service over arms, had sent them to serve the earl. Martin had discovered in the two a depth of talent and loyalty that quickly raised them out of the ranks and into his inner circle.

Tennice was the elder, serious and scholarly, his thin face forever pushed into a book unless one made a chance remark about law or politics within his hearing. He had a remarkable memory, which had imprinted on it everything he had ever read. He was Martin's chief counselor, and thus accompanied the earl on all his business.

On one occasion, after an intense, three-day discussion of matters of royal succession and the peerage, Tennice invited me, quite sincerely, to read law with him. Perhaps I could move in with Julia, whose estates bordered Martin's? I was overwhelmed by the compliment, for it was unheard of for a woman to participate in such intellectual pursuits, and I was surely no scholar. Of course, I had to refuse. My father was newly buried, and Tomas would never permit me to leave home unmarried for such a purpose. But as soon as I returned to Comigor, I began to receive books on law and politics and philosophy, and copious notes in Tennice's own handwriting. I studied them intensely, so I could discuss them on my next visit. I was determined to deserve his regard.

Tanager was Martin's aide and bodyguard and the very opposite of his brother, muscular and rash, exaggerated in every way. No one would plunge into Martin's enterprises with more enthusiasm. His broad shoulders would bear a donkey's head for a Long Night farce or bloodstained armor in his lord's service with equal willingness and enjoyment. Again and again he would lavish his heart and his attentions on a woman, only to plunge into deep depression when she discovered his lack of fortune and abandoned him. The others teased that he should wear his armor in Martin's drawing rooms, as no one ever came out of the conversational battles more bloodied than Tanager.

By the autumn that I turned nineteen, I felt more at home at Windham than at Comigor. . . .

Year 29 in the reign of King Gevron

I arrived in early evening, breathless with the chill wind of the open carriage. Julia met me with a kiss and swept me toward the fire, snatching off my cloak and tossing it to a manservant. "Dear Seri, I'm so glad you're here. I'm in desperate need of an ally. Your cousin is being an ass again."

Martin and a portly noble of similar age were propounding their dismay over the recent visit by one Baroness Lavastre to the Council of Lords. The formidable woman had intruded on the Council's deliberations, insisting that she be allowed to offer opinion on a property ruling being considered by the body, her husband being away at war and his man of business recently deceased. "It's true the woman had an excellent grasp of tariffs and the subtleties of trading-company acquisitions," said Martin, clasping his hands behind his back and shaking his head with such gravity, one might think the woman had suggested Leire surrender a city or two to a wild-haired Isker warlord. "I discussed the matter with her in this very room only last spring. But if we allowed her to speak to the Council, why then next month she would want to vote her husband's shares!"

"And why should she not?" Julia riposted as we joined Tennice, Tanager, and several other younger men who had settled on the couches and chairs near the fire. "A good mind for business with a few fresh ideas could increase everyone's profits."

"Perhaps, if women were allowed to speak, some consideration might be given to the smaller shareholds whose masters are younger and thus all away at the war," I added, not even pausing to give Martin his usual peck on the cheek before joining the fray. "As it is, only those too cowardly or too old to serve are voting. They're running smaller trading companies into the ground. . . ." It was an old argument, and Martin always started it up again whenever a fellow member of the Council of Lords showed up in his drawing room. Did he believe his own pronouncements? I was sure I had heard him argue exactly the opposite way on earlier occasions when Tennice had brought out the points of law that prohibited women's voices being heard in the Council chambers.

We pursued the matter until supper was announced. Almost everyone in the fireside circle had seen his ideas upheld or trounced, and had been called variously a fossil, a libertine, or an anarchist fit only for the mad speakers' corners near the Royal University in Valleor. Only one observer had stayed quiet throughout the discussion—a slender, dark-haired stranger, who stood leaning on the corner of the tall marble mantelpiece, arms folded across his chest. His blue eyes and high cheekbones gave him a slightly foreign look, though I could not guess his origins. He was clean-shaven, and conservatively dressed in a black doublet, high-collared white shirt, and slim black breeches, though in any Leiran house he would be inevitably conspicuous for the lack of a sword at his side. When the supper truce was called, and Martin bent over me for his greeting kiss, my cousin flicked his glance to the man. "Did I not tell you we had a lively forum here, my friend?"

The stranger looked from Martin to me, crinkling his eyebrows as if making a serious study. "Are all the women in Leire so opinionated, or is it only those with fire in their hair?" He spoke in a soft, melodious baritone. "I've lived among many strange cultures, and in few are women allowed a voice until they're at least eighty. Now I think I understand why." If his marvelous eyes had not sparkled with good humor, I might have been offended.

Martin almost choked on smothered laughter. "Lady Seriana Marguerite, duchess-daughter of Comigor, may I present my good friend Karon, a gentleman of Valleor. He is a traveling historian and archeologist on leave from the University, come to study the people of Leire and our peculiar customs. Karon, you must call her Seri or you'll never have a chance to get in a word of your own. . . ."

The gentleman bowed and took my hand, raising it to his forehead in the Vallorean way. I had never seen a man so graceful. He was of an age with Julia—late twenties— and I plagued him shamelessly with questions throughout that evening, even more forward than usual as his air of mystery intrigued me so. But he remained vague about his origins, saying only that he'd spent most of his life moving from one place to another after the death of his parents when he was very young. By the end of my three-day visit, I realized that I had done far more talking than he.

The ensuing months passed much too quickly. Once having met Karon, I never looked back to Evard. Karon's intellect and interests were wide-ranging, embracing subjects far from his specialties. Martin had taught me how to argue, how to poke and prod my opponent with strange ideas and bits of information, twisting and turning words into knots and puzzles, until both of us came out panting with the mental exertion. The purpose of it was never the winning or the losing, but only the exhilaration of the contest. Karon was never averse to taking a position far from his own simply to further the enjoyment of the fray. He reveled in the game, while Evard was interested only in winners and losers.

My year of mourning was almost over, but I was not ready to give up the freedoms it had granted me. When the months had shrunk to days, I decided that I must speak to Tomas.

"The year is up next week," I said one evening, as we sat alone in the Comigor dining room.

"So it is. Will Evard offer for you?" Tomas seemed more interested in the slice of roast pork he was carving to refill his plate.

"You know his mind better than I."

"His mind is on the succession. Gevron grows more feeble each day."

I pushed a compote of currants and blackberries within his reach, watching a drop of the deep purple sweetness soak into the white table linen. "What if Evard doesn't win as he expects?"

"He'll win."

"But what if he doesn't, and I'm betrothed to him?" My own meal sat untouched on my plate.

My question clearly set him thinking. Tomas would feel it disloyal to speculate on Evard's failure—and Tomas was anything but disloyal—but a rich, virginal, and reasonably attractive young duchess was a considerable asset, not to be thrown away even for friendship and loyalty. I knew my worth.

"An interesting question." He said nothing more about it that night or any other night following. But when the year was up, Evard did not offer. After some weeks, I broached the subject once again, but Tomas said only that Evard had agreed he had no time for betrothals or weddings or wives. Not until his position was secure.

That was enough for the moment. I lived for my days at Windham and harbored no illusions about my future. I was a key to Tomas's fortune every bit as much as his strong sword arm. Many brothers would have forbidden the freedom I had, so I treasured my friendship with Karon and all Martin's circle, and I acknowledged nothing beyond it.

Year 31 in the reign of King Gevron

King Gevron fooled everyone by lasting two more years. Though Evard chafed, he was not idle. As he had predicted, an astonished Earl of Vennick was found guilty of diverting tax revenues into his own pockets and retired to his country estate in disgrace. And a witness signed documents avowing that the priest of Jerrat who had presided at the wedding of Gevron's sister Lady Catherine to Sir Charles Colburn was an impostor, unknown to any temple in Leire. Therefore Lady Catherine's son Frederic, Duke of Warburton, was a bastard and had no claim to his uncle's throne.

With no little unease, I watched Evard bind Tomas ever more closely to his fortunes. Evard told my brother that it was time he named his own military staff. As the lord of such a vast holding as Comigor, Tomas should replace the old Comigor captains who were beholden to our father with younger men who would be loyal to him alone. Evard even offered to loan him Captain Darzid.

To think of my father's loyal commanders thus dismissed, seven fierce and honorable warriors who had dandled me on their knees when I was small, who had taught me to shoot a bow and still brought me exotic gifts from their travels, was insupportable. In the past year, as Tomas and Evard had become more engrossed in their intrigues, I had spent a great deal of time with Captain Darzid. I enjoyed his wit and found his ever-sarcastic observations of Leiran courtiers amusing. So, on the night before the change of command, I sought him out at his townhouse and explained my feelings.

He pressed wine into my hands and, once done with his delightful renderings of my brother's shock and the scandalized court ladies' gossip at my secret venture into a bachelor's house, seemed sincerely interested in my pleas. "What would you have me do, my lady? I am ever at your command as you well know. But my refusing the post will not

help the old curmudgeons. Nor should it. Duke Tomas is
absolutely right; your own safety depends on his control of
his troops."

"You're clever, Darzid. I know you care for no one but
yourself"—we had discussed this many times—"but for this
once, bend your wit to a kindness. I'll think of something
magnificent to reward you. I swear it."

He promised to think about it, and indeed on the next
day as the seven were forced to turn in their shields and
strip the four guardian rings of Comigor from their sur-
coats, he presented each man with a fine new sword, a new
warhorse, and a document vouching for his valor and loyalty, so that he could get a new position with another
house.

When I thanked Darzid for extending himself so generously and on such short notice, he looked at me in an oddly
calculating way that left me feeling uncomfortably exposed.
"I would have as soon seen them hanged, lady. But the
prospect of a reward from you . . . that intrigued me enough
to spend a small fortune and a night's work."

Interregnum

By the time King Gevron gave in and joined his forefathers
in the great tomb on Pythian Hill, Martin was first in line
for the throne, and, after him, Evard. Tennice said it was
only a matter of time until some accusation surfaced about
Martin. Even after all I'd heard, I refused to believe that,
either of Evard, who was almost certainly to be my husband, or of Tomas. But a few days before the Council of
Lords was to announce the succession, the Council received
a letter avowing that Martin, Earl of Gault, had sheltered
a sorcerer. The letter named one Alfredo, a resident of
Windham who had died the previous year.

I remembered Alfredo. The rumpled and absent-minded
mathematician had once been Martin's tutor. Martin had
offered the old man a home at Windham when he lost his
last position due to failing hearing and other circumstances
of age. Alfredo often forgot where he was, frequently mis-
placed his handkerchiefs and his books, and seldom dined
with the rest of the household, ashamed of his trembling

hands that could not hold a knife. But, despite his declining faculties, he remained extraordinarily good at chess, and with intense and exuberant joy he pursued his sole remaining purpose in life, designing complex chess problems in hopes of stumping Martin. One could not imagine Alfredo feeding his dark powers on blood, murdering children to use for depraved rites, raising demons to drive men to madness, twisting the beauties of nature into grotesque parodies, or carrying out any other of the evil works popularly attributed to sorcerers. And how could anyone believe that Martin, so wise and perceptive, would give shelter to an abominable heretic? The whole thing was absurd, yet the accusation could not be ignored. The extermination laws would not permit it.

Sorcery was a vile and wicked practice, the last dregs of the chaotic evil from the Beginnings, before the First God Arot had defeated the beasts of earth and the monsters of the deep and given dominion over the world to his twin sons, Annadis and Jerrat. In the past few years, I had learned that a number of intelligent and otherwise honorable Leirans looked skeptically on our sacred stories and rituals. But to countenance sorcery was to invite horror and chaos back into the world, denying the gods themselves— the very gods who stood beside our king and his soldiers on every battlefield.

The announcement of the succession was postponed, and the Council of Lords convened to hear the arguments. The principal witness was a chambermaid who had been dismissed from Windham the previous year. She had been assigned to take care of Alfredo's room, and a terrible burden it had been, she said. No one understood why the earl kept such a disgusting creature about. Alfredo was crude and had foul habits, just as she had always been taught about sorcerers. The old man marked papers with arcane symbols and patterns, and he cursed and murmured over them when she peeked through his door. He would always hide the papers from her and swear that she would never steal his secrets. He ate in his room, she said, not with proper company, and often she would spy him gnawing on meat that was just the size as would be a human baby. I had heard no more ridiculous accusations in my life. Knowing the old man and his preoccupations, every bit of these foolish accusations could be explained.

Despite the people's horror of the practice, and the priests' insistence that the merest taint of sorcery must be thoroughly investigated, Tennice was able to convince the Lords that there was no evidence to convict Martin of so much as discussing the dark arts, much less harboring one of the vile in his home. The Council ruled that Martin was not guilty of the accusations, but that since Alfredo himself could not be examined, it was impossible to determine whether the old man had truly been a sorcerer. That was enough. As long as any doubt remained, Martin would never be king. That was all Evard really wanted.

The afternoon of the verdict was dreary, the autumnal gloom deepened by a miserable downpour. Throughout the hearing, Tomas had sat beside me in the Council Hall, making sure I was seen nowhere near Martin or the others, but after the ruling he went off with Evard, abandoning me with servants to take me home. Instead, I traveled to Windham. Just the six of us were there: Martin, Karon, Julia, Tanager, Tennice, and me. We said we were going to celebrate, but the dinner was dismal. Martin left the dining room before the soup was taken away. The rest of us picked at the meal in silence. After an hour Tennice dismissed the servants, telling them to take the rest of the night as a holiday in honor of the earl's vindication. The five of us retired to the library.

Only two lamps were lit against the gloom. The dark leather of the furnishings and deep, rich reds of the rugs suited our mood very well. "I never thought he cared so much," I said to Julia, who sat staring at the closed door of Martin's study, her eyes shining with unshed tears. "He always treated the throne as such a remote possibility, spoke of it so irreverently, that I thought—"

"It's what he wanted people to think," she said, "to discourage any interest in him. But he lived for it. It's how he put up with all the foolishness and idiocy of court life. Frederic and Vennick had agreed to cede the throne to him if they were named. They'd won a clear majority on the Council to his support . . . until all of this stupidity. The whole world is askew, and he can see so clearly what needs to be done to set it right. It will drive him mad to be relegated to impotence once more, to see Evard in his place, destroying what remnants of civilization linger in Leire."

While Martin remained closeted in his study and the others drank brandy and regaled each other with sporadic bursts of funereal humor, Karon asked if I would walk with him in the gardens. I was happy to get out. Sitting and thinking was the last thing I wanted at the moment.

We strolled down gravel paths that wound through manicured bowers of roses and lilacs and into wild gardens of foxtail and harebells and summerlace. Around every corner was a lovely surprise: a grassy grotto with a stone bench or perhaps a pool or fountain tucked amid the ferns and trees like the presents hidden about houses and gardens for children at the Feast of Vines in the spring.

The evening air smelled damp and earthy from the afternoon rain. After a while Karon lagged behind, and I glanced over my shoulder to see him standing in the middle of the path staring upward, watching the first star emerge from the deep blue of the clearing sky. He was forever dawdling when we walked out, stopping to examine the subtle shading of a primrose, or peer underneath a water lily to see the silver trout hiding there, or gaze for moments at a time at a raindrop poised at the edge of a leaf. I had never known anyone so entranced with nature, with people, with beauty—or so observant of them.

I had no heart for gardens or beauty. A message had arrived just before dinner. Tomas would be at Windham the next morning to escort me to the royal palace in Montevial. My time had run out. The knowledge that I might never return to Martin's house except as Evard's wife dissolved my resolution like frost in sunlight.

"You are extraordinarily quiet," Karon said after a while. "Am I too distracted?"

"No. I wish I could do as you seem to do, take in all this to hazard against an uncertain future."

"Ah." We walked on.

The silence was too heavy. "Will you travel again soon?" I asked.

"Perhaps. I've stayed here much longer than I intended. I should go."

"And where will you go? Whom will you study next?"

As always, his smile illuminated his face as if his inner being had taken fire. "I've heard of a land of flame-haired women—" He never finished the jest.

Tanager burst into the garden from the library doors. "Karon, Seri, come! It's Martin. The blasted fool has tried to kill himself."

We ran through the gardens, up the steps, and through the doors that led into Martin's study. He was slumped in his chair by the fire, scarcely breathing, his lips a sickly blue, his eyes glazed, spittle stringing from the corner of his slack mouth. A glass of wine had fallen from his hand, and Julia knelt beside his chair, staring in horror at a silver vial in her hand. "Oh, my darling, you said this was only for the worst of times, and we weren't there yet. Not yet. How could you?"

Karon took the vial. "What is it?"

"I don't know the name," said Julia, pressing one hand to her mouth and wrapping the other about her stomach. "Martin brought it from Valleor years ago. He said it was made by jonglers, a 'diplomatic gift' he couldn't refuse. They told him it was painless, and that it was always good to have a way out of the worst of times. He joked about it. Never, ever, did I think . . ."

Karon did not hesitate. "Tanager, bring me a knife. Sharp and clean. Just do it! Don't ask questions." He gave Tennice a plain white linen handkerchief. "Rip it into three strips and tie them together end to end. Tight." Martin was limp as Karon lifted him to the floor; his eyes had rolled back in his head, and his tongue was swollen and discolored, threatening to choke off what little breath remained in him.

Hurriedly Karon removed his coat, loosened the left sleeve of his shirt at the wrist, and then knelt on the rug beside Martin. When Tanager returned, Karon took the knife, then glanced up at us hovering close about him. After an ever-so-slight nod of his head, he closed his eyes, opened his arms wide, and spoke with quiet intensity. "Life, hold! Stay your hand. Halt your foot ere it takes another step along the Way. Grace your son once more with your voice that whispers in the deeps, with your spirit that sings in the wind, with the fire that blazes in your gifts of joy and sorrow. Fill my soul with light, and let the darkness make no stand in this place."

He gripped Martin's hand and with a flash of the knife made a deep and bloody gash in Martin's arm. Before any one of us could cry out or pull him away, he pushed up his left sleeve and did the same to himself. He had done it before. His arm was covered with scars. Hundreds of them.

"What in the name of all gods—?"

Karon ignored Tanager's outburst, holding out the knotted handkerchief. "Bind us together. Hurry, if you love him." His command was tight and hard. Cradling Martin's head with his right hand to ease his choking, he positioned his wound over Martin's and had Tanager tie their bleeding arms together as tightly as possible. Tanager's hands were trembling. "Now, all of you stay back." Eyes fixed on Martin's face, Karon whispered, *"J'den encour,"* in a language I did not know.

I sank onto a stool by the fire, stunned and speechless. This must be another of Martin's pageants. Surely in a moment he would pop up and say, "Good joke!" and Karon would show us how the knife was a trick and the blood was not real and nothing out of the ordinary was occurring here. But instead, Karon remained kneeling at Martin's side, the two of them bound together in this strange brotherhood. Karon's eyes were closed again, his head bowed, and for an hour he did not move. Nor did any of us, shocked and terrified as we were. I could feel a charge in the air like a veil of lightning, shimmering about us, ready to strike our hearts still at any moment.

The clocks in the Windham tower chimed a second hour. Just as I thought my chest must burst or my head split, Martin sighed and began to breathe easier, faint pink replacing the morbid blue of his lips. Karon was ashen, sweat pouring down his face. He swayed a bit, and Tanager moved to catch Martin before Karon could drop his head to the floor. But without moving or opening his eyes, Karon said hoarsely, "No! You must not. Only when I tell you." Tanager paled and backed away, clasping his hands tight as if they'd been scorched.

Another quarter of an hour and Martin's eyelids fluttered; his cheeks grew rosy.

"Cut the binding now." Karon's voice was no more than a whisper.

Gingerly, Tennice picked up the knife Karon had dropped and slit the strip of linen. Martin's arm exhibited no drop of blood, no mark; on Karon's arm was only a new pale scar among all the rest. Karon gently laid Martin on the rug and backed away, but remained on his knees, arms folded, shoulders hunched, looking pale and fragile, almost transparent. He did not raise his head.

Martin sat up slowly, rubbing his temples and blinking as he looked about the room. "What's going on here? Why so solemn? Stars and planets, Karon, you look like death."

Karon, eyes still averted, said softly, "I think there are those not far from here who'll tell you that is exactly what I look like."

Martin glanced from Karon to the rest of us, and only after an awkward moment did his puzzled gaze settle on the spilled glass of wine, the silver vial, and Karon grimly fastening his left sleeve as if he could hide what was there. "Oh, my friend, what have you done"—his voice was filled with shock and distress, but no surprise—"and what have I, in my unbounded self-pity, done to you?"

"If Evard is to be king, then he must have someone worthy to keep an eye on him, to be ready when his subjects take his full measure,"—Karon glanced at Martin, his smile as pale as the rest of him—"and we'd miss your entertainments so."

"And did you tell these others what you were about?"

Karon laughed ruefully and blotted his neck with the remains of his handkerchief. "I thought it best to surprise them with it. More in keeping with the Windham tradition of puzzles and mysteries. I thought that if I were to reveal my little secret, I'd best get some good out of it and make sure you were here to defend me." His color was returning.

"And what did you think we would do?" asked Julia, abruptly sitting herself on the carpet between the two men and grasping one hand from each, forcing Karon to look at her. "Such faith you have in your friends!"

Tennice stood behind Karon and laid a long, thin hand on his shoulder. "Have you listened to nothing we've said these past two years? We know what kind of man you are, and nothing you've revealed this night makes any change in it." Then Tanager sagged onto the couch cushions, saying sorcery must not be all it was made out to be, as it looked more like work than the devilish fun he'd been led to believe.

I sat on the hearth stool, trying to comprehend what it was I had witnessed. Nothing was as it had been. The world had changed as surely and irrevocably as if I had been struck deaf or blind, or had been roused from deafness to hearing or blindness to sight. But, just as Tennice had said, I knew this man. "Martin, I think there are some inaccuracies in the lessons I've been taught. I certainly hope someone has plans to set me straight."

CHAPTER 6

Interregnum

The night of Karon's revelation was a night of intoxication. We were four initiates caught up in the heady exhilaration of mystery and conspiracy. As our questions flew about the library like autumn leaves in a whirlwind, Karon pleaded that we had no time to waste. "I must go. Give me an hour. Then go to a sheriff, tell him my name, and report what you've seen. I'll not have you compromised for me. Every moment you delay increases your danger."

Julia was weeping, trying to thank Karon for saving Martin's life, and asking what refreshment might relieve the toll his night's work had so clearly taken on him. Tanager swore to slit the throat of any man who said that what we had seen was anything but holy, and began reviewing the events aloud as if we had not witnessed them for ourselves. "Stars of night, man, you've got to tell us how you do it," he said.

"You can't just leave it." Even Tennice pushed his brother aside and said he'd appreciate knowing one thing: Could Karon just tell him whether it was one of the Twins, or the First God Arot himself, or some unknown god who guided his hand in such works, or was it, instead, some factor of the blood?

I was so filled with wonder, I could not decide what to ask first, so I just kept mumbling that no one in that room could ever be so cowardly as to betray him to the law. He could never have heard me above the clamor. We might have continued all night in such fashion, but Karon looked more distressed by the moment and cast a pleading glance at Martin, even as he tried to disentangle himself from our exuberant circle.

"Silence, all of you!" Martin bellowed. "Karon, step into the garden for a moment—no farther, mind you! We must give these nattering fools a chance to think."

Only when an exasperated Karon had retreated through the garden doors did Martin turn to us. "Sit down and listen, friends. This is perhaps the most dangerous night of your young lives, and I'll not have you go forward without stopping for one moment to give it some serious consideration."

Once we had obediently sat ourselves on the overstuffed couches, sobered by his serious tone, he went on. "This is the law of Leire—and Tennice can correct me if I miss a word or two. To harbor a sorcerer, to knowingly speak with a sorcerer or listen willingly to one word from his mouth is punishable by death—not the unspeakable death Karon will suffer if news of this night's deed escapes this room, but death, nonetheless. To my everlasting shame, my weak and selfish impulse has put him and you in this danger. He has risked the stake, the burning of his living flesh . . . and every conceivable torment that could make even such horror as that a welcome gift . . . to save my pitiful life. Yet I know him well, and the last thing he would wish is to buy his safety with ours. Every moment that we delay in turning him over condemns us alongside him. You must think soberly of your lives and your futures. If you do not accuse him as he insists, then every breath you take from this night forward will have a binder on it, every word you speak will be restricted, every truth to which you swear will be tainted by the shadow of a lie, a secret, a withholding. No soul beyond this room can ever hear this tale, be it husband, wife, child, or lover. Never. Ever. Or we are all forfeit. Now, hold your peace until I give you leave. Think carefully."

We obeyed his command in seeming. But one glance at each well-known face told the answer. No one of us would ever preserve his own life by setting the hounds on Karon. When Martin released us from our silence, we told him exactly that. Yet even as we released our pent-up indignation—that Martin might, in the remotest chance, believe one of us could be such a craven coward—my cousin confronted each of us individually, asking if we would swear to keep Karon's secret, be damned whatever came. Each one agreed. He came to me last.

"And you, my dear cousin. Never would I knowingly have faced you with this circumstance. To require you to carry such a burden into a marriage . . ."

"There is no burden here, Martin," I said. "Every time I'm at Windham my world grows larger. Who better to understand truth than one who might be queen?"

There. I'd said it. The fact that could not be lost in the excitement of the night.

Martin smiled at me fondly. But behind the lines that five and forty years of good humor had written on his kind face was pain and worldly wisdom that I could recognize, though not yet understand. "If I'd only kept that thought in my head a few hours ago, perhaps I could have spared Karon and all of you the consequences of my unforgivable cowardice. Go fetch him, and we'll let him tell you more of truth." Tennice and Julia poured brandy, while I hurried toward the garden door.

I found Karon stretched out on his back in the grass, his arms behind his head, gazing upon the stars that were scattered like diamond dust on the black velvet sky. Not wishing to startle him, I approached quietly, and so I glimpsed the expression on his face before he was aware of me. Not fear. Not anxiety. Only yearning—the same hunger I glimpsed when he walked with me in the garden or at the times when he stepped back from our laughter in Martin's drawing room and embraced our company with his eyes. In seeing him devouring the glory of that night, and in thinking of all I knew of him and all I had witnessed, both the essential question and its answer sprang up wholly formed in my head. I believed I might already understand what he would tell us.

I cleared my throat and sat down on the grass, wrapping my arms about my knees and waiting a moment to see if he would look around. He kept his eyes on the sky, but he blinked and shifted his arms protectively across his chest, so I knew he was aware of me. "You're replenishing yourself," I said, venturing my theory. "Replacing what you spent on Martin."

"Yes."

"That's what it's all about. What you are all about. Beauty, joy, friendship . . . these things you are able to cache within yourself . . . and then spend."

"Life. All of it. Pain and sorrow are wonders, also. But, of course, beauty is easier." He rolled to his side and propped his head on his hand, smiling as one will do to soften a hard truth.

"And the spending . . . is sorcery."

"Exactly so."

"I want to know. About you. About all of it. Why have we been so deceived?"

That sorcery equated with evil was a fundamental construct of the universe, a fact as sure as that time moved forward and not back. No history or science was required to prove it any more than history was required to say the earth was solid beneath our feet or the ocean fluid. Not only our priests condemned sorcery, naming it as one of the abominations of the earth that Arot had tamed in the Beginnings, but our kings and wise men, our mothers and grandmothers, men of science and warriors, believers and unbelievers agreed that it was a perversion of nature. Now, in one short hour everything had changed, and the gap in my knowledge of the world was so vast, so stark, I believed my head must cave in. This man and the healing I had seen him work were as far from evil as anything I had ever known.

Karon sat up and, after one quick glance at me, dropped his eyes and began picking at the grass. "I wanted to tell you—and the others—but because of how things were with you . . . your future . . . it made no sense. And then today, I should have sent you all away, but I didn't even think of it. After so many years, not to think of it . . . Maybe it was because I wanted you to understand." He shook his head wonderingly and expelled a quick breath. "I always thought it would be so hard to explain, but I should have known you would put the pieces together. Even Martin took a while to understand the connection you've just seen."

Why was it that those of Martin's circle were forever underestimating me? "I would imagine that Martin had neither the patience nor the incentive to observe you as closely as I have over the past two years," I said. "There are some things at which a woman is an expert before she is eighty!"

The words came out more prim and bristly than I intended, but Karon burst out laughing and I felt myself consumed by his remarkable eyes. "Oh, gods, Seri, how I love you! What I wouldn't give—ah!" He bit off his words and looked vexed. "Damn! My tongue will not keep still. My habits are all askew tonight."

He jumped to his feet and offered me his arm, instantly sober and contained. "Come," he said softly. "The others will remember all their training and believe I've eaten you." I allowed him to pull me off the grass, but I did not take my eyes from him. Everything was changed yet again by that moment's revelation. Though he avoided my gaze and swallowed his words as if to recall them, nothing would erase what I had just heard. Truth. As clear as the clean-washed night.

We strolled across the garden, up the steps, and into the library, but I might have been treading on cloud or water for all I knew. Only when we halted in the middle of the library did I wrench my eyes from Karon's face. The others were staring at us, sipping brandy, and waiting. I could not think what they were waiting for.

"We thought perhaps you two had wandered into some other garden," said Julia, her head tilted, peering at us thoughtfully.

"This exceptional young woman would not get lost in Hierant's Maze," said Karon, releasing my arm and immediately retreating toward the hearth. "She has been explaining her theories of sorcery to me."

As I sank to the leather couch beside Julia, Martin widened his eyes and waggled his eyebrows at her. I felt the blood rise to my cheeks, but before my cousin could come out with whatever clever jibe he was concocting, Karon drew the group's attention back in his direction. "So have you decided, sensibly, that I must be on my way?"

Oh yes, the grim reality of the night. Somehow I could no longer grasp it.

Tennice snorted. "Seri! You didn't get even that far in almost an hour?" Everyone but Karon and I laughed, and my face flamed hotter.

"There was no time," Karon said, clasping his hands behind his back. "The young lady was busy reading my soul and reciting to me its inner workings, telling me I must explain a few things more so as to advance her education."

"Well," said Martin, "since Seri was distracted from her task, I'll tell you that these young lions have sworn on their lives and honor—and most importantly, their tongues—that your secret does not go beyond this room. They understand the consequences for you and for themselves if it should. So it's up to you. We will take the risk of having you here. If you are willing to take the risk of our silence, then there's no need for you to go."

"I've traveled enough for the present," said Karon, softly, and the great hand which had been clenching my heart and stomach released its grip.

Martin laid his hand on Karon's shoulder. "If you're to be with us for a while longer, and since I don't think any of us are yet ready for sleep, then perhaps, as Seri suggests, it's a good time to tell your friends the history they never learned."

"As you wish."

Another log was thrown on the fire. More brandy was poured. The two starving lamps winked out, leaving the pool of light from the hearth as the only illumination. Karon settled himself on the patterned rug and began.

*   *   *

"I am of a people whose name you've never heard spoken, though we believed the race of the J'Ettanne was once as numerous as the Valloreans with whom we came to share a language. Much of our history has been lost, and I've never heard any explanation of why we were born so different or whether at some time we had a land of our own. Our oldest stories say only that the J'Ettanne scattered throughout the Four Realms because they were constantly wondering what was beyond the next hill or past the next turn of the road. A J'Ettanni man and wife might labor to build a house and plant a crop, only to abandon them before the vines bore fruit, just because a day's sunrise was so lovely that they wanted to see what might lie east of their land. Or another might move to the next town when he heard there was a minstrel there who had sung a new song of surpassing beauty. Our neighbors thought our wandering life odd, for they didn't understand that the accumulation of experience is the essence of J'Ettanni power."

The flames in the hearth set the shadows to dancing about the room.

"And yet, our people were welcomed everywhere, for their only desire was to spend their power for good. Some could infuse new life into herds and crops. Others could build skillfully and beautifully. They could make light or fire from nothing . . . well, their talents could be applied to so many things."

Karon's face was sculpted by the firelight as he spun his tale of wonder, his eyes riveted on the orange flames as if the only way he could proceed was to convince himself that no one was listening.

"The world was much as it is now. Greed and ambition set people against people, and a sorcerer's talents were too valuable to ignore when battle was to be joined. Most refused to join the service of the local warlords. To use their power for destruction violated everything the J'Ettanne believed. But the warlords tried to force them by taking their families hostage or burning their homes. Even if a man aided his lord willingly, he might find himself set against an army wherein his cousin, or his brother, or his sister was forced to serve.

"And so a group joined together, calling themselves the Free Hand of the J'Ettanne, determined that the J'Ettanne be a people who would speak for themselves, not subject to any lord. Deep in the mountains that you call the Dorian Wall lay an ancient stronghold that J'Ettanni legend said was a place sacred to our people. The Free Hand rebuilt the stronghold so that all could have a refuge in time of trouble. The secret of its location was closely guarded, passed carefully from one to another of the Free Hand, who swore on the lives of their children to keep it. They couldn't allow the warlords to discover it.

"About the time the rebuilding was done, there came a split in the Free Hand. A faction calling themselves the Closed Hand thought it was enough for us to have a safe haven, so individuals could choose to serve the warlords or not. Another group, called the Open Hand, looked beyond our own needs and asked why should peasants or knights, any more than sorcerers, be pressed against their will into the service of those who were unworthy? With the gifts of the J'Ettanne, it would be possible to order the world in peace. After long years of disagreement, the Open Hand prevailed, and J'Ettanne rose up all over the Four Realms, proclaiming that there would be no more war, no cruelty, no brutality. No more."

"How was it possible?" I burst out, unable to contain all the questions jostling each other in my head. "The talents you've described are impressive, but not enough to defeat true warriors."

"Let me show you." His gaze flicked around the room as if to make sure we were all still there. His cheeks were slightly flushed, and he quickly returned his attention to the fire. *This is what they did, and what no one then or since has ever understood.*

I heard him speaking as clearly as if his mouth were at my ear. But his lips did not move, and the room was silent save for the snap of a log in the fire. My neck prickled and my mind swelled with a presence that was not the one I carried with me every day. It was gentle and embracing and apologetic, but as undeniable and overwhelmingly powerful as a spring deluge. In that same moment, I felt an overpowering thirst, and I lifted my brandy glass to my lips.

This would not have seemed so extraordinary if Tennice and Tanager and Julia had not lifted their glasses at exactly the same moment in exactly the same motion, all of us stopping in a single movement as if time itself had halted. Suddenly, my knees felt like water.

"So you see," he went on in audible speech once more, "how it might be possible to change many things with such abilities."

Tanager, Tennice, Julia, and I . . . we looked at each other with astonishment, disbelief, and a hundred other emotions that were written on our faces. Tanager downed his brandy all in one gulp and jumped up from the floor to pour himself another. Julia's slender hand seemed paralyzed, and she stared first at Karon and then Martin. Tennice slammed down his glass, sloshing the amber liquid on a small table and jerking his hand away. I forced myself to exhale, hearing the tremulous sound of my own breath as implications and possibilities ran riot in my head . . . terrifying possibilities . . . humiliating . . . violating . . .

Oh, Seri, don't be afraid. No, I've never—not ever—done this to you before. You've had no thought that was not your own. You've felt no desire, performed no act that was not of your own will. And until this moment, I've never let myself hear anything but what has come from your lips.

The words carried so much more than their meaning—a plea for understanding that exposed a part of his most private self—that I found myself thinking, *It's all right; it's all right. I'm not afraid. Not of you.* And I knew it all was real when he glanced up quickly and gave me a tenuous smile.

"You can see how it might be easy to abuse such a gift," he went on, "and why people might come to fear it. That was what happened. For thirty or forty years the Open Hand ruled the Four Realms and corrected all that seemed wrong. But the J'Ettanne were no wiser than other men and no more immune to self-importance, and more and more they liked to order things according to their whims. Those who disputed their rule were punished with nightmares and terrors until the poor souls thought they were going mad. The poor and ignorant were controlled with superstitions—rumors of vile monsters, spirits, and demons. By the time of the Rebellion, the J'Ettanne had enslaved the people they thought to save, and, in their arrogance, had written their—our—doom.''

"But what chance had ordinary people against such power?" Tennice sat stiffly in one corner of the couch with his third glass of brandy, his voice tight, verging on anger.

Karon stood up, folding his arms, a slender silhouette against the fire. "There were so few of us. That was the key. We had been scattered for so long that our numbers had not increased like those of other races. And it doesn't matter if I can listen to what you're thinking, for if all five of you are thinking at once, as loud and discordantly as possible, I can sort it out no better than if you're all babbling at once.''

Tanager had stretched his long legs over the rest of Tennice's couch, and with a wry grin poked one of his outsized feet at his older brother. "That's exactly what Evan and I always did when we were boys. We'd bully Tennice into taking on Father over our last scrape, while we went off and got into another. We'd yell at him until he was so confused, he couldn't think how hard Father was going to come down on him.''

Tennice glared sourly at Tanager . . . and then slowly, reluctantly, his stormy countenance relaxed and he broke into a rueful chuckle. "I had to take up the law as self-defense.''

Karon nodded, laughter dancing across his face like the wisps of summer fire above a midnight meadow. "Quite the same. In our case, it was only the matter of a single year until the Open Hand was overthrown. Those who came to power decreed that no one would be safe as long as any J'Ettanne walked upon the earth. No work of the J'Ettanne could stand and no memory of the J'Ettanne could survive. Thus began the extermination and the law that you know. The priests called us heretics and destroyed everything we had touched, as well as many things that had nothing to do with us. They closed down every temple and shrine, broke every statue, burned every writing, ruined every artifact that was not devoted to Arot and Mana or one of the Twins—''

"That's why the temple rules are so strict about heresy, and priests are so quick to stamp out any talk of lesser deities like harvest gods or shopkeepers' daemons or water spirits," said Julia.

"Exactly so," said Karon. "They couldn't untangle politics and belief and superstition and sorcery. And so they had to destroy it all. Over the past four hundred and fifty years most of the J'Ettanne have been hunted down and killed, though I doubt three people in the world outside this room remember exactly why it's done."

"But where have you come from, then?" I said. "How have you managed to survive without being found out? There have been no . . . no sorcerer burnings . . . since I was a child." The very words were as acid on my tongue.

"I'm getting to that." With a grateful smile, Karon drained a glass of wine Julia had given him. Setting the empty glass on the mantelpiece, he continued. "Though most of the followers of the Open Hand were slaughtered right away, those of the Closed Hand held out for a few years in their stronghold. But they knew their days were numbered. With the hunt so virulent, they were sure to be discovered. So they decided to abandon the stronghold, building secret ways through the mountains and sending out a few families at a time to settle in remote places where they would not be known. These refugees carried with them two tenets: that the gifts of the J'Ettanne were for life and not destruction, and that no mind could be invaded without consent. At least a few survived and managed to escape detection for several centuries. Some prospered, particularly in one Vallorean city called Avonar. My ancestors were among them. As late as five years ago the Lord of Avonar, the Baron Mandille, was a J'Ettanne. He was my father. . . ." His voice faded.

I caught my breath. "Avonar! Evard's triumph. Did Evard know?"

Karon hesitated, glancing at me and then at Martin, who was perched on the back of Tennice's and Tanager's couch.

"He knew," said my cousin in disgust. "I don't know how, but somehow in the last days of the Vallorean War, King Gevron learned that sorcerers lived in Avonar and that they were the last. Gevron promised amnesty to every citizen of Avonar who returned to the city before midsummer's day, proclaiming that he had decided to leave the place a free city because the lord of Avonar had tried to broker the peace between the Leirans and the Vallorean king. The war was over. They all went home. But instead of amnesty Gevron sent the Duke of Doncastre. When Evard sacked Avonar and slaughtered all who lived there, Karon was studying at the University, bound by his father's command to keep his connection with Avonar secret."

Martin paused for breath, and the four of us pelted him with questions, the most particular being how Martin had come to learn the truth about Karon before the rest of us.

"When I was in Yurevan two years ago," Martin said, "I took a few days to visit a professor from the University whom I've known since my own student days. He introduced me to a young colleague who was collaborating with him on a cultural history of northern Valleor. Karon, of course. We enjoyed each other's company immensely and went riding together several times over the course of the week.

"One day we came upon a young family with a newborn babe, the man and woman scarcely more than children themselves. They were starving, riddled with wasting fever, and had taken refuge in an abandoned charcoal-burner's hut in the forest just beyond Ferrante's land. The boy warned us off and, in his last despair, begged us to toss him a knife so he could put an end to his family's misery.

"I would've done it, but our friend here said there was an alternative. He tried to shove me off with some twaddle about medical training and the risks of contagion, but being stubborn, as you all know, and damnably curious, I watched from concealment. And so I saw Karon do his little business with the three of them. Needless to say, he had to spend some time telling me all he told you tonight."

Martin sighed. "We thought we were done with the incident, but didn't the stupid young bastard ignore Karon's requirement of silence and take his healthy wife and babe into town, telling everyone of the miracle that had come about. The fool thought he'd make his savior into a hero, but instead, at Ferrante's house, we hear that a hunt is up for a sorcerer in the district. I managed to smuggle Karon back to Yurevan, meet him properly in different circumstances, and invite him here, never thinking I'd be so stupid as to put him back in the danger from which I had extracted him."

CHAPTER 7

By the time Martin had finished his tale, the sky was rosy and the birds twittering in the garden. Tomas would arrive by mid-morning, and the events of the night would make my departure no easier.

Despite his best efforts, Tanager fell asleep on the floor, while Julia and Martin went to the kitchen to hunt up something for us to eat. Martin had told his stewards to continue the servants' holiday through the coming day. Tennice paced the library, grumbling under his breath and casting such mournful glances over his spectacles at Karon and me ·that we decided to escape to the garden. We walked for a while, but there was nothing to say and everything to say, and we could not even begin. Eventually we gave up trying and joined Martin and Julia in the kitchen.

Just as Martin pushed a knife into my hand and told me to slice the oranges piled in a copper bowl, Tennice burst through the door. "Martin, do you have a copy of the Westover Codex? Surely you do. Don't tell me you don't."

The Earl of Gault was up to his elbows in buttered toast. "You're going strange on us, Tennice. The Westover Codex at six in the morning? Here we've had a night such as friends seldom experience, and you're ready to get back to your books."

"No jest, Martin."

Martin shrugged. "In the vault, then. Black leather case."

Before too long a time had passed, Tennice's head reappeared in the kitchen doorway. "Seri, would you come, please? I need to speak with you."

Wiping my hands on a towel and yielding my sticky knife to Karon, I joined Tennice in the library. He was poring over a fragile parchment spread out on the library table, and when I came in, he whirled about, snapping a pen in his thin hands. I had never seen him so agitated.

"Do you love him, Seri?"

I was taken aback.

"Tell me honestly. Karon—do you love him?"

He was not asking lightly. "Yes. Yes, I do, but—"

"You're not afraid?"

"Of Karon? No more than I'm afraid of you or Martin or the others."

He nodded as if he had expected nothing else. "If, by taking a great risk, you could avoid what is to come with Evard, would you be willing?"

"I'd do almost anything."

"I've found you a way." He beckoned me to the table to look at his parchment. "Evard will likely be crowned this afternoon, no later than tomorrow. It's already been two months since Gevron's death. A thousand noble guests are getting restless at twiddling their thumbs here in Montevial, waiting for us to make up our mind who we're going to crown, while their tenants are harvesting crops and their less honored neighbors are lusting over their unguarded fields and horses. And, most importantly, the fall campaign against Kerotea can't begin until there's a king. So I started thinking about how there's no time for an extended celebration, only the necessary rituals—coronation rituals. And that reminded me of something I'd read." Tennice never forgot anything he read, not even if it made no sense or had no relevance at the time. No one in all Martin's circle had ever been able to catch him up. "You'd risk Evard's wrath. He's not a forgiving man, as you well know."

The three from the kitchen appeared, carrying trays loaded with toast, jam, oranges, and tea. "What's this about Evard's wrath?" asked Martin.

"I've found a way Seri can refuse him and choose"—he glanced up at me—"a life she might prefer."

"Tell me, Tennice," I said.

"There's a codicil buried in the Westover Codex about petitions put before the new king on Coronation Day—the

Favored Ten. To violate the Westover Codex is to violate the very basis of his own power. Evard won't do it. Can't do it. The Council wouldn't stand for it, and he needs them to support his war. And if he accepts the Westover Codex, then he must grant the first ten petitions on the day of his coronation. If you're willing, Seri, you can petition him to marry whomever you will."

When Tomas escorted me from Windham that morning, I told him that I wished to be presented to Evard as soon as he was crowned.

"He'll send for both of us soon enough," said my brother.

"But I should be the first to acknowledge his authority, should I not?" Now I knew of the Codex codicil, there was no stopping. I would not let myself consider what the future might bring; all would depend on Evard's reaction. But, whatever the consequences, I could live with them. Evard, I could not.

Evard, Duke of Doncastre, was crowned King of Leire and Protector of Valleor that afternoon in the presence of the Leiran Council of Lords, every Leiran noble of importance, the high priests of Annadis and Jerrat, and every resident of Montevial who could bribe, wheedle, or sneak his way into the palace precincts. One sullen group of guests dressed in sober finery were noble hostages from Valleor and Kerotea, kept under house arrest in Leire and now forced to witness the succession of their conquerors.

Sharp angles of purple and green light from the stained-glass windows streaked the gray stone floor of the Great Hall of Leire. The carved capitals of the soaring columns were lost in the dim and smoky heights, as were the frescoed ceilings. I stood among the most favored guests to the right of the throne, trying to avoid having my eye put out by the women's stiff headdresses, my skirts snagged by the men's jeweled sword hilts, or my breath choked off by the cloying perfumes. But I squeezed and smiled and elbowed my way to the front where I could see.

The ceremony began with a priest's long-winded recounting of the War of the Beginnings, and most especially of the part where Arot had retired to his mythic palace of Cadore with his wife Mana. While his twin sons guarded the world against the fiends of air and sea, those of us on earth were commanded to defend our own lands and welfare by serving strong, faithful warrior kings. By the time the chancellor was halfway through a recounting of our new king's life, Martin had dozed off. Evard was only twenty-five. This part shouldn't take so long.

For my part, I was neither sleepy nor anxious. In truth I was more concerned with Tomas than Evard, for what I was about to do would be a grievous offense to my brother. We had been our parents' only children, close in age and interests, and forced into constant companionship by the remote situation of Comigor, our father's keep. I loved Tomas dearly, honored him as a warrior and a swordsman, and respected his authority as the head of our family. But he had never once asked me of my wishes, hearing my objections no more than he would hear a complaint from his horse that the flies were becoming a nuisance. To do so had never occurred to him, though I had been frank about my declining opinions of his friend. But Martin had taught me that my opinions were worthy of consideration.

When the chancellor's droning ended, the Council of Lords came forward one by one to swear fealty to Evard. Martin winked at me as he took his place in the queue. I nodded, unable, even in my own anxiety, to forget the pain which had led to his moment of desperation the previous night. If Annadis and Jerrat truly favored Leire as our priests assured us, then somehow Martin would have a say in our kingdom's future.

After the twelve nobles had kissed the new king's hand and sworn their oaths, Evard named Tomas Champion of Leire, the most coveted honor in the realm. The Champion answered any personal challenge made to the king. It was perhaps the only royal office awarded on merit alone. My heart swelled with pride. How I wished my father had lived to see him so honored.

Tomas, dressed in white and gold, quite looked the part. He was as tall and commanding a presence as our father had been, who had been considered the epitome of the gallant soldier. My brother's hair was the same deep red-brown color as my own, shining and thick as it framed his handsome features: straight nose, dark brown eyes, and a battle scar on his jaw just large enough to make court ladies sigh at his bravery. Maybe there was a little too much of the indulged boy-child in his curling lip, but he was intelligent. He would grow into his power and see Evard's flaws. Perhaps his influence with the new king would help moderate those flaws.

When Tomas took his place beside Evard, he leaned over and whispered in his friend and liege's ear. Evard smiled indulgently. He sprawled on the gilded throne as if it had been his from the moment of his birth instead of for a mere quarter of an hour. He waved his hand to get the attention of the assembly, then nodded in my direction. "This fair young lady has asked for public audience upon this occasion, and it is our delight to hear her."

Now to me. There would be no turning back. I could be queen if I wanted. I could submit to the authority of my brother and the desires of his friend, and no one would ever take me to task for it. It was the singular expectation of a woman of privilege—to marry according to her family's wishes rather than her own. I would not be held responsible for Evard's character except in my own mind. After a few years I could most likely take a lover. Evard wasn't single-minded in that regard even now, and I knew how things worked in royal circles. But that was not the life I wanted. Martin had opened up the world to me, and I was not willing to abandon his gift.

So I stepped forward and curtsied, pulled a manuscript from my sleeve, and proclaimed to the assembly that I was making petition of His Most Gracious Majesty King Evard upon his Coronation Day, according to the provision of the Westover Codex known as the Grant of the Favored Ten. Because my parents who would guard the welfare of their only daughter were dead, and because my brother, whom I honored, was almost of an age with me, I petitioned that I be freed from the traditional duties of a subordinate female and be allowed to choose my life's partner for myself.

Evard had to grant my petition. No one at court could fail to know that I had been intended for him and that my petition was a product of my disdain. But for that very reason, he had to be magnanimous. Better to be thought spurned by a proud and willful female than to let anyone know he cared. Many a man in the same position would bully the woman he desired into marriage, but I knew how Evard's mind worked. He would get his revenge some subtler way.

With strained good humor, the king proclaimed, "It is difficult for us to imagine a determined young lady such as yourself ever entering into an arrangement counter to your desires. The unlucky gentleman would rue the day, we have no doubt." The assembly laughed uneasily. "As an impartial observer and your longtime friend and well-wisher," he continued, "we would caution you to heed the advice of your brother, who is perhaps wiser in the ways of the world than a sheltered young lady such as yourself. Whims such as this one can have consequences beyond a moment's gratification. But we can see no reason to deny your petition. Let it be so written."

With a flick of his hand I was dismissed. It was a good thing I had no designs on any courtier. Evard had surely dampened my prospects with his remarks. I had a gracious response prepared, but someone else was already making his obeisance, speaking of dispatching messengers to the Leiran troops to pass on the joyous news of King Evard's ascension to the throne. The line of petitioners, grovelers, and well-wishers stretched all the way through the hall and into the outer ward.

My eyes cast down, I curtsied deeply and backed away into the murmuring crowd. I felt like flying to the ceiling with the pigeons, like leaping atop the long, curved Council tables and crowing like the gold and russet hawks who soared above the roofs at Comigor. I dared not look at Martin or Tennice, lest I burst out laughing or fling myself into their arms and bless them for their gifts. After a suitable time of humble attention to the proceedings—of which I heard not a single word—I worked my way to the back of the crowd and slipped out one of the many side doors to the hall. People were jammed up to every door, willing to suffer crushed toes and bruised elbows to provide themselves with a glimpse of history to carry though their lives—or at least through the next dinner party. I had scarcely made my way through the door when I felt a firm hand on my elbow. "Darzid!"

"Your brother requires your presence, my lady." To my surprise, the dark, deep-set eyes of Tomas's aide glittered with amusement. Did Tomas know his aide took so light a view of my rebellion?

"I'd have thought Tomas would be too busy with his new duties to have time for family visits."

"Oh, no. He's asked me especially to bring you to him. Need I say that he has a most ah . . . pressing . . . desire to have a word with you? Would this be a good time for us to run away together, do you think? You will reap his wrath for an hour, but I have to fight beside the man!"

Despite his smiles and mischievous humor, Darzid's gentlemanly touch brought me back to earth. My visions fled. My wings felt ripped away, my hawk's feathers plucked. I jerked loose from him and smoothed my gown, disheveled by the press of the crowd. "If Tomas thinks to change my mind, he's mistaken."

"I make no estimates of his expectations, my lady. I'll confess that after this day's events, I would not set myself up to predict any action of yours. You're even more interesting than the young woman I've come to admire so deeply over the past years." He swept his hand indicating a path down a broad corridor to the left, and then offered me his arm.

Somehow, I could not bear the thought of touching him again, and so I shoved past him. "Remember your place, Captain."

Darzid bowed and led me to a small, luxuriously furnished sitting room. "I'd recommend you remain here until the duke is able to attend to you." His expression did not register my rudeness. His smile did not change, nor the amused glint in his eyes. He bowed again and closed the door behind him.

I was left to occupy myself with an ivory and jade chessboard. Fingering the exquisite pieces, lost in thoughts of Windham and those who played there, I wondered what I might have to do to keep my friends out of harm's way. If naught else, Darzid had wakened caution. No attention must be directed anywhere near Karon.

An hour later, Tomas burst through the gilded door. "There you are." His face convulsed with fury. "What damnable perversity has made you do this to me?"

I was prepared to hold my tongue, to do whatever I could to mend the rift I'd caused or at least do nothing to make it unmendable. Tomas and I had no family but each other, no aunts or uncles, no one any closer than distant cousins like Martin. But my brother was not to be placated.

"Have I not let you have your way all these years? Have I been extraordinarily cruel or brutal, that you should humiliate me so despicably? Our father must be crying out from the grave at the disgrace you've brought on our house this day." He strode to the center of the room, spun on his heel, and glared at me. "It's Martin, isn't it? He's put you up to it. The Westover Codex . . . faugh! The self-righteous prig, thinking he's got the only mote of intelligence in the universe. This is how he takes his pitiful revenge, befouling all of us because the better man won. He's not strong enough or brave enough to face Evard on his own, so he manipulates a fool of a girl to do his dirty work for him."

I thought he would never leave off.

"You meant to do it this way. The culminating day of my life—everything I've worked for, fought for, bled for— and what have you done? Turned it into a hill of dung!"

"Tomas! Listen to yourself," I broke in at last. "All I hear is how you are humiliated, how you will have to wallow in dishonor, how your triumph has been turned to dung. Did you ever consider me for even a moment? Did you ever think what it is to be deemed of no more value than a plot of land or a chest of gold to be paid out because your brother is loyal? You would pledge your sister to a man she despises. For what?"

"For everything. I would have made you queen, you little fool! We would have been the most powerful family in the Four Realms."

Blast all stupidity, I thought, as Tomas trembled with rage. It was not just for loyalty and friendship. I'd not given Tomas enough credit. It had never crossed my mind that his ambitions stretched beyond Evard.

I tried to soothe him. "You'll have all the power you wish, Tomas. You've been Evard's most devoted friend;

you've fought beside him since you were boys. You are the Champion of Leire, and not just because you're his friend. You're the finest swordsman in the Four Realms and none in any realm will dispute it. But I don't want to be queen, Tomas, not if it means being Evard's chattel or even yours."

Tomas threw up his hands. "You prefer Martin's endless Long Night follies and juggling shows. Are you his whore, too?"

So much for unmendable rifts. I slapped him, leaving a darker red mark on his red face. "Your tongue is as foul as your choice of friends, Tomas, and just as unimaginative. The only foolish thing I've done this day is think that somehow, given time, you might understand."

My brother answered with cold hatred that was far more terrible than his anger. "I will never understand, Seri." He opened the door and flung his last words over his shoulder. "Don't bother returning to Comigor. I'll have your things sent to the townhouse and set up a means to keep you respectably. I trust you'll return to some semblance of decorum after this despicable performance." He slammed the door, leaving me alone in the gilded room.

The anger I had expected. Tomas had been indulged from his first breath, deprived of nothing save the remotest inkling that there were others in the universe besides himself. But the unyielding hatred—that I had not expected. I would have to tread carefully. In one day I had made enemies of the two most powerful men in the land.

Well, I had made my choice and I had no intention of regretting it, though I could see now the painful consequences that must follow. An ornate little desk in the corner of the anteroom housed paper, pens, and ink, so the first thing I did was to write a message to the housekeeper at our townhouse, saying the house must be opened that night, rather than later in the fall as had been the family custom. And then I wrote a letter to Martin.

My dear cousin,
As you have seen, it is done. My fate, at least in the realm of marriage, is in my own hands, and I do not regret my choice. But as with all choices of any signifi-

cance, especially those which tread on the pride of kings and brothers, certain consequences must temper any celebration of success in my endeavor.

I cannot express too deeply my gratitude for the education and friendship you have given me in the past four years. My view of the world has been irrevocably changed by the enlightened company at Windham, but for now my participation in those pleasant activities must end. Though not my desire, this too, is my own choice.

My brother and I have agreed that I will take up residence here in the city. I am well provided for.

You must tell my friends that they will ever be in my thoughts, and for any who go traveling, may the road be filled with nothing but beauty.

Highest regards,
Your cousin,
Seri

It was not enough, but what could possibly be enough to tell them what I wished? They would read between the lines.

Year 1 in the reign of King Evard

I plunged immediately into the social life of the court, renewing girlhood friendships I had abandoned when I had begun attending Martin's salons. I found it ironic that I was supposed to find the "decorum" Tomas so prized in the drunken revelry of idle nobles who could converse on no topic more serious than who was whose mistress, and what were the prospects for the fall campaign, and weren't last year's vintages the most bloody awful in history.

But between afternoon feasts, hunting parties, and evening entertainments, I read and studied furiously. Until the years at Windham I had never been studious, preferring a ride across the downs to reading a book or a game of draughts to composing an essay. Even at Windham, my scholarship had been mostly confined to avid listening, unschooled argument, and persistent questioning. Only Tennice's challenge had sent me to reading. But now that I was deprived of that company, I discovered a hunger for knowledge that I could ease nowhere but in books. In the back of my mind I held fast to something Tennice had mentioned in passing, that one or two women had been allowed to study at the Royal University in Valleor. To make something different of my life . . . I liked that idea. Things more unlikely had come about.

I also hired an elderly gentleman to teach me to play the flute. He was a drunkard, but in the rare times he came without spirits on his breath, he could sear the soul with the beauty of his music. He said he drank because no one would listen. I listened, and I learned.

One morning, as I sat in my library studying a history of the Four Realms, Darzid came to visit. "Just to discover how this new life suits you," he said. "No need to stop what you're doing."

He settled in a chair by the window and seemed to mean what he said. He browsed through the stack of books I had left beside the chair: one on law, one on philosophy, one on the history of Valleor that I was devouring with new eyes, hunting any mention of Avonar. The task of opening a conversation was left to me. The trouble was, I was far more interested in what I was reading. The tattered book in my hand purported to recount the history of "the reign of horror and the noble restoration" some four and a half centuries in the past. I purposely did not offer Darzid any refreshment and did not move from my library table to a chair that might facilitate our conversation.

"You must report to Tomas that I appear comfortable and well fed, and I do not seem to be moping for the loss of his companionship or Evard's."

"Mmm." He thumbed idly through one of the books, but I didn't think he was reading it.

It was tedious to make conversation when you had no heart for it. "So, Captain, are you finding sufficient fodder for your character sketches, since Tomas has dragged you so high? Have you decided to write them down as you threatened? I think the kingdom could do with a good laugh now the war has taken up again."

"The world is absurd. I—" He broke off, threw the book on the table, and sat back, tapping his long finger rapidly on the arm of the chair. Though his dress was as sleek as ever, Darzid didn't look well. The sunny window at his back left his haggard face in shadow. The mischievous glint was gone.

I waited for him to resume his thought. He was not one to dance about a topic or adhere to polite protocols. But the silence stretched so long and so heavily, I felt compelled to say something. "Captain, why are you here?"

A hint of his sardonic smile flashed across his face. "I've missed our dinner conversations. Every fishwife in this city knows of your estrangement from your brother, thus they refuse to seat me next you. You've always brought out my best humor."

"So, is it court life or soldiering that's quenched it?"

"Truth to tell, I've not been sleeping well." He drew up to the edge of his chair and leaned forward. "Tell me, lady, do you ever have the sense that you belong somewhere else? That your life has taken a course you cannot explain?"

"On occasion," I said. Certainly on the night I had learned that the society I believed built on honor had perpetuated a horrific lie—that sorcerers were universally evil and deserved to die in torment. "Usually when I am at some baroness's masque—"

"No, no. This is something else." A gold chain hung about his neck, its links gleaming in the sunbeams. "I visited a village in the far north of Valleor last month, a place where I've never been. The people of the village claimed to know me. To detest me. Old people swore they'd met me in their youth. I thought it an oddity, but at three other villages in the district, it was the same. My lady, they told me of a duel fought there thirty years ago. I killed a local man, they said, a man well regarded in their district. They described the combat in detail. I scoffed at the tale, but they swore to it, mentioning a star-shaped scar left on my shoulder from the incident. I told them it was nonsense, of course. Tomas got a great laugh."

"But you're not laughing." Indeed he was as serious as I'd ever seen him.

"I have such a scar on my shoulder, exactly as they described it." Absentmindedly, Darzid rubbed his left shoulder, as if some ghost pain bothered him.

"Coincidence. You're a Leiran soldier. You have a number of scars, I'm sure. And every Vallorean hates every Leiran ever born."

"But, strangely enough, I can't tell you where I got this particular scar. The whole matter got me thinking. There are a number of things I can't remember: stories of my family, my career, that I've told so often they seem true, and yet when I turn my mind to them, they vanish like movements you see only out of the corner of your eye." He stared at his hands and the ugly burn scars that crossed his palms. "And there are images floating in my head that have no place there, images that have the truth of memory, and yet are so fantastical . . ." He shook his head as if to rid himself of those very thoughts. "Foolishness. You must think me drunk."

"Why are you telling me these things?"

He forced a laugh. "I've no one else to tell of my fancies. Tomas and Evard are quite single-minded, and everyone else in this kingdom gets the megrims from such talk. But you sit here wide-eyed and act as if you hear such mysteries every day. I knew you'd not laugh at me. You are exceptional. . . ."

I'd never seen such a look on Darzid's face—unmasked admiration . . . a request for intimacy . . .

I stood up abruptly. This conversation was going somewhere I didn't want to go. "I'm sorry I can't hear the whole story, Captain. But for now, I'm in the middle of some work. . . ." I waved at my book and a stack of papers on my desk.

Face scarlet, he leaped to his feet and called my butler for his cloak. "My apologies, my lady. I had no wish to make you uncomfortable."

"This thing with Tomas will pass." I said. "We'll sit at many a tedious dinner where you can tell me more." His story was indeed curious, but I had no need and no desire for intimacy with an ambitious courtier. Those entrusted with mortal secrets had to be careful about intimate relationships.

In a flurry of farewells and deprecating humor, he took his leave. "If Tomas fails to come to his senses and you find this studious life as boring as a dinner party, perhaps you will invite me back sometime and restore my wit."

"Anything is possible, Captain."

But in truth, I never invited him back. I cared nothing for Darzid and his humors and his mysteries. Rather, my thoughts remained at Windham, and I would smile to myself and wonder what dusty tomes Tennice had discovered lately, and who would ally with Julia to argue with Martin that women should own property, and was Karon even there or was he traveling again, searching for knowledge and beauty to feed his strange power. Someday I would know more of sorcery. I'd had too small a taste of that exotic fruit.

When I was a child of five, King Gevron had decided that subjugation of the other three of the Four Realms was the only answer to the centuries of bloody disputes with our neighbors, Valleor, Kerotea, and Iskeran. He began with Valleor, the fertile kingdom to the northwest, also the weakest of the three and the one with the longest shared border. Eleven years passed until the day the last Vallorean fortress fell; only the kingdom's vast size—and frequent interruptions from the more warlike Keroteans and Isker—had made the conquest take so long. Gevron spent three years ravaging conquered Valleor, and thus had turned his full attention to Kerotea only in the last years of his reign. That war had gone nowhere.

Evard marched out of Montevial one week after his coronation, bragging that he would finish off the Keroteans in far less time than Gevron had taken to crush Valleor. By midwinter of the first year of his reign, he claimed decisive victories on the Kerotean frontier. But dismal weather cut the campaign short, and gossip was that everything gained would be lost again by spring.

On the eve of Long Night, I decided to stay home. There had been an unending siege of entertainments celebrating Seille—the midwinter season that culminated in Long Night and the ten days until year's end—and I had refused no invitation lest any slight be noted. I flirted with any man who would look at me and made sure there was enough gossip at court that Tomas and Evard would hear of it. The king would be able to blame no man for standing higher than himself in my favor. Eventually, perhaps, he would lose interest and stop listening. But enough was enough. I pleaded the grippe and spent the evening with a wool comforter and a book of Vallorean folk tales, the winter shadows held back only by the flicker of my library fire.

The front bell rang. I assumed it was one of my latest suitors, most likely Viscount Mantegna, pleading with the butler that he would be eternally devastated if he could not drive me out in his new sleigh. Mantegna was a slobbering pup, but amusing enough. Luckily I had Joubert, the butler, well trained. "No" meant *no*.

There came a tap on the library door, and Joubert entered with a long, thin parcel in his hand. "Your pardon, my lady. A gift has arrived."

The arm-length bundle of green silk was tied with a gold ribbon and had no card. Unrolling the layers of silk revealed a rose . . . in the middle of winter, a single, perfect red rose. The tips of the scarlet petals curled out, on the very instant of bursting open. Poised on one of them was a single dewdrop, no stray snowflake or ice pellet melted in the warmth of the room, for as I gazed upon the flower, wreathed in its sweetness, I smelled the dew-laden gardens of Windham. Enchantment . . .

I ran to the foyer to see if he was there, but the front of the house was dark and deserted. I was overwhelmed with disappointment, but only until I touched the rose again. Then I smiled, put it in a crystal vase, and set it on a low table where I could see it from every angle. The rose was message enough.

Spring brought the Month of Winds, when we celebrated Arot's wedding to Mana, the wind maiden who had given birth to the Twins. On each day of the Month of Winds, parents gave children presents and sweets in remembrance of the gifts Mana had given to the creatures of forest and sky at her wedding, hiding them around the house and gardens as Mana had hidden nuts for the squirrels. Midway through the month came the Feast of Vines, supposedly the most propitious day of the year for engagements and betrothals. Certainly it was a propitious day for wine-merchants.

On a rainy afternoon five days after the feast day, I attended the funeral rites for the Duke of Gamercy, a jolly, hard-drinking, foulmouthed old man who had been one of my father's closest friends. Gossip said the old man had enjoyed the Feast of Vines a bit too much for one in his sixty-seventh year. Tomas did not attend the funeral, being at Evard's side on the new campaign in Kerotea. Martin was present, though, sitting across the cold stone expanse of Annadis's temple with Tennice at his side. It was the first time I'd seen them in the seven months since Evard's coronation. Neither of them looked my way.

After the incense-filled hours of songs and stories commending the old warrior's name to the Twins as worthy to be entered on their lists of earthly heroes, the guests retired to the duke's townhouse for refreshment and reminiscence. Though I wanted nothing more than to fling myself into Martin's arms and beg for news, I followed his lead. My cousin engaged himself with a serious group of men I didn't know, making no move to approach me. Tennice left early after speaking with the widow and no one else.

As I took my own leave of the duchess, a footman presented me with the customary engraved commemorative card, folded so that the duke's arms and martial history were scribed on the outside, and the tale of his lineage on the inside. It wasn't until I got home, lonely and disappointed, that I discovered that my card had a scrap of paper inserted. The note was not signed, but two years of handwritten tutorials on the law enabled me to recognize Tennice's hand quite easily. The text read like someone's random, philosophical musings, but to me the choice of words was not at all random.

> *The wisdom of the fair sex is proved.*
> *Safety for the traveler lies in prolonged absence.*
> *Four is not enough for true diversity of opinion.*

The first line confirmed my belief that Martin's failure to discourage my withdrawal from Windham was a recognition of its necessity. I wondered if he had more concrete evidence of my wisdom than did I myself. I had only instinct.

The second told me that Karon was gone. I couldn't decide whether it was more difficult to think of him traveling in some distant, unknown land than it had been to think of him at Windham, so close, yet a place I could not be. I could not consider the prospect that he might never come back. Not after the rose.

The third told me that I was missed, and that made it all very hard.

Summer brought the fascinating news that Evard was betrothed to the daughter of Dagobert, the last Vallorean king. It was a brilliant move on Evard's part—the legitimization of Leiran dominance over Valleor. Princess Mariel was sixteen and had been "sheltered" in a remote temple school since the day her entire family had been beheaded in front of her.

Though Leirans did not usually execute women, out of respect for Arot's holy wife Mana, spared by the monsters of earth and sky in Arot's battles in the Beginnings, they had made an exception for the Queen of Valleor. As her husband's and sons' severed heads yet stared up at their executioners, Queen Margereth vowed to lie with the first healthy Vallorean man she could find, whether noble or peasant, and thus produce an heir to Valleor more legitimate than any Leiran king. She was beheaded straightaway. But King Gevron had allowed the girl child to live, as long as she was locked up tight in a temple school and never allowed to look at a man. Perhaps even marriage to Evard would be better than that sterile prison and never tasting life at all.

The wedding was in late summer. The pale-haired girl was lost in the opulent finery Evard had selected as suitable for his bride. She was short and thin, with a long, angular face and large eyes that blinked constantly. No one was impressed by her. I wished her a tolerant heart and a self-sufficient nature; she was like to need both.

Tomas attended the wedding, of course, handsome as always and appearing to have lost no standing with Evard because of my folly. He had stood as Evard's champion three times already, and word had it that he was undefeatable. When we crossed paths near the refreshment tables, his face hardened bitterly. He spun on his heel and walked away. No healing there. Darzid, at his side as always, bowed, but did not follow my brother. He made as if to speak with me, but I excused myself politely before he could say anything. Martin was in attendance also. He greeted me with a formal bow, then turned back to another conversation. So it was not time yet.

Year 2 in the reign of King Evard

In the second autumn of my "exile," I turned twenty-three. I returned home early on my birthday evening, no more lonely being by myself than in a crowd of people with whom I shared no sympathetic interests. I found increasing pleasure in practicing my music and thought it would be a satisfactory celebration of the day. When Joubert opened the front door for me, he pointed to the library. "A parcel has arrived for you, my lady. I've put it in the library. I'll return to light the lamps as soon as I've hung your cloak."

"No need for the lamps. I'm just going to play for a while."

I entered the shadowy library, wondering who among my acquaintance had recalled it was my birthday. On the polished table was a long, thin bundle of green silk, tied with a gold ribbon. My pulse quickened. The rose was white this time, with a blush of pink at its edges, the crystalline dewdrop like a tear of joy at its perfection. I stood in the firelight, inhaling its sweet fragrance and reveling in its beauty—and even more in its meaning.

"I didn't know whether red or white was more to your liking," came a voice from a chair in the corner, "and having been tempered in the fires of the Windham debating society, I would be the last to risk your displeasure by making unsupported assumptions. So I thought I'd best come gather evidence for myself."

I whirled about, ignoring the thorn pricks in my fingers, and out of the shadows stepped a sorcerer, come to conjure the desire of my heart on my birthday.

CHAPTER 8

"Aeren, who are you?"

The young man had turned away, not seeing what he had done and not hearing my urgent question. He was furiously launching rocks down the hillside.

I took a deep breath and went to take a closer look at the knife.

Jacopo croaked, "Don't touch it! Oh, demonfire, Seri. There's no crack there, no opening."

"It's all right, Jaco. It's done." But it was not all right. My eyes had not deceived me. The blade was firmly embedded in solid rock.

"Aeren," I called again. Flushed and agitated, he dropped his stones and joined me beside the spring. I pointed to the knife, and he shrugged his shoulders, not surprised at all. What in the name of the stars had I stumbled onto? It became even more impossible to deny what had happened when Aeren yanked the knife from the stone. No mark, no slot, no chip marred the stone, and the weapon itself was neither scratched nor bent.

As I stared at the uncompromising evidence, the trees began to thrash in a rising wind, and shadows raced over the ridge top, draining the warmth from the wavering sunlight. Afternoon storms were typical of summer in the region, though drought had kept them rare the past four years. Yet no storm of nature's making had ever afflicted me with such profound unease. I shuddered with the sudden chill and found myself looking over my shoulder and scanning the horizon. Stranger still, although the sun's disk hung just over the hilltop, and the evening sky was unmarred by haze or cloud, neither my body nor Aeren's nor Jacopo's cast a shadow.

Aeren grabbed my arm and Jacopo's, and, before we could question or protest, dragged the two of us down the slope toward the wood, shoving us roughly into the thick brush under the trees and motioning us to silence. I crouched low, and soon the entire physical substance of the world was reduced to the dusty twigs beside my nose and Aeren's muscular arms, pressing me into the thicket. Dread seeped into my bones. Time twisted in a knot and turned in upon itself. The wind stank of smoke and ash—the scent of soul-searing desolation . . .

The weights lifting from my spirit and my back told me when the shadow had gone. A beam of sunlight pierced the forest roof, stinging my eyes. The still air smelled properly of hot pine needles and dry leaves, and a jay's raucous chattering roused the other birds. Jacopo and I reacted as one.

"Aeren, what was that?"

"What madness is this, Seri?" I had never heard Jacopo afraid.

"I don't know, Jaco," I said. "I don't know."

A frowning Aeren paid no attention to my question, but urged us down the trail toward the cottage, casting frequent glances toward the ridgetop. I had no mind to argue with him. Whatever we had experienced, I wanted no more of it. But by the time we reached the meadow and the cottage, the event was already fading into insubstantial memory, a lingering revulsion like the taste of spoilt milk. What had really happened besides a cloud passing over the sun?

Aeren himself was of far more interest to me. One language I had not tried with him. I knew only a few words, for most were long buried in the depths of history, and I had believed no one still living in the world could understand them.

"Aeren, J'Ettanne ý disé?"

Though he shook his head, his face came alive in a way I had not yet seen. I tried a few more words, and he recognized some, but not all, as if this was a language of which he, too, knew only fragments. Did he mean that he was not J'Ettanne or that he didn't know? I couldn't seem to make my question clear. One more thing to try. I formed a question in my mind with absolute clarity, sweeping aside every other thought and concern until the words stood alone like stone pillars in the desert, and then I took Aeren's hand and laid it on my temple, inviting him, with the gesture Karon had taught me, to read what was inside. He yanked his hand away and shook his head angrily, then rapped his clenched fist rapidly against his brow. So he couldn't do it, but he knew exactly what I meant.

I could hardly contain my excitement. Excitement—how strange it was. I should be terrified. No one could get wind of this or all of our lives would be forfeit: Aeren's, mine, Jaco's . . .

The old sailor sat on Jonah's bench beside the cottage door, staring at the horizon, his wide hands braced stiffly on his knees. I sat down beside him and laid my hand over his gnarled fingers. His skin was cold.

"Jaco, I'm so sorry. I'd never have gotten you involved if I'd suspected this."

"Can he truly take our souls? Was that what he was doing up there? Evil, Seri. I've never felt such evil."

"I'm not sure exactly what happened up there. The first part, when he did the magic, yes. When you felt prickly and alive. But what came later—the stink, the feeling of snakes slithering up your back—that was outside my experience. But I swear to you that sorcery itself is not evil, and, though he is surely dangerous—wild, half-mad, I think—I don't believe Aeren means us any harm." A sorcerer . . . one of Karon's people . . . How in the name of all gods had he happened to come here? "I'm not sure what to do."

"They'll arrest you if they find out, little girl. They'll finish what they started. You can't let him stay."

"What they'd do to me is not half what they'd do to him, and the way he is, I'm not sure he would even know why."

Aeren roamed restlessly across the meadow. I caught up with him, determined to get some explanation. "What was up there?" I gestured toward the hilltop.

He picked two blades of grass, one green and healthy, one brown and withered. Holding the green blade in the fingers of one hand, he passed his other palm over it, leaving only the withered blade exposed. That was clear enough. When he pointed to the trees and the cottage and folded his arms over his head, I gathered that such were places to hide. When I pressed him further, he shrugged and walked away.

The J'Ettanni language had defined no simple word for sorcery. It had been no more necessary than for other men to have a word for what it is that makes them get up in the morning, set one foot in front of the other, or inhale and exhale. But for my own safety and Jaco's, I had to teach Aeren the difference between sorcery and other actions. He demonstrated no sense that there was anything unusual about what he had done and no understanding of the dreadful consequences if others saw such things.

I caught up to Aeren again and persuaded him to follow me. Taking a large rock from the stream, I demonstrated that I could not make my knife penetrate the stone. He was surprised. Stars in the heavens, where had he been? When I handed him the rock and my knife, and indicated that I wanted him to try it, he looked puzzled. But with a shrug, he stabbed my knife into the rock with no more effort than if it were a lump of cheese.

Though I had been prepared for it, my heart crashed against my ribs. I took Aeren's hand and made him look at me. "Sorcery," I said. He frowned and gestured for another word. I pointed to the rock and said its name, and I pointed to the knife and did likewise, but I pointed to them joined and said, "Sorcery."

What else could he do? He was not a Healer; I would have seen the scars. Karon had borne so many. Lifegiver, his people had called him. I dragged Aeren to the garden and showed him the bean vines that had wilted in the heat. "Can you make them grow?" I asked, miming my words as I spoke. "Make them healthy like the rest?" He thought what I wanted was ridiculous, but I insisted that he show me. He brushed his fingers over the plant, touching leaves and stem gently. A few of the leaves took on a deeper green, and for a short distance the vine became thicker, but most of the plant remained limp and withered. After only a short time he ripped the vine out by the roots, threw it down, and ground it beneath his sandaled foot.

"It's all right," I said, trying to remain calm and keep him the same. I retrieved the vine and pointed to the leaves he had changed, saying again, "Sorcery."

That piqued his curiosity. With his eyes narrowed, he bade me come to the fire ring in the dirt near the cottage. He piled up tinder and kindling in the ring of blackened stones, and then he blew softly across his palm and passed his hand over the little mound, staring at it intently. After a few moments, a smoky tendril curled upward, and then another joined it, and another until a tiny flame poked its head above the dry stuff. Though the flame went out almost immediately, Acren looked satisfied and gestured to me that he wanted the word.

"Sorcery," I said, and he smiled with a brilliance that dimmed the day.

So the first hurdle was done. He knew what kind of things were sorcery. Now to convince him that he mustn't do any more of it. As I tried to explain, he acted puzzled, like a child suddenly told not to walk after being so praised for the accomplishment.

Poor Jacopo watched all these activities uncomfortably. Though they had known the crimes of which I had been accused, I had never discussed sorcery with Jacopo, Anne, or Jonah. Why distress them? I had fought my battles and lost.

But on this strange afternoon, I stepped back into the fray. I cared nothing for anyone; I would not cross a road to save a life. For ten years I had believed that human beings were the most despicable of creatures, vile, murderous hypocrites who would slaughter their own. Even the J'Ettanne, who so piously celebrated life, had taught their children that their destiny was to die, refusing to lift their hands to stop it. Yet in the end I was as bad as the rest of them, manipulating others, endangering lives to serve my own ends. I pressed a mug of ale into my only friend's hand and told him that my curiosity and my hatred were going to put him in mortal danger. "I've decided what to do next," I said, my cheeks hot, my limbs so light they might have belonged to someone else entirely. "I'm going to find this man who's searching for him."

I owed the J'Ettanne nothing, but Aeren was a sorcerer and Darzid was hunting him. I would kill Aeren myself before I allowed Evard to burn another man.

*   *   *

Though Aeren was clearly unhappy about my decision to leave the valley, and Jacopo grumbled endlessly about my decision to venture my mission alone, I bade farewell to the two of them early the next morning. Grenatte was five leagues to the south, but I had walked it before. I followed a narrow track across the meadow, and when I reached the intersection with the main road just south of Dunfarrie, I found a surprise—a skinny, grimy figure perched on a pile of boulders waiting for me.

"Paulo! What are you doing here?"

"Not my idea."

"I wondered why Jacopo found it so urgent to go down to the village last night. How much did he pay you to tag along?"

"Secret. Promised."

"And what are you supposed to do? Protect me from highwaymen?"

The boy straightened his back. "Might. I know a bit."

"Of course you do, but it's a very long way." I didn't want to shame the boy, but I failed to see how he could walk so far with his twisted leg.

"Done it before. Faster'n you."

I grinned. "Think so? Well, we'll see then." I started briskly down the road, Paulo scampering along beside. Jacopo was no fool. Having an extra hand, a pair of youthful eyes, and a trustworthy messenger was not a bad notion.

"So Paulo, does your gram know where you are?"

"She's down drunk again."

"Oh."

His father had been hanged for thievery when Paulo was small, and his mother had disappeared only months after, leaving Paulo to be raised by his grandmother when she was sober and the rest of the village when she was drunk. He had no trouble keeping up. I thought it would be exhausting to twist with each step as Paulo had to do, but he seemed tireless, and though his body was far from perfect, his hearing was excellent. After an hour of good progress, he halted abruptly. "Horses. Wagon. Behind." He cocked an eye at me. "Jaco says maybe you want to be private."

"That's true," said I, "but I don't hear anything."

"Four or five of 'em. I'll swear on horseflesh."

He was so sure of himself that, despite feeling a bit foolish, I motioned him over behind the sprawling blackberry bushes that lined the roadway. He promptly began stuffing berries in his mouth while I crouched itching and sweating in the prickly thicket. About the time I was convinced that his warning was only a ploy to get a rest, the boy put a purple-stained finger to his mouth, and I heard the jangle of harness.

Two heavily armed men rode and two equally tough-looking women walked beside a wagon driven by a hard-faced boy about Paulo's age. Their cargo was barrels of the type commonly used for sugar—a valuable load. Dangerous. I allowed the party to take a substantial lead before setting out on the road again.

"I'm glad you're here, Paulo."

The boy trotted ahead of me. "Best keep up!"

The road stayed close to the river for a while, then angled southwest, passing through a trailing remnant of the great northern forests before breaking out into the rolling grasslands of southern Leire. I disliked the few-league passage through During Forest. The giant oaks and ashes grew together so thickly that they blocked the sunlight, leaving their lower branches bare and brittle. Little grew on the forest floor to disturb the ancient piles of rotting leaves and tangles of fallen trees. We had been walking beneath the grim forest canopy for almost an hour when Paulo stopped again.

"Riders. Three of 'em close behind. And there's men in the woods up ahead. Quiet."

My skin crept. Highwaymen. Paulo and I quickly retreated into the shelter of a lightning-split oak, settling ourselves carefully so that no breaking twig could betray our presence, and so that we could not be seen from the road. Then we watched.

The three horsemen wore priests' robes, two of them in gray, one in black with a heavy gold chain about his neck. Their horses were richly caparisoned with red and gold, blazoned with the rising sun of Annadis. Intricate decorative goldwork hung from the bridles, jingling softly as they passed.

I had little use for the priests of Leire, resenting all the years I had listened to their drivel. They taught that the Holy Twins had no interest in the daily trials of mortals, only in deeds of honor and glory that reflected their own. Priests of Annadis had sanctioned what was done to Karon and my son. I was not interested in gods who found honor or glory in such doings. And for the common folk, honor and glory meant working themselves to exhaustion, paying the exorbitant temple fees and royal taxes without complaint, and dying cheerfully in the king's everlasting wars. No surprise that village shrines all over Leire were neglected, and the great temples deserted except on high feast days when the priests gave out alms.

The highwaymen slipped out of the trees and blocked the way of the hooded travelers just as the riders passed our position. "Hold!" commanded a short, stocky man. He wore a yellow rag tied around his head and carried a long knife. His four companions were variously armed with a cudgel, a spear, a dagger, and a crossbow, cocked and ready. "Dismount." The priests obeyed in silence. Two of the outlaws caught the reins of the horses, while their companions stood guard on the hooded priests.

The stocky man examined the horses carefully, running his hand down the withers of a well-formed bay. "Such fine beasts are not the usual for traveling holy men. And such trappings . . ." He jingled the gold linkwork dangling from the bridle, and then strolled up to his victims and ran his eyes up and down the still figures. "Turned out quite grand for priests, are we not?" With a swift movement of his knife he snatched the gold chain about the neck of the priest in black and deftly twisted it about the long knife blade, leaving the point of his blade at the man's throat. The three priests stood perfectly still and perfectly silent.

"Quiet lot, you are. Never met a holy man could keep from telling me how wicked are my ways, and how the Twins want my blood and my coin. Tiresome. Perhaps you're not born to it." He took another twist in the gold chain. "But you've prospered, nonetheless. Mayhap it's time you shared a bit with the poor."

I was prepared to see murder done—highwaymen had nothing to lose, being already condemned—but not in the way it happened. With breathtaking suddenness, the three horses screamed and reared, crushing one of the outlaws and entangling another in hooves and reins. In the ensuing confusion, the two gray-robed priests whirled about with blinding speed and precision, overpowering their guards. The one in black pinned the leader of the outlaws to the ground under the point of his own knife. With simple ease and no hesitation, the priest drove the knife home in the bandit's chest, and then jumped up to join the larger fray.

It was over in moments. Three outlaws lay on the road unmoving. The two gray clad priests held the two remaining highwaymen, pinning their arms behind them so cruelly that I expected to hear a bone snap in the sudden quiet. The priest in black approached the defiant captives. His hood had fallen back to reveal thin, light-colored hair and an angular face with jutting nose and brow. "You should have been more selective as to your prey, my little wolves," he said evenly, his voice the more unsettling for its complete lack of emotion. And before the outlaws had a chance to savor a last breath, he whipped his knife across each throat. The two bleeding bodies were released and slumped to the ground.

The priest in black jerked his head around and stared into the trees, exactly in our direction. I dared not breathe until he pulled up his hood, turned, and clucked at his horse. A fallen highwayman moaned. The black-robed priest snapped his fingers. One of his fellows picked up the dropped spear and plunged it through the injured outlaw, pinning him to the road. The spear shaft was still quivering when the three priests disappeared down the road south.

"What, in the name of all gods, was that?" I shivered. The midday heat felt harsh and bitter. My mouth tasted of ashes.

"Filthy, bloody damn." Paulo never had a lot of words.

We crept out onto the road. I told Paulo to wait for me while I stepped cautiously to each of the five men that lay on the hard-packed dirt.

"Are you loony?" said Paulo. "Get away!"

"I need to make sure they're dead."

"It's only thieves."

"They're men." Well, they had been men. Now they were all quite dead. Outlaws, yes, murderers themselves, no doubt, many times over. Yet I found myself with an odd sense of sympathy. If I had been empowered to choose the victors in that battle and entangle my fortune with theirs, I would have, quite irrationally, preferred to take my chances with the highwaymen.

As a child I had adored my family's winter stays in Montevial. The crush of people and society in the city, the music and torchlight and carriages, even the spine-chilling sight of criminals hung up in cages or locked in pillories had been a thrilling change from our dull castle in the country. But now I found the stench and din of even so small a town as Grenatte made my head throb. Wagons of hay and wood rumbled noisily through the cobbled streets, and the walls of a blacksmith's shop bulged with deafening clatter. A leather-aproned tradesman stood in the door of his shop, arguing loudly with a driver over a wagonload of hides, while a slack-mouthed girl drove a herd of bleating sheep through the square and yelled lewd insults at a man locked in the stocks and emitting a thready moan. The prisoner had evidently borne false witness; flies crawled on the bloody void where his nose had once been.

I sat tiredly on the stone steps that encircled the public well in the center of the town square, having bidden Paulo go to every inn in town, giving out the story that he had been paid to deliver a message to the person seeking a stolen white horse. The message said to meet the sender, a dark-bearded man wearing red, in the Green Lion common room at sunset. I had no intention of confronting the stranger right away, only to get a look at him. At the end of an exhausting day, my motives were far less clear than when I'd set out.

An army of beggars, the crippled remnants of Evard's Kerotean war, groped at passersby on the peripheries of the square. The Kerotean campaign had been murderous. The Keroteans were a fiercely independent, religious people, sturdy warriors who believed their mountains were the fortresses of their god. Only the sheer numbers of bodies Evard had flung against the heavily fortified Kerotean cities had conquered them. Rumor had it that twenty-five thousand Leirans had died to take Kallamat, the city of golden-domed temples where butter lamps burned to the Kerotean god every hour of every day, a city perched so high in the mountains that men could not breathe the air. Evard had told his men there were chests of gold in every house in Kallamat, but no common soldier had ever seen a single coin of it. And the people of Leire had seen only these armless, legless, or eyeless veterans, if they saw any result at all of twelve bloody years.

In less than half an hour, Paulo came streaking back through the late afternoon crowds, narrowly avoiding tumbling into the well. "Found him."

"What was he like?"

"Dark. Small. Dressed fine." Paulo screwed up his face thoughtfully. "He don't fit."

I wasn't sure what he meant, but could garner no clearer explanation. "What did he say?"

"Tried to grab me, but I nipped off like you said."

"You should stay out of sight for a while. Have you anything to eat?"

"Got a biscuit." Paulo touched a limp cloth bag hanging from his belt. I was sure the boy never got enough to satisfy a growing appetite.

I dug into my pack and pulled out a small cloth bundle. "Here's jack and cheese. I'll get a room and we'll see what comes. Jacopo did me better service than he knew when he sent you along."

"I can do for myself. Innkeeper said I could sleep in the stables if I mucked out the stalls." He hadn't touched my offered bundle, though his eyes had not left it since I mentioned its contents.

"Go on, take it. I brought enough for both of us."

Before I could blink, the boy grabbed the bundle and was gone. The light was fading as I shouldered my pack and made my way to the Green Lion. It seemed a decent enough place, with less grease and soot than most Leiran inns. A wide, flyspecked window looked out on the docks. I told the innkeeper that I was a widow, hoping to catch a skiff going south so I could return to my family in Deshiva.

"We've lost ten local boys to the war already this year," confided the stout, bearded proprietor, who introduced himself as Bartolome. "No one can hardly work the land

no more, for lack of hands to hold the plows. More widows
like you than children. Don't know who they'll take next
for soldiering. I've a hope they're not desperate enough for
fat innkeepers!" His thick, hairy fingers traded a mug of
ale for a copper coin, even as he talked. Fat or no, I had
the sense that he would not even need to see the coin to
know whether or not it was genuine. "Shall my wife send
supper up to your room? Ladies often prefer it when traveling alone."

"No, I think I'll sit in your common room. I've been
alone too much and could use the sight of people."

"As you wish. Becky there will see to you." He waved
at a barmaid and was soon deep in conversation with another customer.

Fifteen to twenty people sat in the smoky room: some
lone travelers eating soup ladled from the common pot, a
few laborers and tradesmen finishing the day with a tankard
of the Green Lion's ale, and a prosperous-looking couple
with two small, neat children in stiff collars, casting surrep-
titious glances at the other guests. No one fit my quarry's
description.

I settled myself at a small table in the dimmest corner
of the room, where I would be able to see anyone who
came in the door or down the stairs. The ruddy-faced barmaid brought me a bowl of hot broth, thick with barley and
spiced with pepper. The inn was busy; customers flowed in
and out like a noisy, thirsty tide. Laughter blared from
tradesmen sharing a bawdy story, some tankards were
spilled, causing tempers to erupt and two men to threaten
fisticuffs. Bartolome shoved the drunkards out the door,
and the prosperous-looking family fled up the stairs.

As the light outside the window dulled, a man descended
the stairs. I almost laughed. Paulo's description had been
so right. He didn't "fit." He had the look of a Kerotean—
dark, almond-shaped eyes, straight black hair, and close-
trimmed beard sculpted to a point—and he was dressed
in the flowing trousers and colorful, brocaded vest of the
Kerotean aristocracy. But his skin was the color of dried
oak leaves, not milk. More significantly, his head would
only reach my shoulder, and there lived no Kerotean aristo-
crat so diminutive in size, not even the women, who aver-

aged a full head taller than me. Kerotean nobles killed any of their children that were defective in any way, including those born undersized.

The fidgety little man whispered to the landlord, and when the portly Bartolome shook his head, took a seat at a table not too far from me. His dark eyes darted about the room, and I concentrated on my soup. When next I dared look up, the man was sipping from a tankard of ale. Another mistake. Keroteans drank no ale or spirits of any kind. I had thought to observe the man for a day or two, perhaps question the landlord and servants about him, but my plan suddenly seemed foolish. Paulo and I could wrestle this fellow into submission if he gave any trouble.

But before I could make a move, everything fell apart. The stranger's head jerked up and his eyes grew wide. My gaze followed his. Coming down the stairs were three robed priests, two in gray and one in black. When I glanced back at the table beside mine, it was empty, its occupant already halfway out the front door of the tavern. Judging by his wide-eyed terror, he wasn't coming back.

To be this close . . . I could not lose him. Jumping up from the table, I dodged tables and benches, patrons and barmaids to follow the hurrying man. But when I pulled open the door, ready to dash into the night, I stood face to face with Graeme Rowan, Sheriff of Dunfarrie.

CHAPTER 9

Year 4 in the reign of King Evard—summer

"Are you sure you won't go with us, little girl? Don't like to leave you here alone."

"I won't starve, Jonah. Anne's left me more than I could

eat in the space of a week. I won't set the house afire or ruin your garden or break anything. And the weather's fine, so I won't freeze, even if I can't get a fire going."

"You'll learn the touch of flint, little girl," said Anne as her dry kiss brushed my cheek. "Just as you've learned so much already." She climbed up to the wagon seat. "You know the way down village if aught frights you. Jacopo will take you in."

Five months with the old couple had taught me one thing for certain: No one had ever been so inept, so useless, as I. Fires were lit by servants, not coaxed grudging from bits of metal and chaff. Food was brought on trays from warm kitchens, not grubbed from the dirt with raw and bleeding hands. I had only played at gardening. I knew nothing of rocky soil, wire-like weeds, or cartloads of stinking manure hauled from the pigsties in the village to feed the impoverished earth. Clothes were always clean and never had to be mended in candlelight with dull needles that tormented raw fingers. And there was always plenty to eat, even in spring when winter stores were depleted, so your stomach never gnawed at you until you were ready to eat sticks and weeds. Indeed I had learned a great deal in five months. Now it was time for me to learn to be alone.

"Be safe," I said and got on with my lesson.

Just past dawn on the third morning after Anne and Jonah's departure, I lay abed, deciding whether a hot breakfast was worth the hour's struggle with the fire, when I heard a hail from outside the door. "Jonah? Are you in?"

No one but Jacopo had visited the cottage since I'd come to live there, and the unusual stillness had the power to unnerve me. I pulled up the rag quilt and prayed the visitor would go away.

"Goodwife Anne? A word, if you would. And I've brought some oranges from Jaco. Washed up from the barge that wrecked upriver last week."

I shoved back the quilt with a silent curse. If the man was a friend of Anne and Jonah, it wasn't right to refuse him their hospitality. Hurriedly I pulled on the ill-fitting black dress Anne had given me, smoothed my ragged hair, and opened the door.

The man holding a splintered crate on his shoulder had

sand-colored hair and green eyes and looked to be a few years older than me, perhaps as much as thirty. His face was serious, with regular features, a broad forehead, and the network of thin lines at the corners of his eyes that came from spending long hours in the sun. Unremarkable in height, dress, or manner. A ragged scar creased one side of his face from cheekbone to unshaven jaw.

He set the crate on the bench by the door. A dark blue jacket lay crumpled on the top of it, likely shed on the warm journey up the path. "Good morrow, miss." He did not seem surprised to see me. "I've come to speak with Jonah if I may. Or Goodwife Anne."

"They've gone to Montevial and won't return for several days more." Surely he would go now. "May I offer you ale or tea? I'm sure they'd wish it."

"Ale, then, and I'd thank you for it. The day's gone warm already." He retrieved the jacket, straightened it a bit, and flopped it over one shoulder.

I snatched a mug from the shelf, filled it from Jonah's little barrel, and shoved it into the man's hand, remaining standing in the doorway lest he decide to stay a while.

He raised the mug slightly and nodded as if answering a question I'd not heard. "I'd be Graeme Rowan from Dunfarrie." I couldn't remember any mention of that name, but his provincial inflections were much thicker than Jonah's or Anne's, so I couldn't be sure. He downed the ale quickly, but, to my distress, seemed in no hurry to go. "Perhaps I ought tell you why I'm here," he said, propping one foot on the bench beside the sand-crusted crate. The rotting, fishy scent of river-wrack overpowered any smell from the battered green and yellow fruits. "Aye, it's probably better I speak with you."

I didn't like the way he looked at me so intently, his expression revealing so little. And his slow speech, as if he weren't quite sure he wanted to say anything, left my jaw tight with impatience.

"I've heard Anne and Jonah had a visitor these few months. Some in the village say it's their granddaughter Jenny, come home after so many years lost." The moment stretched. His gaze picked at my face. "Last night, three men come to the village. They're the sort who look as if they'll burn their shoes when they leave your town and think no one in a place the size of Dunfarrie can understand words of more than one syllable."

The long pauses and his unreadable expression goaded me to speak. "And what did these men want?" The planed edge of the doorframe dug into my back.

"They were looking for someone, someone they badly want to find, though they vow they wish her no harm. Told me only that the one they hunted ran away from her family five months ago, that she's five-and-twenty, tall for a woman, and has brown eyes and red-brown hair, cut shorter than the usual. They claim it be a matter of law. The time was the same as when Jonah and Anne came back from Montevial in the spring, so I thought to come up and ask what knowledge they might have of the question."

As if an executioner's hood had been dropped over my head, the brightness went out of the day. "What did you tell these men?" My voice came out no more than a whisper.

His gaze did not waver. "Naught as yet. But they didn't know who I was. They'll find that out this morning."

"And who are you?"

"I'd be the Sheriff of Dunfarrie."

Bile rose in my throat. No matter what claims were made about maintaining order or protecting the citizenry from theft and murder, a sheriff's first duty, the very reason for his existence, was to exterminate sorcerers. And though he was appointed by his lord, a sheriff's first allegiance was to his king. Evard's man. Evard's anointed killer.

Coldly, no longer in a whisper, I said, "So you'll tell them about Anne and Jonah's guest."

"I'm god-sworn and king-sworn to uphold the law."

I spat at his feet. "That for Evard's law!"

The slight hardening of his mouth and eyes reflected his judgment of me. "You've no business here, madam."

No matter that he was a damnable villain, he was right, of course. I couldn't hide behind the old couple's kindness, and I didn't think I could run. Karon had told me about that kind of life, and I had neither the determination nor the skill for it. Survival was not that important to me. But Anne and Jonah were. "So you'll hand me over?"

One might have thought I was some kind of dungworm. "I ought. But they've given me no warrant, no grounds, not even a name. For all I know this is just a game for ones like you and them—causing trouble for ordinary folk. But unless you give me some reason not, I'll tell these men what I'm required to tell them, and they'll have no such scruples."

I stood mute. I would not tell a stranger—a sheriff—of my life. He snorted, slung his jacket over his shoulder, and started down the path.

The world was already cold and shadowed even before I stepped out of the sun. I straightened the quilt on the pallet that Jonah had crowded into the corner by the hearth, put away the cup I had used the previous night, and folded the mended towel I used for washing. When all was tidy, I sat on Jonah's bench and stared at the sun-drenched meadow long enough for the sheriff to be well on his way. Then I rose and walked down the path toward the village, expecting never to come back.

The common room of the Wild Heron was dim after the glare of summer morning, so it took me a moment to see the four men seated at a corner table: the sheriff, two soldiers in red livery, and a dark-haired man in black, who had his back to me.

Rowan noticed me first. His expression did not change. One of his companions touched the arm of the dark-haired man, who whipped his head around. Darzid. I thought I might vomit.

He remained seated, his shiny boots resting on the table, as he inspected me. "Well now, my lady, you've come up in the world, I see. From sorcerers to pig farmers. What next? Gravediggers? Cutpurses?"

"What do you want of me, Captain?" I said, forcing my voice even.

"Only word of your safety and health to carry back to your friends and family. Your brother grieves for your company."

"Rubbish."

"Also, you have something that belongs to your king."

"Impossible."

"Ah, dear lady, only by his sufferance do you live."

"I'm sure I'm very grateful." What kind of game was this?

"Gratitude is not enough. There's a price for the king's parole."

Parole. I caught my breath. "He wouldn't dare!"

"Oh, yes. The first day of autumn is only three weeks away. This exemplary sheriff has been charged with the responsibility to see that you fulfill your duty on Sufferance Day in this and every year of your life." I started to speak, but Darzid raised his finger. "You'd best not compound your past offenses with treasonable words. Such an example it would be. And from a duke's daughter, one whom rumor claimed was to be our queen! Do the good people of this place realize the honor to which they are privy, having such an exalted personage in their midst?"

One of his companions nudged him and said, "Not from her dress, would they, Captain?"

Darzid chortled merrily. "Perhaps not. But her manners are so fine. I'm sure she curtsies to the swine, or perhaps she discusses fine points of law with the sheriff here." He waved Rowan and the men in livery toward the door. Then he stood and straightened his dark purple tunic and vest. "Have you any message for your brother, my lady?"

As I was awash in the bitter implications of his news, it took me a moment to realize I was not to accompany him.

He propped one boot on a chair and used the hem of his cloak to flick away imaginary dust. "Quickly, madam. If we stay here too long, we'll begin to stink. A message for the duke?"

A message? For Tomas the executioner? Even in the moment's relief, my hatred boiled over. "Tell my brother he cannot wash them enough."

Darzid crinkled his eyebrows in puzzlement and shrugged. "As you wish. Don't think to run away again." With mock solemnity, he wagged a finger first at the sheriff and then at me. "It would go hard with anyone who's given you aid. And the first day of autumn—on your life and the lives of everyone in this charming sty, do not forget." Darzid and his soldiers left the tavern without closing the door behind them.

*   *   *

The autumn equinox—the Day of the King's Sufferance. The law stated that on the first day of autumn all those who lived by the king's sufferance must appear before him and swear they had not trespassed on his favor during the past year. The event was a favorite of those who enjoyed displaying moral superiority without fear of rebuttal or retribution. Observers could question the petitioner about anything, whether related to the past crime or no, and the penalties were severe if one answered untruthfully. A horrid custom. Humiliating.

At dawn on the last day of summer, I met Graeme Rowan at the Dunfarrie Bridge to make the daylong trek to Montevial. He waited on the seat of a rickety farm cart. A lantern gleamed from the seat beside him, revealing, among other things, a gray smudge in the center of his forehead. No surprise to discover he was a pious man, one who would pray at the shrine of Annadis before a journey, marking himself with earth to remind the god of earth and sky that he was his servant no matter where he traveled.

I climbed into the seat without a greeting, and the sheriff put out the lantern and slapped the mule. Only after half a league of the bone-jarring ride did Rowan first break the silence. "I'm sorry this isn't the kind of carriage you're accustomed to," he said after a particularly hard jolt.

"You have no idea to what I'm accustomed."

"Those men told me of your crimes." His eyes were fixed on the road ahead—or perhaps the mule's rump.

"And are you properly appalled at the affront I am to lawful society? Afraid of my arcane connections? Afraid Jerrat will send a lightning bolt to strike me while I'm sitting next to you?"

"I thought it right you should know."

"You have a highly developed sense of honor—for a sheriff." For a man with so much blood on his hands.

Jacopo had told me how the sheriff had come by his office. Rowan had saved our local lord's life while serving in Evard's first Vallorean campaign back in King Gevron's time. That campaign, of course, had included the slaughter at Avonar. I glanced at Rowan's hands that gripped the mule's reins—short, work-hardened fingers, wide backs with a layer of wiry, reddish hair. Ordinary enough. But I could not look at them without imagining those hands binding women, men, and children to the hastily erected stakes, throwing piles of sticks at their feet, waving the blazing torches close. . . .

Rowan slapped the reins hard. I didn't think the beast could go any faster. "It's true I have no rank, neither dukes nor earls nor even a lowly knight in my pedigree, but I manage to keep some sense of right and wrong about me."

"Do you think that's why I'm allowed to live? Because of my rank? Does that offend your belief in the law?"

"I'm not your judge—"

"I think I'm glad of that."

"—but I tired long ago of those who take or leave the law at their will."

"Rest easy, sir. I would not think of challenging your sense of right and wrong while in your charge. Any man who burned the children of Avonar would surely have no mercy on a depraved soul such as my own."

His features might have been carved from the oaken planks of that cart. He said no more. In fact, we traveled the entire day without twenty more words between us.

We arrived in Montevial after nightfall. Rowan had started fidgeting a league from the walls. As we pressed through the travelers crowding across the Dun bridge, trying to get across the sluggish river and past the city gates before they were closed for the night, his eyes flicked from side to side, and he moved almost imperceptibly toward the center of the wagon seat. The flickering torchlight made the lines about his eyes and the creased scar in his cheek seem deeper. Once he stopped the wagon, jumped down from the seat, and spoke quietly to a constable who was patrolling a street of shuttered shops. When we at last came to a halt in the muddy stableyard of a cheap riverside inn, he kicked the crowding beggars away from us and snapped an epithet at a ragged girl. The sheriff seemed to think she was trying to steal the mule, but she had only come to take the beast into the rickety stable. I don't know which of us was more relieved that the journey was over.

When Rowan appeared at my door the next morning, he wore his usual sober garb of tan breeches, a country man's canvas leggings, and a dark blue coat, cuffs frayed and thin at the elbows. We walked through the city in a mournful drizzle, the crowds growing thicker as we neared the palace. Rowan started at the bump and jostle of the passersby and gripped my arm tighter the farther we walked, as if I might be tempted to run away now I was in the bastion of Leiran aristocracy.

I tried to keep my eyes away from the palace towers that dominated the cityscape and the red banners with gold dragons that swelled limp and heavy from the walls, but as Rowan's firm hand steered me toward the center of the city, my steps slowed.

"What is it?" asked Rowan.

"I cannot . . . not that way. There are other ways to the Petitioners' Gate." Much as I despised myself for revealing anything to a sheriff, I could not hide the wave of trembling sickness that had come over me.

"Isn't this the quickest route? I should think you'd want to be done with it."

"Please, Sheriff, I beg you. Another way." Some places even pride could not carry me.

"As you wish. As long as we get there."

The Petitioner's Gate in the south wall of the king's residence at Montevial was opened twice a year: on the first day of autumn for the Sufferance Rite and on the last day of the year for the Feast of the Beggar's Penny—the day when legend said that in the days of trial before he was granted dominion over the earth and sky, Annadis the Swordsman had given his last penny to a poor beggar in the depths of winter, only to find out that it was his own father, the First God Arot, in disguise. Soldiers in red livery guarded the gate, and a line of soberly dressed men of all ages and sizes was waiting to pass through. The men in line—there were no other women—were mostly prosperous merchants or officers. The poor could not afford the king's parole.

Rowan released my arm at the edge of the plaza that fronted the gate.

"Are you not to hand me over?" I asked when he motioned me to go on alone.

"My duty was to assure your attendance. You'll find me here when your duty is likewise done."

"But surely your duty does not extend to taking me back?" I was genuinely surprised.

"My duty, madam, is to uphold the law."

The sheriff's fiery emblem glared at me from his blue coat. Revolted, I left him and made my way to the line of petitioners, wrapping my shabby cloak tight around me.

The queue moved slowly through a small courtyard littered with leaves blown in over the walls. No one would ever bother to clean them up for such traffic as passed through the Petitioner's Gate. Beyond the courtyard was a waiting room crowded with wooden benches. I squeezed onto the end of a bench and fixed my gaze on the muddy stone floor. One by one the names were called. I felt lightheaded. Perhaps I should have eaten something.

An hour passed. I could do this. For Anne and Jonah who had saved my life, for my freedom, I could do it. What could they ask me that had not been asked during the weeks of interrogation before Karon's trial?

"Look deep inside, Seri love," Karon had told me. "Look at the beauty you've stored up there, the life you hold, the spark that is no other. They cannot touch it."

I would not let them in. Karon had built himself a fortress of peace to protect his own spark of life, and in the end, it had failed him. He had died screaming. But I was a warrior's daughter, and I knew of fortresses. To withstand the assaults of the world, you could not afford peace or sentiment. You couldn't afford to care about anyone or anything. I would give these people no satisfaction.

"Seriana Marguerite of Comigor."

The heavy-jowled man wore red robes and carried a guide-staff with a gold dragon on its head. Neck straight, eyes forward, I rose and followed him down a passageway, through a tall arched door, and into the Great Hall of Leire. Hundreds of people were crowded along each side of the vast room, their gaily colored dress garish beside the somber, ancient stonework. Cold light fell through the high windows.

At the far end of the hall, scarcely visible through the murky light, twenty men sat at a long curved table. Evard slouched in his gilded chair at the center of them. Sitting on either side of him were others I knew: the Chancellor Villarre, the Dukes of Pamphile, Aristide, and Greymonte, the Earl of Jeffi, an old hunting partner of my father's, his leathery wrinkles sagging in distress. So many who had once been part of my world. On either side of the table were a few rows of observers of high enough rank to jockey for chairs, those like the priests, who had a special interest in those who violated the sorcery laws. Everyone else stood, whispering and murmuring behind fans and jeweled fingers.

About fifteen paces from the table, the heavy-jowled steward stuck his staff out in front of me, barring closer approach. He spoke sideways through his teeth. "Obeisance. Complete. Now." Surely he was joking. No one of noble family made complete obeisance. The king was the first among equals. And to Evard? Never. I made a deep curtsy as was proper, keeping my head unbowed. My father had sat on the Council of Lords. My mother had been maid of honor to Queen Theodora.

As I rose, I glimpsed Tomas watching stone-faced while a fair, rosy-cheeked young woman clung to his arm, giggling and whispering with other women around her. His wife's name was Philomena.

The heavy-jowled man whispered from behind me. "Obeisance. Complete. Now." I stood firm.

Evard's relaxed posture was belied by the edge in his voice. "It is the custom for those who live by our sufferance to make a respectful approach."

"Your Majesty, I bear the honor of all who hold the rank I have been privileged to share. Acquiescence to such a custom would draw the structure of society into question. If such were my intent, I would most assuredly begin at a different place."

The crowd drew breath as one. Evard slammed his hand on the table. "The only rank of those who enter the Petitioner's Gate is the rank of supplicant. You will follow the custom or you will be forced to follow it."

It would have been easy, though repugnant, to grant Evard what he wanted, but as with most bullies, it would only leave him with expectations I was not planning to fulfill. I stood quietly while Evard jerked his head to the heavy-jowled man. Three red-liveried guards surrounded me. Two of them grabbed my arms and spread them in the supplicant's gesture. One forced me to my knees and bent my head forward until it touched the floor. After a moment they released me, and I stood again. Tomas was livid. What did he expect?

The chancellor spoke first. "Seriana Marguerite, you have been adjudged guilty of the most serious crimes: consorting with enemies of Leire, conspiring to hide criminals, participating in treasonous activities, plotting to place on the throne of Leire one who knowingly harbored . . ." I did not even listen until Evard began the questioning.

"Where have you spent your time since you so ungratefully repudiated your family's concern?"

"A village in the south, Your Majesty."

"And who has sheltered you?"

"Peasants. No one of importance."

"Do these peasants know of your crimes?"

"They know of what I have been accused. I acknowledge no crimes. My husband was a healer who shared a blessed gift with all who needed it."

The observers gabbled in disbelief. The high priest of Jerrat, a tall man with a craggy face, jumped from his chair. "Insupportable!"

Evard pounded on the table for silence. "Stubborn still, are you? We would advise you to restrain your insolent tongue. It would be easy to overreact to your heedless provocation and do that which might give us indigestion tomorrow. Tell us, madam, in these months since your judgment, have you had contact with any person who has at any time or in any wise practiced, studied, or tolerated the repugnant and unnatural rites of sorcery?"

"I have not."

"Have you, in any other way, broken any law promulgated in our name?"

"I have not."

Evard then turned the questioning over to those in attendance. It went on for well over an hour. Had I worked charms or spells? Did I know how? Where had we held the god-cursed rites? Was it true the late Earl of Gault was himself a sorcerer? Had I been intimate with a man since I ran away? The women's questions were the worst.

Tomas looked as if he might burst as the farce played out. His face blazed when one of his friends asked me if a sorcerer could "magic his prick bigger" during the act of love. And when his own wife asked if I pleasured myself, as no man would have a woman befouled by a sorcerer, I thought Tomas might throttle her. Darzid sat just behind him, watching thoughtfully.

I would have gotten through it quite well if a sober Graeme Rowan had not been standing by the door as I was escorted out. But when I thought of him hearing all I had been forced to answer . . . I was truly humiliated.

The journey back to Dunfarrie that evening was even more awkward than that of the previous day. Rowan never shifted his eyes from the road. I could not look at him without anger and embarrassment, and then I cursed myself for caring what a murdering sheriff had heard. We arrived at the Dun bridge near midnight. Honor required me to acknowledge the escort; he could have left me to walk.

"Thank you for bringing me back, Sheriff."

"I'm surprised you'd wish to return to peasants of no importance."

Stupid man. Couldn't he see it was better not to interest Evard in this place? I turned to go.

As I started up the path, though, he called after me in a very different tone. "Tell me one thing. What was the place in the city where you wouldn't walk?"

What was one more question on this day? He could have asked it at the rite, and I would have been required to answer. And he had honored my request. "It was the command, Sheriff. Surely you know of it. The heart of any Leiran city where public rites and performances are held and proclamations posted. In Montevial, the place where sorcerers are burned. For a year, as a warning, they leave it there, the pyre, the stake . . . whatever is left. It is the law." Words could not pain me. "I heard that Avonar looked like a burned forest."

*   *   *

From that day on, every year on the last day of summer I met Graeme Rowan at the Dunfarrie bridge. Neither his sober expression nor his stiff propriety varied from one year to the next, nor did we speak beyond the minimum necessary. The smudge of the gods always adorned his brow. Each year, he listened as I was questioned, and then we returned to our separate lives, duty and the law satisfied.

CHAPTER 10

"Rowan!"

"You! What in blazes . . . ?"

Only a few times in my life had I been at a loss for something to say. The only clue to Aeren's identity was slipping away from me into the night, and standing in my way was one person who absolutely must not know of my mission. Possible explanations raced through my mind and were discarded just as quickly. Graeme Rowan was not stupid.

The sheriff took my arm firmly and propelled me backward into the shadowed alcove between the outer door, the staircase, and the wide entrance to the common room.

"Release me at once. You've no cause to hold me," I said, in a furious whisper.

"I've every right to investigate suspicious behavior, and I find your presence here extremely suspicious." Rowan spoke quietly also, in tones that brooked no dispute.

"You have no jurisdiction here, Sheriff. If I should scream that I'm being brutalized, you would have no more rights than any other bully."

His sober expression did not change, though the sun lines at the corners of his eyes crinkled a bit. "I disagree. Barnard, the local sheriff, knows me quite well. He would most likely be interested in the activities of known lawbreakers in his town."

"You wouldn't!"

"Test me. Or would you rather tell me what you're doing here? I know there are few things that pain you more than having a word with me, but I really must know what's brought you here."

And this, of course, was where I was out of words. I couldn't think fast enough. The long day's journey, the terrible doings in the forest, the odd little man running away . . . "Can we step outside, Sheriff?"

"As you wish."

Beggars, carters, and drunkards crowded the torch-lit lane, but the stranger was nowhere in sight. *Curse the man!* "Have you nothing better to do than bother honest citizens, Sheriff? You should leave me alone and clean up your own district. Take care of the murderous highwaymen that prey on travelers." To my dismay, my voice faltered a bit as I recalled the brutal scene in During Forest.

If there was any lack of will on Rowan's part to pursue our confrontation, he dismissed it instantly. The pious mark on his brow glared at me like a third eye. "Madam, what do you know of highwaymen?"

Cursing my loose tongue, I folded my arms and looked away.

"Blessed Annadis, give me patience!" he said. "How do you propose I take care of my district if every person in it is so high and mighty as you?"

"Perhaps your district would be better off without a sheriff's care."

His face flamed, but he gritted his teeth and kept his voice down. Once could not mistake his sincerity. "Five men were slain in During Forest today. They were no ordinary highwaymen, but the most ruthless that ever plagued this road. They've survived for twenty years and were cut down in an afternoon. It's something I must understand. If you refuse to speak what you know, then you've no right to demand anything of me. I ask you again, madam, what do you know of highwaymen?" I had never heard so many words from him all at once.

My distaste for the upright sheriff and my revulsion at

his past did not entirely cloud my perceptions. As Jacopo often reminded me, Rowan was neither excessively brutal nor grasping in his day-to-day duties, as were so many of his ilk. And if his unquestioning adherence to a flawed notion of law set him at odds with the ruthless travelers I had seen in the forest, I would not argue. However uncomfortable it might feel for me, reason was on his side. After all, the priests might have nothing to do with Aeren. Perhaps the almond-eyed man's fear of the three had its origin, as mine did, in their handiwork of the day.

"You're right," I said. What was pride but another garment to be discarded when you had grown past its use? "Not about everything . . . but about this. Yes. I witnessed what happened in During Forest. Quite by chance."

"And will you tell me of it?"

I glanced about the dark lane. "Can we walk away from here just a little?" Rowan started to protest, but I interrupted. "I promise, I'll tell you why."

Just down the lane two empty crates sat outside a poulterer's shop. My feet felt as if someone had taken a hammer to them. Making sure I could still see the door of the inn, I sat on one of the crates and propped my heavy boots on the other, leaving Rowan to decide whether to sit on the filthy ground or remain standing, unable to see my face. He squatted, looking uncomfortable.

"I was on my way to Grenatte on private business," I began, and without mentioning Paulo, I recounted what I had witnessed that afternoon.

"And these priests are in the Green Lion?"

"That's why I was leaving in a hurry," I said. "They unnerved me, though I don't believe they saw me in the forest, and though one could say they were entirely in the right in the matter. How can I explain it?"

He nodded thoughtfully. "The kill was not cleanly done. Yet, as you say, it's not against the law to be good at defending oneself. But any who can take such men down easily are worth my attention, for rarely are they less dangerous in their turn."

"So what will you do?"

"I'll speak to these priests and see what they're about."

"You'll not tell them who you are?"

"Surely this is no concern for my welfare?" he said.

Graeme Rowan's welfare was his own concern. "It just occurred to me that a casual encounter might be less risky than telling them you're a sheriff. In fact"—a scheme began taking shape—"to make things easier, I'd be willing to accompany you while you speak to them. We could say we are cousins."

"I see no purpose in deception. In this matter, at least, they've no reason to fear me." He straightened to his full height, looking down at me quizzically. "But if, for whatever reason, you'd like to be present when I interview them, I'll not prevent it. I certainly don't intend for you to leave Grenatte until we can discuss other matters . . . such as what you're doing here."

I bridled. "There's no need to assume that because I answered a few of your questions, I'll allow you to question me on my private business."

"Madam, I would never presume to expect anything from you."

I did not respond to his goading. I was already planning what to say to the priests.

As soon as Rowan and I entered the inn, the landlord bustled up to us, eyeing the sheriff suspiciously. "Is the gentleman bothering you, madam?"

"No. Not at all, Goodman Bartolome. Thank you." I would not allow Rowan to control the situation. "In fact, this is my cousin, Graeme, come unexpectedly to meet me." I ignored the sheriff's darkening brow. "Can you tell us, innkeeper—there's a gentleman in your common room, one who wears the robes of a priest—do you know his name, sir? He looks quite like the priest who wed my sister Catherine to her man, but I'd feel quite foolish asking if it were not the same priest."

"The fellow's name slips my mind," said the innkeeper, "but the three of them come from a temple school in Valleor. Don't know much else."

Through the door of the brightly lit common room I could see the priests seated at a table near the center of the room. "That could well be the same Pere Franze, don't you think, Graeme?" I said, indicating the three. "I believe he'd be interested to know Catherine has produced five healthy boys in five years. His offering of Mana's blessing was most efficacious!" Producing the Twins was Mana's only role in our holy legends, and the First God's wife was interested only in sons.

The sheriff peered through the opening and then dragged me back into the shadows. "I think you should come away immediately," he said in a tight whisper.

"What think you, innkeeper?" I said, paying Rowan no more heed than a doorstop. "Should I speak to them?"

"Well, now, they seem right enough fellows," said the innkeeper, shrugging his massive shoulders.

"I can't imagine they'd have an interest in such trifles," said the furious sheriff. "You—"

"My cousin always thinks I am too forward."

Rowan tugged my arm so forcefully, it was difficult to hold my ground. "And so you are. You should not bother either the priests or our host with your foolishness."

Bartolome thoughtfully scratched the hairy chest bulging above his apron. "Well, I can't see as how it would hurt to ask. I always take it fair when someone says I've done a decent job, even if I'm not the one as done it."

"Exactly!" I said, and I yanked my arm out of Rowan's grip and marched through the doorway and across the smoky, crowded room. "Excuse me, Your Honor, sir. Might I have a word?"

When the man I had seen slit two throats and pierce a man's heart with skill and relish turned to look at me, it took all my resolution not to step away. There could be no soul in him. Neither beauty nor life had ever graced those pale eyes, nor had any human feeling with which I had kinship. I quickly averted my gaze.

"How may I help you, madam?" His voice was coolly friendly, not at all like his eyes.

"It's most likely foolish, sir, but my cousin and I have had a disagreement, and the only way to resolve it is to speak up. I say that you are the very most honored Pere Franze that has wed my sister Catherine and her husband David in Deshiva these five years past, and that it is my duty to tell you of the most efficacious blessing of Mana you performed on that happy occasion, being as Catherine and David have five healthy sons in five years"—I spoke much too fast, trying to bolster my faltering resolve—"but my cousin, who lurks in yonder shadows with our worthy innkeeper, says I should not bother a weary traveler with such trifles, though to my mind such a blessing that gets five healthy sons is no trifle!"

Though a smile played on the thin lips, it did not warm his emptiness. "Much as I would like to lay claim to such a success, I cannot. I've never traveled to Deshiva. Giano is my name."

"My apologies for disturbing you then, Your Honor. I was so hoping you might be Pere Franze, for I was thinking of asking Annadis's warding for our travels back to Deshiva. After what we saw today . . ." I shuddered.

"And what was that?" Early frost enfolded the summer night.

"Oh, sir, I'd not wish to offend you with the description of it while you're at table."

"Travelers should share their wisdom and experience, madam, so as to ease the road for their fellows," he said coolly. "I think it imperative. Don't you agree?"

I wasn't sure I would have been *able* to disagree. Though not invited to do so, I drew up an extra chair, sat down, and leaned across their table. To avoid his eyes, I kept my own focused on the gold earring he wore in his right ear. "True enough, sir. Indeed it was the most dreadful sight that ever I hope to see. Five dead men, brutally cut down and left to lie on the road through During Forest. Highwaymen, so I've heard, and so better dead, but a fearsome sight nonetheless. I feel quite faint when I think of continuing our journey tomorrow."

Pere Giano's slender fingers lay quiet on the table, one hand upon the other, no residue of blood on the pale skin. "We've heard of this discovery, also, and are shocked by it. We've been sent to Leire to build a school to teach young warriors the service of Annadis, but such doings might hasten us back to our quiet temple life."

So they were going to lie about it. No surprise.

"It would be a great honor to have a temple school in western Leire." No student of *my* acquaintance would be sent to such a tutor.

"Unfortunately, our plans have been upset," he said, leaning closer, his words slithering their way into my head. "Thieves are not always found in the forest, but often in the very bosom of one's family. A faithless servant has absconded with the small endowment with which we were to build."

And there it was . . . the connection. Though I dared not allow him to note my satisfaction, my heart quickened its pace. "Have you notified the authorities? Perhaps my cousin should summon Barnard, the local sheriff, so your servant may receive just treatment from the law." A faithless servant . . . Were these men, too, seeking an 'addled groom'?

"It's against our custom to bring down the law on our servants, but we've seen nothing of him in a fortnight. We believe that if we could but find the youth, we could persuade him to rethink his wayward behavior."

What persuasions might be imposed by a man with no soul? Enough to chase a man out of his clothes? Out of his voice? Out of his mind?

"My cousin travels widely in his business, your honor. Why, he's most likely visited every hostelry and inn in five districts in the past month, as well as having wide acquaintance. Can you describe this fiend who is so wanting in decency as to steal from the Swordsman's holy servants? Perhaps my cousin has taken note of him."

"A young man. Tall and light-haired, fairly made, but wicked and hasty in temper, and weak in the mind, full of grandiose delusions. I think the gods have sent him this weakness to make him humble, but alas, though we at the temple have nurtured the boy since childhood, our care seems to have gone for naught."

"A sad story," I said. He was so smug in his lies. "All too common among those who depend on the charity of holy institutions. I'll ask my cousin if he's seen anything likely. I've neither seen nor heard of anything myself."

"Even so." The priest picked up his wine cup and leaned back in his chair. He was done with me.

I craved to wheedle something more from him—a name, a province—or some hint of whether he knew of his "faithless servant's" talent for sorcery. But I had lived enough years to know when I had pushed my luck as far as was profitable. "I'll bid you and your companions a good night, sir. My cousin is known for being sometimes too free in his ingestion of spirits in such a friendly house as this. I wish him to be alert on the morrow!"

The man in black nodded and turned back to his silent, hooded companions. I believed I saw the trace of impatience on his narrow face, but I couldn't bear to look at him long enough to be sure.

I left the common room sedately, slipping past the shadowed foyer and up the first flight of stairs. But no sooner had I got out of sight of the common room and bolted for the second landing, than Rowan stepped out in front of me, grim as a headsman. "That was very foolish."

"But revealing, don't you think? Did you listen? The poor servants of the Swordsman whose money has been stolen, though they wear gold worth an earldom at their necks. Not a word about the events in the forest." And such a strange story about their missing servant.

"You're fortunate. These men are clearly not to be trifled—"

"I thought you might have more mettle than to eavesdrop from the stairs like a scullery maid. Quite a man of the world is my cousin Graeme."

"A little forewarning might have helped." Was he more annoyed with my interference, or that it was *I* who had done the interfering?

"I didn't think it necessary. Did I not play it quite well?"

"I'm surprised you'd think of it as play, having seen what you did in the forest today. Were all your questions answered satisfactorily? Perhaps you'll condescend to enlighten me as to your purpose in the matter and what else you might know of these people."

"We should not discuss this in the passageway of an inn."

"I suppose there's no question of a cousinly chat in your room or a walk in the evening air?"

"I'm asleep standing, Shcriff. And, of course, I've no interest in this matter. I was curious because of what I saw, and willing to help you, because . . . you were right that I should. Good night."

Rowan bowed stiffly. "I'll remind you that the conditions

of your parole require your obedience to the command of
any sheriff, and the nature of your crimes makes me responsible for your actions. We have not finished our business, my lady. You're not to leave your room, and you'll
have no commerce with anyone until I give you leave. I'll
see you first thing in the morning." The insufferable prig
started down the passage, and, to my chagrin, I could not
think of hateful enough words to throw back at him. As
he disappeared down the stair landing, he called over his
shoulder. "And you may tell Paulo that his sneaking about
has left his gram half-frantic with worry, and that if he
doesn't get himself wrung out by highwaymen or conspira-
torial women, then it will most likely be by me."

As well he turned a corner just then and that my knife
was tucked away under my skirt.

Rowan would have been well satisfied had he been able
to read my thoughts in the next hour. As the exhilaration
of the evening's encounter wore away, I started shaking,
almost sick as I thought of the slaughter I had witnessed
and the empty eyes and pale hands of the one who had
worked it. What was I doing? I had no business there. Only
after I had made a vow to scoop up Paulo at first light and
run as fast as I could back to Dunfarrie was my tired body
able to sink into sleep.

Sometime in the hours after midnight, a scraping noise
across the dark room brought me abruptly awake. I slipped
my knife from the sheath under my pillow and held still
until a freckled face rose above the windowsill like a
grubby moon.

"Paulo!" I pulled him through the window, and he
landed on the floor in a disheveled, ripe-smelling lump.
"What are you doing here?"

"Found him!"

"Who?"

"The one we come here for."

"Yes, I found him, too, but he ran away before I could
speak to him."

"Nope. He's close. Got his horse from the stable and
rode off, but didn't go far."

My feet were already in my boots. "Take me there." All

terrors were dismissed, all vows forsworn in the prospect of the chase.

The inn was dark and quiet, lying fallow like a well-managed field in the hours between closing and breakfast. We slipped down the stairs, then sped through deserted streets until we reached the southern outskirts of town. A jumble of squat, dark shanties crowded the dirt lane until it broke free into open country and wound up a shallow rise. Atop the rise, silhouetted against the moonlit sky, was a crumbling finger of stone, an abandoned watchtower once used for observing the road and the river.

Paulo pressed a finger to his mouth as we approached a gap in the curved wall. The wooden door had long since rotted away from its rusty hinges, allowing a narrow band of moonlight to penetrate the interior. We stepped inside. From across the circular darkness came the scent of a horse. I felt the soft solidity of its presence. Paulo tugged at my arm and pointed to a mound huddled against one of the curved walls. We tiptoed closer, but before we reached the dark form, Paulo lost his balance and fell against a pile of crates that clattered onto the stone floor.

"Who comes?" The voice from the direction of the dark mound quavered a bit.

"Friends," I said.

"I have no friends here. Who are you? What do you want with me?"

"You ran away before we could be properly introduced."

"I know nothing of mundane women."

"Come, sir, let us speak in a civil manner." *Mundane* was as good a description of me as I had heard in a while, but how would he know? "You're searching for a missing horse, and I may know something of it."

I pulled one of the fallen crates into the path of moon-light from the door and sat on it. After a moment the slight figure emerged from the shadows to stand in the moonlit rectangle a few paces from me. Straw clung to his flowing trousers and Kerotean vest, and his high-necked tunic was twisted awkwardly about his neck. He stood up very straight, narrowed his almond-shaped eyes, and stepped toward me.

"Not too close!" The man and I both nearly shed our

skin when Paulo yelled and popped out from behind me with a good-sized stick of wood on his shoulder.

"The messenger boy!" cried the stranger, his eyes darting from Paulo back to me. "You are the one who summoned me . . . a woman, not a man. Why have you lied? The Count de Mangerit I am, and no one must lie to me."

I had to smile at his posturing. "As I said, I have news of your horse."

"Grasping mundane. Think you to extract some reward?"

"Not a reward, but information. If I learn what I want, I may be able to tell you what you want to know."

"I don't believe a mundane—a woman mundane—could know anything I want to hear." Clearly *mundane* meant something particular to this man.

I had hoped to save my trump card for later. I sighed, pulled a twist of paper from my pocket, and showed the man its contents. While Aeren lay ill, I had trimmed the brambles from his matted blond hair. "Is this lock perhaps from your horse's mane, 'Count'?"

The stranger sagged to his knees and covered his face with his fists, pretense shed like unwanted clothing. "All honor to you, Vasrin Shaper, Vasrin Creator," he whispered, "he has been found." After a moment he lowered his folded hands to his breast. "Please, woman, tell me that he lives." He did not yet look up.

"He lives. And my name is Seri."

I thought he was going to cry. Whether it was because Aeren was alive or because he'd had the audacity to do it with a "mundane" woman's help—I wasn't sure.

"I want to know who he is and who you are," I said.

He straightened his head proudly. "I am not permitted to tell you those things. You must take me to him."

"You're quite mistaken. I'll take you nowhere near him until you persuade me that you're his friend. And if you are not his friend, you'll not live to harm him." Paulo blanched a little, but to the boy's credit, his stick did not falter.

"You cannot understand, woman," said the man. "You are a mundane. He is—This is impossible!" He was entirely flustered. "He is my servant, my groom. He has taken my prize stallion. White. You are required to give him to me, as he has stolen my possession."

"You may leave off your playacting, sir. If you think to impersonate nobility, then you must learn more of their customs. Uncountable clues tell me you have never been to Kerotea, never laid eyes on a Kerotean, and most likely never had a groom. Now, answer my questions or I take my leave."

"No, no. You must not go without telling me where he is. Let me think. I must think. Good Vasrin shape thoughts of sense in my head." The man began pacing, fingering a tassel dangling from his belt as he mumbled to himself. "I *will* not say. I *cannot* say. I am sworn. But I must get to him. Why me? Yes, it happened fast, but Bendal was designated. So what if he was wounded? Bendal wounded is worth ten of me. A mundane woman. I am cursed. But he lives, and the Zhid are close. The timing is all. . . ." He stopped his pacing and sat himself cross-legged on the dirt in front of me. "You'll not take me to him if I do not speak?"

"Correct."

"And you will have this ferocious boy bash me senseless if I try to extract answers from you?"

"Absolutely correct." I worked to keep my face sober.

"So you force me to tell you."

"Prove to me that you are his friend."

The small man cocked his head. "Why do you care for him? I can give you a reward, a substantial reward, if you take me to him and ask no questions."

"It's a long story. I care nothing for either of you, and even less for your reward."

"He is well?" He hugged his knees and looked at the ground.

"He had a wicked knife-wound in one shoulder, but it's healing well."

"But he's told you nothing? Perhaps you have harmed him." He glanced up and, for just a moment, his dark eyes were daggers. "Perhaps you lie." The moment's ferocity vanished as quickly as it had appeared. "He would not trust you. He too has little experience of women or mundanes. Of anyone, if truth be told." He shook his head in resignation. "He's never been easy. . . ."

"It's not just that. For one thing, he is incapable of speech."

"Incapable . . . ?

"And for another, I don't believe he can remember anything to tell me. He doesn't know who he is. He can't remember his people, or where his home is, or why the king's men were pursuing him through my valley. He needs a friend who knows him."

"Ah, my sorrowing land . . ." Tears filled the almond eyes and rolled down his cheeks. He dashed them aside unashamedly. "The foul Zhid have done this!"

"Tell me who you are," I said, more gently this time, hoping not to fluster him into complete incoherence. "And who is your friend? Truly, I wish him no harm."

"My name is Baglos. And you are correct. I was never meant to wear the dress of nobles." He wrestled off his brocade vest and threw it into the dirt. "And I was never meant to be the Guide. I was meant to cook: to braise succulent fish, to baste roasting quail, to mix and blend and season. But the one who was designated as his madrissé was wounded. When it was decided that D'Natheil must make the crossing immediately, the Zhid attacked, and all was chaos. It's why we became separated, not just that I am inept, though that is true. I thought my duties were ended before they had begun, and that our last hope was dead because only Baglos was available to guide." He sank into a melancholy silence, leaving me at a loss.

"Please. You must explain a little more. I've understood none of this except that your name is Baglos and that you're a cook. Is that right?"

"Unfortunately true."

"And you have been made Aeren's 'guide' . . . because someone else was wounded?"

"Aeren?" His head popped up from where it rested heavily on his fist. "Who is Aeren?"

"Your friend. He heard the cry of the gray falcon that we call an aeren, and he indicated to me that such was his name. Is that not true?"

For the first time, Baglos smiled. "D'Natheil means *falcon*. D'Natheil is his name. The Zhid have not taken his name. That is good, very good. Thank you for telling me."

I was glad to hear there was something good about the confusing mess. But the fellow's enemies had me worried; I'd never heard of "Zhid." And there was the matter of his talent. . . .

"There was an afternoon when Aeren—D'Natheil—became quite afraid, but he couldn't tell me why." I hesitated, then forged ahead. "The light was . . . very odd . . . that day. It smelled wrong. Felt wrong."

I expected ridicule at this or at least puzzled curiosity. But Baglos jumped to his feet as if stung by a scorpion. "We must go to him. Please. The Seeking of the cursed Zhid is already touching him. And they are here, so close."

"The three priests—the men you ran away from—are they these Zhid? Your enemies?"

"Zhid are the warriors of Zhev'Na, the enemies of all who breathe, of all who live unfettered. They'll find him if we don't hurry. Such danger stalking him, more than you know if they find him too soon. Please, woman. He is our last hope."

Though I was no closer to understanding his words, I believed Baglos. There was no pretense in his quivering anxiety, no deception in his concern for the young man. And he didn't seem very threatening, though the memory of the silver dagger embedded in solid rock could not but leave me wary of both Aeren and his friends.

"All right," I said. "Let's go."

CHAPTER 11

Baglos was not happy at the idea of my returning to the inn before leaving Grenatte, and I myself had more than a few sharp words ready for Graeme Rowan and his self-righteous snooping. But if I failed to meet the sheriff, I had

no doubt the man would be sitting on my doorstep with
Aeren under arrest by the time I could walk back to
Dunfarrie.

The fading moon was setting and the sky was gray with
approaching dawn when I left Baglos and Paulo at the edge
of town. The streets near the marketplace were already
busy, and the smells of hot bread and sizzling bacon from
Bartolome's kitchen reminded me that I was ravenous. I
was crossing the innyard, ready to wheedle an early breakfast from the good innkeeper, when I spied two men shaking hands close by the entrance to the stable—two men
who should be in no wise so friendly. Dismayed, I slipped
around the outside of the innyard into an alleyway separated from the stable only by a wooden wall. Though I
could no longer see the two, I could hear very well.

"You'll not forget our agreement," said one. "We're re-
lying on your utmost discretion. It has come highly
recommended."

"I am a servant of the law and take my duties seriously.
I was surprised to see you here. You told me yesterday
that you knew where to find him."

My eyes had not lied to me. One voice was Rowan's,
and the other belonged to Giano, the pale-eyed priest of
Annadis.

Giano laughed. "We expect to have the business done
within the day. You'll be rewarded handsomely."

"My reward will be in seeing a scoundrel brought to
justice."

"One item of information we yet require . . . ." The voices
faded away. The two men must have stepped inside the
stables.

I was furious, more at myself than Rowan. Trusting one
who wore Evard's badge, giving credence, even for a moment, to his words of higher motives, justice, unclean
murder—I should have known better. He'd been working
with the priests all the time. Were these Zhid naught but
sheriffs, wearing a holy disguise as they went about their
despicable work? They must have had a good laugh at my
performance, thought themselves quite clever. Well, I
would provide no more entertainments.

My appetite soured, I sat in the common room brooding

until a grim Rowan burst through the door. "There you are!"

Tempting to spit at the devil's lackey. "Did you think I'd left Grenatte without you, Cousin?" I said.

"The thought occurred to me. I think we should take some air this morning. A walk would be ideal." He took me firmly by the elbow and escorted me into the lane without so much as asking me if I was willing. He propelled me between a wagon load of squawking chickens and a knot of people gawking at a merchant beating his bondsman, and into a narrow alley well away from the door of the Green Lion. "And so, my lady, do you know where they are?"

I wrenched my arm away. "Do sheriffs not breakfast before interrogations? Bartolome can take rightful pride in his fare, and it is always such a pleasure to spend time with you."

Though he didn't touch me, the sheriff backed me into the soot-stained wall, propping one hand against the wall on either side of my head, "I ask you again. Do you know where they are?"

"They?"

"Either of them. The one you came here to find or the one that seems to have the whole countryside in pursuit of him—the weak-minded servant."

"A servant? How could I know anything of servants? And why would I care? I despise weak-minded people . . . and devious ones." I ducked under Rowan's arm and proceeded down the alley at a brisk pace until I emerged in another busy street.

The sheriff was close at my shoulder. "What of the other one, the small, dark, odd-looking man? You remember, the one who's looking for his prized horse, but can tell me nothing but that the horse is white; he's also disappeared. But then you know that already. Bartolome says he was in his common room last night and rushed out shortly before I arrived, only moments before I met you hurrying out the same door. You told me it was the priests that frightened you. Did they frighten him also?"

"This has nothing to do with me."

Rowan was forced to let a well-guarded flock of geese

pass by and then shove his way through its trailing mob of anxious buyers to catch up with me again. "This has everything to do with you," he said, anger snapping like sparks on a frosty night. I had never seen him display such intensity of feeling. "I learned also of the messenger that came here yesterday, asking after the man who sought his stolen horse. The messenger was a freckled boy who limped. I'm no idiot, madam, despite what you think, and I don't forget that Jacopo would be the only person in Dunfarrie I told of the strange little man who didn't fit his impersonation."

I threaded my way through the crowd that was rapidly filling the streets, and stepped around a shapeless beggar who had crawled into the muck-filled ruts and had the lack of consideration to die there. "Coincidence," I said. "If you must know, I'm here to see if the local dyeshops will buy some of my plants. Several of them grow only on Poacher's Ridge." A glimpse over my shoulder twisted a knot in my stomach; the dead beggar was a woman, her thin face an artwork of bruises and sores, sculpted by starvation and the brutal world. She might have been twenty or seventy. Wasted life. Useless death. I wrenched my attention back to my companion. "As you've so often noted, I'm accustomed to living better than I do at the moment."

Rowan did not yield. He stepped in front of me and halted, forcing me to look him in the face. "In no measure would this be coincidence, and in no way do I believe a word of your story. I've learned enough in these ten years gone to know when you tell the truth. You've said yourself these priests are not what they claim. That I do believe. Who is this man they seek? It's someone you know, isn't it?"

He knew . . . curse the man forever, he knew that Aeren was a sorcerer. A fiery heat that had nothing to do with the growing sunlight coursed through my veins. "Why ever would I tell you? And how dare you judge my truth? I think you know very little of truth."

"I will find out, you know—or someone will who's even less to your liking. There have been other inquiries about this 'groom.'"

"I've no need of your concern."

Our voices had risen through the conversation, but Rowan's next words were spoken quietly. Only their edges were hard. "Ah, but others might. Jacopo and Paulo have no noble relations to protect them from the consequences of their actions. If you have any feeling for them—if you are capable of feeling—you should consider your course carefully."

As the threat hung in the air like smoke from summer grassfires, the sheriff took my arm again, and steered me down the road to a stable where his horse stood saddled and waiting. "Time to go home, 'Cousin,'" he said, gesturing me toward his horse. "No more foolish playacting and no more sneaking about Grenatte. You will take yourself and your young accomplice back to Dunfarric, and you will remain there until I return."

"You're not planning to drag me back yourself? What if I, in my fiendish perversity, dare to disobey?"

"No, you go alone. I've business in Grenatte today. You'll swear to me that you'll do as I say, and I'll believe you. But of course if I should find out you've disobeyed me, you'll spend the rest of the week in the gaol."

"You wouldn't dare!"

"You've told me many times that your rank has made no difference in your punishment. I live by your words." Rowan unslipped the reins from the tether rail and stuffed them in my hand. "Take Thunder. He'll carry both you and Paulo. I'd rather not have to dig any more graves in During Forest tomorrow, and mounted travelers are at less risk. Tell Paulo to bring Thunder back to me first thing tomorrow morning and I might not whack him for tormenting his gram."

I wanted to refuse any gift tainted by Rowan's hand, but simple reason curbed my tongue. Amid all the confusion of the sheriff's motives, one thing was certain. Aeren and his friend must be long gone before Rowan's return. If riding the cursed sheriff's horse helped that happen, then, by holy Annadis's sword, I would ride.

We made good time on our return journey. Baglos had his own mount and rode skillfully. I was unable to question him along the route as I had planned, for he raced north along the dusty road as if the doom of the world were indeed riding with him.

When we turned onto the narrow track that led up to the meadow, we had to slow, for the track was all dry gouges and ruts, left from some long-ago year of harsh rains. "Is it much farther, woman?" asked Baglos, his voice reflecting my own anxiety.

"No. Just over that rise."

"Is it a safe place? A large city, a village? This village I have visited before?"

"It's only a cottage. Dunfarrie is an hour's walk."

"Are there trees, then?"

I thought the question curious. "A whole forest of them. Aeren—D'Natheil—sleeps under the trees. And when the light was so strange, he took us into the wood, but we never saw anyone."

Baglos brightened considerably. "So he knows to go to the trees. Perhaps he's not forgotten as much as you think."

The drought-starved meadow was just as I had left it the previous day, an ocean of limp gray-green rippled by the hot breeze, cheered here and there by a clump of stareye or stately stalks of pink and silver lupine. The cottage sat squat and peaceful in the middle of it.

Paulo gave a whoop and let Thunder race the last distance across the meadow. Jacopo came out of the house to meet us and steadied me as I slipped from the saddle. "So Paulo has brought you home riding, eh? He's quite a boy, wouldn't you say?"

Paulo grinned and led the horses off toward the copse and the spring.

"Where's Aeren?" I said.

"He's been poking about the woodpile all morning. A strange one, he is. Never know whether he's going to break your neck or shake your hand." Jaco peered over my shoulder at my companion, who was straightening his tunic and straining his eyes about the meadow. "Looks like you've been successful in your business."

"Yes, this is Baglos, a friend of Aeren's. Baglos, this is my friend Jacopo. . . ."

Aeren strolled around the corner of the cottage carrying a forearm-sized piece of wood. At the sight of us, he increased his pace straightaway. Giving Baglos not so much as a passing glance, he planted himself just in front of me and, with unpleasant grunts and most explicit gestures, expressed his displeasure at my long absence.

Before I could respond, Baglos crowded in between us. He dropped to his knees, grabbed the young man's hand, and kissed it. Aeren growled and jerked his hand away, waving the kneeling Baglos aside. When a confused Baglos failed to move, Aeren snarled and raised the piece of wood over the man's dark head.

"Ce'na duvonet, Giré D'Arnath! Detan eto." As he cried out, Baglos raised his arms to shield himself.

Aeren paused and dropped his hand, flicking his fingers toward his own ears and then toward the smaller man's mouth, as if he'd heard something in the exclamation that interested him.

Baglos showered Aeren with words in a flowing musical language, most of them shaped as questions. Aeren understood the words, which seemed to soothe his dangerous irritation, but I saw no light of recognition in his eyes, and to none of Baglos' questions did he answer other than in the negative.

After a goodly time of this, Aeren pointed to his mouth and then to his head with a most humorously eloquent gesture, telling Baglos that the two appendages were equally useless. Aeren's changing humors were as spring on the northern moors, a continual race between sunlight and storm. Baglos bowed and backed away, gazing sorrowfully on the young man who sat down in the grass and turned his attention to his limb of birchwood, peeling off the bark as if he were expecting to find something underneath, but wasn't quite sure what it might be.

"Ah, woman, I did not believe it possible that D'Natheil could have truly forgotten himself," said Baglos, holding his clasped hands to his chest, the color of his complexion gone sallow. "But your surmise is entirely correct. He recognizes nothing I speak of. We are lost if he cannot remember. And I cannot guide if he has forgotten the words to command me." He tugged at his disheveled tunic, straightened his shoulders resolutely, and bowed to me. "But this is not your burden. I will take him away now, and we will trouble you no more."

"No!" I blurted out the word more forcefully than I intended. "You can't take him away yet. We should eat something before you go. He's been ill. . . ."

"He does not belong in this place. He has duties. In the name of the Dar'Nethi Preceptorate, I thank you for your kindness." The forlorn Baglos cast his eyes down and walked back to Aeren, bowing once again. *"Ce'na, D'Natheil"*— Aeren's head popped up as he spoke—*"ven t'sar—"*

"Baglos, look," I said. "He recognizes his name."

Baglos had already noticed and dropped to his knees beside the young man, chattering rapidly. An exasperated Aeren soon clamped his hand over the smaller man's mouth and toppled him over backwards.

"Give him time," I said, helping Baglos sit up and brush the grass and dirt from his shirt. "Take it more slowly."

But the little man waved off my help. "Foolish woman. There is no time. Everything is prepared . . . waiting . . . This was not part of the plan. The Zhid have done this—I felt their icy breath at the crossing—and I've not the skill to reverse it. Everything depends on me, but with this . . . I don't know what to do." Such profound distress surely had origins somewhere far beyond irritable masters and momentary confusion. *Our last hope,* he had said.

"He understands your language. Perhaps if you were to tell me more of him, then, between the two of us, we could make him remember what he needs to know."

The little man sighed and rubbed his brow with his fist. "If only remembering were enough. Since the ruinous attempt to send him, he has not been capable—" Baglos glanced over at Aeren, dropping his voice though the young man was preoccupied with his wood-shaping. "He never regained even the small skills he had as a boy. You would not understand the importance of these skills, as they are not abilities your people possess."

"Skills?" I approached with caution. "What kind of skills? He seems to be a talented warrior and very intelligent."

"I speak of what a mundane would call magic. Sorcery." Baglos spoke as casually as one might mention a gift for poetry or painting or baking.

I breathed a prayer that my instincts were correct. "He has done magic here."

Baglos sat paralyzed, eyes stretched almost round. "How is that possible? And why didn't you tell me?"

"I wasn't sure if you knew he could. It's not a thing to mention lightly. The law of the Four Realms . . . surely you know that." I told him of the knife and the plants and the fire.

"What knife is this?" He sprang from the ground like a new-vented geyser.

"We found it on the hilltop and believed it had some connection to Acren because of the symbol on it. It's the one he uses even now." Aeren had pulled out the dagger and was diligently scraping his piece of birch.

Baglos's eyes now filled half his face. "You told me that he wore nothing and carried nothing, but this is the Heir's dagger, D'Arnath's dagger . . . our safety . . ." His olive skin paled even further to the color of milky tea. "The sword . . . he carried no sword, did he? Please tell me he did not."

"I've seen no sword. He's been looking for one."

Baglos exhaled deeply and shook his head. "You say he does not recognize the knife, but he was able to penetrate the rock with it. This is astonishing! He was never able to do these things since his injuries when he was twelve. It is one reason we are so afraid. That he will never be capable"—he snapped his teeth together. "Yes, woman, we will stay for a while and learn more of you. The Preceptors are wise beyond the ways of the Dulcé. Perhaps this is not entirely the work of the Zhid, for if D'Natheil has done magic . . ."

I shrugged my shoulders at Jacopo—no hope of understanding everything at once—and sat down near Aeren, patting the turf beside me. "Please sit down, Baglos, and start at the beginning. Who are these Preceptors? Who is D'Natheil?" I motioned the younger man to pay attention.

Baglos began his tale, speaking first in his own language to Aeren, then in Leiran for Jacopo and me. Setting aside his occupation, Aeren listened carefully to the little man's words, the afternoon breeze rippling his light hair.

"There are things of which I am permitted to speak and things of which I am not permitted to speak without D'Natheil's command. And there are many things I do not know at present. Do you know anything of the Breach or D'Arnath's Bridge?" began Baglos.

The young man shook his head, and I did the same.

"Well, I cannot tell you that part, because I don't know it properly today, and truly it is a great mystery that is beyond my understanding, even if it was a time when I could tell you of it. D'Natheil could tell you if he could remember, or I could tell you if D'Natheil would command me, but I don't know how we will teach him of it if we do not know it correctly." Baglos was in despair again, here at the beginning.

Unable to construct anything sensible from this rambling, I tried to get him to start again. "Just tell us about Aeren and how you come to be here. You honor him as a lord, and I've seen enough of his manner to know it must be true. What is his family? Where do you come from? Has he truly grown up in a Vallorean temple school with those priests?"

"Certainly not! He has not lived with the Zhid. Zhid lie as easily as they breathe. They are no priests of any god I know, which is, of course, only Vasrin of the Two Faces: Vasrin Creator, who squeezed nothingness in his mind's fist to create matter, and Vasrin Shaper, who formed matter into the shapes of her dreaming—earth and sea and those of us who walk here. D'Natheil is the Heir of the royal line of D'Arnath, a prince you would call him. The mark on the dagger—it is the shield of his family."

"A prince. I knew it."

"We have had no king since the mighty D'Arnath. His successors see their highest honor in being named his Heir. For a thousand years the Heirs of D'Arnath have held the safety of Avonar in their hands. They have walked the world Bridge through the darkest perils. They have led us in the war against the Lords of Zhev'Na and their warrior Zhid. They have ruled with strength and justice and honor, bearing the hope of our people—both Dar'Nethi and Dulcé—that the Breach would one day be healed and the Wastes restored. But since the Battle of Ghezir, when the Zhid stole D'Arnath's sword and dagger and closed the Gates, our hope has waned, for the Bridge cannot be maintained while the Gates are closed. D'Natheil is the sixty-third Heir of D'Arnath. Since the Gates were closed, thirty-four Heirs lived and waited and died in vain, for we had become too weak to reopen them. We hoped against failing hope that the Exiles might open the way, to aid the Heir in his task as is their duty."

I was at a loss already, grasping at bits that were comprehensible, even if they made no sense. "A thousand years! What family can be traced back a thousand years? Not even the Kerotean priest-kings claim such lineage."

"Yes. His family is very old, but he is the last. All the others of his line are dead. That has been our great dilemma. When the Gates were opened against all expectation, D'Natheil had only just come of age and been anointed. There was a great dispute among the Preceptors that day—the Preceptors are our wisest and most powerful leaders, who advise the Heir in all matters of power and talent—matters of sorcery, as you would say. Some thought to send D'Natheil immediately to walk the Bridge for fear we would lose the chance to repair and strengthen it, but Master Dassine argued that the boy was untrained and, at only twelve years, too young to survive the attempt. The other Preceptors overruled Dassine, and D'Natheil and Baltar were led to the Gate, but when they attempted the passage, D'Natheil was thrown from it with terrible injury, and Baltar, my cousin, lay dead.

"In the chaos that resulted, Master Dassine cried out that those who were not traitors deserved defeat for their stupidity—a charge not fairly given, and he had no call to chastise the other Preceptors. But Dassine picked up the young prince in his arms, took him to his own house, and posted wards that would allow no one near D'Natheil without his leave for all these years. Though many disagreed with Master Dassine's course of action, all could see that the premature attempt had harmed the boy in ways they could not understand. The hope has been that as D'Natheil grew older, he would learn the things needed to accomplish his purpose and develop the talents with which he was born."

"Talents for sorcery?" I said, fighting to untangle the knot he was making of my head.

"He is not a bootmaker, woman. He is the Heir of D'Arnath." Baglos's indignation was worthy of a jilted bride.

I sighed. "Go on."

"So we in Avonar have fought to retake D'Arnath's sword from the Zhid and to defend the Bridge and the

Gates until D'Natheil could reach maturity. But we have
seen no further sign from the Exiles, and the Zhid have
grown more powerful. Eight days ago even Master Dassine
agreed the Bridge was in imminent peril. D'Natheil himself
fought on the walls of Avonar that night—for the first time
since his injury as a boy—and he slew fifty Zhid. We heard
the terrible rumor that he lay near death after it, but clearly
that wasn't true. On the next morning Master Dassine announced that D'Natheil and his Guide must make the crossing before the Gates could be closed again.

"The rites were rushed and confused, for there was fighting in the city streets. Bendal was wounded"—Baglos' nar-
ration faltered briefly—"and Master Exeget performed the
madris so that I might serve the Prince as his Guide. But
at last D'Natheil reached the palace and stepped through
the Gate. The Zhid must have broken into the chamber
just as Master Exeget pushed me after the Prince, for three
of them followed right on my heels."

Baglos took a deep breath, as if only now recovering
from the terror of battle, and when he continued, he spoke
with resolve and conviction. "The Zhid and their masters,
the three Lords of Zhev'Na, will do anything to destroy
the Bridge. Anything. They believe it will give them their
victory, that it will complete the Catastrophe of their making. As the Heir, D'Natheil is sworn to defend the
Bridge . . . to preserve our land . . . and so he must do.
Now do you understand? Our people stand at the verge of
annihilation, and he it is who must save us all."

As Baglos repeated this last for Aeren, my mind was
flooded with questions. And caught up in the words like
flotsam on the tide were words and images that tweaked
my memory, but would not explain themselves: the Breach,
the world Bridge . . . I had tried so hard to erase the past,
to get on with my useless life, forbidding the horror of my
dreams from lingering into day. But one of Baglos's bits
and pieces had washed up on the shore and lay in plain
view where I could not ignore it.

"Your land," I said. "You call it Avonar?"

"Our land was once called Gondai and encompassed
many realms, but now that only our royal city and the Vales
of Eidolon are left outside the Wastes, that name gets little

use. Avonar—the City of Light. I fear that I may never again gaze upon its beauties."

My throat could hardly give voice to my question. My skin felt tremulous, cold and hot and numb all together, as if I'd had too little sleep. "Where is this Avonar, where such things as sorcery are the custom?"

"I cannot tell you where, except that it is in the mountains beyond the Wastes," Baglos said. "At some other time perhaps or if D'Natheil could command me to do so, I could tell you of it."

"There was a city in Valleor called Avonar, but it was destroyed almost twenty years ago." The hair on my arms was standing on end. "Tell me, Baglos, who are these Exiles of whom you speak?"

"The Exiles were dispatched right after the creation of the Bridge, long before the Battle of Ghezir. Twenty Dar'-Nethi were led across the Bridge by D'Arnath's beloved brother. It is part of the story of the Bridge that I cannot remember today. To be sent so far from their home and abandoned with no hope of return seems a cruel punishment, but they are great heroes and not criminals. We never knew their fate, but our hopes that they would be able to open the Gates had long faded. When at last they accomplished it, our hearts were lifted."

How impossible it was that I should be sitting in this meadow and talking with this odd stranger about such things, that of all the places in the Four Realms it should be Poacher's Ridge where D'Natheil would appear out of nowhere. For who else but I, out of so many thousands, would be able to see the connections I saw amidst the incomprehensible strands of Baglos's story? Even the symbol on the knife—at last that connection had resolved. Change the rampant lions to smooth curves, reduce the design to its elemental forms as a thousand years and imperfect memory are wont to do, and one could see the simple rectangle with the arced triangle inscribed, and the three stylized flowerets. The mark of a ruling family . . . just as it had been the mark of Karon's father, the Lord of Avonar. How could this be?

"Do you know, Baglos, what was the name of the one who led your Exiles, the first one those hundreds of years

ago?" I could not have said whether it was day or night,
so intent was I on his answer. I would not have noticed a
whirlwind had it settled in our midst or a storm of fire
raging in the trees. The storm was within me.

"Everyone knows that. He holds honor next to D'Arnath
himself. J'Ettanne was his name."

The universe shifted underneath my feet. This was not
coincidence. It couldn't be. "Your people are called Dar'-
Nethi, then?"

"In our land we are of two peoples, Dar'Nethi and
Dulcé. You can see clearly that my parentage differs from
that of D'Natheil, for I am of the Dulcé. Dar'Nethi and
Dulcé have lived in harmony since the beginning of time,
for our gifts are very different."

D'Natheil sat in the golden light of afternoon with his
chin on his knees, his face expressionless. How much he
understood, or whether any of the strange story had
touched a familiar chord, it was impossible to tell.

My own difficulty was where to begin my questioning.
Bridges seemed clear. Breaches—chasms—made sense.
What were these gates of which Baglos spoke?

The Gates marked the two ends of D'Arnath's Bridge,
so Baglos told me as the sun settled westerly—the Heir's
Gate in Avonar, the Exiles' Gate in this land. Found deep
in a chamber accessible only to the Heir or those to whom
he has given the magical key to unlock its wards, the Gates
appear as a wall of fire through which one must pass to
walk upon the Bridge. Baglos had been prepared for a journey of horror at the crossing, but in truth he must have
fainted, for a great fracturing burst upon him just as he
stepped through the wall of fire. The only remaining entry
to the Heir's Gate was located in the royal palace in Avonar, and that was where he and D'Natheil had begun their
crossing. Baglos had no idea at all where any entries to the
Exiles' Gate could be found. "Not today at least," he said.
D'Natheil should have emerged at the principal entry to
the Exiles' Gate; such had been the expectation. And he,
Baglos, should have been with the Prince, but this "fracturing" had separated them. He had awakened in the middle
of a wheat field with a pounding head and had begun to
search the countryside for D'Natheil. For three days he

walked in circles, but he couldn't find the Prince. Thus he had begun visiting towns and villages, used his silver to buy a horse, and revealed himself to strangers so as to inquire after his missing lord.

I tried to digest the idea of a "fracturing,"—an earthquake, perhaps?—but quickly decided to go on to more urgent matters. "Tell us of these Zhid, Baglos."

Baglos wrinkled his face in disgust. "The Zhid. The Empty Ones. Servants of the three who are called the Lords of Zhev'Na. We are taught that the Zhid, and even the Lords themselves, were once Dar'Nethi or Dulcé like us, their souls lost when the Catastrophe laid waste all the lands beyond Avonar. But I believe they were a terrible mistake of Vasrin Shaper when she put form to the life Vasrin Creator had made. Zhid feed on fear and destruction and despair. And they are powerful warriors, though their Seeking is more to be feared than their swords."

"This 'Seeking' is something of sorcery, then?"

"It is their most terrible sorcery. It withers a man, binding him to the Lords in service, sometimes taking his name and leaving him empty or mad, sometimes making him like to the Zhid in all of their evil. A forest can shelter you from them, as can some dwellings, because a forest is of all places the one where life is thick and rich. And if the dwelling is a home where there have been births and deaths and people living there who care for each other, the Zhid can destroy the house itself, but their Seeking cannot penetrate it."

I asked Baglos much more, but he seemed incapable of answering anything beyond what he had already told us. "On another day," he kept saying. "Ask me again and I could tell you." His knowledge was so spotty, his physical capabilities so unprepossessing, and his emotional state so volatile, that I doubted that he could keep D'Natheil alive, much less do anything in the way of guiding him. He obviously cared for his young lord and his people very deeply, but, aside from his remarkable fluency in my language, he demonstrated no power of intellect or intuition to support his duties, especially when one thought of the dangers D'Natheil faced from the law of Leire, as well as his own enemies.

"What must you do now, Baglos?" I asked. "What were you and D'Natheil to accomplish in Leire, if all had gone as you planned?"

Baglos looked at me like a child who has just heard from his parents that he must teach them to walk, instead of the other way around. "I do not know."

"Surely there was some goal, some deed to perform?"

"I do not know."

"You are called a Guide. To what place were you to lead him or in what activity? You speak of his duty to 'walk the Bridge.' Is that it? What does it mean?"

"I know my own duties, woman, but as for D'Natheil's course and his purpose and what he must do to further them, I cannot say."

"Have you lost your memory, too?"

"I have not!" Baglos was indignant and turned away from me in a pout.

I exploded. "Then why in the name of all that lives were you sent? If you don't know these things today, you're not going to know them tomorrow. How wise can your Preceptors be to put someone who knows so little in this position? It's madness!"

Baglos turned back to me with an expression of long suffering. "No, no, woman. You do not understand the Dulcé. Did I not tell you our gifts were different from the Dar'Nethi? It is not required to know all these things. If the Heir were to command me, then I would know what was necessary, and I could teach him or lead him as he desired."

My head was splitting as I tried to understand. "It doesn't make sense. How could you tell him anything you don't know?"

"Such is the gift of the Dulcé: to make connections when commanded by our madrisson—one with whom we have been linked by the rite of the madris. If D'Natheil commanded me to lead him to some great city, even if I had never seen it, I could discover the best way to take him there. If he commanded me to teach him the lore of the stars as practiced in your land, then I could do so, but I could not tell you of it now. If the information is to be found, then I can acquire it. But he it was who knew his course and his purpose. It was not necessary for me to be told." The Dulcé leaned close and his strange eyes hammered at me. "You must help me, woman. We must find a way to make him remember and to finish his preparation, for if we do not, D'Arnath's Bridge will fall and the Lords of Zhev'Na will feast on the souls of your people as well as ours. We will see no beauty and no joy ever again."

Though I believed he spoke truth, I wondered about the many things the Dulcé would not or could not tell us. His story was impossibly strange. And woven through it all were the magical names. J'Ettanne. Avonar. Just as they were woven through the life I had fought so hard to forget . . .

CHAPTER 12

Year 2 in the reign of King Evard

In the season of Seille of the year that I turned twenty-three, Karon and I were wed. The true ceremony took place in the grand drawing room at Windham, Martin's elegant silk tapestries, crystal, and brass softened by garlands of fragrant evergreen and the light of five hundred candles. Only our four closest friends were there to witness it. I wore dark green velvet and carried roses that Karon had grown for me. Martin placed my hand in Karon's, and it was difficult to tell which of our company radiated the greatest happiness. Julia swore adamantly that it was Tennice. For my part, I believed that good Arot himself, in that first Long Night at the beginning of the world, could have been gifted with no better friends and no more perfect joy.

I notified Tomas of my marriage. In return, I received a

letter from his man of business. My marriage portion was to be the townhouse and *a settlement sufficient to ensure the Lady Seriana's position cannot be seen as a reproach to the family. The Duke of Comigor has no wish to enter into any negotiations with any parties, and since his consent to the marriage was not required, he will assume that the consent of the suitor is not required as to the settlement.*

Though I knew Evard would have claimed the sizeable dowry my father had set aside for me, I didn't argue. Karon and I had more than enough. Tomas had not been stingy, and Karon had a gentleman's income, set up anonymously by his father when Karon had first gone to the University.

Our more public wedding was in Montevial, where my circle of acquaintances had come to know Karon as the new Leiran Commissioner of Antiquities. My former beau, Viscount Mantegna, had told me of the post, vacant for several months since its most recent occupant had died, and I had pestered Karon until he applied for it. My new husband had returned to Montevial with some vague notion of using his income to buy a house in some out-of-the-way place so we could be together, but to leave Montevial made no sense when I held title to my family's townhouse, a much finer home than anything he could afford. Evard's marriage and Tomas's flourishing career had eased the fears that had forced both Karon and me into self-imposed exile, and even Martin agreed that a respectable position and Karon's intention to forego any privilege of rank would preclude any closer inquiry as to Karon's origins. Though we would always need to be careful, we believed we had weathered the storm. And truly, the court posting was perfect for him.

The antiquities collection was a conglomeration of cultural rarities and worthless junk dumped haphazardly into the vaults of the royal treasury after every Leiran military victory. No one knew quite what to do with it all. Only the suspicion that abandoning the hoard would somehow subject Leire to the scorn of foreigners, who seemed to value such things, convinced the administrators to replace the deceased commissioner. Karon did not care about the political purposes of the treasure, but considered the position an unparalleled opportunity for anyone with an interest in history and culture. To care for such treasures as they needed to be cared for, to have unlimited access to study and write about them, to have the charter to seek out whatever might be available to augment the collection—he admitted that no position was more suited to the nature of a J'Ettanni scholar. So much to discover.

We kept up a social life in keeping with my rank and Karon's position, though with far fewer engagements than I had in my year alone. Marriage made me dull, I heard it said. Acquaintances whispered that I had married beneath me, but then it was a fact that I was getting on in age for a first marriage. Indeed, most men would shy away from anyone with my uncomfortable relationship with King Evard, so perhaps I couldn't afford to be too selective. I cared not a whit for what anyone said.

I still had a thousand questions about sorcery and the J'Ettanne, but Karon was unused to speaking of his secrets, and I was reluctant to begin our life together by forcing him out of his habits. When he was ready, he would tell me everything I wanted to know. I had never felt so deliriously happy, so much at peace, as in those first weeks after our wedding.

Karon reveled in his work, and I delved into my studies with renewed fervor, determined to share in the intellectual pursuits he valued. But as the winter deepened, I noticed a disturbing change in him. It began with a growing restlessness that no amount of walking, riding, or other occupation seemed to satisfy. He would sit with me of an evening to write letters or read, but instead of luring me into two hours' conversation with some anecdote from his reading, he would throw down his book or his pen after only a short time and stand staring into the fire. No teasing or question, no puzzle or activity or entertainment of any kind could hold his attention, and though his affection seemed undiminished—far from it, in fact—he expressed less and less of it with words. Even after the act of love itself, he could not speak or sleep, but would excuse himself and go walking alone.

I refused to pry. I had observed a similar behavior in his years at Windham; it had always passed without explanation, and I had promised myself to respect his privacy. But on the evening he broke off our planning for Tanager's thirtieth-birthday celebration, circling the library like a trapped beast and muttering that he couldn't concentrate, I decided I could no longer wait for explanations. . . .

"Karon, what is it? You'll wear holes in the floor with your pacing."

He looked up, his expression that of a deer facing a hunter's bow. Every terrible fantasy a new wife could invent raced through my mind: he didn't love me . . . he felt he had made a mistake . . . I had displeased him in some way.

"Tell me," I said. "Whatever it is."

"Oh gods, Seri. I thought I could be rid of this. With all you give me, I must be a fool." He paced across our library and picked up a book, riffling through its pages. Without looking at a line of it, he tossed it down again. He crouched and threw a log onto the fire, and then cursed himself when it rolled out, scattering ash and sparks across the rug. He reached for a hearth brush to scoop up the mess, but I snatched it from his hand and pushed him to the floor, seating myself on the rug just in front of him.

"I am your wife. Tell me."

He breathed deeply, his face sculpted with such distress, I had to force myself still. "Not two months ago I pledged I would never leave you, and here we've scarcely begun. . . . I swear to you, Seri, my feelings have not changed, nor has my intent, but I'm afraid my vow must bend." He took my hands in his, as he unleashed the flood of words. "Do you remember, in those early years at Windham, how I would leave for a few weeks from time to time?"

"Your research trips. Interviews and observations."

"Well, that wasn't quite the truth. But of course you didn't know about me. If I'd told you I had to go because my blood was on fire, you would have thought me mad."

"Most likely."

He tried to smile. I could not even attempt it. His hands were near scorching my own.

"To describe it so would have been . . . would be . . . no exaggeration. This gift I have is forbidden by every law and custom in the world, yet would be far easier to ignore my eyes or my heart or to forgo speech or breathing than to abandon it. The journeys I made from Windham were to every manner of place. In such times as ours, it's not difficult to find those who need what I have to offer. Though there aren't ten people on this earth who would knowingly accept healing from a sorcerer, many are desperate enough to ask no questions."

He kneaded my fingers, then bundled them up and enfolded them in his own. "What I'm trying to say in this stupidly muddled way is that I cannot stop. I thought I could after I came back last autumn. After a year of wandering, of doing little else but healing, I was spent. I thought that perhaps I had done enough, and from then on, it could be only when I would choose. I swore I'd never do anything to endanger you, even if it meant I never used my talents again. But that's impossible. Neither my body nor my mind will allow me to ignore what I am. If I'm not on this earth to heal, then I cannot understand the purpose of my life. And if I fail to heed this call, then I'm afraid you may wake one morning to find a lunatic in your bed. I have to go, Seri, until I can settle again."

"Will you come back?"

He drew our clasped hands to his burning forehead and breathed the words. "I swear to you that I'll come back as soon as I quiet this demon in me."

I had planned that my life would be different from the lives of other Leiran women. How often my mother had heard my father say, "My duty is to my king. I cannot take my ease in bed with you when there are battles to be fought and won." She, as all warriors' wives, had spent her life waiting for her husband to come home from war. But as a girl, I had nurtured dreams of fighting my own battles, of leading merchant caravans, or exploring the wild lands beyond our borders—a life of more purpose than waiting.

And so, as Karon told me haltingly of the strange fever that grew in him the longer he denied himself use of his power, I began to envision possibilities: travel together, adventure, not bloody combat with swords and severed limbs and looted cities, but secret kindness and magical escapes. I could help him tend his patients, divert suspicions, watch his back while he was occupied with his magic. When he fell silent, looking a little puzzled, I burst out with my ideas. "Well, at least you needn't go alone anymore. . . ."

But Karon dismissed my fantasies as quickly as they'd

grown. "The places I go are not for you: battlefields, border villages, the poorest quarters of any city, disease and danger in every corner. And the way I have to manage it, in secret, always hiding, in disguise, ready to run at any moment. It would be impossible for two. I've no love for putting myself in jeopardy, but I cannot—will not—endanger you. I'll not take you."

I argued with him all the rest of that evening and into the next day, as he gathered a few things to take with him on his journey: some plain and sturdy clothes, a worn brown cloak with deep pockets on the inside, a supply of food, and a flask of wine. But despite my best reasoning, my escalating accusations of his mistrust and his disdain of my abilities, and a serious threat to bar him from my bed when he returned, he would not even tell me where he was going.

"I tell you again," he said, "you are the most capable, most intelligent, most determined person I know—man or woman. I trust you with my life every hour. But this is for *your* safety. If I were to— If anything were to happen— which I promise it will not—you must have no idea where I've gone. You can say that I was a typical blockheaded man and refused to allow a woman to know of my business. Be ignorant and blame me for it. Promise me. . . ." Even with all his peaceful ways, Karon could be stubborn.

Only as he led his horse from our stable and kissed me did I relent. "Then I suppose this is the way it must be," I said. *But only for now,* I thought. I was stubborn, too.

He did come back, after only five days away. Four weeks later, he had to leave again. Sometimes he was gone for a week, rarely more than two. He would return home tired, sometimes grieving, but always at peace. And after a few weeks, the restlessness would begin to grow in him again. I came to recognize its onset before Karon did.

At first, he did not speak of his journeys even after he came home. I quite pointedly refused to ask about them, acting as though he'd not even been away. But after one four-week absence that had left me so frantic with worry that I could not pretend indifference, he broke his silence. Late on the night of his return, after a singularly desperate lovemaking, he held me in the dark of our bedchamber and began to tell me of a poor, isolated village near the Kerotean border that was devastated by a wasting sickness that had left three quarters of its people and all of its children dead. I let him talk until he fell asleep. He never spoke of it again.

But as time went on he did open this most private part of his life to me. He told of towns rife with fever, of Kerotean settlements ravaged by bandits, of streets where children grew malformed because their food had been taken for soldiers or because their childhoods had been sold for labor in mines or quarries. He would work until someone asked questions or until he had done all he could do.

So many of us lived our lives without accomplishing anything of worth. I could only marvel at the stupidities of a world that would call such a gift, so freely given, evil.

Deep on one night in early spring, when Karon was away on one of his journeys, I was awakened by the soft pad of footsteps crossing the wood floor of our bedchamber. Beyond the bed-curtains a faint light moved from the direction of the doorway to the far wall where a washing cabinet stood between the windows. I huddled silently under the bedclothes, cursing my foolish presumption that just because I shared a bed with a sorcerer I could forego the Comigor custom of hanging knife and sword above the bed. A medley of strange sounds came from the room: a bundle laid down, a quickly silenced ring of metal, the clink of glass. Time passed. My terror turned to puzzlement. No one had murdered me. Thieves would have taken what valuables I owned and fled. Pouring liquid . . . ripping cloth . . . a man's muffled curse . . . Karon . . .

I yanked open the bed-curtains and saw him standing shirtless by the washing cabinet, dabbing at his side. "Seri! Gods, I'm sorry. . . ." He tried to hide it from me with a ripped and bloody towel. "I didn't want to wake you."

"And did you think to sneak away again once you'd ruined all my towels?" I said, pulling his hands away to see a long, blood-crusted gash in his side. Ugly and painful, but not too deep at least.

"I just wanted to clean up a bit before you saw. You mustn't worry."

I motioned him to a chair, lit a lamp, and brought towels,

a healing salve, and a linen bandage I kept in a drawer, and then set to cleaning the wound myself. "Not worry? Better ask me not to breathe. The law of Leire is— Stars of night, Karon, you were a prisoner!" I held his hand up to the light, my skin crawling at seeing the rope burns on his wrists.

"This was thieves, not the law. They saw my heavy cloak and my decent horse and thought I might fetch a good ransom. It was quite clear there was nothing extraordinary about my skill in avoiding them," he said, grimacing as I tightened the bandage about his middle. "And since I can't heal myself, they had no cause to suspect me of anything else."

"And how did you get away?"

"Well, they had to sleep, and I was able to conjure myself out of their ropes, leaving them only the most convincing evidence that I'd got hold of a knife and cut myself free." He stroked my hair. "It could happen to any traveler at any time, you know. I was just able to get out of it easier."

I jerked my head away from his hand and dumped the bloody water into the waste jar. "You live in Leire, not Valleor. You must wear a sword from now on," I said. "No Leiran noble would ever walk the street without a weapon, much less travel that way. You might as well ride naked."

"I cannot."

I gaped at him uncomprehending. "Cannot . . ." My father and mother, my brother, everyone I knew, both male and female, and I, too, lived by the sword. I'd known how to wield a blade since I was ten, prepared to use any weapon to defend myself and those I loved. The brocade knife sheath strapped to my thigh was never empty. "Well, then"—I scarcely knew what to say—"you don't have to use it, only look as if you are capable."

"Oh, I'm quite capable. I was trained just as any youth. But I gave up carrying a sword when I realized I could never use it. I'm a Healer, Seri. How could I?"

I could think of several points of debate, but I had already learned that Karon's deepest-held beliefs were immune to reasoned argument. "There lives no more stubborn beast than a man of conviction," Martin had once told me. Karon took me in his arms, and we said no more about it, but I never again rested easy when he was away.

As the months passed, Karon taught me more of sorcery and the life of the J'Ettanne in Avonar. There was no day he could remember, he told me, when he could not do things I would call magic: to light a candle with the brush of his mind, to make a rose bloom from a dormant shrub, to call a bird to sit on his hand. And on every one of those days he knew he could be burned for it. It was as if I had grown up knowing I could be executed because my heart was beating.

In Karon's youth, several hundred of the J'Ettanne had lived in Avonar. They had learned through hard generations how to live a dual life, to suppress their talent until they were in safety or to use it so subtly that no one would ever know. They were merciless with their children, he said, for it was the only way to keep them safe. Whenever a sorcerer was taken, seven of the J'Ettanne, always two of them children, would stand in the command of Montevial or the Imperial Amphitheater in Vanesta and watch while their friend or kinsman burned—so they would never forget.

But the children were also taught the skills and the love of life that were bound up with their heritage. Never did they deny who they were or reject the difficult course laid out for them. Never was there any suggestion that they forsake their Two Tenets and revert to the practices of their foolish ancestors. Many J'Ettanne became quite facile at using their talents. The ordinary citizens of Avonar never suspected that the reputation of their city for having the most exceptionally beautiful gardens and fountains and the most skilled craftsmen in all of Valleor rested in large part on the community of sorcerers that lived among them.

"Of course, our life was happy," Karon told me one evening as we worked in our own tiny garden, tucked away behind the townhouse. "Quite happy. There were always 'aunts and uncles' to care for you and to listen when you were troubled. And we weren't isolated from the rest of the children in the city. We couldn't be or it would be noticed. We just learned how to manage it."

"Could everyone do the same things you do? Heal, I mean. Tame birds. Make light."

"Basic things, yes, like the candles and the birds. But it wasn't until age sixteen or so that your primary talent would manifest itself. A bit terrifying when it happened. You would go to sleep as a modestly capable boy or girl, plagued with the normal confusions of being neither child nor adult, and then awaken the next day as a Gardener or a Builder or a Metalwright or a Healer. There were those who could melt silver without fire and shape it into marvelous creations with only their minds. There were the Speakers—not many, as truth-telling was always a rare gift—and there were the Word Winders and the Singers. My mother was a Singer. When she sang, the image of her words was brought to life right in the room with you, not just in your mind, but a shimmering vision in the air before you, alive with color and motion. When she sang you to sleep, you would dream her songs."

I shoved a stick-like tree into the hole Karon had dug and wished I had some magic to make it grow faster, so that it would shade this corner of my garden before I had white hair. Some days, my own life felt truly useless. "What of you then?" I asked, pounding the dirt about the tree to hold it straight. "When did you discover you were a Healer?"

"I was seventeen. All that summer I had lived with the growing fear that I had no talent beyond the ordinary, that the Way would never be laid down for me. On rare occasion that would happen. No one knew why. One day my brother Christophe and I were out tramping in the mountains. He was just thirteen and very much determined to show he was my equal in climbing. We were hoping to find a new route to the top of Mount Karylis that day, but had begun to think it impossible. Then Christophe found a narrow chimney that looked to reach a ledge we'd been trying for, and before I could discourage him, he was up it. He fell, and . . . well, the details aren't important. He landed on a rock and caved in his chest. There was no one to help—no one within two hours' walk."

Karon's attention drifted into the realm of story and memory that was always as vivid as present daylight for him. "I had watched J'Ettanni Healers perform the blood-rite and prayed for years that whatever my gift, it would not be that one. But on that day my desire was reversed, and I had no choice but to try. Otherwise Christophe was dead and would cross the Verges long before I could get him home. Our people had many theories on how specific talents developed; perhaps my gift might have been different if my need had not been so great. I did what I had to do, holding Christophe close to me so the blood would mingle as it must and taking myself into him so I could put right what had been damaged. More than half a day it took me." He laughed and squeezed my hand, returning from his journey of remembrance. "I was not very skilled and caused both of us more grief than was necessary. That scar is my constant inducement to humility."

When I asked him, he showed me the long, ragged white mark that had been his first.

"Can you remember them all?" I ran my fingers over the tracery of white that criss-crossed his left arm. Hundreds of scars.

"Every one. You cannot forget. The sense of completion . . . of purpose . . . of wholeness . . . is indescribable. There's been nothing in my life to compare to it . . . until I met you."

And then were both talking and gardening interrupted for a while.

Later, as we walked into the house in the moonlight, I asked him what he meant by "crossing the Verges." He wrinkled his brow and said, "Nothing in Leiran cosmology corresponds to the concept. The J'Ettanne call the place where souls reside after death L'Tiere, the 'following life.' We know nothing of its nature, but we believe that between the life that we know and L'Tiere, there exists a boundary which the living cannot cross and from which there is no return. After death there is a time—from a few moments to a few hours—when the soul has not yet crossed this boundary and can be returned to the body. It's why time is so critical to a Healer. With skill and effort and luck and the gift I have been given, I can return one who is dead to life again, but only if the soul has not yet crossed."

I was fascinated by all this, but uncomfortable, too. Death was rarely a topic of discussion in Leiran society. Warriors lived forever in legend and story, of course, and the Holy Twins would inscribe their names on their lists of heroes when we recounted their noble deeds in temple rites. And the families who nurtured such heroes shared in this immortality, as Mana shared in the glory of the First God Arot. Otherwise, Leiran gods had no use for the dead. Living a life of honor was what was important.

"It was not so very different in Avonar," Karon said, when I mentioned my discomfort. "We had a somewhat more optimistic view of whatever is to come, but Healers were never the first ones that came to mind when one was making a guest list. Reminders of mortality are never welcome." He gave an exaggerated sigh. "I suppose now you'll want to banish me to the kitchens when you entertain."

"I'd already planned it so. It was your conversation that attracted me, you know, and I'm hesitant to put your social graces on display lest another woman be singed by the same flame!"

As Karon flourished in his more ordinary profession, I spent more and more time with him at the antiquities collection. Here we had no arguments, but reveled in the unending variety of human creativity. Among the bins and boxes we found man-high statues of Kerotean marble and tiny fetishes of wood and ivory from cultures so primitive that nothing at all was known of them. There were Vallorean tapestries, illuminated manuscripts, helmets and armor and swords of a thousand varieties, maps and glassware, jewelry and silverwork, rugs woven of the hair from exotic beasts. Most of these articles had been stuffed into musty vaults in the royal treasuries with no regard for their fragile nature. Armor was thrown on top of crumbling manuscripts, paintings laid face down, ivory and jade statuary left where dampness had made stagnant pools.

Shortly after assuming his post, Karon had several large, well-aired workrooms set aside for his use. He had his small staff of assistants bring each item to the workrooms, so it could be judged, and then it would either be disposed of or sent to be cleaned, repaired, and packed away more carefully.

Our delight was to find an article that was unmarked and unknown and to unravel the mysteries of its origin. We would seek some idea of its history from the pieces stored alongside it. Then we would attempt to trace the materials, the paint, the stone, the paper, the ink, the yarn. Karon would search the royal libraries for references to anything similar or write letters to scholars or collectors who might have information. If we were still lacking information, I might take the piece to the market, and inquire of visiting merchants or travelers if they had ever seen such a thing.

Evard's lord high chamberlain heard of the new commissioner's work and sent his secretary to ask if there might be articles suitable for display in the palace. Evidently Evard had decided that some ornamentation might better suit his role as the supreme monarch of the civilized world. Perhaps his decision was connected with the rumors that the young queen considered Leirans, including her husband, to be barbarians. And so, when we found a particularly fine piece, I would write a card describing it, pack the card with the vase or statue or tapestry, and send them to the chamberlain with the commissioner's compliments and a recommendation as to the object's placement and method of display.

The only activity I avoided was accompanying Karon down into the vaults. I blamed my deep-rooted horror of dark, confined spaces on Tomas. Once when I was but five or six years old, I was playing hide and seek with Tomas and two of his friends through the dank cellars and musty storerooms of Comigor. Tomas decided it would be a great joke to abandon the game without telling me. He and his friends took themselves off riding, not knowing that the ancient cupboard I had discovered deep in the darkest cellar had a faulty latch and that I could not free myself. When I failed to come to supper in the nursery, the governess assumed I was out riding, too. Only when the boys returned at nightfall did the alarm go out.

It was two days until they found me, pale and terrified and perfectly quiet, huddled in the pitch-blackness of the cramped old cabinet. I had been afraid to cry out when I heard the searchers, for our old nurse had always told us that there were demons in the dark who would devour crying children to feed their sorceries. I had decided it would be better to starve than to risk such an awful fate. Years passed before I could sleep without a lamp left burning, and the fear of confinement had never left me.

The first time Karon took me into the vaults, eager to share the wonders of his treasury, I convinced myself that my childish megrims would surely be banished now I was a married woman. But as luck would have it, halfway down the ancient stairway our lamp ran out of oil, and it took no extraordinary talent for Karon to discover my terror. I almost tore the sleeve off his coat. In an instant, without regard for the risk, he conjured a light for me—a soft white glow emanating from his hand that faded only when he led me into the daylight and wrapped his arms about me to calm my shaking.

"Ah, love, you need never fear the demons again," he said, after I'd told him the tale. "Is it not true that you have married one of them, who, now he is in your power, can well hold his fellows at bay?" It became a joke between us about the demons, and indeed I discovered that as long as Karon was with me, I could survive a venture to the vaults. Only rarely did I go, however, and I always checked the lamp oil carefully.

It was while delving into the crates of booty hauled from Valleor after its conquest that Karon came across a legacy from his ancestors. One summer afternoon, I came to Karon's workroom as I did several times a week to help sort and number the artifacts. I had suggested a cataloging scheme, so we could have a record not only of what was stored in the vaults, but also where each item was located and what other items might be related to it.

On this particular day I was recording a description of a crate of mouse-chewed books, a set of erotic stories written and illustrated by a Kerotean noble for his bride. I was hoping the woman had possessed a strong stomach and an exotic sense of humor. Karon appeared in the workroom doorway, and I waved a greeting, but he didn't seem to notice me. He was dusty and disheveled, not an unusual state when he'd been working in the vaults, but the expression on his face was his "storytelling" look, as if, despite his body being in the room, he traveled in some faraway

place. Where ordinarily he would see fourteen things needing his attention, he seemed at a loss.

I left my list with a workman and threaded my way
through the workroom clutter. "Karon, what is it? Have
bodies come popping out of your rusty armor?"

His eyes caught mine for a moment. "Yes . . . well . . .
in a way."

A young man, whose nose, mouth, and chin came to such
a sharp prominence as to be vaguely reminiscent of a rat,
called out from across the room. "Lord Commissioner,
should I discard this helm? It's quite ordinary—Leiran, and
not even a very nice one. I think it must have belonged to
the fellow who collected this lot." Racine had been the
secretary for the previous Commissioner of Antiquities, but
had been required to do little more than carry notes to
the man's mistress. Karon was pleased with Racine's keen
interest in the new procedures and how quickly the eager
assistant's eye had become discriminating.

"Whatever you think, Racine." Brought out of his distraction a bit by the exchange, Karon spoke quietly to me.
"Can you come? I'd like to show you. I don't know what
to do with it."

"Of course."

Karon told Racine to carry on and led me to the steep,
winding stair. "We have to go down. Will you be all right?"

"I'll manage," I said, touching his hand and remembering
his magical light. "My demon is with me."

He took me deep into the far corner of the vault to a
pile of rolled carpets. Setting the lamp on a nearby crate,
he dragged a cracked leather trunk from underneath the
pile. The trunk was full of old clothes. From deep beneath
the jumble of faded silks and satins he pulled out a flat,
wooden box. The wood was polished dark and smooth by
years of handling, the plain brass hinges and latch tarnished. Karon raised the lid and reverently removed the
contents, one by one.

First, a silver knife, the finger-length blade and curved,
ornately worked handle black with tarnish. Next a threadbare strip of cloth, a scarf or sash perhaps, more like a
spiderweb that threatened to dissolve at a touch. Then a
round, button-like piece, also made of silver, blackened by

time. Karon laid each thing in my lap, and I could not mistake the wonder in his eyes.

"They're not very old by the standards of many things in the collection," he said, "but they're quite rare."

"What are they?"

"Tools. The tools of a J'Ettanni Healer. One can use things that were originally designed for other purposes, as I do when I work, but there was a time . . . well, the custom was to have your own tools always ready: a knife of silver, cast with your own proper enchantments to keep it keen-edged—there is no way to make that part of it easy or pleasant, but a sharp knife is always better than dull—and a strip of white linen for the binding—it's dangerous to lose contact in the middle of the rite, as I've told you. You can get dizzy. And in this"—he showed me how the button was actually a tiny cup with a hinged lid—"you would keep indiat, a paste made from herbs, quite rare and expensive, but it would ease the pain of the incision for the one you were to heal. The rite can be very hard, especially for children."

As always, I had a hundred questions but I wasn't sure he would even hear me.

"It's incredible enough to find these things, but they're not all." From the wooden box he pulled a small book, hardly bigger than his hand. Its leather cover was half rotted away, the stitching gone, leaving it little but a stack of pages of precarious thinness. Faded ink filled the pages, words of a language I didn't recognize written in a bold hand.

"The Healer's journal," said Karon. "See the symbol of the knife on the front. And here"—with utmost care, he opened to the front of the little book—"a list of names and places, and what I think must be a description of the circumstances for each healing he did. It's written in the old language of the J'Ettanne, which went out of use long before bound books. I know so little of the language, it's hard to read it. But look at this entry." His face was that of a child on Long Night. "*Garlao, the miller. Mycenar*— that must be the village—*hand caught in*—something. *J'dente* means healed. It's so important for a Healer to remember. There are times when it's not right to change the outcome, times when death is not an enemy to be thwarted, times when sickness must be left to burn itself out, and so you must constantly look back at the judgments you've made to see if your course is straight. This man did it this way." Karon's whole posture begged me to understand what it meant to him to find these things. He believed he was the last living soul of his own kind.

"It's a connection both to all those who came before you and to one particular man who was a Healer like yourself."

"And even more than that. You see, he's marked the book into days. Some are skipped; some are just noted by a symbol." He turned the delicate pages carefully. "This one he's marked Av'Kenat. I think the text must be a description of it . . . by one who was there."

Av'Kenat was the "Walking Night," the late autumn celebration when the ancient J'Ettanne would come together to celebrate the passing of summer, the harvest, and their belief that life was a formless essence, given shape by the crossing of our paths as each of us walked the Way laid down for us. It was a time for storytelling and family reunions, for betrothals and weddings, reunions and feasting, and magical games and displays of all kinds.

Karon's face glowed in the lamplight. "All I've ever heard is legends, passed down so many times one never knew if they were true. Our people never dared join together on Av'Kenat. Only in the heart of the family could we have any celebration, and that contradicted the whole meaning of the feast. If I were to work at it, I could read of the real thing from one who witnessed it."

"You could learn things that even your own family didn't know."

He nodded, but the glow was already fading, and his brow quickly settled into a frown. "But I'm required to destroy the journal and the other things. The law explicitly forbids these words, this language, any mention of these events and activities."

"If you were not married, would you consider destroying them?"

He glanced up quickly. "Of course I would. The risk . . ." The flush of his cheeks spoke truer.

"How dare you use me as an excuse for cowardice! I

don't recall making any vow of safety when I married you. Nor do I recall requiring you to make any pledge to relinquish your life, your history, or any of those things that make you who you are. Besides"—I grabbed his chin and shook his frown away—"these are treasures that belong to the royal collection, and it would ill become the Commissioner of Antiquities to destroy anything in his charge."

"Ah, Seri." His pleasure illuminated the dim vault. "It would take me quite a while to decipher it all. What I've thought is that I could first transcribe it. Then I could return the book here and work at the translation as I had time."

"Not at all efficient, Lord Commissioner. If I were to transcribe it for you, then you could begin work on the translation before the transcription is complete—tonight, if you wish."

For the rest of the summer, I seldom came to the storehouse of antiquities. Not only did I transcribe the fragile pages onto decent paper, but I also made separate notes of word usage and combinations that appeared frequently. Karon taught me the words as we worked, and I developed the rudiments of a dictionary comprised of both words and symbols. Never had any work satisfied me so.

The Healer often wrote in symbols, many of them representing J'Ettanni talents and offices. Karon told me that in the Healer's day it was the custom to have the device painted on the lintel of your house: the knife for the Healer, the lyre for a Singer, the bridle for the Horsemaster, and so on. "If my father had lived in those days, he would have had his own Word Winder's spiral, as well as this one." He was sitting at our library table, and in the margin of his page of translation, he sketched a rectangular shield with two curved lines set into it, and a stylized floweret in each of the three regions scribed by the lines. "This is the symbol of a ruler. Christophe inherited both the talent and the office from our father—"

I was standing behind him and leaned over his shoulder to look closer. "But you were older. Why was your brother to inherit?"

"Our elders had ways to discern who was gifted in that

way. Perhaps they could see I had no stomach for ruling. Christophe was to be officially named my father's heir on his twentieth birthday in the autumn Avonar was destroyed. I planned to go home for it. If the Leirans had attacked two months later, I would have been in Avonar with the rest of them.

I tugged at his chin, forcing him to look at me. "But you were not—for which I bless the hand of fate every hour. Does it bother you? Make you feel guilty that you weren't there with them?"

He smiled. "No. That would not be very J'Ettanni, would it? Such was the Way that unfolded for us; we had escaped the ravages of the Leiran war for a long time as it was. But I miss them all and wish very much that they could meet you. All except Christophe."

"And why not him?"

"Ah. He was very much closer to your age than I, and altogether more handsome and charming."

"Impossible."

"Every young woman in Avonar was in love with him."

"And did they not recognize the charms of his older brother?" I took the pen from his hand and threw it on the desk, crammed the stopper in the ink bottle, and pulled him from the chair.

"Let's say I was fortunate to meet you before you knew of my true profession. Few Healers ever married. Though you, I think, would have defied the common wisdom. . . ."

The hunger was growing in him again. His easy laugh told me that he didn't sense it yet, but his skin was hot, and when I wrapped my arms about his neck, I felt the quickening of his heart. I closed my eyes and drew his arms around me like a shield.

CHAPTER 13

Year 3 in the reign of King Evard

By my twenty-fourth birthday the king and queen of Leire had produced a daughter, the Princess Roxanne, and my transcription of the Healer's journal was complete. I had copied every word, drawn every symbol and diagram just as the author had penned them. Karon had replaced the journal in the wooden box and buried the trunk under piles of carpets, marked with a number that appeared on none of Racine's lists. The translation was progressing well. Karon was able to puzzle out enough of the words to make some sense, and I would carefully record each newly deciphered word in my dictionary. We had come to think of the ancient Healer, whom we called the Writer, as an acquaintance just as real as Martin or Tennice.

The Writer had lived approximately four hundred fifty years ago, during the time just before the Rebellion when the J'Ettanne ruled Leire—the *unholy usurpation,* Leiran historians called it. He had traveled the roads of Leire and Valleor, taking his skills from village to village, spending his power until he had no more to give. Even in those days the gift of healing was rare, and the need for his help far outstripped his capacity.

Karon told me that a healing such as he had done for Martin, using the blood-rite to bring someone from the very brink of death or beyond it, was all the sorcery he could work for a matter of several hours. Lesser healings were easier, not needing the heavy investment of lifegiving, but the effects on the Healer were cumulative. Many Healers would not even attempt small hurts or illnesses, husbanding their resources for more serious needs, afraid the process of replenishing their power would be too slow.

The Writer had not been one of these. He would take all comers until he could do no more. There had come a night when one of his own children had wakened with a virulent fever. The Writer had spent all of his power that day and had nothing left with which to heal her, and so his small daughter had died. He wrote of his profound grief, but did not change his ways.

I was appalled. "Bludgeon-headed man, why didn't he learn from his mistake? He should have saved something back for his own children. What a cold fish he must have been."

"Not at all," said Karon. "Read how he wrote of the child. He cared very much. But he didn't see it as a reason to change. When you give a gift, you cannot retain part of it. It is either yours or the other's. No in-between. Sorcery and healing are not some oddity or aberration that alter the paths of life. They are a part of it. I was able to heal Christophe because it wasn't time for him to die, and Martin the same. If I'd spent what I did on Martin, and then Tennice had needed me, it would not be my part to say, 'If only I had not . . .' That's a sure route to madness."

"But you said you must constantly look back at your judgments."

"And so you must. But in each case on its merits alone, not on what the circumstances of life have made of it. Such is the Way."

I couldn't see it. "It makes no sense. If you see your way blocked by the enemy, you don't keep marching down the same road. You withdraw and change your tactics. It was his own child. He was responsible."

As with so many of our arguments, a kiss ended, but did not settle it.

When winter came and another Seille, we celebrated the first year of our marriage. Karon gave me a delicate gold locket, engraved with a rose. Inside it I put a crumbled bit of the enchanted roses he had grown for me. I gave him a chestnut stallion. He named the horse Karylis, which in the language of Valleor means *sunlight*. Karylis was the name of the mountain where he had healed his brother and come into his calling.

On one quiet night in midwinter, I sat nestled in an oversized chair by our library fire, plodding through a story written in Vallorean, trying to bolster the smattering of language skills I had neglected so sorely in my girlhood. I was finding myself easily distracted, in the latest instance observing how the pool of lamplight lit Karon's high cheekbones so delectably as he sat at the library table poring over the journal transcription. So I was not too startled when he sat back and burst out, "Mother of earth! Seri, come see what I've found." His high color made the lamplight pale. I hadn't seen him so excited since the finding of the journal.

I abandoned my chair and lap robe to lean over his shoulder and see what page had revealed such a dramatic secret. It was a diagram labeled with odd symbols. "I never expected we'd make any sense of this one," I said. "Have you deciphered it?"

"I've not interpreted the diagram or the symbols, but I know their purpose." He turned back a few pages and traced his finger over my writing. "The Writer has been getting more and more worried about the terrible things being done by the Open Hand. He says that on Av'Kenat, one of the rebellious cities was beset by a 'legion' or 'army,' or something like that, of *nethele. Nethele* means 'the dead.' Evidently this ruler, Zedar, whom he has mentioned before, sent the spirits of the dead to frighten his subjects into submission, filling their minds with 'the most pernicious mortal dread.' The Writer is horrified at the perversion of Av'Kenat, and it looks as if it inspired him to action. What do you think he's done?"

I squeezed his shoulder and jiggled it. "Don't make me guess."

"He's gone to the elders of the Closed Hand and asked for refuge in Vittoir Eirit, the J'Ettanni stronghold. And he's written down the route they told him."

"He wrote it down? I thought it was the most closely guarded secret." More and more I was losing any wonder at how powerful sorcerers had given up a kingdom so easily.

"It was. But the Writer never trusted himself to remem-

ber everything he needed to keep straight, so he encoded
the instructions. It's the reason for the symbols. Seri, if I
can unravel his code, I might be able to find the stronghold.
Can you imagine it?"

"Surely there would be nothing left."

"Hard to say. The stories we told in Avonar came from
people sent away from Vittoir Eirit when the elders decided
to abandon it. My ancestors never knew what became of
the stronghold, and they were forbidden to seek out any
other of the J'Ettanne, so they had no way to find out.
They assumed it had been discovered and destroyed. But
even if it's ruined, think how fine it would be to discover
its location. To walk in Vittoir Eirit . . ."

Karon had taken on his dreaming look again, and I
tugged at his hair. "Give it up. You'll not unravel a four-
hundred-fifty-year-old puzzle without the key to his code."

"True. But we've already learned that the Writer is not
a complex man. The key will be here in his journal."

"And birds will fly upside down and Evard will develop
a heart." I flopped back in my chair and picked up my
book, but my eyes did not leave Karon's glowing face.

The search for the key to the Writer's code occupied the
entire spring, but by the beginning of our second summer
married, we were no closer to the answer. The diagram
consisted of five symbols, connected by straight lines. We
assumed the lines were roads or trails and the symbols
landmarks of some kind. We pulled out maps of Valleor to
see what roads might fit the pattern, but too many years
had passed, and even in our present day, maps were notori-
ously inaccurate. And, too, we had no idea if the distances
between the symbols on the page were at all in proportion
to the actual distances involved. The five symbols were no
more enlightening. One was almost certainly a foot, one
looked something like a trunk or chest, another resembled
a hunting horn. The other two looked like a man's face
and a rabbit. We investigated the names of towns and villages, rivers and landforms, and tried a hundred other
ideas, seeking some correspondence, but to no avail.

Karon proceeded with the translation, learning more of
the Writer's travels and his life with his wife and six re-

maining children. The man wrote of his garden and his animals, of the difficulties of teaching his children to read and finding mentors for their emerging talents. He wrote loving and lengthy descriptions of their games and childish follies. We laughed when we read of his five-year-old daughter's attempts to install the family pig in the house in the dead of winter. She was afraid the beast would be cold and succeeded in inducing it to follow her about like a tame dog. It took all of the family together to overcome the little girl's enchantment and persuade the agitated pig to retreat to the cold barnyard.

As Karon read this passage, he sat beneath a tree in our garden, and I lay on the grass with my head in his lap. "When do you know . . . with a child?" I asked.

"If they have magical talent, you mean? When one of the parents is not J'Ettanne?" I felt him move under my cheek. I loved the way Karon's body came to life when he spoke.

I nodded.

"Five or six years." Karon touched my cheek, and looked down with a smile that made my heart swell. "It won't matter you know, if and when such a marvel occurs. The child is the miracle. And the love that creates it. Nothing else."

"Were there marriages like ours in Avonar?"

"Yes. We were so few. We could not marry just within our own kind."

"And the children . . . it really didn't matter? Not even to them?"

His eyes drifted out of focus. "There was an old J'Ettanni Healer named Celine. She became my mentor after my day in the mountains with Christophe. She was married to a candlemaker who was not J'Ettanne, and one day I asked her if her children had talent or not. She said that one of her sons had looked to be a tamer of horses since he could walk, and he had grown into the most renowned horsetamer in Avonar.

" 'Eduardo, the Horsemaster?' I asked her. Eduardo's power was renowned among us. 'Aye,' she said. 'But my other son showed no magical talents at all.'

"And in the fullness of my newfound J'Ettanni manhood, I asked her, quite solicitously, was it not terribly difficult to see one son so talented and one so . . . ordinary. Celine nodded gravely and said it was one of the trials of parents to see children unequally blessed. Her other son had worried about it a great deal when he was a youth and didn't want to listen to those who told him that his own talents were of no less value than J'Ettanni sorcery. But while Eduardo was in the fields with the horses, Morin read and studied, talked with the elders, and made what he could of himself.

" 'Morin?' I said. And she smiled slyly and said, yes, Morin was the name of her unmagical son. Well, Morin was possibly the wisest man I have ever known. He was my father's chief counselor and the most respected man in Avonar. Of all that was lost to the world in the destruction of Avonar, the loss of his mind was perhaps the most grievous. Even now, I always begin to sort out a problem by thinking how Morin would approach it. So, you see, I learned my lesson early what gifts were important. It really doesn't matter."

For Karon's birthday I gave him a walking stick made of cherry wood. "It's quite the fashion at court, in case you haven't noticed," I said that evening in our library. "And I had it made especially for you." Despite his avowals of delight and appreciation, I did not imagine that he was anything but puzzled at my choice. We were not at all bound by court fashion. Karon would sprout wings before he gave up the high-necked shirts and muted colors of provincial Valleor.

He brushed the richly colored wood and twirled the stick about his head. "Am I to use it to fend off your frustrated suitors, then?"

"Not my suitors"—I snatched the stick from the air, rotated the ebony ring set into the shaft, and held the implement where he could see the sharp steel blade that now protruded from its lower end—"only those who mean you harm." I had failed miserably in trying to persuade him to carry a sword when he traveled and thought perhaps a weapon that did not invite confrontation might be more acceptable.

"Ah, Seri . . ." It took no mind-speaking to tell me right away that I had failed again. He was still smiling, but his delight had gone.

"I'll have it taken out," I said, retracting the blade, unable to look at him any longer. I could not bear the thought that I had disappointed him. "I should have known better."

The distance across the room between us suddenly yawned very wide. "I can't be what you want," he said. "In every other matter, I will follow your lead, become whatever you wish, but this one—"

"You are everything I want," I said as I fitted the stick back in its wooden case. "I just thought . . . I just want you to have something more reliable than sorcery to defend yourself. Stars of night, Karon, what if you've used up everything . . . all your power . . . and you're taken?" I could scarcely say the words, and even as I said them, I shoved them out of mind. "No matter. You are as you are, and I adore you, and Martin and the others are waiting for us with your birthday feast."

I started for the door, but he did not follow. His stillness forced me to turn around. He was standing where I'd left him beside the hearth. His eyes were locked on me, and he wore a look of such distress that I hurried back to him and tried to wipe it away with my hand. But he gathered my hands into his and gripped them hard. "Seri, I've wronged you sorely. All these years I've known I would have to explain this. The Way of the J'Ettanne—this path that I choose for my life—is very hard. Coward that I am, I've told myself that my choices will not harm you if I'm careful enough. If I'm strong enough. If I love you enough. I've ignored the truths of our future and soothed my guilt by saying that I cannot rob you of the power to choose your own way. If your choices endanger you, then that is the Way laid down for you." He sat down on the couch and pulled me down beside him. "But I've been fooling myself and you. I'm so afraid. . . ."

Afraid? The fingers that stroked my own so softly were cold. I felt as if someone had crammed the walking stick down my throat. "Tell me."

He took a deep breath. "When the day comes that I am discovered, I'll not fight."

"I don't understand."

"I mean, I cannot use my power or any other weapon to take life or inflict an injury. Not to save myself. Not to save you. Not for anyone. The gift I have is for healing, for lifegiving, and I cannot use it otherwise. It's ingrained in me so deeply, it wouldn't be possible. You have to know that."

I came near blurting out that this assertion was ludicrous, an impossibility for a man of honor. And Karon's honor was unquestionable; he constantly risked his safety to care for people whose names he didn't even know. I could understand his reluctance to inflict bodily injury, having lived so intimately with the pain and suffering such violence caused. Yet it was inconceivable that a man would not use whatever weapon he possessed to defend his family and friends, and in Karon's case, defending us meant defending himself.

But Martin had taught me how difficult it was to argue with an idealist. "A small dose of hard reality will always make idealists into practical men," he had once said. And so, rather than disputing Karon's professed beliefs, I argued with his more speculative point. "Then we'll just have to make sure you're not discovered. Martin is wait—"

I tried to rise, but Karon would allow me neither to leave nor to divert him. "It's more likely than not, and the result will be terrible. I've seen what they do to sorcerers, Seri, and what they do to those who consort with them. The image never leaves me. And I'm telling you that I can't protect you from it."

"I am perfectly aware of the risks. I just don't want to think about them."

"But you must. If you have me in your life, then I'm afraid you'll have that in your life, too."

"I won't let it happen."

"If anything gives me hope that it won't, it's your determination. But you're the daughter of a Leiran warrior, and you've been taught that failure to fight is despicable cowardice. I'm a J'Ettanni Healer, who's been taught that the crooked paths of life are the most marvelous. You were so young on that night when Martin and the others chose to have me stay. . . . I'll not sneak away and pretend I don't love you, but I can't ignore this anymore. I'm asking a great deal of you."

And, of course, because I loved him and it was his birthday, I said I would accept whatever came and whatever he could or could not do about it. But somehow I would persuade him to carry a weapon.

In early summer Karon and I rode out to a jonglers' fair that had grown up in the hills just outside the walls of Montevial. Jonglers were wandering entertainers who usually traveled in small family groups, but who would stop for a few weeks in summer here or there, gathering in ever-greater numbers to exchange stories, wives, and horses, and generally to enjoy each other. Though jonglers were widely regarded as thieves and liars, people would travel from nearby cities and villages to enjoy the risky marvels of their fairs. The colorfully dressed women told fortunes by casting painted sticks, and wiry, shirtless men in pantaloons swallowed fire. They told tales, sang songs, fought mock battles in wildly colored costumes, and painted portraits on bits of wood and glass. Their ragged, scrawny children were the envy of every child in Leire who dreamed of living in eternal entertainment without the restraints of propriety or lessons or labor.

"Are you sure you're not ready to head home?" asked Karon, giving me his hand as I jumped over a running ditch, left full by an afternoon cloudburst. "This isn't the safest place to be after nightfall."

"We couldn't go before she finished the sketch," I said, the dim light forcing me to squint at the few coal-drawn lines on the split shingle that evoked an astonishing likeness of Karon's face. "And there's still the fire dancers. A jongler fair is so much more exciting after dark. Tomas and I were once confined to our rooms for a month after we sneaked out to a fair that had grown up near Comigor one summer, and we never regretted the punishment. They actually plunge the torches right down their gullets, while everyone around them is whirling and stomping." Some delights one just never outgrew.

"Then we'd best circle around this muck, rather than crossing straight through it and having you in wet shoes the rest of the night." Karon led me along the dark peripheries of a field trampled into ankle-deep mud by a jousting demonstration. The flaring torches of the main venues were far across the field from the shanty where an acquaintance had told me I could get a portrait of Karon so like I would swear there were two of him. Forced by the mud to take a circuitous route, we threaded our way through a ragtag village of tents and lean-tos, currently dark and deserted except for a few bony dogs. Periodically a great cheer went up from the distant fire-glow of the central fair, so I almost didn't hear the child.

"Agren. Agren. Wake up, Agren. Come on." The quiet pleas were interspersed with sniffs and sobs. "Don't be dead. Please don't."

We slowed our steps and peered into a shed of canvas hung from wood beams that had been roped together in a box-like shape. A ragged little girl of some six or seven years knelt beside a dark form sprawled on the ground. She was shaking his shoulder, but he was not responding to her pleas, likely something to do with the knife hilt protruding from his back.

Karon tried to drag me away, but I wouldn't budge. "Wait," I said. "Aren't you needed here?"

"Not while you're with me," he said, glancing grim-faced at the child as he urged me toward the distant light. His hand was hot on my bare arm. The fever pained him when it grew too fierce, and the child's quiet desperation would make it worse.

"Karon . . . do what you must. I'll keep watch."

Another cheer went up from the distant revelers. He shook his head. "We're too close to the city. Too many people about."

"Who's there?" The girl's voice quavered as she twisted around to look out of the flapping doorway. "Is it you Deft? Don't frig me, Deft. Agren don't like it."

"What happened here?" I said, loosening Karon's fingers, ducking my head under the low beam, and stepping into the shelter. "Are you all right?"

The man lay on his belly. His beard was matted and dark, his long dagger still sheathed. Though I felt no breath when I placed my cheek by his mouth, his skin was still warm. "Who are you?" asked the child, glaring at me ferociously as she huddled beside the body.

"Fairgoers. My husband is a . . . physician. Perhaps he can help."

"Somebody shivved him." Her chin quivered. "I think he's dead."

"Perhaps he's not dead. I thought I felt a breath." I gathered the child to me and drew her away, nodding to Karon, who stood outlined against the doorway. "Come, let's give my husband some room to work."

The girl—Nettie was her name—sat on a barrel outside the shed and told me of Agren—maybe her father, maybe not, she wasn't sure—and how he'd gone off to meet a man about a gambling debt. When he didn't return to the fair, she'd come hunting him. Through the dangling canvas, I glimpsed Karon kneel beside the man and, after a brief examination, yank the dagger from his back. Though he was but a shadow against the gray night, I recognized the next movements: unbuttoning his sleeve, scoring the dead man's arm, the moment's stillness as he cut himself and then wrapped the man's own long scarf about their joined arms.

I stroked the child's braids, sticky with the oil her people used to make their hair shine in the torchlight, and let her chatter on about the jonglers she liked and those she feared. Karon's back was still. A warm breeze flapped the canvas walls.

"Nettie!" A rasping whisper came from the darkness. "Here, girl . . ."

"Agren?" Eyes the size of saucers, the child jumped down from the barrel. I grabbed for her arm to prevent her seeing what Karon was about or touching him or her friend, but she squirmed free, scuttered into the tent, and dropped to her knees on the dirt across the body from Karon. Right on her heels, I bent down to lift her, only to have my hand fall slack in horrified astonishment.

"Vengeance, Nettie. It's Deft done this. We'll poison the sodding bastard. . . ." The hoarse voice, the vicious and brutal words came from Karon's mouth. Anger and hatred twisted his face until it was almost unrecognizable. "We'll take him ere morning. I'll cut out his heart. . . ." As vile, murderous epithets poured from him, Karon's expression convulsed and his shaking hand gripped the knife he had pulled from the jongler's back.

"Karon!" I dared not touch him. He'd told me of the

explosive enchantment, the dangerous unbalancing that could damage both Healer and patient when the link was disturbed. So I squeezed the squirming child to my breast, hiding her eyes while I did nothing but speak his name.

The quivering knife moved laboriously upward, drawing my eyes and breath with it. I was ready to shove the child aside and leap, but the blade fell so quickly, I could do nothing but cry out. "Holy gods!" Three . . . four . . . five more times the knife slammed into the corpse.

When all was quiet again, Karon was bent almost double, his right hand still holding the knife embedded in the jongler's back. *"Maratathe . . . maratachi . . . maratakai,"* he whispered in his own voice, repeating the words over and over. When he had gained control of his trembling, he said, "Unbind us."

One arm still wrapped about the squirming child, I drew my knife and sliced through the dirty scarf holding Karon's left arm to that of the jongler. After a moment, Karon got to his feet, took my arm, and pulled me up to his side. Nettie remained on the ground beside the dead man.

"I'm sorry," Karon said softly to the gaping child, as he drew me away from them. "I couldn't help him."

We walked straight to the carriage row and drove home, Karon neither speaking nor looking at me the entire time. Though my curiosity was near bursting, I waited for him to begin. Only after he had bathed and dressed the unclosed laceration on his left arm did he come sit beside me on the couch in our candlelit bedchamber, leaning his head back on the cushions and closing his eyes. "Agren did not like being dead. Coarse, corrupt, filled with so much greed and jealousy and hatred . . . In a hundred years, you could not imagine it. Instead of entering his own body again, he took mine. Celine told me of such souls, ones that longed so for life that they refused to cross the Verges and would turn on the Healer. I've never experienced it before, and never will again, I hope. Stars of night . . ."

"The knife . . . what did you do?"

Karon opened his eyes and rolled his head toward me, revealing a rueful smile. "I convinced him that he could only come back as himself. Which meant, of course, that he was truly dead, for his body had failed beyond revival.

He wasn't happy about that. You saw the result. I'm glad he took it out on his own body and not on you or the child or me."

"I wonder what will become of the child."

He shuddered. "She'll be better off, no matter what."

We sat up together the rest of that night, falling asleep on the couch only when dawn was peeking in the window.

A few weeks later Karon took a small party to Valleor to investigate an ancient tomb exposed by an earthquake. The royal governor of Valleor's southern district had notified the Antiquities Commission of the find that lay near the city of Xerema, reporting that the site appeared to have relics of great value.

Karon took two of his assistants on the trip to learn what might be necessary to mount a full-scale excavation. He was only to be gone a few days, and so I chose to wait and accompany him on the larger expedition he planned for autumn. I was working at my language studies again, helping Tennice translate an Isker manuscript for Martin, and I hated to abandon him in the middle of it.

Three weeks passed with no word from Karon. It wasn't like him. This was a public journey, not one of his private ones. A few more days and I had difficulty concentrating on Tennice's project and couldn't settle at anything else. When the fourth week passed, I went to the palace to see if Racine or Sir Geoffrey, the administrator of the royal archives, had news. But there was nothing. Never had I been so worried; every morning when I woke alone in bed, I felt nauseated.

Martin came to our house only rarely, so when Joubert interrupted my pacing one afternoon to announce the Earl of Gault, the sea of dread burst through the feeble dike I'd built to contain it. "News out of Valleor," he said, taking my hands, his calm voice belied by his somber face. "Nothing specific to Karon, but we've had word that there's been another earthquake. They say Xerema has been leveled."

"He wasn't to be in the city. . . ." One has to say the words.

" . . . and I'm sure travel and communication are difficult," said Martin. "Tanager is already on his way. He'll send word as soon as he knows anything."

I hated Martin for sending Tanager without me. I had to sit and eat and walk and wait, counting leagues, counting days and hours, imagining horrors . . . After ten excruciating days, a cryptic message arrived with a Windham footman. "News. Come." I was in the carriage before the footman's voice fell quiet.

Martin was waiting when I hurried up the steps. Without wasting time on a greeting, he led me to a sitting room where Tanager sprawled on a couch, shirtless and producing snores of prodigious volume. One arm was bound to his chest, and his head was bandaged. Julia was cleaning dried blood and filth from an ugly gash on his leg.

"Tanager insisted that he must explain with his own mouth what he found," said Martin, shaking Tanager's shoulder, "but we thought he should stay put for a while. Here, lad, Seri's come."

"I didn't see him," Tanager mumbled, as I knelt on the floor beside the couch. "But I'm convinced he's alive." His broad face sharpened as he forced himself awake. "Sun and thunder, I've never seen such destruction. If a thousand armies had taken a thousand battering rams to those walls for a thousand years, they couldn't have caused so much. Not more than a tenth of the place is habitable, even if you could bear the stench of the dead." With his unbound arm, Tanager shoved himself to sitting, not seeming to notice Julia still working on his wounded leg. "Thousands were buried alive in the rubble. Those lucky enough to get out dug without stopping, trying to get to the rest before the governor's men set fire to the ruins. I rode out to the place of the tombs, and there was nothing left. Half the mountainside had come down on it."

I thought I might suffocate.

"Listen to me, though." Tanager's broad hand gripped my arm. "No one could tell me anything of the Leiran party that had come to excavate the tombs. But then they'd start speaking of their own troubles, and I kept hearing of a stranger who had appeared in the midst of the destruction. Time after time he managed to find men and women and children buried in impossible places, yet they lived. Unhurt. Everyone wanted to find this stranger to come pull out their relatives and friends, for luck walked with him, and he might find them alive when there was no other hope. They called him the *Dispóre,* the saving hand. They couldn't describe him. Some said he was milk-skinned like a Kerotean; some said he was dark and had the tilted eyes of an Isker. But all marveled at his strength, his luck, and his skill."

"So you see why we have hopes?" said Martin. "It sounds as if our Healer just can't pull himself away."

Tanager nodded. "By the time I left, they had burned the rubble. But the tales of the *Dispóre* hadn't died out. They say he's in company with those working with the sick and injured. I tried to find him, but the place is chaos, and he was always a step ahead of me. I only hope he doesn't stay too long. I got tangled with a mob who decided to share out my horse for supper. In thanks for saving his neck, the beast brought me home without much guidance."

I wanted to believe that the stranger in the tales was Karon. He would indeed find it difficult to leave a place where he was so much needed. There was nothing to do but wait.

Seri . . .

On a moonlit night a week after Tanager's return, I had fallen asleep in a chair, having stayed up reading far too late as had become my habit when Karon was away. The call startled me awake, but a glance about the dark library quickly confirmed that I was alone. The glass doors to the garden stood open, the scent of balsam hanging on the summer night. Moonbeams laid a silver path across the rug. The lamps were long cold, and a breeze ruffled the pages of a book I'd left open on the table.

Dreams, I thought, or perhaps some midnight noise from the lane beyond the garden wall, but as I gathered my shawl and my dropped book, ready to head up the stairs to bed, the call came again, faint, but clear. *Seri. Hear me!*

"Karon? Where are you?" I was wide awake now, and sure the voice was his, but I couldn't fathom where he could be for it to sound so faint.

My love, I need your help.

"Where . . . ?" And then I realized why I couldn't find him. His voice was only in my mind. Not since that first night of revelation in Martin's study had Karon spoken in my thoughts. I was unsure how to answer, but he seemed to know I heard him.

Be at the Inn of the Bronze Shield at Threadinghall, to-morrow. Bring Karylis for me. If I'm not there by nightfall, on your life do not stay. Ride for home and tell no one.

"I'll be there," I said. It seemed so foolish to speak aloud. "Can you hear me? Are you well?" But I heard nothing more.

The full moon allowed me to leave well before dawn. I carried only a bit of food and wine in my saddle pack. With Karylis's halter attached to my saddle—Karon never rode him on his travels for fear of losing him—I rode northwest as fast as I dared, avoiding the main road and all other travelers. I had never ridden so far unaccompanied, but I had surely read more maps than books in my life. Only in isolated spots did I stop, and then only long enough to rest the horses. And in those short intervals, my hand never left the slit right pocket of my riding skirt, where I could reach my dagger, secure in its brocade sheath. I would not fail.

CHAPTER 14

Year 3 in the reign of King Evard

Threadinghall lay about ten leagues northwest of Montevial, set in a heavily forested part of the kingdom, about forty leagues from the Vallorean border. The baron who held the region was a nasty man with a nastier wife and a son who was known to hunt starving Valloreans for sport. By midafternoon I was riding into the little town, a mournful sort of place with a clock tower in the center of it. The streets were narrow, the tall houses pressed close together, and the people as pale and shaggy as the moss-covered trees that surrounded them so thickly. I inquired of a stringy-haired sausage vendor as to where I might find the Inn of the Bronze Shield.

"Where the trees take the road," said the girl, pointing to the west.

I didn't quite catch her meaning, until I found the inn. It was the last structure in the town, and the forest did indeed appear to have swallowed whatever of the town or the road that had ever existed beyond it.

Leaving the horses with a ragged boy I found sleeping on a mound of hay beside the stable, I took a deep breath and walked into the inn. The common room was gloomy, lamps already lit despite the early hour. Five roughly dressed men sat at a large round table in the middle of the room, drinking ale and regaling each other with raucous commentary on a hunting trip gone awry. One of the hunters, a bear-like man with a red beard, whistled through his teeth, bobbed his head at me, and elbowed a sinewy youth beside him. Halting in midsentence, the youth looked me up and down, grinned wide enough to show a mouthful of stained teeth, and tipped his hat. The elbowing and crude politeness completed the circle of the table. I smiled back at them and dipped my head, from habit as much as anything. I had grown up around my father's soldiers. Rough manners often masked good hearts.

I sat at a table near the door and asked the proprietor for a cup of cider and a bowl of whatever he had simmering over his cookfire. He hovered near my table once he'd brought my refreshments, asking me three times if he could do anything for me. Women rarely traveled alone.

"I'm supposed to meet a party of friends here," I said. "My cousin, young Lord Elmont, with his friend, and his sisters. Two women and two men."

"Got no party of that description, miss." The man retreated a step at the mention of the unsavory local nobility.

"A messenger then? They'd send a messenger ahead if they were to be late. Are there any strangers about?"

"None save the two in the corner there. Shall I ask them if they're sent to you?"

I hadn't noticed the two men in the dim corner farthest from the fire. "No, certainly not." I sniffed and wrinkled my nose. "I'm sure Lord Elmont would not have used any common messenger. I'll wait."

"As you wish."

I dawdled over my meal. A few local tradesmen came in. A thin, twitchy man in a many-colored coat ordered a mug of ale. The tradesmen called him Weaver and teased him for being away from his loom in the middle of the day. The thin man turned scarlet and said he was waiting for a cartload of wool due in at five. The hunting party grew louder in their cups. The two from the corner left. By this time I'd sat for two hours and began to feel conspicuous, so I left a coin for the proprietor and strolled into the yard. The sky above the trees was still ruddy with late afternoon, but in the premature darkness of the forest, the lamplighter was already flitting about like an oversized firefly. *It's not nightfall yet. Not yet.*

I wandered back to the stables and explored a path that led around behind the ramshackle building and through the encroaching trees. As I approached the fence and the little gate where the path returned to the stableyard, I heard quiet voices.

"Don't look like aught's comin', Sheriff. P'raps you got a bum turn."

Sheriff . . . The word froze my steps.

"When the clock strikes, we'll have him. Lynch drives his route as regular as clockwork." The dry chuckle held no mirth. "Remember you're only to hobble the beast, so he can do no harm until we have him properly restrained. Kill him and your own life is forfeit. Understood?"

"Aye. I've never seen one, you know. A priest told me they can set a man afire with their eyes."

"He can do no harm if you're quick and do as I've told you. There's reward enough in this to pay well for any risk."

Heart racing, I crept back along the stable wall until I could peer around the far corner of the stable into the yard. Like two great spiders, the strangers from the common room lurked in the shadowed niche where the tall wooden fence met the stable building. One of the men wore a broad-brimmed hat with a feather. The flaming sword blazoned on his cloak glared boldly in the failing light. The giant body of his companion slouched against the fence. That one's leather vest, worn over a long tunic and baggy trousers, along with his wide belt with a short sword dangling from one side and an iron bar from the other, named him a hireling thug of the sort one could find in the alleys of Montevial. He would have four more knives hidden in boot top or sleeve, and perhaps a vial of lye tucked in his sleeve. A soft cap was pulled low over his brow.

When the clock strikes . . . Lynch drives his route . . . And the weaver was expecting a wool cart at five. I imagined I could hear the grinding of the gears in the clock tower. How long had it been since the last quarter struck? No time to plan.

Yanking the narrow brim of my hat lower to shade my face, I marched out of the trees toward the sleeping boy. "You lazy beggar, I'll have you flogged."

The poor lad sat up, rubbing his eyes.

Calling to mind every tantrum of spoiled nobility I had ever witnessed, I stamped my foot and yelled. "Idiot boy! If I miss my reunion with Uncle Charles and Aunt Charlotte because of you, I'll personally remove your ears! My whole life is at stake—my inheritance, everything—and to have it ruined by a filthy stable beggar is insupportable."

As the bewildered child shot up and ran into the stable, I hurried across the yard to the two lurkers. "I commanded this lazy, insolent boy to have my horses ready so I can leave this dunghill before nightfall, but he's not even got them saddled. And my cousins have contracted for a reliable guide to lead me out of this pestilential forest. I suppose there's no possibility that either of you is my guide?"

"No possibility, madam," said the cloaked man. His eye sockets were almost flat, his eyes protruding like those of a fish. His bulbous lips, protruding from a thicket of dark, wiry black beard, curled in disdain.

Several passersby stopped to see what was the disturbance. Good. I wanted a crowd. "Good fellows, I'm not an unreasonable woman. I'll pay you well. But I must insist— Ah, you, sir!"

The sallow-faced proprietor had stepped into the stableyard, looking annoyed.

"I must have an escort, hostler," I said. "My party has not arrived, my cousin is laid up with the gout, and your fool of a stable boy is only now saddling my horses, though I've no one to ride with me." I dragged the speechless proprietor into a position that would prevent the two lurking men from leaving their corner without walking over us. From the lane, a plodding horse's hooves clopped on the cobbles, and the wheels of a wagon creaked and slowed. I forced myself not to look. "Tell these two to escort me. If I don't get satisfaction at once, I shall remember the poor service I received in Threadinghall and at the Bronze Shield, in particular. You'll get no more trade from my family. . . ."

The jolly hunters from the common room had wandered out into the yard, as the proprietor scratched his head and questioned the stable lad who had just returned with my horses. The poor boy was likely more befuddled than ever, having remembered how I'd specifically instructed him *not* to unsaddle the pair when I'd arrived.

The creaking wheels turned into the stableyard. The two strangers stiffened and shuffled their feet. Grabbing the reins from the boy, I maneuvered the horses to where they would block any view of the yard.

"Sirs, are you honorable men?" I said to the two. "Does your road take you north? I know I'm bold to ask it, and Aunt Charlotte will be horrified at the impropriety, but if you deliver me to my relations at Elmont Castle this night, you can demand a prince's ransom. I've an extra horse—"

"Get out of the way, woman, and your filthy beasts with you," said the sheriff. "We've business with this wagon."

"Curse you, black-hearted villain," I shouted as loudly as I could, praying that Karon was listening. "What business with this wagon could possibly be more important than my inheritance?" I backed away from the men, keeping close enough to prevent any passage around my horses, and clapped my hand to my breast. "Why, I'll wager you plan to rob it! Help! Thieves! Driver! You on the wagon! These two plan to rob you. Beware!" My brother had always accused me of having the most piercing scream in the Four Realms.

Several bystanders closed in on the two angry men, who

were now trying to force their way past me and the horses. The situation quickly degenerated into chaos. "A pox on you, whore!" With a bone-cracking grip, the fish-eyed sheriff shoved me backward into the horses. "I am a king's sheriff. Get out of my way."

I pulled back just enough to make room for the hunting party who had crowded up behind me growling. The cornered pair tried to push their way out of the ring, but my rescuers had drunk enough ale to make their courage and honor invincible. The red-bearded storyteller quickly pinned the sheriff against the wall. As I slipped backward, the pushing and shoving gave way to serious fisticuffs. The crowd was large enough and confused enough and drunk enough that no one could tell who was who.

Oh, please, Karon, be ready.

The proprietor was shouting at the combatants over the heads of the crowding observers, and I thought matters were well in hand. But as I led the horses away from the melee, the sheriff's thuggish companion dodged the flying fists and squeezed along the shadowed edge of the stable toward the yard, where the wagon had come to a halt under a spreading oak.

A dark figure dropped lightly from the back of the wagon. The thug crept up behind him, iron bar in one hand and a loop of heavy chain in the other.

Karon! Watch out! No one was watching. Everyone was occupied with the brawl. Holy Annadis, he didn't see. . . .

I drew my knife. Ducking between the two horses, I called up every skill my father and his soldiers had taught me and let fly my weapon. With a harsh expulsion of air, the brute straightened and pitched forward into the dirt. Satisfyingly still.

Heart and stomach threatening to choke me, I dragged the horses toward the wagon and the newcomer, who had slipped behind the bole of the great oak.

"Please, madam"—I flinched and spun backward, but it was only the flustered proprietor who had popped up at my side—"forgive this misunderstanding. Allow me. . . ." He gestured toward the horses and offered his hand.

Taking a quick breath, I stiffened my chin and raised my foot purposefully. The proprietor quickly linked his hands and gave me a leg up. "Since my honest guide has not arrived to escort me, I suppose I must ride alone," I said.

"So sorry, madam, but for me to leave the inn—"

"I am the guide hired for you, madam." The figure in the hooded cloak stepped out from behind the tree and bowed, interrupting the innkeeper before he could grovel further. "My apologies for my tardiness."

"Hold up there," yelled the grizzled driver of the wagon, as he stood shading his eyes and peering into the noisy fracas. He waved his arm toward the corner, but the sheriff was fully occupied, and Karon was already on Karylis's back.

In moments, we were racing out of Threadinghall and down the forest road, back the way I had come earlier. The full moon lit our path with the brightness of day.

For an hour we rode without stopping and with no possibility of speech. When we emerged from the dense trees into the rolling moonlit meadows, Karon pointed to the right branch of an upcoming fork in the road. We thundered down the dusty track, winding through gentle hills until at last we came to a grove of willows bordering a wide stream. The water rippled merrily in the silver light.

We pulled up, and I slipped from the saddle straight into Karon's arms. I whispered into his neck, "I was so frightened for you."

"I'm so sorry," he said, stroking my hair and pressing me fiercely to his breast. "I had no idea. Never, never would I knowingly call you into such danger." He was trembling.

I pulled away and laid a finger on his lips. "Judge on the merits of the deeds alone, not on what the circumstances of life have made of them. Have I got it right?"

"Yes. Of course you do." He smiled weakly. "My chief counselor never forgets anything that can be used to refute a fool's premise."

"Should we not ride on now? I can go farther, you know."

"We should, but I can't. I have to rest for just a bit." Karon's trembling was not just the released anxiety of the evening's events. His skin was hot and dry, a fever that had nothing to do with sorcery, and his rigid posture told me that sheer strength of will kept him upright.

"What have you done to yourself?" I asked, stroking his haggard face.

"Nothing that a year of sleep and a lifetime of you will not take care of. And to my great regret"—leaning on my arm, he sank to the spongy ground of the willow thicket—"a little of the sleep must come before anything else." His eyes closed as he mumbled. "Just an hour, no more than two, then we must go. . . ." And while holding my hand as if it were his last connection to life, he was asleep.

For a long while I sat and watched him sleep, knowing full well that the night's events had changed my life forever. Karon had come a finger's breadth from capture. I had killed a man to protect him. Full of uncomfortable musings about what else we might have to do to keep him safe, I pulled his cloak around us both and fell asleep.

The moon hung like a huge yellow lantern low above the mountains in the west when I woke. Karon slept unmoving, his scarred left arm thrown over me. "Wake up," I said, shaking his shoulder. "You said two hours, no more."

He buried his face in my tunic and emitted a muffled groan. "But this feels so marvelously fine."

"Our own bed will be much nicer, and perhaps you'll be clean. Happy as I am to see you, there is definitely an aura of the stable about." At least his fever seemed to have cooled a bit.

He rolled over wearily. "I was the only passenger in Lynch's cart, but chickens, and sheep, and pigs had most definitely preceded me. I was in no position to be choosy."

I pulled out the provisions from my saddle pack. That roused him a bit. First he drained two waterskins. Then he downed half a loaf of bread, a knob of cheese, and three apples, and did not protest more than once when I gave him my portion, too.

"The man who laid the trap was a sheriff. He knew about you."

He rubbed his neck and stretched his shoulders. "I was sure I'd shaken them . . . careless . . . unforgivable—"

"I told you, it's all right. You're safe. That's all that matters."

We didn't return to the main road, but continued on a longer, less traveled route back to Montevial. As we rode, I told him Tanager's story, and then he told me his own.

"I'd gone into Xerema to hire guards to protect the site. It was a fabulous find—at least seven hundred years old, built deep and hidden to protect it from graverobbers— but, of course, it's all gone again now. I was on my way back to the site when the earthquake struck, out in the open. Though I used everything I knew to find Rinaldo and Damon, I had to give it up early on; I sensed no hint of life and had no hope of digging through that mess.

"But I couldn't leave the area without trying to help. Unlike at the mountain, there were pockets in the city ruins where people could survive for a little while. Whatever I did, it wasn't enough. Every few hours I'd have to forgo use of anything but my hands, and I could still hear people screaming and crying. But somehow I managed to do more than I could in ordinary times. As did everyone."

The beautiful morning seemed at odds with his dreadful tale. Hawks soared through the haze of dayfires, hanging over the patchwork grain fields. Karon stared at the weedy path ahead of us, lost in the telling. "After a week or so, there was no one left living under the stones, and no one who hadn't crossed the Verges, and I thought I'd come home. But I met up with a surgeon named Connor. We'd worked together at several sites, and he had guessed there was something out of the ordinary. He asked if I had medical training, and I told him I did, though perhaps different from his own. He said that if I'd continue working with him, he'd ask no questions."

Karon looked up at me with a sadness that tore my heart. "He was extraordinary, Seri. Never have I met anyone who gave so much of himself. For days he would go without sleep, treating all who came to him: nobles, beggars, peasants, soldiers. Never did he lose patience or fail to treat even the least of them with kindness and respect, as if each were the most important person in the world. And he was skilled beyond any physician or surgeon I've known. I would assist him as best I could, and when he found something he couldn't handle, he'd ask if I might have some insight into the case beyond his own. If I thought I could do it, he would find a private place and see that I was not disturbed. . . ."

"You speak of him in the past."

He nodded. "There was a little girl. Only five years old or so. A beautiful child. We got to her too late. With all of Connor's skill and all of mine, we could not undo what had been done." He spoke as if the terrible scene still lay before him. "The child's father went mad. His wife and five other children had died in the earthquake, and the little girl was all he had left. When Connor told him she was dead, the man pulled a knife and stabbed him to the heart. It happened so quickly"—Karon's face was a portrait of grief—"and just as with the Writer and his daughter, it came at a time when I had nothing left to give him. Before he died, he whispered that he had hoped he could at last witness what it was I did. Oh, Seri, would that I could have saved him. It was very hard to keep my own teaching in my mind."

"Because he was an uncommon man and a friend in terrible times."

"More than that. The murderer was a man I'd brought back from the dead."

We rode in silence for a long while. What ordinary words of comfort could ease such extraordinary sorrow? But eventually Karon took up the tale once more, shaking his head as if to rid himself of his own thoughts. "That was about twelve days ago, I think. I knew I couldn't keep up the work indefinitely. Someone would see or guess, and I was very tired, sick enough that I was endangering people I wanted to help, seeing two of everything or things that weren't there. And without Connor my work was far more difficult. A day or two after I buried him, I began to suspect I was being followed. I've been running ever since. Every time I thought I was clear, that sheriff would turn up again. Finally I heard about this carter that plied the Leiran road, so I believed I could get to Threadinghall. I'd be safe there. But I knew I could go no farther without help—"

"—and you called me."

"Inexcusable. I should have known they'd find me again. But I was at the end of my resources, and you were so much in my thoughts. I don't think I could have spoken to anyone else at such a distance. I couldn't conjure a broomstraw after it. Still can't. The certainty that you would be waiting was the only thing that kept me moving yesterday. But invading your mind, stealing your thoughts—it violates everything I profess . . ."

"Would it make a difference to you if I said it was all right? If I gave you my consent to speak to me in that way any time?" The idea had been with me since I had first heard him in our library. "Last night, I needed to warn you. I wanted you to hear. I trust you, you know, and I welcome you into every part of my life. It doesn't frighten me."

"Gods, Seri . . ."

We reached home without incident and with no evidence that Karon's pursuers had any clue as to his identity. He believed they had never seen his face. He worried that I'd be recognized, but I assured him the light had been poor and my face shaded by my hat. For good measure I burned the clothes we had worn.

I didn't tell Karon that I had killed to protect him. Keeping the secret caused me far more guilt than the killing, but I told myself that I would reveal it as soon as time had blurred the event. Perhaps by then Karon, too, would realize that the Way of the J'Ettanne was not the way of the world.

Karon's illness passed quickly with rest and decent food, but I had never seen him in such a desert of the spirit. In the weeks after his return, he ventured out of the house only once—to visit the families of his two assistants, offering them his sympathy and what help he could in dealing with their loss. Though he hadn't asked me to do so, he seemed relieved that I discouraged visitors. The effort of communicating with anyone was so monumental that even a quarter of an hour's company left him pale and sick. He had spent everything he had five hundred times over. Now smiles and laughter and even words came hard.

But on one morning in early autumn I awoke to find him gazing down at me, head propped on one elbow, a sober demeanor belied by a sparkle in his blue eyes. "There's something you're not telling me, my lady."

"What do you mean?"

"Are there more secrets than this one?"

"Who ever said you were to know everything that goes on?"

"But I believe I have an interest in this matter."

"Have you been prying with this fiendish talent you have, sir?"

"I confess to it. You've seemed unwell these few weeks, and I was worried."

"And so you've deprived me of my surprise?"

His face lost its shine for a moment. "Does it really bother you? I thought—"

I rolled over into his arms. "Not a whit! I was just waiting to be sure." An astonishing thought came to mind. "What else can you tell about it?"

His laughter was bursting with joy and life. "Do you really want to know?"

"Everything you know. If I have no secrets, neither can you."

"It is a son."

The months that followed were the sweetest that life can provide. Whether caused by delight in our child's new life, or the newfound intimacy of our mind-speaking, or the summer's brush with mortality and dread, that golden autumn was wrapped in aching beauty. It was as if nature itself had decided to grant us a season of perfection long after a normal year would have lost itself in snow and ice. We walked and rode in the intoxicating air of the countryside. We read and we laughed. Karon delved into his work, and I with him, and we marveled at each new treasure we dragged out of the bottomless vaults of Leire.

Our son would be named Connor Martin Gervaise. So many names for a being so tiny, said Karon. Every night he would close his eyes and lay his hands on my belly, whispering the proper words, and, after a moment, he would smile and tell me all was well. Sometimes he would say it with words, and sometimes he would look into my eyes and speak with his other voice. Words were only a pale shadow of that other voice, no more representing the wholeness of speech than notes of one octave can represent the wholeness of music.

The J'Ettanne of Avonar had only rarely used their talent for mind-speaking. The gift carried an immense emotional burden, for it had been their downfall. Its use was rigidly constrained by the Two Tenets of the J'Ettanne. Thus it was only with the freedom granted by my offer that Karon was able to explore his strange talent for the first time. Eagerly he experimented with all its various aspects, working at openings and barriers, contacts and distractions, until I thought that he must turn his head inside out—or mine.

We practiced enough that it became easy, Karon speaking to me and then listening to my thoughts in reply. But once we mastered the skill, we used it only rarely. Karon said it would be too easy to misstep, demonstrating knowledge of something one had no business knowing while in the company of others. It was the same reason he used his other magical abilities so sparingly. Habits. Though I believed no one would ever learn of what we did, I did not complain as I might have a few months earlier. Karon's safety was the one subject on which I no longer offered any dispute.

Karon made no healing journeys that fall. At my urging he would take Karylis out to run in the countryside long after I felt too uncomfortable to ride, but he would always be back before nightfall. Each time he would say that perhaps the groom should take the horse out for exercise from then on, so he would not be away too long. But I told him, laughing, that he should not deprive himself of his delight in riding, for I had bribed Karylis to make sure he always came home.

CHAPTER 15

As Baglos recited the tale of his mysterious land and people, the afternoon waned gracefully. The meadow came alive with birdsong and a soft breeze. While I sat picking at the dry, weedy grass, giving thought to our next move, D'Natheil used my ax to split the thick chunk of birchwood and shorten it. Baglos stood nearby, chewing his lip and watching D'Natheil uncertainly, as if he weren't quite sure what to do next either.

Jacopo stood up, rubbed his backside, stretched his shoulders, and then promptly squatted down again beside me, rapping his thick knuckles on his boots. "I should go home," he said, eyeing my two visitors uncomfortably. "I'm feeling down in the leg after all this hill climbing, and I left Lucy Mercer with the shop. The old biddy's overgenerous with my money. Got no eye for a bargain."

"You should go," I said. "Paulo, too. Better if you're both out of this."

At some time during Baglos's astonishing story, Paulo had finished with the horses and fallen asleep in the shade of my woodpile. He could not have heard much and was surely not in the habit of volunteering information to anyone. But Rowan seemed to have an eye on Paulo, and the prospects for a lame, illiterate boy from Dunfarrie were bleak enough without tainting him with talk of sorcery.

"I don't feel right to leave you. Fearful business—all this talk of madness and murder and men with no souls. And I can't say as I trust these two as you do. Come along home with me, Seri."

"They'll not be here for long. Wherever their mysterious duty takes them, it's not likely to be Dunfarrie." And I couldn't run away. My search for reason and order in the universe had long succumbed to defeat, but I was coming to the conclusion that I had to do something about D'Natheil. When fate opens a chasm underneath your feet or shoves a lava-spewing mountain into your path, you cannot ignore it.

Jacopo laid his thick fingers on my knee. "I know better than to try to keep you out of their business if your mind is made up. And I'll do your bidding in whatever way a disbelieving old man can do. But I'll ask you one thing, Seri girl. You must tell Graeme about all this. He's his own man first, not the king's nor Lord Marchant's. If those villains are as wicked as this Baglos says, then Graeme's going to get himself killed or worse. You know he'll not leave off."

Rowan was definitely a puzzle. Did the sheriff even know that the priests were sorcerers, too? Was he corrupt, or merely stupid, or was he a wily villain, planning to lure the priests into the fire once they had led him to other sorcerers? Whichever one, we could afford no dealings with him.

"I can't tell him anything, Jaco. His duty is to exterminate sorcerers. He lives by the law, no matter the consequence, and by the law, he must turn all of us over to the king. I won't let him do that. Assuming Paulo wakes up by tomorrow, he'll take Rowan's horse back to Grenatte. By the time Rowan returns to Dunfarrie, D'Natheil and Baglos will be gone. Even if the sheriff is determined to be pigheaded, it'll do him no good."

"Ask for his help. He'll listen to you." Jacopo scratched his grizzled chin and grinned, "I love you dearly, little girl, but if there's one of you that's been pigheaded, it's not Graeme."

Jacopo's grin raised my hackles, and I answered more sharply than I should have. "I don't trust any sheriff. You shouldn't either. Don't you dare let him drag you and Paulo into this."

Before we could argue any further, a bone-cracking slap and a sharp cry sounded from the direction of the cottage. I turned to see Baglos staggering backwards, his hands shielding his face. D'Natheil's hand was raised for another strike.

"Bence, mie giro!" cried Baglos. *"Ne stes damet—"*

D'Natheil's second blow knocked Baglos to the dirt. Blood dribbling from his brow, the Dulcé vainly tried to scramble out of harm's way, but his master's foot caught him in the backside and sent him sprawling.

"Stop it!" I cried, jumping to my feet and running toward the men. "What are you doing?"

Another kick caught the fallen Dulcé in the side. *"Mie giro, stes vyn—"* Another, and Baglos could only grunt instead of finishing his plea.

I stepped between them, trying not to flinch as the back of D'Natheil's hand flew toward my face. His fair complexion darkened to yet a deeper shade of purple. But the blow did not fall. Rather, he snarled, shoved me aside, and went after Baglos again. He did not continue the beating, but rolled Baglos to his back and yanked something from the Dulcé's belt—his own silver knife. Glaring darkly at his cowering servant, D'Natheil sheathed the weapon. His blood-streaked fingers twisted the Dulcé's purple vest and pulled Baglos's upper body from the ground until the small man's face was only a handspan from his own.

"Don't you *dare* hurt him again," I yelled. "That's enough!"

D'Natheil shifted his cold blue stare to me. Lip curling, nostrils flared, the young man gathered the wad of satin tighter. He needed no power of speech to tell me that he could break the Dulcé's neck without reservation, without remorse, almost without effort.

"You. Will. *Not*," I said, biting each word and spitting it at him. It seemed to be the only language he truly understood. "You are his prince. You are responsible for him. Tell him, Baglos. Exactly as I said it."

From his precarious position, the Dulcé closed his eyes and murmured hoarsely.

The moment expanded to fill the space between us. Then, with a hiss of disgust, the Prince slammed Baglos to the turf and walked over to the wide stump where lay the ax and his birch limb. I watched to make sure he planned to use the ax on the wood and not our heads. But he was soon lost in his work again, using the blade to hack long slivers from the chunk of birch. After each cut, he would explore the wood's thinning shape with his fingers, examine each piece for who knew what, and then raise the ax again.

Baglos had rolled to his side and curled into a ball. "Stupid, stupid, stupid," he mumbled. "Did I think he wouldn't notice?"

"Are you all right?" I knelt beside him and laid a hand on his dark hair. He jerked at my touch and tried to sit up. "No, stay down for a moment, until we see how he's hurt you," I said. "Jaco, bring some water." My friend was already on his way to the stream with a pail and a rag, and soon I was blotting the Dulcé's bruised and bloody cheek.

"What Dulcé was ever so stupid?" He waved off my hand, struggled to sitting, and took the rag, pressing it under his nose, which was bleeding profusely. But even the blood paled beside his skin color. Stars of night, he was embarrassed!

"You picked up his knife. He has no call to beat you for it."

"He thought—" Baglos changed whatever he was going to say. "It is D'Arnath's blade. I could not see it left in the grass. Dropped. It should not even be here . . . but in Avonar. D'Arnath's weapons are—they bear immense—" He took a breath as if to quiet his stumbling. "It was a misunderstanding. He is young."

"You're more forgiving than he deserves. To serve a master so unworthy of his position, no matter how important his duties, requires a more generous spirit than mine. When your friend was wounded, you should have let someone else have the 'honor' of being D'Natheil's Guide." I regretted that D'Natheil could not understand me. I would have told him what I thought of people who beat their servants. "You needn't make excuses. I've known him for a brute since I first encountered him."

Baglos shook his head. "It is not his fault he is this way. His life—" He glanced at the oblivious D'Natheil and quickly dropped his eyes to the ground. "My lord's mother died when he was but a babe. Avonar was at war, and no one had time to see to a boy who was wild from his earliest days. No one worried about his poor training, because it was his oldest brother D'Joran that would be the Heir after his father, and then D'Seto next. Never had a third son been named Heir. But the war worsened and one after the other his father and brothers fell. Then all attention turned to D'Natheil, who had been left to play in the alleys, sleep with the dogs, and eat with the warriors on the walls."

The Dulcé sighed and blotted his nose again. "He was only nine years old when he became the Heir, a full three years before coming of age. The Preceptor Exeget was named his mentor and guardian. D'Natheil was insolent and prideful and would forever run away. He had no desire to learn of his gifts, or the art of ruling, or the history of his people and their past glory. Master Exeget disciplined him harshly, until the other Preceptors begged him to go easier on the boy, but the master said only that the Zhid would not go easy on the Heir, and one could not disagree with that. And so, my lord progressed . . . only slowly . . . in anything but his fighting skills."

And when the boy was only twelve, so Baglos had told us, his desperate people had sent him into a magical war for which he was unprepared. I rinsed the bloody rag in the pail of water, wrung it out, and gave it back to the Dulcé. "He has no right to hurt you, Baglos. Many people have terrible childhoods and impossible duties, but they live their lives with grace." How could this callow hothead be kin to the J'Ettanne? "Is he even capable of what's needed to save your people?"

Baglos was a long time answering, his face hidden in the rag. "He is, dear lady. Whether he wishes it or no."

One might have thought the Dulcé's cuts and bruises magically vanished when I asked if he felt well enough to prepare a meal for us. While Baglos busied himself with my pots and poked about in the garden, the meadow, and the larder dug into the hillside, Jacopo and I hauled water to my neglected garden.

"Does Emil Gasso still have extra horses?" I asked as we splattered the contents of our pails onto the dry soil.

Jacopo had relaxed a bit, now he was busy with something not smacking of sorcery. "He does. Old buzzard figures he'd best get gold for 'em soon or the king'll have them for the war."

"If we're to get these two out of here in good order,

they're going to need another mount. Maybe two. I'm not
sure if Baglos's horse is reliable." I was not yet willing to
tell Jaco that I was planning to accompany them. My plan
was still too flimsy to expose to the daylight.

"Gasso's got at least three good mounts, so it shouldn't
be a problem."

"Would he lend them? It would take far more than I
have to buy even one."

"Not likely. Emil Gasso is as penny-pinching as a body
can be, so he'll not let the beasts out of his sight without
the coins in his purse."

Baglos interrupted, asking for salt, so I went to show
him, while Jacopo finished watering the garden. There
wasn't room in the cottage for all of us to eat, so I had
Jacopo help me move the table outside, and then sent him
to drag Paulo from his nap in the woodpile while I
fetched D'Natheil.

The Prince was no longer behind the cottage or anywhere that I could see, so I walked over to the copse where
the horses were tethered. He was kneeling by the spring,
frantically scrubbing at his hands. Curious at his odd frenzy,
I held back and watched. After drying his hands on his
breeches, he wrapped his arms about his face and head and
bent over until his elbows almost touched his knees, releasing a quiet groan of such heart-tearing misery, such private
and profound despair, it seemed to swallow the last light
of the sun. Disdain and condemnation died on my tongue.
Any man in such pain was suffering more than any reproach of mine could cause him. And so I retreated. Even
if I had cared to ease him, I had no remedies for that kind
of wounding.

Not long after I had returned to the cottage, D'Natheil
came striding across the meadow, haughty and composed,
displaying no remnant of the emotion I had glimpsed at
the spring. I motioned him to the table, where Paulo leaned
on his elbows yawning and a frowning Jacopo tapped his
knife idly on his empty bowl. The sky had deepened to a
rich blue, and I set out candles that flamed against the
evening like two new stars. An odd company we made:
a peasant sailor, a village urchin, a disgraced duchess, a
diminutive cook, and a mute, half-mad prince. I sacrificed

the flask of wine that I kept for emergencies, shared it out, and when Baglos set his fine-smelling dish on the table, I raised my cup to the company. *"J'edai en j'sameil.* To life and beauty everlasting!" I said the words first in the archaic language of the J'Ettanne and then in Leiran.

D'Natheil's eyebrows lifted slightly as he raised his cup and tipped his head in gracious acknowledgment. The season had changed yet again.

Baglos's mouth fell open, and he almost dropped his cup. "The Avonar feasting wish! Where have you learned those words, woman? And spoken in the most ancient tongue of the Dar'Nethi! Has D'Natheil—How could he have taught them to you?"

"He hasn't. It's my story, Baglos, and I'll tell you some of it, but right now we feast on your magic. What incredible thing have you done with my bits and pieces?"

Whatever the shortcomings of the little Dulcé, they did not include his cooking. Thin slices of ham were rolled up around a savory filling made of bread and nuts and onions. Tart monkberries from the hillside were sweetened with honey and made into a sauce to go over it. To top it all he brought out apples, baked in the coals with butter and honey. Hard to believe they were the hard early apples that were always so tasteless. None of us could get enough. From what conversation went on during the meal, one might think we were all as mute as D'Natheil. Paulo came near bursting with unbridled ecstasy when we gave him the last bites, as well as the pot to scrape.

Jacopo left for Dunfarrie soon after we were done. He bowed politely to Baglos, but granted D'Natheil only a disapproving stare, his terror of sorcery momentarily superceded by disgust at the Prince's unmanly behavior. The pleased Dulcé returned the formality. D'Natheil ignored him. Jacopo set out across the moonlit meadow, stopping to wave just before disappearing into the trees.

"That ranks among the finest meals I've ever eaten, Baglos," I said as we cleaned up the mess, "including those at the tables of kings and nobles. Any great house in Leire would make your fortune were you to agree to manage its kitchen."

"Please excuse me," said Baglos, as he wiped the pots

and stacked them neatly by the hearth, stood on a chair to hang the net bag of onions in the rafters and set the small tin of salt on my shelf. "But I have great curiosity. What woman who lives . . . excuse me . . . as you do, has ever dined with kings and nobles? And how is it possible that you know the ancient language of the Dar'Nethi?"

While the moon rose above the eastern horizon and a dry breeze nipped at the candle flames, I perched on the table and told the Dulcé and D'Natheil something of myself and something of the J'Ettanne and something of how I had come to live as I did. Not so very much. Only that the descendants of J'Ettanne knew nothing of these things Baglos had told us, that they had been exterminated, and that it was possible my own husband, a Healer, and my son, a newborn infant, had been the last of them.

Baglos was in shock at my story, exclaiming his horror even as he translated it for the Prince. "The Exiles all dead . . . and their gifts outlawed. Burned alive . . . slaughtered at birth . . . Vasrin guide our steps from this place. I think the Lords of Zhev'Na have already won!"

"You see why I believe you've been sent to me? It's possible there's no other soul in the Four Realms who even knows the name J'Ettanne."

"That seems indisputable."

"And you see why D'Natheil must do no magic where anyone can see? Make sure he understands that. Our law is absolute."

"Much is now explained. Will you not tell us more, woman? About J'Ettanne's people, about their life in this land? Why did they no longer come to the Bridge?"

"I told you, they had no lore of a Bridge or of a kingdom such as yours. I've no answers that can help you. As for their life—it doesn't matter anymore." The past was done. Karon and the J'Ettanne were dead. Dwelling on their stories would not repair that. I hated speaking of them.

When Baglos told D'Natheil all of this, the Prince indicated that he remembered my teaching. He displayed no fear, of course. Bullies never believe they'll experience the kind of wickedness they parcel out. He retrieved his birchwood—now a slender chip the size of his palm—sat himself in the light spilling from the cottage doorway, and began carving on it with the tip of his silver dagger. Once I felt the slightest stirring in the air, a faint sigh that was not the cooling breeze, and I looked over to see him running his fingers over the blade of his knife. I wondered if he was invoking some enchantment, but I wasn't about to ask.

Baglos and Paulo moved the table back into the cottage. Paulo mumbled something about seeing to the horses and strolled into the night with his hands in his pockets. The boy would not consider taking Thunder down to Dunfarrie. The sheriff had told him to ride the horse as far as Jonah's cottage, and Paulo was unwilling to jeopardize his privilege by straying one finger's breadth from the instruction. A fine meal, responsibility for Rowan's horse, mysterious princes, and talk of sorcery—Paulo had likely never had such a day in his thirteen years.

A short while later, as I dumped out the water we had used to clean the dishes, D'Natheil suddenly jumped to his feet, dropping his woodcarving into the dirt. Grabbing my pail and throwing it aside, he shoved me toward the doorway of the cottage, and then, with vehemently expressive hands, demanded to know where Paulo was. Just like him not to notice anyone else until he wanted something for himself.

"What do you want with—?" Before I could finish my question, D'Natheil bellowed in frustration, waved his hand to the sky and the meadow and the wood, and then slapped his fists together ferociously. *Danger.* Even as I squinted at the darkening edge of the trees, trying to see what bothered him so, a gray haze shadowed the moonlight, and the cheerful flickering of candlelight faded, though the moon was unclouded and the candleflame yet burned. An alien wind swept through the valley, leaching the warmth from the summer night, bearing on its back the scents of smoke, ash, and decay. "He's with the horses." I pointed to the copse.

With long, graceful strides D'Natheil dashed across the stretch of grass to the dark grove, and soon returned with a squirming Paulo over his shoulder. The young man pushed me farther into the house, dumped Paulo on the floor, and slammed and barred the door. Breathing hard, he leaned his back against the door, and his defiant chin challenged me to argue.

Baglos said, "What is it? Wild beas—? Holy Vasrin! The Zhid!" He cast his almond-shaped eyes to the roof and the walls, climbing onto my bed to close and bar the shutters.

Paulo picked himself off the floor, rubbing his arms. "He's balmy."

"Never mind it, Paulo," I said, urging the boy away from the Prince and toward the fire. "There's danger about, and he wants you safe. It will pass."

"What of the sailor?" said Baglos. "How far had he to travel? I pray Vasrin he is not out."

My heart stopped for a moment in fear for Jaco, thinking of him on the exposed lower slopes of the Dunfarrie path, but then I considered the time and shook my head. "No, it's only an hour's walk to the village, and it's been at least two—"

"—and he is not the one they seek," said Baglos, patting my arm. "Build up the fire and do not think of what passes outside the door. In Avonar, we would tell stories when the Zhid were seeking, hoping to bar them from our thoughts."

The wind gusted and howled and pawed at the cottage, rattling the door and shutters, seeping through the log walls. Beneath its bluster was an undertone of uttermost desolation, a song worthy of a world mourning for a dead sun or a race lamenting its lost children. I needed no urging to build up the fire. "If there are to be stories, someone else will have to tell them," I said, pulling a blanket about my shoulders. "I don't think I can."

D'Natheil sat on the floor beside the hearth, eyes narrowed and head cocked to one side, his senses fixed on something far beyond the fire. As the rising flames gnawed at the logs, his expression gradually lost its intensity, as if he were mesmerized by the play of light and colors.

"Mie giro." Baglos sat down on the worn woven rug beside his master and plucked the Prince's sleeve. *"Mie giro, ne pell don . . ."* D'Natheil ignored him. His narrow face tight, the earnest Dulcé persisted. He spoke softly to his master, shaking his head and pressing a fist to his heart, coaxing and cajoling until D'Natheil dragged his gaze from the fire, blinked, and nodded.

"The Prince has agreed that I may tell a story of his childhood to distract him from the Seeking. I hope it might make him remember." Baglos spoke first to me and then to D'Natheil, as before.

"When my lord was six years old, he was a wild boy, who wished to do nothing but fight. He greatly admired his older brother, Prince D'Seto, a young man both honored for his courage and fighting skills and beloved for his great good humor. One day D'Natheil stole a sword from Prince D'Seto, not understanding that it was only a flimsy ceremonial sword that his brother had enchanted so as to make the one who carried it irresistible to the ladies and tireless in . . . ah . . . adventures of the heart. D'Natheil was so small that the strength of the enchantment acted on him like an excess of wine. . . ."

Baglos proceeded to tell us a long series of D'Natheil's embarrassing adventures among the warriors and ladies of Avonar. The Dulcé was a fine storyteller. I found myself shaking my head in amused disbelief, Paulo giggled, and even D'Natheil was flushed and smiling. And amid the humorous escapades, I caught vivid glimpses of a cultured city and a courtly people bitterly scarred by war.

After a while, however, Baglos's tale flagged. He struggled to continue as if a lead weight were attached to his tongue, and as his voice faded, so did our laughter. I huddled deeper in my blanket, cursing my foolish imagining that I might be able to help anyone avoid horror. I hadn't even been able to keep my own child alive. D'Natheil took up his listening posture again. He watched the fire, and Baglos watched him, gingerly touching his sleeve or his knee, whispering in his ear, but unable to distract him. Only Paulo remained serene. He fell asleep, curled up on the wood floor.

After perhaps half an hour more, the Prince startled me by leaping to his feet and yanking open the door. The moon was bright, casting silver-edged shadows over the meadow. The wind was gone along with the morbid chill. Evidently, the Seeking had passed.

The past two days had been exhausting. I had been awake since well before dawn, and I managed to keep my eyes open only long enough to tell the others that they should remain in the house. "This won't hurt my reputation," I said, when Baglos expressed concern at three men sleeping in the house with an unmarried woman. "I've none to worry about." It would be crowded, but only for a night. "Tomorrow we leave for Valleor. I know someone who may be able to help you." Then I curled up on my bed and knew nothing until dawn.

Paulo was off to Grenatte with the sunrise. As he proudly mounted Rowan's black horse, I loaded him up with jack and hearthbread. "Whatever the sheriff asks you, tell him only the truth. But carefully, Paulo. You've heard some strange talk here, and you must be cautious about what you repeat of it . . . lest someone get wrong ideas."

"I mostly hear more'n people think," he said, "but my head's too thick to keep hold of much." The boy gave me a sideways grin, and then he and the horse were racing down the trail to the south.

I set off for the village shortly after, trying to decide how to broach to Jaco the news that I was leaving Dunfarrie. He was limping about the shop and grumbling about the mess Lucy had left him. "Busybody," he said, before I'd even had time to wish him a good morning. "Don't have nothing better to do than try to set everything to rights. Junk shops aren't supposed to be set to rights. Who'll ever think they've found a treasure if it's all laid out in front of them like I've looked at it careful? She even cleaned the window. Fool woman. If I wanted more light in here, I'd of lit me a lantern. Blasted leg is seized up good this time or I'd be up there smoking up the glass again." He pointed at the clean window with his walking stick.

"Jaco, stop this. Listen to me. Did you see anything strange on the way down last night?"

He wouldn't stop fussing about. "Nope." He limped slowly to the back room and returned with a roll of chain.

"The shadow came again after you left. Like we saw on the ridge, only worse. Closer. The night went dark even though the moon was up. The wind was cold and smelled like death."

"I saw nothing like that. It was a fine night. I walked down, sat and smoked a pipe for a while, stopped in at the

Wild Heron. It's your imagination all roused up by these two strangers. I've a hard time even remembering what it was like that day on the ridge. The more I think on it, the more I believe all this magical business is just foolery, and we really didn't see nothing at all. This Aeren—or whatever his name—is addled from his fever. And there must've been a crack in the rock." He dumped a barrel of neatly folded clothes on the floor, kicked them into a muddle, and then stuffed them back in the barrel.

"No. It was real then, and it was real last night. We stayed in the house as Baglos said, and he told us stories to take our minds away from it. He says these Zhid feed on fear."

"Listen to your foolish talk. You must be rid of those two, Seri. Send them away." He unstacked a nest of iron pots. Into one he threw some bits of rope. Into another he dumped a wadded cloak, three spoons, and a battered tin of tea.

"Exactly so. I'm taking them to see a man I know in Yurevan. Jaco, you—"

"Taking them? Yourself?" For the first time I seemed to get Jaco's attention. His head shot up from his puttering. "Never heard anything so foolish. Why would you do that? Who is this man?"

"Someone who might be able to help unlock D'Natheil's confusion."

"You need to tell me . . . who is it? What's his name?" His brow was creased, his face red. "So's I can find you if need be. Maybe I ought to go with you. Yes, that's what I must—"

"His name is Ferrante, a professor at the University who knows about the J'Ettanne. He used to live just outside of Yurevan. I don't even know if he's alive."

Only after I so stupidly blurted everything out did I think what a predicament I was leaving Jaco in. "Listen, I know the sheriff is your friend, but you mustn't tell him any of this. Rowan fought at Avonar. Leiran soldiers slaughtered everyone in the city just because some of the citizens were sorcerers. They burned the sorcerers and their families and friends. Even their children, Jaco. Rowan helped them burn the J'Ettanni children."

Jacopo stopped his work and pulled out his pipe. His fingers were shaking as he worked to fill it, spilling the fragrant tobacco all over the floor until he threw pipe and bag down in annoyance, and sank onto one of his wooden stools, his back to me. "No. I won't say aught to him. I've been thinking you're right. It's not such a good idea to bring in Graeme. He's still got to take you to Montevial in the autumn, and I don't know he could lie to the king."

Though he had finally yielded to my opinion, I was astounded. Jacopo had been after me for ten years to trust Graeme Rowan. He must be truly afraid. I laid a hand on his hunched shoulder, but he didn't turn around. Perhaps he was weeping or embarrassed to show his fear. "Autumn is months away, Jaco. You mustn't worry so much. This mystery has got my blood running again. That can't be a bad thing, no matter what comes of it."

"Give up this sorcery business, girl. It's vile. Wicked." His plea was a plaintive chant such as a child might use to ward off evil spirits. "Send this prince away. He'll be the death of you."

"I detest D'Natheil," I said to Jacopo's back. "He's a bully and a brute, and I can't get rid of him soon enough. But I won't give him over to Evard or Darzid or the sheriffs of Leire. And that means I have to go with him. He and Baglos would be lost or arrested within a day, and Ferrante won't trust messages—not in this matter." And now for the awkward part. "I do need your help, Jaco. I've got to have two of Emil Gasso's horses."

"The horses"—Jacopo scratched his head slowly with his wide fingers—"yes, I'll get you the horses. A loan, mind! But you'll have to wait a day, as I can't deal with Gasso until tomorrow. Too much to do here; boat due within the hour." He glanced toward me, and then stood up and went to work again, sticking his head deep in a barrel of rusty tools and tossing one after another onto the floor. "I'll bring you the horses tomorrow midday. It'll do you good to rest up before traveling so far."

To wait another day was a dreadful risk, but I couldn't press Jacopo's generosity any further. "You're a good friend, Jaco. We'll meet you tomorrow at the spring on the ridge. We can't be at the cottage when Rowan returns." I waited for him to answer, but he only grunted and dropped an old pump handle on the floor. "Tomorrow then."

I had to pass Emil Gasso's stable on the way out of town, and on a whim decided to stop in. Gasso was a small-time horse breeder who had been hit hard by the constant levies for the Isker war. When I told him that Jaco would buy his horses and tack for a reasonable price, he was so delighted that he said I could take the horses with me. He would trust Jacopo for the money. I couldn't believe my good luck.

One of the horses was a huge chestnut with powerful legs and fire in its eye. The other was a smaller roan who nuzzled my hands and my pockets. "I think we'll let D'Natheil ride your friend, and you'll stay with me," I said to the roan. I considered going back to tell Jacopo about Gasso's generosity, but the morning was escaping. So I started up the trail to the cottage, riding the sweet-tempered roan and leading the chestnut.

CHAPTER 16

Less than an hour after my return from the village, I led D'Natheil and Baglos onto an obscure track that led over the ridge and down into the deep forest. D'Natheil rode as I knew he would, as if he'd been born in the saddle, a primitive exuberance in the man matching that of the fire-eyed chestnut. As for me, what I had told Jacopo was the truth. My blood raced as it had not in ten years, and I spent a great deal of the day marveling at what a short time it had been since Midsummer's Day, when I'd believed I would never feel anything again.

By early afternoon we came to the crossroads at Fensbridge. At Fensbridge market Baglos traded an unmarked coin of silver for boots and sword for D'Natheil, the latter old-fashioned and dull, but decently made. The young man hefted the weapon and grunted in satisfaction, if not pleasure.

From Fensbridge you could cross the river and travel the main road south back to Dunfarrie and Grenatte or ride north to Montevial, as Rowan and I did every fall, or you could take one of several roads west into the foothills of the Dorian Wall. Straight west would lead to the high, rugged country at the base of the mountains. Our northwest route would take us through the forested, rolling borderlands all the way to the Valleor highroad, a well-traveled way across the border. Those who wished to avoid border checkpoints could leave the highroad and find innumerable secondary paths into Valleor. Karon had often used them on his private journeys, and such was my intent.

By nightfall the morning's excitement had long dissipated. I was saddle-weary, and a day's contemplation had convinced me that my plan had more holes than a moth-eaten cloak. I had no assurance that Ferrante was even alive, much less residing in the same ivy-covered country house where Martin had first met Karon. And I had only the most faint supposition, entirely unsupported, that Ferrante knew whether there had been more than one J'Ettanni survivor of the slaughter at Avonar. And yet, the history professor had been a close friend of Karon's father, the one person outside of Avonar that any of the sorcerers would go to for help. I hoped he would tell me what I needed to know without my having to recount Baglos's fragmented stories of Heirs and enchanted bridges.

We camped for the night in dense forest. The air was humid and still, smelling of old leaves and moldy earth. We would see rain before morning. D'Natheil worked at sharpening and polishing the battered sword. After some rapid speech and hand gestures from Baglos, the Prince began to run two fingers over the weapon slowly, touching every part of the dully glowing surface. I believed enchantment flowed from his touch.

Watching the Prince intently, the Dulcé retreated to the log where I sat by the fire. I leaned toward him and whispered, "What's he doing?"

Baglos jumped, as if he had forgotten I was there. "Oh, I told him—It's just—to keep its edge and strengthen it . . . to enable it to serve him, a Dar'Nethi warrior can give a weapon his blessing. He has lived his whole life with swords," he said softly, "and wielded them as a man when he was scarce taller than the weapon. But never before has he managed to do this. It was said that he would try too hard, get angry, and stop before he could get the rhythm of it. Now . . . I'm not sure he understands what he does." After a while, Baglos sighed and set about cleaning up the supper things and laying out D'Natheil's blanket.

The night passed undisturbed for the most part. In the middling hours of the night, I woke from dreams of suffocation to an unsettling scent of cold ash. But after an hour of anxious watching, I was convinced that it was only the result of our own fire being doused by the onset of the rain. We were well away from Dunfarrie and safe under the trees.

Over the next few days we traveled into the cooler hill country that bordered Valleor. As we rode through thick forests of dripping pines and birches, and between rocks covered with thick green moss, a constant drizzle seeped through the collars of our cloaks and the seams of our boots, leaving us as wet and miserable as if we'd been caught in a deluge. Baglos pestered me with questions: about the Four Realms, about the forest, about politics and trade, clothing and geography, weather and cooking and growing vegetables. Everything was which and where and how and why, why, why. Half a day of this and I was ready to scream. When I asked, "Could we not speak of something less trivial?" he began asking me about Karon and the life of the J'Ettanne. For example, was not it a sore trial for a Dar'Nethi to be wed to a mundane?

"My husband and my life are my private business, Baglos. Do you understand the word *private*?" I had given Baglos and D'Natheil my sustenance, my peace, such as it was, and my safety. They would get no more from me.

In deference to my ill humor, Baglos shifted his attention to D'Natheil and spent the afternoon speaking exclusively in his own language. I rode behind them, pronouncing my relief at being left alone. But two hours of unintelligible monologue did nothing to improve my irritation. When I asked the Dulcé what he was telling D'Natheil, he said that he was describing royal Avonar, its people, and things he knew of D'Natheil's childhood, hoping to prod his young master's memory. I hinted that I could use such information as well. But the Dulcé found the constant translation too awkward to keep up, so I was abandoned once again to my own thoughts. Annoying. As seemed to be my experience of late, what I asked for was not necessarily what I wanted.

On the next day, when the whole sequence repeated itself, I asked Baglos if he would teach me something of the Dar'Nethi tongue. To my satisfaction I picked up a few words quite readily. As I demonstrated the first results of my lessons, D'Natheil seemed pleased and motioned insistently to Baglos to teach me more.

When we camped that night, D'Natheil went through his martial exercises again, but this time with his sword. I had grown up surrounded by soldiers, but never had I seen anyone move with such grace or such ferocious intensity. He would make even Tomas look like a newly vested squire.

Near midday on the fifth day of our journey we came to a good-sized town called Glyenna. It was market day, a drab, colorless affair, where the animals were sickly and the wares of the poorest and most utilitarian kind. The sour-faced crowds milled about the poor display as if they had been sentenced to attend as punishment for the sin of cheerfulness. We planned to stay only long enough to fill waterskins and buy food, though Baglos had shown himself an incessant conversationalist at every stop and seemed to enjoy nothing more than coaxing information about anything and everything from anyone he could get to speak to him. But as I paid a peasant woman for our supplies, I caught a glimpse of a sandy-haired horseman in vehement discourse with a man wearing the colorful badge of a local constable. Rowan! The still, heavy morning suddenly closed in. I backed away, turned, and ran.

D'Natheil had stopped to gawk at a cockfight, and when I touched his sleeve, he growled and slapped my hand away,

craning his neck to see better. As always, Baglos was gab-
bling with the raucous onlookers about why and how they
watched such things and what kinds of fowl were best to
use and all manner of useless information. Despite my
whispered warning, I had to drag the reluctant pair away
from the bloody, vulgar spectacle, watching for the sheriff
as I led them through the crowd.

We were almost to the edge of the marketplace when a
disturbance broke out just behind me. I looked over my
shoulder, and, to my dismay, D'Natheil was sitting atop a
filthy, ragged man. He had the man's head dragged backward into an impossible angle and his dagger poised at
the man's bared throat. Two burly townsmen hung on to
D'Natheil's arm, a temporary reprieve for the squirming,
whimpering victim. Baglos was babbling at the Prince and
trying to pull him away.

"It's just Hekko, the beggar," shouted an old woman.
"Meant no harm. Didn't take nothing."

A tradesman in a leather apron bawled for someone to
bring the constable, as Hekko had been trying to steal the
stranger's silver dagger. More townspeople were gathering
by the moment.

With a ferocious bellow, a powerful wrench of his shoulders, and a backhand sweep, D'Natheil dislodged his restraints, sending the two men and Baglos sprawling. His
knife flashed toward the beggar's throat.

"No!" I yelled, lunging toward him and grabbing his
knife arm with both of my hands. "By the stars, you must
not." Though I had not the least faith that he could hear
my angry remonstrance over the uproar, and my physical
strength was surely no more threat than that of a child, the
mad fire in D'Natheil's eyes faded instantly into bewilder-
ment. He loosened his grip on the moaning beggar and
allowed Baglos and me to drag him away.

"He's been to the war," I said to the grumbling men
pressing close as I shoved the Prince toward our horses.
"It's left him high-strung . . . touchy . . . you understand."
I jerked my head at Baglos, who pulled out a copper and
tossed it to the bruised and shaken beggar. While the old
woman continued her screeching, and two ragged boys in-
expertly tried to pick my pockets, the rest of the onlookers

nodded and shrugged and murmured about the war. By the time we were mounted, the crowd had begun to disperse.

"Wait! Stop those three!" Over my shoulder I glimpsed Graeme Rowan struggling to get to us through the milling throng.

"Go!" I screamed, and we kicked our horses to life, leaving the bewildered citizens gaping.

We raced westward along the heavily wooded road, not slowing until the night was so dark we dared not risk the horses. We had left Glyenna a considerable distance behind, but I insisted that we walk another half a league into the thick trees before stopping. What a spectacle we had made of ourselves! My fury at D'Natheil's folly had not cooled by the time we made camp.

"You will tell him exactly what I say," I commanded Baglos as we unsaddled our horses in a high, rocky grotto. "Some things other than sorcery are frowned upon in Leire, at least among people of rational mind. To attack a beggar is the act of a coward, and to call attention to yourself in such a way is utterly stupid. Our lives are at risk because of your childishness. You will control yourself if you want any more help from me. Do you understand?"

D'Natheil, his face blazing, turned his back on me.

Baglos tried to smooth it over. "Madam, you must understand that D'Natheil has been trained as a warrior since he could walk. He is considered to be one of the finest—"

"That's no excuse." Annoying little twit. I wanted to strangle him and his master both. "It's quite possible to control one's reactions, no matter how finely honed. Warriors should be somewhat larger of mind than animals. Tell him that, too. Exactly as I said it."

Baglos paled, but did as I asked, speaking softly to his master's rigid back. The silence was long and awkward as we made our camp. D'Natheil threw his pack to the ground and kicked away the rocks that lay where he planned to make his bed. He kept to himself for the rest of the night.

With Rowan so close on our trail, I made sure we were on the road early and took extra care that we were not observed by any other travelers. Whenever I sought information about roads, I asked about Vanesta or Prydina, re-

lying on my own geography skills to set us right and hoping
that the sheriff would follow the wrong path. I considered
taking the wrong direction for a while, and then looping
around in hopes of throwing off pursuit, but I dared not
delay. If Rowan was in company with the sorcerer Zhid,
they might be able to follow us anywhere.

The journey would have been dismal even without the
close pursuit and the rainy weather. The border villages
had suffered the most in the years of the Vallorean War,
and in few of the rotting settlements that were still occupied were there any men at all between the ages of thirty
and sixty. Strangers, especially sturdy young men of military
age, were regarded with scarcely controlled hostility, and
only grudgingly were we allowed to avail ourselves of
food supplies.

As stiffness and saddle sores took their toll alongside the
discomforts of constant rain, cold food, and sleeping on
hard ground, I thought regretfully of my childhood when
Papa would take Tomas and me on three-day riding excur-
sions to see the site of his grandfather's victory over Vallorean raiders or the hill where legend said that Annadis spent
his vigil night before being named Arot's successor. Twelve
hours a day in the saddle had seemed life's ultimate delight.
My brother and I would sleep with the horses and dogs
while Papa's soldiers cooked, told stories, and stood watch
for wolves. Rain just made our treks more adventurous.
What dreary tricks fate can play on us.

After Glyenna, D'Natheil refused to engage in any conversation. He rode, he ate, and he brooded, and when we
stopped at night, he practiced his swordwork and took his
share of the watch. The Dulcé was anxious to pursue his
teaching further but had learned not to press. His master's
anger was quick and heavy, though, in truth, D'Natheil's
withdrawal seemed to restrain his intemperate hand along
with everything else. After a few days, Baglos might have
welcomed a blow just as evidence D'Natheil was listening
to him at all.

"Was D'Natheil always so changeable?" I asked Baglos
one night when the Prince had disappeared yet again as
soon as he had eaten his share of the night's meager fare.
"On one day I'm sure he's going to put a knife in me as I

sleep. The next, I could be the muck on his horse's shoe for all he cares. And then . . . well, before I yelled at him . . . he would surprise me with one of those smiles, and I'd think he was going to ask me to dance."

Baglos was scraping the last of the boiled turnip from the bottom of our cooking pot. "In addition to physical strength, intelligence, and extraordinary power, the family of D'Arnath has always been blessed with those amiable qualities which allow men to lead others in difficult times. In the matter of aggressive temper"—he glanced over his shoulder at the empty clearing—"they have been variously gifted . . . or afflicted as one might view it. As you see, D'Natheil was born with a full measure. When he was eleven, D'Natheil had a swordmaster who was quite serious about his task and rigorous in his discipline. D'Natheil scorned him, complaining that his skills were inferior, and grew increasingly impatient that no better master was brought in. One day the master was found dead in the sparring arena from a sword wound in his belly. D'Natheil claimed it was an accident in their practice, simple proof of his contention that the man was unfit to be his tutor. No one witnessed the incident, and nothing more was said. But I've heard the man was hamstrung."

On the afternoon of the seventh day we dropped down into the high plains of eastern Valleor. Southward, to our left, soared the peaks of the Dorian Wall, needle-sharp spires piercing the heavy clouds. To the far west a lesser range called the Vallorean Spine split Valleor down the middle, and before us and stretching far to our right lay the valley of the Uker River, endless vistas of gentle hills and lakes, dotted with the darker green of patchy forests, eventually rising into craggy highlands many leagues to the north. It was beautiful country, the fertile heart of gentle Valleor, on that day pooled with fogs and mists.

King Gevron had raped the fields of Valleor, stripping them bare to feed his armies and then slaughtering any who tried to work them. Now, anything grown in the Uker valley must be shipped instantly to Leire. Only then could it be purchased, properly taxed and at highly elevated prices, for distribution in the subjugated land. The starving

Valloreans had to watch as heavily laden grain wagons rolled past their villages, and never did they see even one-tenth of their land's bounty returned to them.

Three more days brought us to Yurevan, the oldest city in Valleor, and Ferrante's house, Verdillon, some half a league outside the city walls. The professor was the second son of a Vallorean count. Though unable to inherit the title or lands, he'd had a decent enough portion to escape the poverty of most University dons. As it turned out, his had been the luckier inheritance, for his brother the count had been hanged and the family's traditional holdings confiscated after Gevron's victory.

I managed to find the proper road, and my heart thumped a bit when I caught sight of the stone walls, thickly covered with vines of lush green. The gate was standing open when we arrived, and the grounds were as I remembered from my single visit long ago: sprawling cherry orchards, roses of a hundred varieties, spreading carpets of green grass. The gravel carriage road wound through the lovely parkland to a classic beauty of a country house.

The day was inordinately quiet, no sound of groom or gardener, dog or bird. Perhaps the heavy mist rolling in from the forest had deadened the noise on what should be a normally active day about the property. When we reached the flagstone courtyard before the front door, I dismounted and rang the bell. Ferrante had to be there. To have come so far to find only strangers would be too cruel.

D'Natheil stepped past me and pushed on the massive doors. They swung open easily. Wariness and foreboding shadowed his face, quieting my protest. The foyer was just as I remembered: highly polished oak floor, graceful, curving staircase, the display case still holding Ferrante's greatest treasure, a thousand-year-old brass bowl dug up from the tombs at Doria. The air smelled of the cut roses that stood in every nook and the cleaning oil used on the dark mahogany tables.

"Hello!" My greeting seemed muted by the richly colored tapestries hung on the dark wood paneling. No lamps were lit to chase away the gloom of the afternoon. Bustling servants should have been taking our sodden cloaks and wiping our damp footprints off the fine floor, but no one came.

"Professor Ferrante? Is anyone here?"

Baglos whispered anxiously, "Perhaps we should go, woman. Though your rank would permit it, we do not look like we belong here, coming in the front door."

Something was certainly amiss. D'Natheil could sense it, too. I started up the stairs toward Ferrante's study on the second floor. "Hello," I called again. "Professor?"

When we reached the upper gallery, D'Natheil pointed inquiringly at a pair of satiny walnut doors. I nodded. Quietly and carefully, the young man pushed open the door and led the three of us into the professor's study.

Tall, paned windows welcomed the gray afternoon into the book-lined room, revealing the comfortable furnishings of thick rugs, brass lamps, and deep chairs. Professor Ferrante sat at his wide desk, but the brilliant, gentlemanly scholar would never again answer anyone's questions. The front of his gray morning gown was drenched in blood, and his eyes gazed out at us, fixed in a horrified stare.

My skin crept. "We need to leave," I said.

"I don't think so," said a man's voice from behind me. I whirled about to see Baglos's eyes bulging. A long, thin arm was wrapped about the Dulcé's throat, and the point of a knife was poised at his belly. The hand that held the knife was shaking, but there was no mistaking its intent. The owner of the arm and the voice was obscured by the shadows behind the door. "Have you come back to review your handiwork? Pull down your hoods. Let me see those who would so foully murder a man of peace and intellect in his own home." Anger and grief left the man's voice hoarse. "Do it now—before I skewer this one!"

As I lowered the sodden hood of my cloak, ready to proclaim our innocence, I heard a sharp intake of breath. "Seri!" Baglos stumbled to the side, the knife fell to the carpet, and from the shadows stepped a bespectacled man, thin and slightly stooped, gray at the temples with creases at the eyes from too many years reading in dim light. A graying goatee lengthened his narrow face, causing a moment's uncertainty before I recognized him. Then a small eternity of disbelief passed before I could convince my lips to say his name. "Tennice!"

In movements so swift one could see only the result,

D'Natheil's sword was drawn and touching Tennice's belly, pressing him to the wall.

"D'Natheil, no!" I cried. "Baglos, tell him no. This is my friend . . . a friend who's come back from the dead."

Baglos spoke quietly and insistently to D'Natheil. After a long moment, the cold-eyed young man released Tennice, but he did not sheathe his weapon.

"Is it really you, Seri?" Once it appeared that he was not going to be spitted on D'Natheil's weapon, the ghost lowered his hands and touched my cheek with his cold, but quite substantial fingers.

"He heard you die," I whispered. "They made him listen. All of you were dead." Now I was shaking. Dead was dead.

"And so I was or so close as to be thought so. I can tell you what happened and must hear the same from you, but first"—he turned to the grisly scene in the library and ran his fingers through his thin hair—"I've got to take care of Ferrante."

"What happened here?"

"I've been in Vanesta for several days, searching for a book for Ferrante. An hour ago I rode in and passed four strangers on the service road behind the house. I thought nothing of it. Students are in and out all the time. But no servants were about, no grooms in the stable, and then I came up and found . . . this. When I heard your call, I thought you must be students or tradesmen. But when I stepped out and spied you coming up the stairs, I thought the murderers had come back. Who would do this to him? They didn't even steal anything!"

This murder left me with a horrid, creeping sickness . . . a sensation well beyond that caused by the vile deed itself. I glanced at Baglos and D'Natheil, then down at my own soggy cloak, and my revulsion took on more substance. "What made you believe we were the murderers?"

"Your long cloaks, I suppose, and the colors. Two of those I saw riding away wore gray, one of them black. Like you, they had their hoods up, so I couldn't see—"

Baglos caught the connection. "Great Vasrin, the Zhid! It's a trap. We must be out of here!" He was already out of the library door, dragging D'Natheil like a fierce sheepdog, bullying his charge away from the wolf's lair.

"What's he saying?" said a bewildered Tennice.

"We've no time to explain. We must go, and you must come with us."

"I can't leave him this way. I have to notify someone . . . the University . . . his friends."

I grabbed his arm and pulled him toward the door. "Please, Tennice. You mustn't be here if the killers return. You can't do Ferrante any good."

Reluctantly, my friend allowed me to drag him down the stairs. D'Natheil listened carefully at the front door, then motioned us to stay back. Watchers, he gestured. Our horses nickered restlessly. A quick exchange of words and gestures between Baglos and D'Natheil, and the Dulcé announced that D'Natheil would fetch the horses and take them around the back. The rest of us should meet him . . . where?

"Tennice, does the blacksmith's shed still link the kitchen garden and the stable?" I asked. He confirmed it. "Baglos, tell D'Natheil that the stable is just past the carriage house east of the kitchen garden. We'll meet him there. And tell him he can fight today."

Baglos translated, and D'Natheil nodded. He put his hands up to raise his hood, and, for the first time in a fortnight, he smiled, the piercing brilliance of it reflected in his marvelous eyes. For that single moment, my fear vanished, and all the annoyance of the journey was forgotten. Then he disappeared into the back of the house.

From a window that opened onto the courtyard, we watched D'Natheil slog slowly around the corner of the house from the direction of the stables. He looked shorter, bent in the back, and had acquired a slight limp. He untethered our horses and led them back toward the corner of the house, as if he were taking them to the stable to stay the night. No hurry. No hesitation. Melting into the scene every bit as much as the paving stones or the dead leaves heaped in the corners of the courtyard. It was difficult to focus on him. One's eyes kept slipping off into the background.

"Who is he?" whispered Tennice. "One would almost think . . ."

I thought I glimpsed movement in the shrubbery beyond

the courtyard, but the harder I stared, the less I saw, and finally I forced myself to look away. "I'll tell you about him once we're safe. Now it's our turn."

Tennice threw on his cloak and led us through the dark, silent passageways and the deserted kitchen into the kitchen garden. We crept through the muddy garden, hugging the high stone wall, and slipped through an iron gate that led to the blacksmith's shed. The dark enclosure smelled of coal and ashes and cold dirt floor. Carefully, Tennice cracked the wooden door that opened onto the stableyard, and we peered out. Far across the yard the stooped figure shambled toward us, leading our horses. Tennice whispered that he would meet us in the stableyard, and then he vanished into the adjoining stable. I was beginning to think our elaborate precautions foolish when a gray-robed figure stepped out of the rainy gloom behind D'Natheil.

"You! You with the horses. Who are you? All the servants were dismissed today." D'Natheil didn't stop, but he didn't hurry either. Every sense was screaming at me to run out of the shed and get away. But D'Natheil was still too far away.

"You! Come here!" The voice was cold, like jaws of ice gnawing at the heart.

D'Natheil paused and looked around as if he had all the time until world's end. He waved at the hooded figure and continued on his way to the stable, limping slowly. When the Prince was some twenty paces from the stable, the gray-robed man started running. I needed no signal. I thumped Baglos on the shoulder, and we burst from the shed. D'Natheil snatched me off my feet and catapulted me into the saddle, then did the same for the Dulcé. The man in gray attacked D'Natheil before the Prince could mount his own steed, but D'Natheil raised his arm and backhanded him. The gray-robed man staggered backwards. Two rough-looking men in leather jerkins appeared from the front of the house and ran toward us, swords drawn. D'Natheil drew his own sword and ran one of them through in a single motion. The second, he upended with a blow so hard, the man's jaw cracked like dry wood. Two more men leaped out of the bushes.

As D'Natheil threw himself onto the chestnut, shouts rang out from several directions. Tennice shot from the stable astride a fine-boned bay, crying, "This way!" We raced down the carriage road, following him through the wet fields and gardens.

At least three horsemen gave chase. Whisperings of horror teased at my back: *might as well stop now . . . the race is over . . . you'll never elude them. . . .* Tennice moaned and pulled up on his reins, and Baglos, too, began to slow, but D'Natheil roared and slashed at our horses, and the four of us thundered down the road and through the back gate of Verdillon. Beyond the park boundaries Tennice led us off the road and into the thicker trees, and more quickly than we could have hoped, our pursuers and their creeping horrors had vanished. We pushed on, not daring to stop too soon, scarcely able to see through the rain and the failing light. Raindrops stung our faces and soaked our clothes.

At last Tennice pulled up somewhere deep in the forest. He gave me a hand down from the lathered roan and kicked open the door of a squat hut made of poorly joined logs. "We lost them, I think," he said, urging me through the doorway. "No one knows about this place."

Baglos tethered the horses on the lee side of the hut. While Tennice and I carried our packs inside, the Dulcé and the Prince tended the beasts, rubbing them down with a blanket Tennice had used for a saddle. Before long, Baglos joined us in the hut.

Shivering, the Dulcé and I pulled out blankets and what little we had that was dry, sharing with Tennice. After a brief glance inside, D'Natheil remained standing in the doorway, staring out into the rain, one hand peeling strips of soft wood from the rotted facing. When Baglos offered him a plain silver flask pulled from the leather bag he always carried over his shoulder, he shoved the Dulcé away and stepped outside, striding across the soggy clearing to a low brick wall, part of the abandoned charcoal oven. He perched sideways on the wall, drew up his knees, and rested his head on them, letting the cold rain pour over his head and back.

For myself, I appreciated Baglos's offering. The potent, sweet wine left a trail of fire down my throat.

Tennice broke the tired silence. "And now can someone explain all this to me?"

"I can try," I said. "If you've no wish to be . . . involved . . . I couldn't blame you."

"I've just left my friend and employer wallowing in his own blood, and I've been pursued through the forest by those who make me feel like someone else is living in my skin. And in the midst of it all appears a woman I believed ten years dead, who happens to be in the company of two most unusual strangers. Not likely I can just leave it."

"The ones who murdered Ferrante are called Zhid," I said, as I tried to get my thin, damp blanket to make a double layer around my cold feet. "They, as well as my two friends here, come from . . . someplace else. I'm not sure where. Clearly you've guessed some of this as you watched D'Natheil—that surly one who prefers the rain to our company. I seem to have gotten myself mixed up with sorcerers again."

"I knew it. . . ."

I told him how D'Natheil had come to me, and the evidence that led me to believe that it was not by chance. ". . . and so, even though for the past ten years I believed myself as dead as the rest of you, I have now been selected, coerced, or summoned to play nursemaid to a mute, half-wild princeling who can scarcely remember his own name. And this other one—the good Baglos—says he's been appointed as D'Natheil's 'Guide,' but he knows nothing of where he is to guide him, and cannot tell me where their home lies, and in fact knows very little unless his master bids him. And somehow D'Natheil must remember how he is supposed to go about saving the world."

"This makes no sense."

"Absolutely correct. I'll confess that it's more than a little unnerving to listen to these two and attempt to find some logical conclusion to it."

Even Tennice's puzzled expression could not persuade me to voice the absurd speculation that had been running around the back of my head for the past few days. Where had D'Natheil and Baglos come from? From a land called Gondai that appeared on no map I had ever seen in my father's vast collection of maps, nine tenths of it laid waste embroiled in a war that had lasted a thousand years. From an Avonar that was not Karon's Avonar, but far older, a city of sorcerers. Across an enchanted bridge that connected Gondai to a land with no sorcery, a land that the people of D'Natheil's Avonar considered exile. We in the Four Realms were indeed turned inward, giving scant attention to the vast reaches of the world beyond our borders. But how could such places exist and our people not know of them? Enchantment . . . sorcery . . . another place . . .

Tennice took a long pull at one of our wineskins. "Who are these Zhid? And what does Ferrante have to do with any of this?"

"From what I understand, the Zhid are the ancient enemies of D'Natheil's people . . . Karon's people. And Ferrante—" I puzzled over it again, the intricacy of the puzzle distracting me from my unnerving ideas. "Baglos claims he is unable to explain more than I've already told you, and that D'Natheil is the one who must explain their mission. And he says that D'Natheil's condition—his inability to speak and his loss of memory—is certainly new. And so I decided that the only hope to discover what's locked inside D'Natheil's head is to find someone to read what's there in the way Karon could."

"But Ferrante was no sorcerer."

"Another of the J'Ettanne could do it."

With every justification, Tennice stared at me as if I'd gone berserk. "They're all dead, Seri."

"Are they? When Karon first went to the University, his father told him that in time of trouble he should go to Ferrante, that Ferrante was the only person outside their community who could be trusted implicitly, that he was sworn by the most sacred of oaths never to reveal a J'Ettanne to anyone. Ever. In that last autumn before he was arrested, Karon began to wonder if perhaps the professor was *unable* to tell him the truth, that Ferrante took his oath so seriously that he wouldn't even reveal one J'Ettanne to another. He never had the opportunity to confront Ferrante with his theory."

Tennice's eyes had grown wide as I said this, and when I paused, he spoke in quiet excitement. "The list of those who are left . . ."

"What?"

"I can't believe it. You're right. Karon was right. It's so obvious now." His eyes glittered behind his spectacles. "Ferrante had records of all the students he ever taught over the years. Hundreds of them. Under each name he would list the topics they had covered, thesis titles, research projects, and the like. He was forever asking me to find out who had done the work on the Battle of Horn's Cavern or written a discourse on the Honneck Invasion. On one of my delving expeditions, I came across three instances of Karon's name. Two entries were quite typical, one from his student years when he first came to Yurevan, the other from his second sojourn, when he was studying archaeology and Martin met him there. But the third entry had nothing beside it but a mark. Several other names were on that list, most with the same mark beside. I asked Ferrante about those entries, and he said only that it was 'the list of those who are left.' Stupid me, I never understood. I'll wager frogs to elephants, they were J'Ettanne. There's your answer. . . ."

"But we can't risk going back for it." The disappointment was crushing. To be so close . . .

Tennice bumped my chin with his bony knuckle. "Have you forgotten so much? Though I never had Karon's intelligence, Martin's wisdom, or Julia's wit, I possessed one skill that was out of the ordinary. These cursed eyes don't see so well as they did, but the head to which they're attached is the same."

"Your memory!"

"Four names were still unmarked: Lazari, Bruno, Kellea, Celine."

"And was there any clue as to where these people might be found?"

"Not in the book. Bruno, I never ran across again, nor Celine. But until a year ago, someone named Lazari wrote often from Kallamat. And Kellea"—he looked as though he might burst. "Well, there's an herb shop near the University—I'm not sure exactly where. But once a year, Ferrante had a little box of a rare herb sent to Verdillon to ease his old cook's gout. He said he could get it nowhere else, but that Kellea had a gift for finding things."

"She's here in Yurevan!" I jumped to my feet, unable to

contain my excitement though cold reason told me we could not set out right away. Even if the shop was easily found, and the woman still there, we dared not leave the forest. Night was falling. The Zhid would be seeking. Even D'Natheil had come indoors at last, settling in a corner, where he was cleaning his knife and his sword with his sodden shirt. "I wonder if this house ever held people who cared for each other in a way that would hold back the Zhid?" I said.

"I don't know about all those who've lived here," said Tennice. "But a family stayed here once. This is where Karon healed the family of plague, and where Martin watched from that window and saw what he did."

"Here?" I pushed the shutter wide open and leaned on the damp sill of the crudely cut window. Gazing into the darkening forest, I heard Martin tell once more of the strange and poignant sight that met his eyes as he watched the young sorcerer work his magic on the dying family. Karon had been here in this room, worked his magic, given of himself. I looked afresh at the crude walls, the dirt floor, the cold firepit, the timber roof, as if somewhere in their grime and splinters might be scribed a reflection of the past, one glimpse . . . oh gods, one glimpse of his face. Such a dagger of grief pierced my breast at that moment that I almost cried out with it.

"He stayed with me, you know. In my head, through it all." Tennice, sitting on the dirt floor and leaning tiredly against the wall, twirled his spectacles in his thin hands. D'Natheil watched us from his corner, where Baglos sat beside him, listening to our talk and murmuring into the Prince's ear. "I would have lost my mind otherwise. I held onto him like one drowning, though what they did to me was nothing to what they'd done to him. After everything else they decided to finish me off with a sword. I suppose I was boring next to Martin and Julia. I told them everything I knew in the first day, said everything they wanted me to say, and signed whatever they wanted me to sign soon after. At the last I lost consciousness, believing and hoping I'd never wake again."

He drew up his knees and rested his long arms on them. "There was a guard—he never told me his name. You know how you could never go anywhere without meeting someone who'd been one of Tanager's 'bully comrades.' That held true even in the foul pits of our foul king. Instead of hauling us out for the gravediggers, this man carried the two of us to an out-of-the-way cell. He cared for us as best he could and sent word to Father—"

"Tanager! Is he—?"

Tennice shook his head. "It must have taken a great deal to break him. I believe he was dead already. For certain he died long before Father's men could retrieve us. I, for whatever reason the mad gods dreamt up, did not."

"That's why your father refused to claim your bodies." For all these years I had cursed the old baron for abandoning his dead sons.

"The guard would have had to produce two corpses, and he had only one. It was weeks before I knew anything. Father told me of Karon's death, and he tried to find out what became of you. Oh, damnation, Seri, we thought you were dead. Father was told that both you and the child were 'taken care of.' When I recovered, I came here and never looked back. Ferrante heard that my brother Evan was killed two years ago in the war, so Father is left alone now. I daren't write him, though. To protect him, I must be dead, too."

"Is it your choice or his?"

"He believes it's his, and that's enough."

"Be sure, Tennice."

He glanced up, his face wrinkled into a rueful smile. "You sound like Karon.'Everyone must choose their own danger.' I hadn't thought of it so . . . the Way of the J'Ettanne."

My skin grew cold. What was I thinking to speak such drivel? "This has nothing to do with the Way of the J'Ettanne." The Way of the J'Ettanne brought only death. Wasted, useless death. There was no "following life," no greater good, and, for those of us left behind, no reprieve from the cost of such wretched, foolish idealism.

As Baglos shared out bread and apples, I told Tennice of Anne and Jonah and my life in the past ten years. The story didn't take long. There wasn't much else to say. We were all exhausted.

Frightful dreams plagued me that night. Each time I

woke, I saw D'Natheil standing in the doorway of the hut, his unshaven face hard and fierce, lit by the traveling moon. I woke again when the sky was just beginning to lighten, and he was no longer there. He must have given in to sleep at last. But as I turned over, hoping to find a more comfortable position and wrest another hour of sleep before the day to come, I glimpsed him sitting in the shadows, his eyes fixed on me.

CHAPTER 17

Year 4 in the reign of King Evard

Evard's war was going badly. Only a month into the fourth year of his reign, his armies had been repulsed at the very gates of Kallamat and driven into the mountains. Even the weather seemed to side with the pious Keroteans, for a ferocious winter storm had assaulted the already decimated Leiran troops. Five thousand soldiers died of starvation when supply wagons foundered in chest-high snow. Five thousand more froze to death, the injured men abandoned by their comrades in fear of the bloodthirsty pursuit. The remnants of the Leiran army straggled into Montevial on the heels of winter, Evard and his household among them.

Baron Hesperid, a young noble who had lost his right arm in the spring campaign, publicly accused Evard of mishandling the war, of proceeding too fast and too far. He hinted that the king had promised his friends new leaseholds of Kerotean lands before taxes were due in the spring. Only intervention by the Council of Lords prevented Hesperid's execution for treason. Instead, Evard stripped him of his lands and title and banished him from Leire for thirty years.

"Lucky, I think," Martin said. "Luckier than the rest of

us who were less pointed in our criticism of this course of stupidity. I wouldn't want to be in the way when Evard decides who'll be the scapegoat for this mess." But, of course, he was. We all were. . . .

"Of course, it's the cursed sorcerers. Kerotea is ruled by barbarian priests. They claim to speak for this vile horse god or frog god, or whatever it is. . . . Come, Seri, you'd know. Your husband studies these barbarian things."

"Ilehu is half-man, half-wolf." *Stupid, ignorant woman.* I restrained my hand from knocking away the wineglass the countess was waving in my face.

"Just so," she said to the three other women who stood gawking at her idiocies. "The savages claim this Ilehu commands them to destroy any of their children born defective or weak. I've heard they eat the hearts of the dead babes, just as sorcerers do! It's a mercy King Evard survived their magics."

Yes, Karon had taught me about the Keroteans. They believed that their terrible custom was a mercy for those who had to survive in their harsh mountain kingdom. But Leirans had never understood such ways, and so every unusual behavior was wrapped in the mantle of the evil they'd been taught to abhor above all others—sorcery.

"I've heard—" The sparrow-like young baroness on my left was twitching, her thin fingers flitting over her mouth and chin. The black dots of her eyes darted about the crowded drawing room, and then she leaned forward, drawing the other women close. "I've heard they walk among us again," she whispered. "Sorcerers—"

"Excuse me," I said. "I think my husband is ready to leave. A lovely evening, Countess. Karon is thrilled with the addition of your artifacts to the antiquities collection."

"Well, I don't see how such a gentleman as your Karon can enjoy mucking about with such refuse, but I told Fenys that I wouldn't have them here any longer. What if there were spells on them? My dogs have been acting most strangely of late. . . ."

Within hours of Hesperid's banishment, rumors had begun flying that the Keroteans had orchestrated their victory by means of sorcery. In a matter of days one could not walk down a street without hearing some demagogue ranting that the Kerotean priests were devilish wizards. Survivors of the campaign swore that snow monsters had appeared in the Kerotean mountains to steal their supplies and mesmerize their comrades. Frost wraiths had lured Leirans into blind-ended valleys, and spells of paralysis had overwhelmed the soldiers to make them lie down in the snow until they died. Every misfortune of that winter battle was attributed to diabolical influence.

I was maddened with it. . . . and with Karon, who kept trying to ease my worry. "Come now, I look less like a Kerotean than does Evard himself, and, besides, I hate winter travel."

I didn't laugh.

"Come here"—he gathered me into his arms—"I *will* take care. I promise."

On one such occasion, as he tried to placate me with more empty assurances, I told him at last of killing the man at Threadinghall. "I would do it again to protect you," I said. "But now I can't see who's creeping up on you, and I'm going to go mad with it. How can you live this way? You need to take responsibility for yourself."

He was not angry at what I had done. Not revolted, as I'd feared for all these weeks. Shocked, yes; he had not seen the man fall. Grieved, yes, that I had done so ponderous a deed and felt I could not tell him, bearing the weight of it alone. But my accusation of irresponsibility cut deep. He stood beside the garden door, its panes garlanded with snow, his face as pale as the flakes still falling so softly. "I can't tell you how to live, Seri," he said after a long pause. "You are who you are, and I would not change you. Your love, your goodness, and your courage are the joy of my life, and this act tells me nothing about you that I have not known and treasured all these years. But you cannot ask me to make the same choices. My calling, my power, demand different things of me. Stars of night, do you think this is easy?"

I listened only to my own fear, not his. "Sometimes it's easier not to fight. To follow the rules, to let your ancestors make your decisions, to let terrible things happen and claim it is for the greater good."

"Sometimes fighting destroys the thing you're fighting for."

I hated this discussion. "Then either way I'll lose you, and I can't bear the thought of it." And then I was in his arms, and he was stroking my hair and promising again to take care. But nothing had changed.

Whether responding to my prompting or his own caution, Karon stayed close to home as the days grew shorter, venturing only to the antiquities workrooms. We no longer practiced mind-speaking. He said such things were better left for easier times.

After several Valloreans were arrested and executed for spying for the Kerotean sorcerers, Karon said he would neither work any sorcery nor speak of it again, not even to me. "Habits," he said, as he knelt by the hearth and burned his translation of the Writer's journal, along with my transcription and all our notes. "They're the key to safety. If your mouth is trained to say nothing of sorcery, then words cannot betray you. If your mind is trained to forget all you know of it, then you cannot inadvertently slip a reference into a discussion." He traced a smile on my face with his finger. "I've become too comfortable, relaxed my vigilance, but I can build the wall again. I just need to work at it, and so will you. No one need find out." When the hunger to use his power came on him, he walked and rode and exhausted himself with work, staying out of my way until he could suppress it.

I wanted to refuse any invitation into society, but Karon reminded me of what I already knew. Such blatant change, in one's habits would draw unwanted attention. We had no reason to think any suspicion should be directed Karon's way. But he would never have burned the work on the journal if he were not concerned. I wondered if perhaps we should consider leaving Montevial. Going away . . . somewhere.

Midwinter brought the usual round of Seille entertainments. In lengthy and elaborate temple services held to appease and flatter holy Jerrat, whose storms had so tested our troops, priests had reminded us of the first Long Night, when Arot lay sorely wounded. The gifts of music and food and human companionship had raised the god from his winter of despair and prepared him to resume his battle with the beasts of chaos at the coming of the new year. Thus, Evard commanded his courtiers to celebrate lavishly, reassuring the common folk that the Leiran spirit was not darkened by the unnatural deviltry of our enemies. And so, at night after night of entertainments, noblewomen dressed in elaborate finery and laughed in shrill gaiety at jokes devoid of humor. Men played the buffoon, drank too much, and spoke too loudly of the glories of war.

A fortnight before Long Night, Karon and I were invited to a musical entertainment at the home of Sir Geoffrey Larreo, the administrator who had engaged Karon to develop the antiquities collection. I saw no way to avoid the occasion. Evard was to make an appearance as a favor to Sir Geoffrey—or rather as flattery to Sir Geoffrey's relatives—and anyone with a court posting would be expected to attend.

Sir Geoffrey was a distant cousin of the late King Gevron, but had no landed titles of his own. He was a kind man, a bachelor much given to birdwatching and other gentle pursuits. Evard ridiculed him publicly and would have ignored him altogether if Sir Geoffrey were not regarded so fondly by Gevron's family.

"Would I had given Sir Geoffrey our regrets," said Karon as he waited for me at the bottom of the stairs that night.

I'd had a new gown made for the season, not to follow the frivolous fashion of society, but to accommodate my changing shape—not too noticeable as yet except to me. The gown was dark green silk cut low at the neck, falling loosely to the floor from a high waist. The narrow wedge of underskirt in front showed a darker green brocade. My hair was caught in a loose braid that fell halfway down my back, and my only other adornment was the gold locket engraved with a rose.

"Am I too awkward to be seen in public already? You'll want to avert your eyes in a few weeks more!"

He took my hand as I descended the last steps. "On the contrary. I'm only reluctant to share such loveliness with the rest of society."

"I wonder if you'll still say such charming things when

we pass two years married this month, or will flattery run its course as quickly as the time has done?"

"There is only truth between us." That, at·least, was one good thing that had come from our argument. The killing at Threadinghall had burdened me more than I had been willing to admit.

"Not only truth," I said, wrapping my arms about him. "Young Connor Martin Gervaise is rapidly taking up a most prominent position between us."

Karon threw back his head and laughed. "I shall begrudge him every moment!"

"You know, my love, you look quite fine yourself," I said, as Joubert announced the hired carriage, and Karon helped me with my cloak. He was dressed simply in a loose white shirt of the finest cambric, full-sleeved and buttoned high at the neck in the Vallorean fashion. No puffed satin breeches, fluted neck ruffs, or slashed brocade sleeves, as Evard's courtiers wore, but simple, well-fitted black breeches and black velvet doublet, embroidered in silver. His dark hair was pulled back from his face, setting off his deep-set eyes and high cheekbones. I loved it that he remained adamantly clean-shaven, defying Evard's fashion of close-trimmed beards and narrow mustaches.

Joubert opened the door, and Karon threw on his own cloak that buttoned high on one shoulder. "I care for nothing but that it please you, my lady." After a gallant, sweeping bow, he kissed my hand and led me into the winter darkness.

Sir Geoffrey often had musical evenings at his townhouse, inviting small groups of selected acquaintances to hear a singer, instrumentalist, or ensemble. He had a good ear, and it was a considerable benefit to an artist's reputation to be invited to play for him. Music and theatrical performances were a new fashion in Leire—Martin joked that it was all his doing—and few people knew quite how to judge talent for themselves. On that night carriage after carriage emptied its elegant occupants at Sir Geoffrey's front door.

"He must have invited half the court," I said, dreading the heat and the crowd.

"Everyone's heard the king is to be here."

"I wonder if he's come to make sure we're all celebrating joyfully as he's commanded."

When Karon and I were announced and directed into the music room, we found over two hundred guests already seated on red velvet and gold-leaf chairs. Intermingled with the scent of expensive perfumes were traces of the pine, laurel, and balsam boughs that were stuffed into great jars and vases and set in every corner, crack, and crevice. The house blazed with candlelight. While gold-liveried servants scurried about with wine and extra chairs, the ladies' diamonds and the gentlemen's swords scattered glittering reflections.

More guests streamed through the side doors. A young woman in a white gown took her place in an island of red carpet at one end of the music room, twisting her fingers and glancing anxiously toward the opposite end of the room where the wide main doors remained closed. As we were seated, she was joined by a hollow-eyed young man with a harp and an enormously large man with a flute, who settled his bulk on a precariously fragile chair. The ensemble did not look promising.

The entertainment could not proceed until the king arrived. Sir Geoffrey circulated among the guests, joking about the wait. "Worth it, as you'll hear," he said. "I picked up this one in Valleor. Such a find! She was the favorite of a Vallorcan merchant until his palace fell in on him in the earthquake last summer."

Karon shifted in his chair, peering between the heads in front of us. I felt his arm stiffen, but before I could question him, the double doors were thrown open and a royal herald stepped into the room. Everyone rose.

"His Most Gracious Majesty Evard, King of Leire and Valleor, and Protector of Kerotea."

Evard strode into the room. An ermine-lined red velvet short cloak was removed by one of his attendants to reveal a tight, gold-encrusted doublet, its exaggerated point dipping all the way to his groin over puffed breeches of gold brocade. A shirt of red and gold patterned silk poked out at his wrists and at his neck in great ruffles, above a wide, flat collar studded with sapphires and rubies. As did the rest of the ladies, I dipped my head and curtsied as he passed. Karon and the other gentlemen bowed. Evard's fair hair drooped rakishly across his brow as always, but the hard gray eyes underneath peered about uneasily, as a fluttering Sir Geoffrey guided him to a seat on the front row.

The queen did not accompany him. Tomas and Darzid followed just behind him, however, as did at least twenty aides and serving gentlemen.

I had not seen Tomas since Evard's wedding, though I'd heard the news of his marriage to the seventeen-year-old daughter of Evard's chancellor. Though as stiff and wary as his royal master, he looked well, apparently none the worse for the Kerotean disaster.

Darzid alone seemed relaxed. He strolled through the aisles greeting every high-ranking noble as if he were himself a duke, whispering in ladies' ears, sharing a laugh or a word with the gentlemen. His behavior brought to mind a recent comment of Martin's. "It seems as if, nowadays, when you turn over any slime-covered stone in Leiran society, Darzid slithers away. And I don't believe it's your brother that sets him to it." I wished we had not come.

The performance began, and, for a while, royalty, politics, Darzid, and the unnerving reference to the Vallorean earthquake were easily forgotten. The music was glorious. A find, indeed. The girl's fidgeting evaporated with the first silvery note of the flute, and when she answered the ringing note with her own clear tone, I thought it might be difficult to tell which was which. But as she began to weave her voice about the music, it became clear that the instrument could not rival the purity of her voice. She wrapped this loveliness about a song of love undying, a song not out of the ordinary way, but when she was done, few eyes in the room were dry. For the next hour the anxieties of the past weeks were forgotten, as if the noble assembly had heaved a great sigh. As Karon's mentor had taught him, nature bestowed many gifts that magic could not surpass.

Karon was entranced, his rapt expression telling me that he was storing up the beauty against the day when he could use his power again. But when the music ended, and the guests rose and began to crowd their way toward the supper rooms, he whispered in my ear. "The girl will know me."

Dread wrapped cold arms about my heart. "Then we must go," I said.

Karon nodded. His face was calm, but his grip on my arm was tight as he guided me against the flow of the crowd toward the outer doors. Acquaintances attempted to turn our course, but I pleaded an unsettled stomach as the reason for an early departure. A quarter of an hour and we were almost clear, but just as we reached the doors that led to the foyer, Sir Geoffrey waved his hand above the crowd and called after us with a hearty voice. "Karon, my lad, where are you going? His Majesty has asked for you." The old gentleman forged through his milling guests and clamped his hand on Karon's shoulder. "I inquired how he liked the Dorian monolith standing at the entrance to the Crown Vault, and he asked was it the new commissioner's choice? I said it was either his or his lady's, and he said he would like an opportunity to express his appreciation."

"I was just going to take Seri home," said Karon. "She feels a bit ill tonight."

"But of course you can't refuse His Majesty's summons. Perhaps your lady would like to lie down in a guest chamber. Or I could supply an escort to take her home."

Karon looked at me, questioning.

Only one answer was possible. "I'll wait with Karon, Sir Geoffrey. Perhaps it will shorten the formalities. The evening has been exceptional."

"It has, has it not? Misara will be the most brilliant star of our musical firmament for a generation." He laid one arm across Karon's shoulders and crooked his other arm for my hand. "Now come. This could be excellent for our plans. I've been worried that the discouraging military news might preclude our proceeding with the expansion, but if His Majesty himself is taking an interest . . ."

Evard was holding court in the drawing room beside a pink marble mantelpiece carved with dolphins. Above the mantel was a gigantic mural of a naked Jerrat holding a lightning bolt, surrounded by crashing waves, sea monsters, and storm-wracked vessels. As Sir Geoffrey forged our way through the glittering company like one of the brave ships in the painting, Karon gave me his most reassuring smile. *All will be well,* it told me.

I didn't believe it.

The king was tapping one foot, looking anywhere but at his companion, a beribboned matron pontificating on the virtues of her gangly son, who looked, conveniently, just old enough to be knighted. Evard himself appeared older than the last time I had been near him, his gray eyes harder, his face more angular, even his blond beard more wiry and pointed. Perhaps life was not going as he had planned.

My brother stood next to Evard and took no notice of me. One would think he was seven years old again, trying to show his displeasure at some slight. He, too, looked older than when I'd seen him last. Regret at our estrangement still bubbled its way to the surface of my heart. Karon stood close and squeezed my hand.

Sir Geoffrey quickly swept the fond mother and her goggle-eyed progeny to the side. "Your Majesty, may I present the Royal Commissioner of Antiquities—"

"I'm sure your lady has told you of our long and . . . intimate . . . acquaintance." Evard scarcely glanced at Karon and did not acknowledge Sir Geoffrey's presence at all. The full weight of his attention fell on me.

"An honor, Your Majesty"—Evard twitched a finger and Karon rose from his genuflection—"and my wife has indeed told me of her privilege to be a friend of your youth." Despite my apprehension, I had to smile. Was this meeting just curiosity or did Evard hope to plant some seed of discord by his implications?

"You've likely not been introduced to her brother, the Duke of Comigor. Tomas, have you met your sister's chosen lord and master?"

"No, sire." Tomas raked Karon with a glance. His lip curled slightly. Karon bowed, but the courtesy was not returned. Tomas jerked his head at his lieutenant. "My aide, Captain Darzid."

"A delight, of course." Darzid smiled cheerfully as he bowed to me, and, in a surprisingly intimate gesture, offered Karon his hand. Karon did not rebuff him, of course, and as they touched, Darzid stared with unabashed curiosity. When he finally released Karon's hand, Darzid grinned at me in his most charming and mischievous manner. "Sorry I can't stay," he said. "My lord's business calls."

He genuflected gracefully to Evard, bowed to Tomas, and leaned toward me with a not-at-all-private whisper. "I wish we had found time to talk about my dreams, my lady. Too late now, I'm afraid." He bowed to me and left the group.

Sir Geoffrey, courteously ignoring the awkward greetings, reminded Evard of the matter which had drawn his interest.

"Ah, yes. The monolith. An interesting choice to guard the Crown Vault." His lack of interest in artifacts was quite apparent.

"Such was its function in the Dorian Empire, Majesty," said Karon. "It seemed proper."

"It serves." Evard drew two fingers along my jaw. "You look exceptionally well, my lady. Town living must suit you. At some time during this cheerful season, we must dine together."

I curtsied, which put my face nicely out of his reach. "Thank you, Your Majesty. My husband and I would consider it a privilege to dine with you. We wish you and your queen a fair Seille." *That for you, you sly devil. Two can play these games.*

I had begun to think that all might actually be well, for Darzid was gone, Tomas distracted, and Evard already engaged by a giggling young woman who looked as if she would be thrilled to have the king's fingers trace her jaw. But before we could withdraw, Sir Geoffrey bustled toward us again, towing someone in his wake. "Karon, Lady Seriana, don't leave yet. Your Majesty, may I present the belle of the evening, Misara, the Lark of Valleor?"

Karon quickly slipped behind me, as if to make room for the singer.

The girl made full obeisance in the Vallorean way, which was the way of penitents in Leire, kneeling, arms spread wide with the forehead touching the floor. Evard frowned and gestured to one of his attendants to pull her up. "No penance is necessary for such a performance as we've heard this night," he said. "Now you must excuse us. We have other business."

The guests bowed or curtsied as Evard moved toward

the supper room. We were almost free. But as we rose from our genuflections, the singer came face to face with Karon. *"Mi Dispóre!"* she cried. Dropping to her knees, she grasped Karon's hand and kissed it.

At the young woman's exclamation, Evard glanced back and saw what she did. "What's this?" he said, scowling over his shoulder.

Misara, tears streaming down her face, said in broken Leiran, "It is the *Dispóre,* Majesty, the saving hand. After the earthshaking, my family were dead, their house fallen. But this one digs . . . so careful . . . all night. Pulls the stones away, crawls in the tiny passage, earth still shaking, again and again, and we thought he was to be dead, too. Such a long time. But then each one he brings out: my father, my mother, Leno, Jasra, Tegro, Niste. All living. Five days were they under the stones, Majesty."

Sir Geoffrey leaned toward Evard. "Karon was in Xerema to examine an ancient tomb site and was himself injured in the terrible earthquake."

"I am in your forever debt, *mi Dispóre.* Command me," said the singer.

Karon spoke softly, looking only at the girl. "Everyone who could so much as stand or lift a stone did the same."

Now quiet your tongue, foolish girl, I thought.

But she would not stop. "Not like you, sir. You were everywhere bringing hope. I sought for you to save my family because I heard of you. Everyone knew. It was a miracle . . . the *Dispóre.*"

Evard cut her off. He flicked his hand in dismissal, spun on his heel, and murmured to Tomas, loud enough that we could hear. "Might have expected Seri to dredge up a paragon."

My hand was already on Karon's arm, my feet moving toward the doors. "Dear boy, one more thing." When Sir Geoffrey accosted Karon yet again, I wanted to scream. "I do wish you would view this manuscript given me earlier today by Jahn Gronne who is just back from Iskeran. I must value it and return it to Gronne by morning, so if you could spare one more moment before escorting your lovely wife home . . ."

Karon pressed my hand and smiled at me with encouragement. "Only a moment." Then he followed Sir Geoffrey to his library.

I remained by the hearth, not at all cold, but most definitely shivering. What if the girl had seen Karon work his magic or mentioned the rumors of the supernatural that had floated about Xerema?

Karon was back in a quarter of an hour. "Good night, Sir Geoffrey. A marvelous evening."

"I hope you will soon feel yourself again, my lady," said the old knight.

I curtsied. "I'm sure I will. Thank you, Sir Geoffrey."

Once more Karon and I moved determinedly toward the exit doors. I breathed easier when we walked into the cooler air of the spacious, lamplit foyer. But no sooner had the porter summoned a footman to fetch our cloaks than two men appeared between us and the outer doors. One of them was Darzid. The other was the fish-eyed sheriff I had last seen in the innyard at Threadinghall.

No time to think. Frontal assault was always the surest tactic. "Captain Darzid," I said. "I was beginning to wonder if you were a separate being from my brother, and now I see you are attached to someone else. It's refreshing to know you've not taken root upon my family tree. Introduce me to your friend."

Darzid glanced at his companion. "I believe you have already met Maceron."

"Oh, yes," said the sheriff. "No doubt of that."

"I don't think so," I said. "I never forget an acquaintance." I approached my brother's lieutenant, all the while screaming in my mind for Karon to run. But instead, I felt him stroll up behind me. His hands would be clasped behind his back as always, as if waiting patiently for the cloaks and his foolish wife. "So what mischief are you about, Darzid?" I asked, fighting to make sure the man could not read my terror.

The sheriff was not to be fooled. "I'm sure of them both. The woman is the whore from the inn, and the man"—his thin lips parted in a smile of purest hatred—"the man is the sorcerer."

The devastating accusation hung in the air like a hawk poised on the wind, ready to dive for its prey. Karon put his arms around me from behind, bent forward, and softly kissed my hair.

A moment later, green-clad guards ripped him away, and I whirled about to see such love and regret in his blue eyes that I thought my heart might crack. Maceron shoved me aside, and while two guards pinned Karon's arms cruelly behind him, the sheriff smashed a brutal fist into Karon's face. I cried out, "Stop!" and reached for Maceron's arm. But Darzid grabbed me and held me fast. A second blow left Karon dazed and with a bloody gash above one eye.

"There's an easy way to confirm our contention," said the sheriff. "If we're right, he'll be wearing his perfidy, not on his sleeve, but inside it."

Karon shook his head groggily. "Wait—"

The fish-eyed man struck Karon again, this time across the mouth, and then pointed one thick finger at me. "The next blow will fall on the woman."

I wrenched my arms from Darzid's grip and found my voice, shaking though it was. "What is the meaning of this, Captain Darzid? How dare you lay hands on a daughter of the house of Comigor or an official of the king's household? Where is Sir Geoffrey? Where are the guards? My brother—"

"Ah, no." Darzid raised a finger in warning. Never had I seen such cold darkness as his gaze. "I learned years ago not to underestimate you, my Lady Seriana, so you needn't fear I've left anything to chance. Your brother has been properly notified of my suspicions, as has His Majesty. They are awaiting my report. If I'm wrong, then the mistake was an honest one . . . but I'm not wrong, am I?" He knew. Blessed Annadis be merciful, he stripped the truth from me even as I stood there. A wintry smile brushed his narrow face.

Darzid pushed me into the hands of one of the guards. Drawing his knife, he slit Karon's left sleeve from shoulder to wrist, exposing the scars for the crowd that had begun to gather by the music room doors. No assault could have been more devastating. Karon, blinking and trying to shake off the blows to his head, struggled to pull his arm close in to his body, but he could not move.

"Take them to the king," said the sheriff, motioning to the heavily armed soldiers who had appeared behind him. "Have a care with the man. He is dangerous beyond your imaginings. Bind his eyes. Keep four spare guards ready at all times."

Darzid took my arm again. "If he utters a sound, I'll kill the woman."

We passed a blur of wide-eyed onlookers, including a bewildered Sir Geoffrey, as Darzid propelled me down a softly lit, wood-paneled passageway and into a comfortable sitting room. Evard slouched on a brown velvet couch, and Tomas stood stiffly behind him.

"Your Majesty," said Darzid, with a deep bow. "The information provided by Sheriff Maceron has proven correct. It is no paragon of virtue to whom the Lady Seriana has gotten herself wed, but to a sorcerer—if such a sublime state as matrimony can be said to apply to a fiend." Underneath his display of shock, I felt him laughing.

Four soldiers shoved Karon into the room. A scarf of incongruously bright green was tied about his eyes. Blood soaked one side of it.

"Your Majesty, I beg you right this injustice," I said. "Is this the way your servants treat members of noble families or men who hold positions in your household?"

Evard looked past me to Darzid. "He is incapacitated?"

Darzid nodded. "He'll not be dangerous as long as we control him, prevent him from speaking, and keep his eyes covered. And as long as we have the woman." He was as cool and matter-of-fact as if he were discussing the finer points of a new horse.

Nodding, Evard rose from the couch, walked over to Karon, and stared at his arm. "Oh, Seri, my dear girl, what have you done? You could have been queen of the Four Realms. Instead you've chosen to consort with a demon." He bent over to examine Karon's scars more closely. I wanted to scream.

"He's bewitched her," burst out Tomas. "This is all Gault's doing."

"Gault will be dealt with."

"Is that what this idiocy is all about?" I said, desperate to gain some foothold. "Martin has long relinquished all claim to the throne. You've no need to manufacture some fantastic plot to discredit him. Tomas, can you believe I would marry a sorcerer? I had the same tutors as you."

But no one was listening to me.

"And so, Sheriff," said the king, straightening up again. "What is it that such creatures as this do?"

"These scars indicate that this one claims to be a healer," said Maceron, moving to Evard's side. "In fact, sorcerers of his kind can indeed pull a passing spirit from the brink of death. What could be a more disgusting distortion of nature than depriving a soul that is done with life of its proper end? The sorcerer does it, not out of generosity, of course, but to create a spirit slave who has no choice but to do his foul bidding."

"And it causes this?" Evard curled his lip as he touched Karon's arm. Karon jerked away and the guards twisted his arms tighter.

"In all its perversity, it's quite an impressive show. Would you like a demonstration, your Majesty? There would be no danger in it as long as Captain Darzid and I control him. He can do only one working at a time. And it would be inarguable evidence at his trial."

I looked from one to the other, trying to understand what they were saying.

"I don't see how you could make him do it." Evard flopped onto the couch again, looking skeptical.

"I know a very good way," said Darzid. He whipped off Karon's blindfold and nodded.

Karon blinked, and his gaze flicked to something behind me. For the first time since I'd known him, I saw fear in his eyes.

"Karon, what is—?" Fire exploded in my back, and roaring erupted in my ears. Karon yelling . . . Tomas, somewhere far away, cursing. My head spun. I couldn't get a breath, and my knees turned to water. Only as I felt warm wetness spreading across my back did I begin to comprehend. "No . . . don't . . ." I tried to warn Karon, but my tongue refused to obey me. There would be no going back if he did it. They had no proof unless he gave it to them.

My knees gave way. Someone caught me. "Damn you. Damn all of you. Get a surgeon in here."

I floated in and out of awareness, the words and shouts drifting through my spinning head.

". . . a knife, clean and sharp."

No, Karon, no. They'll not let me die. My tongue wouldn't work.

". . . grace your son . . ."

"Damnation, what is it he does?"

". . . fill my soul with light . . ."

Fire ripped my arm. *No, Karon . . .*

". . . death to touch either one of them while he . . ."

"*J'den encour,* my dearest love. . . ."

I had been so cold sleeping, but now all was warm again. I lay on my back. A smile crossed my face. Connor Martin Gervaise was getting big enough that sleeping on my back was becoming uncomfortable. And the bed was so hard. I tried to roll over, but couldn't. Karon was there. I felt him breathing. *Tassaye, tassaye,* he whispered. *Softly. Softly.* He was holding my arm so tight. I couldn't move it, and my eyes fluttered open to see him leaning over me. What had happened to his face? Was it from the earthquake? Such terrible bruises . . . and blood all over . . . one eye swollen shut, and he was so pale . . . almost transparent like the day at Windham. . . .

It all came flooding back to me. "No," I said weakly.

His eyes flicked open . . . such love in them. When he smiled, I felt the warmth of his life flowing in my veins. "Cut it now," he said to someone over his shoulder. And to me, "It is a wonder. All of it."

My arm was released, but before I could reach out for him, they dragged him away, and there on Sir Geoffrey's fine carpet, they beat him until he was insensible. Fear lent weight to their fists.

I sat unmoving on the floor where they'd left me, and stared at the door through which they had at last taken him away. Someone came up behind me, and I flinched, but the hands that lifted me up and led me to the empty brown velvet couch were not rough hands. Tomas sat me down and knelt in front of me. No one else was in the room. "By Annadis's holy sword, Seri, what is he?"

I fingered the place on my arm where Karon had made the incision. There was no remnant of it but the fire in my memory. It would have been too difficult to hold me around the back where the knife had gone in. Better to make a new place to mingle the blood . . . the blood of life.

Tomas spoke as if I were a child. "Has he bewitched you? Silenced you with some ensorcelment? Is that what happened three years ago? Did he control you even then?"

I stared at my brother, trying to comprehend what he was saying. My mind was in chaos, horror and wonder entwined in a mortal embrace.

"Seri, tell me you're all right." Fumbling, he examined my back. My gown felt damp and scratchy—stiffening as the blood dried where Maceron's blade had gone in. "Holy gods, it's impossible."

Finally I gathered words. "Tomas, you must help him."

Awkwardly he put his arm around my shoulders. "I'll take care of you, Seri. We'll find out what must be done . . . the priests . . . to purify you. Are you free of him now he's away from you?"

"No. You don't understand. . . ." I tried to tell him about sorcery and the J'Ettanne. But the longer I spoke, the farther he withdrew from me, and by the time I noticed, it was too late. I had told him about our child.

Tomas spoke in muted horror. "You let him do that to you? Plant you with his venomous seed? How could you live? Was there no knife, no sword to put an end to your debasement?"

"Tomas, you've heard nothing I've said."

"I've heard enough. This is an entirely new situation. Evard must be told that taking care of the sorcerer is insufficient."

"Tomas!"

"You'll not burn. You'll not die. You're still of the house of Comigor, and Evard has sworn to me. But you've consented to evil beyond my imagining, and it will be undone." He stormed out of the room, leaving me alone in the library.

Sometime in the night I was taken to the palace and

locked in a bare, cold room, such as scullery maids might live in. My locket and my wedding ring were taken from me, and my bloodstained green silk was replaced by a muslin shift and a plain black dress. I would not weep. I would not.

CHAPTER 18

The morning dawned cool and gray, as did most summer mornings in the Uker valley, but the rising sun burned off the fog early. I awoke cramped and tired from the night on the dirt floor of the charcoal burner's hut, and the lingering disturbance of my dreaming was hard to shake. Stars of night, why could I not be rid of it? Perhaps if I could get the unpleasant prince and his annoying servant on their way, I could go back to Dunfarrie and bury it all again. Yet I wondered. My cottage now seemed as remote as D'Natheil's Avonar.

Tennice and Baglos were quiet that morning, too, brows furrowed and shoulders tight as we passed around chunks of dry black bread, spread with a paste of beans and leeks that was long past fresh. D'Natheil showed no interest in breakfast, but sat in the open doorway, intently scribing his wood chip with the point of his knife.

"What is it he makes?" I asked Baglos, as I smoothed my still-damp clothes into some semblance of order.

"I've asked, but he does not respond."

"Is he well? He looks ill . . . or, no, maybe thinner somehow." The growing sunlight revealed a tracery of lines around D'Natheil's eyes. I'd not noticed them before.

Staying out of arm's reach, Baglos questioned the Prince. D'Natheil shook his head, but rather than lashing out at the Dulcé as was his morning habit, he graced Baglos with his smile, the smile that was everything of good humor and unsullied delight.

The smile was the only constant in D'Natheil. I had never known anyone to change so rapidly, not only in the seasons of his mood, but in his physical appearance as well. I could no longer envision him as he had been on that day he appeared naked in the woods behind my cottage, but I would swear by everything I valued that it was not as he looked today or yesterday or a week ago. I had thought him little more than twenty, and from the Dulcé's tales I judged that close to accurate. And yet on this morning he looked almost of an age with me, as if these past days had laid brushstrokes of years and care on the canvas of his face.

Baglos denied it. "He is as he is, woman. Anything else is only your imagination."

I told him that my imagination had been unused for so many years it wouldn't know how to invent such a business. But, then, after a fortnight without, the Prince had shaved his face this morning. Perhaps that was the difference.

It took me a while after entering the gates of Yurevan to decide what had changed about the city since I had last visited. The mottled stone buildings of the University still dominated the city from its hilltop site, their cloisters welcoming the brightest thinkers from all the Four Realms. The winding brick streets were marked only by time, not war. Ironwork of intricately designed flowers and beasts still ornamented balconies and walls, and the flowers still bloomed in their charming niches. Quaint, tall houses peered down on passersby like old grandmothers inspecting their children's children. It was the people were different, I finally decided.

In the past every street corner had been occupied by a speechmaker haranguing the populace about excessive taxation or the indenture of children, or a student debating society arguing points of history or the origins of the universe. No tavern had lacked an aspiring poet to serve up verses along with his ale, and no sausage cart had failed to employ a young philosopher ready to argue about whether your sausage truly existed beyond your desires. And everyone had taken time to listen.

No more. Now the citizens of Yurevan hurried about their business with averted eyes, and vendors offered no word beyond your transaction. Only on one corner stood a wild-eyed, shabbily dressed man, preaching that the stars foretold the doom of Leire and the coming of a philosopher-king. Mothers pushed their gawking children past the man quickly, and while Tennice and I bought sausage and cheese to take back to D'Natheil and Baglos, green-clad guardsmen dragged the man into the street and beat him silent.

"Yurevan's no different from any Leiran-ruled city any more," said Tennice, hurrying me through an alley to avoid the guardsmen, who were laughing as one of their fellows relieved himself on the crumpled body of the madman. "Evard has set up his own man to run the University. He claimed rebels were using it as their lair, disturbing the freedom of the academics. He's come near 'protecting' the place to death. Ferrante wouldn't lecture there any longer. One of his friends after another disappeared when rumors of sedition touched them, and he decided it was safer to take only private students at home."

"I had no idea." Conquerors had always paid deference to the University, even when the cultural centers in other cities were looted and burned, even in the death throes of the Vallorean kingdom. I had come to think it was some deep-rooted yearning to share in the wisdom tangible in its cloisters. "I always imagined that no matter what madness enveloped the rest of the world, Yurevan and the University would be exempt from it."

"That belief is what brought me here. But we were wrong. The madness is everywhere."

Thinking that four together would be too conspicuous, Tennice and I had come alone to seek out the J'Ettanni woman. We'd left our horses at a hostelry and made our way through the narrow, twisting streets that climbed University Hill. Tennice stopped at a bookshop that he frequented and asked the owner if he knew where he could find gymnea, a medicinal ointment used for failing eyesight. The bookseller directed us to an herbary two streets west and four streets north. They had a good selection, he said, though the shop was run by a "right prickly sort of woman."

Halfway along a bustling lane we found the tall, narrow shop with a wooden sign over the door that read HERBS, TEAS, MEDICAMENTS . The storefront sported two windows, each with its wooden planter box crammed with aromatic flora, and when we opened the shop door, we were almost bowled over by the hodgepodge of scents. The tiny room was filled floor to ceiling and on every wall with row upon row of shelves, each crammed with neatly labeled glass jars and tins and paper bundles. Two worktables crowded the rest of the room so that it was almost impossible to move. On one table was a stack of thin paper, a ball of string, a mortar and pestle, measuring cups and spoons, and a small brass balance. On and under the other table lay heaps of plants, stacks of jars and boxes, and innumerable trays of roots, leaves, stems, and flowers spread out to dry.

Two well-dressed women stood by the weighing table chattering about the ague and the grippe, and the annoyances of servants who forgot themselves enough to get laid up. A small, dark-haired young woman measured a quantity of black seeds into one pan of the balance. She transferred the seeds to a sheet of paper, briskly folded the paper into a small packet, and exchanged it for a coin. "Anything else, Madame LeDoux? Have you fenugreek tea for Nidi's throat?"

"Plenty for now. Perhaps next week if she's no better."

"Good day, then."

"Good day, my dear."

The two ladies fluttered out the door, and the girl turned to Tennice and me. "What do you need?" Her dark hair was cut short, and it hung straight, framing her high cheekbones and light eyes. Her well-defined chin and short, straight nose complemented her blunt manner. She could be no more than eighteen. When the girl stepped around the table, eyeing our disheveled clothing impassively, I was astonished to note that she wore trousers. I had thought my own split skirt bold.

Tennice spoke up. "We're seeking the owner of this place."

"Why?" said the girl.

"We have business with her."

"You may tell me of your business."

"No, young lady, this is private business."

"The owner does no private business with strangers." The girl's words snapped like dry sticks.

Tennice whispered to me, "Speak to her, Seri. You know I've never been adept at handling women." An understatement to be sure. Though neither kings nor dukes nor judges could faze Tennice, a timid serving maid could throw him into a fluster.

I started again. "Perhaps, if you'd be so kind, you could give the owner a message from us?"

"I might."

"Tell Kellea that we were recommended by a friend. He says this is the only place to buy a rare herb to treat the gout. We would appreciate a word with her."

The girl looked at us strangely. "What word would you have with Kellea? If all you want is mycophila, then I can get it for you."

"Please, we wish to consult Kellea on a confidential matter. You understand. A bit embarrassing to talk about . . . Is there a time when we could find her here or perhaps a place where we could meet her? Our friend recommended her especially."

The girl shrugged her shoulders. "You're speaking to her already. I'm Kellea."

No, no, no. The girl was too young. It had been almost twenty years since the destruction of Avonar. "There must be some mistake. Is there someone else by the same name? Your mother, perhaps? Or perhaps another herb shop? We were expecting an older person."

"There's no other Kellea. My mother had a different name and is long dead, anyway, and this is the only herb shop in Yurevan. What's your business? Tell me the name of your friend."

Tennice and I looked at each other in confusion. "I must have been wrong," he said.

"Kellea!" called a croaking voice from beyond a narrow doorway.

"What is it, Grandmother?"

"Tea, dear heart. Could you bring me a cup of nine-leaf tea?"

"I have customers who are just leaving. As soon as they're off, I'll bring it."

I looked sharply at the girl. "Your grandmother. Is her name perhaps the same as yours?"

"I told you, I'm the only Kellea. If you have business with me, state it." She folded her arms tightly across her breast, her hostility shoving us out the door before our feet had moved.

I hated abandoning our only clue. Kellea was the only one of the four—Then it struck me. The herb shop, shelves laden with medicines. The names. "Kellea," I said, scarcely restraining my excitement, "what is your grandmother's name?"

"This is ridiculous. What could you possibly—?"

"It would be a great kindness. It's very important."

I might have been dragging the answers from her with red-hot pincers. "Her name is Celine."

Context. How is it we can stand in two different rooms, hear the same combination of letters and sounds, and our minds construct such differing images? Tennice had spoken four names, but I hadn't listened in the proper context. "Celine" was not a vanished stranger, one more unmarked name in a list of the uncountable dead. I knew her. "Please, Kellea. May I speak with your grandmother? My information was in error, and she's the one I need to see."

"My grandmother sees no one. She's quite feeble."

"I swear to you that I mean her no harm. I'm a friend of her friends. Take her the message I give you, and if she commands us go, we'll go." I took a deep breath and reached backward. "Tell her I knew a student of hers from long ago. He learned many lessons from her, but the most important one was to look at the whole person before judging the worth of their gifts."

As rigid as an iron spike, the young woman disappeared into the back room. She returned quickly. "She'll see you. But only for a moment. You mustn't tire her. She turns ninety next month."

Tennice and I followed Kellea into a tiny room that smelled of lavender and mint. A sunny window flooded the room with light and air and myriad other scents from a courtyard crowded with planter boxes and baskets of herbs and flowers. In a chair by the window sat an old woman, so withered and dry that it looked as if the slightest breeze could swirl her away like dust. Her head nodded continuously in the way of the very old, but her blue eyes blazed with curiosity. "Who is it speaks of long ago?"

"My name is Seri, madam, and this is my friend, Tennice of Verdillon. I cannot say how honored I am to meet you. Never did I believe I would have that privilege."

"That's all very nice, but you haven't answered my question."

"My husband was your student. His name was Karon, eldest son of the Baron Mandille, Lord of Avonar."

Celine showed no fear. No hesitation. But she was listening, surely, awash in stillness. Even her head had stopped its bobbing for the moment. "And what has this to do with me?"

"He told me of his mentor whose name was Celine, and of how she took a frightened and awkward boy and taught him the beauty of his calling. And when he became cocky, as young men do, she taught him the grace to look for the gifts in everyone. He told me of your candlemaker and your sons, and how, whenever he had a problem, he would think first, 'What would Morin do?'"

The old woman extended her hand, her head nodding again as if I had recited my lesson correctly.

"Grandmother!" said Kellea.

But the old woman's handclasp was firm, and she examined me with unclouded eyes. "Karon. Such talent he had—and the heart to match his skill. Lifegiver, we called him. I didn't know he lived past the dark day. But I see in you that he has gone the way of the rest of them."

"Ten years ago. He was discovered."

"I was old when he came to me. Who would have thought I would outlive him? I suppose I've outlived them all." How familiar was her speech. Not querulous or sad, but only wondering at the mysterious ways of life, rejoicing, even in grief, at the interleaving of joy and sorrow and pain and beauty. "And you were his wife. You were not of Avonar?"

"No. We met several years later."

"You knew what he was?"

"Yes."

"It's no easy thing to love a Healer—to share with a

thousand others what should be yours alone." She touched my cheek with her warm, dry finger. "You laughed with him?"

"Very much."

"Good." Celine settled back in her chair, shaking her head solemnly. "No. No easy thing to walk the Way with a Healer."

Kellea stood watching like a new-honed knife, ready to slice the first thing that came in its path.

"So this is your granddaughter?" I said, wanting to leave the past behind and get to our business.

"Great-granddaughter. Morin's granddaughter, newborn only a week before the dark day. On the day the Leirans came, I had taken her for a walk in the hills to give her mother a rest. I watched from the hilltop as the soldiers burned Mandille and Christophe and Eduardo and everyone else of the J'Ettanne, and they put my Carlo and Morin and the rest of the people of Avonar to the sword. Now, why are you here? Not to reminisce. Not after so many years."

"We found you through Professor Ferrante."

"I'm surprised at that. He was sworn. Why?"

"The story is so long. I hate to tire you with it."

"I've nothing better to do. Kellea runs the shop. I sleep here in the sun or watch the flowers bloom. Soon I'll be in L'Tiere and have all the sleep I'd ever want. Keep me awake for a while."

Through the long afternoon I sat at Celine's feet and told her the story of D'Natheil and Baglos, and the reason I sought a J'Ettanni survivor. Whenever the bell on the shop door rang, Kellea would disappear and tend to her customers, and then she would return to her post at Celine's doorway. At every half hour, she would tell me that Celine needed to rest.

"Hush, child, and listen," Celine said to her after the third time Kellea ordered us out. "These are matters of concern to you." And then to me. "Kellea is greatly gifted, but she has never known any of the J'Ettanne but her old grandmother, has never heard the stories told on Av'Kenat, never had a mentor for her talent. I could not be all things to her."

"I need none of those things, Grandmother. Just you. I want you left in peace."

"Did you not hear the story, girl? If we don't help, then even such peace as we know may be swept away."

"Why do you believe them? Because they say familiar words and names? You've taught me to trust no one, and now you open your door to these people without a question. It could all be lies."

Celine patted my arm as she spoke to her granddaughter. "If you cannot tell truth from lies when you're ninety, then you've made a great waste of your time and deserve no better than you get." She gave me a thoughtful glance. "It's quite a thing you ask, Seri, for me to read this man. It may not turn out as you wish."

"But you'll try?"

"I've seen my friends slaughtered and my sons and grandsons put to the torch. I've held life in my hand as few ever have a chance to do, with the choice to give or take. I've listened to the voices of my ancestors for ninety years. If you think I would miss the chance to find out why, then you should bottle me in one of my own glass jars and sell me as a specific for inducing madness."

"Grandmother, you can't!" But Kellea's horrified exhortation was drowned in Celine's hoarse laugh, and as Tennice and I joined in, the girl stormed out of the room.

"Now the two of you be off," said Celine, wiping the tears that rolled down her dry cheeks. "Let me soothe the fears of my sulking child and take myself a nap. Bring your silent friend tonight after dark. Then will we investigate the mysteries of the universe."

When we reclaimed our horses at the hostelry, one of the grooms was saddling a large black horse. The shape of its head, its legs . . . the trim of mane and tail . . . the saddle I had shared with Paulo on the ride from Grenatte to Dunfarrie . . . Rowan's horse. I urged Tennice to hurry and did not breathe easy until we were lost in the press of traffic heading for the outer gates of the city.

CHAPTER 19

Year 4 in the reign of King Evard—midwinter

For endless hours I sat on the hard bed in the dark and tormented myself with "if only." I remembered Karon's birthday, the night when he had explained how he could not use his power for harm, even to protect himself or me. I hadn't believed him then, sure that if this test ever came, he would strike as would any other man. When I had told him about killing the man in Threadinghall, and he had remained steadfast in his resolve, my confidence that he would do what was necessary had not been vanquished, only shaken. But the apology in his eyes as he was dragged away from me had withered my heart. No matter the horror to come, he would not fight. His last words to me had confirmed it. *It is a wonder. All of it. . . .* part of a humorous J'Ettanni story that was the very expression of their acceptance of the vagaries of life—the path "laid down" for them. Damn them all! I wanted to shake Karon's father and his grandfather and every cursed one of the J'Ettanne and scream that it was possible to lay down your *own* path in this world. No wonder they all were dead and forgotten. And now my Karon would be dead, too, for no one was going to listen to him and learn of the beauty and grace he brought into this horrid world.

I could not allow it. If Karon could not fight, I would have to do it myself. I just needed a little time. Plots and schemes fed one upon the other in the dark, until I fell into a exhausted sleep.

Seri . . . help me . . .

The cry startled me awake in the deepest hours of that

dreadful night. It was a time of second memory, as if I had lived the exact event before: Karon calling out to me in the darkness. Surely I would open my eyes to silver moonlight streaming through the library door, my book pages fluttering in a summer breeze scented with balsam and thyme. But this room was cold and barren. No light of any kind shone through the window, a small rectangle of lesser darkness high on the wall above my bed. "Karon?"

Help me. He was on the verge of screaming. I could feel him struggling to hold it back.

"Tell me what to do."

Talk to me. A tale, a song, an image, anything I can hold on to. Please, love, quickly.

I fumbled about for a moment, trying to think what might serve, trying not to think why he might need a distraction so desperately. After a few abortive attempts—too short a tale, too abstract a concept, too shallow a subject— I began to speak of Comigor, the ancient keep that had been my childhood home, the windy heath that attracted storms, but had repelled all would-be conquerors for six hundred years. I explored every passage, every cellar, every attic, every map in its library. As he had taught me, I used audible words to force my thoughts into a single pattern, not allowing worry or distraction to muddy what I left for him to find in my head. Every once in a while I would pause, listening. I heard nothing, only felt his desperate presence in my mind, as surely as if I could hear his harsh breathing or feel his sweat. So I continued.

I considered my warrior father, so distant, so strong, bewildered by his children, yet so gentle with my fragile, lovely mother. Her image was hazy, but I remembered her stories and her garden, and I explored those things, too. I described my bedchamber at Comigor, where I had imagined myself an astronomer, unraveling the mysteries of the heavens, or a minstrel, traveling the land singing songs of heroes that would ignite a warrior's soul. As the high window spilled dead gray light into my room, I told how I had stood on Comigor's highest tower, pretending I was a captive princess, waiting to be rescued by a handsome knight.

This time the princess has done the rescuing.

"No, no. You rescued me long ago," I said, crossing my

arms on my breast as if to hold him to me. "When you stepped from the shadows in my library with a rose in your hand."

Seri, you must tell them I misled you, that I ensnared and deceived you with magic.

"I'll do no such thing."

You must. They've proven to me that they're quite serious about all this.

"Don't worry about me. Tomas has sworn to protect me, just as I've always said he would."

Karon's relief surged through the night. *Good . . . oh, gods of night . . .* He sounded so hurt. His voice in my head, usually so intense, so vibrant and colorful, was almost unhearable.

"What have they done to you?" I said.

It's no matter, he told me. *When I'm with you this way, it's easier. But I don't think you'll ever call me fine-looking again.*

I told him stories until I could no longer speak, and then continued by closing my eyes and thinking of the things I wished to say and see. Yet, deeper still, in a small place yet available for rational thought, I made my plan of battle.

My strategy was simple—political power. Those who wanted Karon convicted would manufacture what evidence was necessary, and, truly, eight people—Tomas, Evard, Sheriff Maceron, Darzid, and four soldiers—had seen Karon heal the stab wound in my back. The only thing that could overrule such testimony was a counterthreat to Evard's war . . . and ultimately his throne.

I could not use Martin. He was in enough danger. But I could contact ten high-ranking nobles that had been close friends of my father and ten more that owed him life-debts, plus I had friends of my own, men with wealth and status, women with influence over husbands or brothers or fathers. All paid levies to support Evard and his war. All knew of Evard's frustrated plans for me. They would believe me when I said that jealousy was behind the king's accusations, and that if Evard could manufacture evidence against me and my husband, then no one in the realm was safe from him. All were honorable Leiran nobles and would come to my defense. I just needed a chance to speak with them.

I could not even begin. They confined me to my room
with no paper, no pen, no book, no possible way to send
a message. The serving sister who brought my meals and
washing water was mute, and the guard who accompanied
her forbade me to utter a sound in her presence, his drawn
sword indicating that the woman's life would be the price
of my disobedience. The guards might have been deaf for
all the notice they took of my pleas for justice or my promises of gold. I was allowed no implement that could con-
ceivably be turned into a weapon. The serving woman was
required to comb my hair, and the lamp was taken away
whenever I was left alone, so that I spent every hour of
the long winter nights in darkness. I was permitted no visitor save priests and royal inquisitors, and they always came
in pairs lest I somehow corrupt them.

The priests treated me as an innocent, possessed of evil
spirits raised by sorcerers. They deafened me with prayers
and exhortation, lectures and sermons, encouraging me to
repudiate the sorcerer. Arot, the First God, had laid down
the law of the world: His sons Annadis and Jerrat were to
hold dominion, and they reserved the powers of earth and
sea, sky and storm to themselves. Sorcerers tried to steal
that power for their own . . . the ultimate blasphemy.

The inquisitors treated me as if I were myself a sorceress.
They threatened me with imprisonment and torture, demanding that I confess my depravity and that of the Earl
of Gault and his friends.

Tomas never came to me. Not once. Nor did any other
friend or acquaintance. I kept thinking that surely someone
would question where Karon and I had been taken. But
then I would remember the faces in Sir Geoffrey's hall
when Darzid exposed Karon's arm . . . and a cold weight
would settle heavier in my belly where I should have been
feeling only the warmth of our growing child. Who would
have courage enough to defend us?

Through all the days and nights of that winter, I felt
Karon with me. Some days he could converse with me in
our strange way. Some days he could only listen, and I
suspected that his captors were interrogating him . . . tortur-
ing him. I would force such dreadful speculation out of my
mind and talk to him about whatever I could think of: art
or music, or philosophical speculation, or the Writer and

his coded map that we had never managed to unravel, or my plans to study at the University someday when Connor did not need so much of my time.

That will be the worst, Karon said, in a rare moment of sadness. *Never to see him.*

I did not take the foolish course of saying that, of course, he would see our son. Neither of us was stupid. We had been imprisoned for over a month, and I had accomplished not one step to help him. I kept a barrier in my mind as Karon had taught me to do, a private place where I would not allow him to go, and there I kept my fear and grief and my guilty hopes that Karon would abandon his convictions and save himself. "There's still the trial," I said. "When they transport you to the King's Bench, there might be some opportunity . . . a distraction . . . and you could change yourself and walk away."

Ah, Seri, if willing could make it so . . .

He could not break chains with his magic. He could not unlock the doors of his prison. I knew that. The only way for him to be free was to invade a mind . . . to force his will upon another with torment and fear . . . to take a weapon and slay those who would harm him. Exactly the things he could never do.

"And the trial itself. Several of the lords on the Council are intelligent, thoughtful men . . ."

Yes. Well. Don't get up any wild hopes about the Council.

"Wild hopes are no more unreasonable than wild hopelessness," I argued. "I can cite many historical references to prove that wild hopes are the only way anything useful ever gets accomplished."

I should have learned long ago never to make any absolute statement to a woman with flame in her hair.

How strange it was to carry on these dialogues without seeing each other. Though I spoke aloud to help me focus my thoughts—whispering, so that the guards outside my door could not hear—we could have continued without a single audible word. Eventually we found it possible to share jests, as well as our deepest thoughts about life and death. I came to hate sleep. Such a waste of time. Karon rarely slept. He said his captors hadn't made it easy for him, and that he rested better when he was with me. He told me he could listen to my dreams.

"I wondered why mine have seemed benign, considering our circumstances," I said.

I can't change dreams, only drown them with other visions if I worked hard enough at it. I would never do that, though. There are those who say that dreams are how our minds work out their difficulties. There's so much I'd like to learn about the mind. Our knowledge is so limited. Perhaps the J'Ettanne could have done better had we understood more about such things.

We talked for a long time that night about the nature of dreams.

The trial would not begin for weeks yet, but as the tally of the new year began to run, I could feel Karon getting weaker. When anyone came to question me, I would ask how my husband was being treated. "He is a son-in-law of one of the oldest families in Leire. The law forbids starvation or maltreatment of any person who has not been convicted of a crime. I can cite the reference in the Westover Codex."

No one listened to me. Once Karon mentioned that it appeared my good offices had gotten him an extra ration of water. *Have you gained a sympathizer as I deeply hope, or have you just bullied someone so long they'll do anything to quiet you?*

"Hold on," I said. "I'll find a way."

But nothing changed. I might as well have been spitting on the palace towers, hoping to wear away the stone.

Year 4 in the reign of King Evard—winter

A week before the trial was to begin, Karon came to me in the middle of the night. *I'm sorry to wake you, but I needed to talk.*

"I'd much rather be with you," I said, sitting up on my bed and quieting my jangled thoughts so I could communicate clearly as I spoke.

I think they've decided I've told them all that I will, so I've had little to do but think.

"And what have you been thinking while I so lazily slumbered?"

Why I'm here.

"I don't understand."

If I'm really the last, then it's a matter of some import when I die—beyond the small matter of a J'Ettanni healer of two and thirty years that no one but you will miss. No, I'm not teasing for you to tell me who'll miss me, though it is a comfort. But it would seem that if I'm the last, and nature has consented to it, then, in some way, something will have been completed. I'd give much to know what it is.

"And has some insight come to you through all this thinking?"

Perhaps I'm losing my reason. I can't tell anymore. That's why I had to talk to you now. I've spent these days and weeks doing my best to deny that my body exists, and as I close off the outside world, I've found out how large and mysterious is the inner one. Alone in this darkness and feeling this way, I found something. It must have been buried in me long ago . . . or maybe it's not in me, but in that part of me that is my father or my mother or my grandfather. . . .

"Go on."

It's a word of power, like the words I use to heal.

"A word . . . what does it do?"

I don't know. Maybe nothing. But I can't get it out of my head, and there are images entwined in it, much in the way engravings of birds and beasts and flowers are worked into an illuminated manuscript. A white city stands surrounded by green mountains, and beyond it lies a great chasm, so deep and dark, I can't see into it. Something . . . broken . . . I don't know. Likely it's all madness. . . .

"You're not mad. You are not. You are the one I know in every way. Do not doubt it." I was up and pacing my room like a caged beast. It was so little I could give him. Only my conviction.

That's what I needed to hear. Perhaps I'll find out more about it as things go on.

"We'll find out together."

With only a few days left before the trial, I was still trying to find someone to help in Karon's defense, but neither the priests nor the inquisitors were of any help. No one would ever defend a sorcerer, they said. Why ever would they?

"Because it's just," I said.

"I cannot comprehend why King Evard even permits a trial," said a slight, balding priest of Annadis who had visited me several times. "To let a sorcerer live even one day is an intolerable affront to the Twins. The people demand to see him burn. They say he's a spy for Kerotea, most likely working deviltry on their behalf, even imprisoned."

That, of course, was why the whole business was being drawn out so long. Karon was to be fed to the people to whet their appetite for Evard's war, to supply fighters for his spring campaign.

"Pere Glasste, I must go to the trial. I must be allowed to speak for him."

"Oh, I've no doubt you'll be there, my lady. The king swears he's never known you to lie."

Though I thought it curious that Evard was touting my virtues, I took that bit of news and nestled it to me as if it were the most precious thing in the world. Hope. One splinter of hope. I would be able to speak for Karon. Martin had always said I could persuade the sea god Jerrat himself to drain the ocean. I wished the wizened little priest would take his quivering young acolyte and leave so I could savor hope, so I could think and plan what to do with it.

"We only hope you'll be free enough of the sorcerer that the truth will not burn your lips."

Bold with promise, drunk with infinitesimal possibility, I responded as if the priest might actually listen to me. "I've spoken only truth to you and your fellows all these weeks. And my husband speaks only truth. Listen to him, hear his story, and you'll recognize it."

The pale, scrawny man squirmed distastefully. "I would never listen to a sorcerer. That was your downfall, my lady: to hear the evil that got you into this dreadful obsession. Thank the Twins and the great father Arot that no one can ever again be taken in by this sorcerer's devilish speech."

"What do you mean?"

"Why, because they cut out his tongue. Just yesterday. They couldn't let him bewitch the king or the Council of Lords at his trial."

The goggle-eyed acolyte joined in. "It's the same reason they burnt out his eyes and crushed his hands on the night of his arrest. So he couldn't use them to ensnare his inquisitors with evil signs and spells. We've had no instance of bewitching from this sorcerer at all!"

I felt as if the earth had given way beneath my feet. Backing away from the preening little beasts, I turned to the locked door and hammered my fists on it until blood streaked the pale wood. "Guards! Curse you forever. Guards! The gods curse you all. Remove this vermin from my room. I must see the chancellor or someone in authority. I demand to speak to my brother. Crimes are being committed in the name of the king. King Evard must be told!"

In moments the door was opened and the gaping priests scurried out, trembling like frightened rabbits. The acolyte dropped his lamp, and when a guard threw his heavy cloak over the burning pool of oil, I tried to push past him. But his comrade shoved me back inside the room and slammed the door. I screamed my outrage until I had no voice left, but no one was sent, either then or later, to listen to my grievances.

Shaking, hoarse, scarcely able to think through my sickness, I dropped to the floor and buried my head on my bed, fighting for control. I had not spoken with Karon since the previous evening—since they had done this new horror—and as the silent hours passed, I began to fear he was dead. His eyes. His tongue. His sweet hands. Oh, gods have mercy. . . .

The wheeling of the light outside my high window witnessed that time had not stopped. Morning came. Someone left a tray inside my door. I did not move to touch it. The angle of the beams shifted to afternoon. The tray disappeared. Only when the last sallow rays of the sun were swallowed once again by the gray of evening did I hear his call. *Seri . . .*

"I'm here," I said, and filled my mind with the images I had readied for him, hoping and praying he could find some small comfort in me—thoughts of gardens, of riding his great horse, of mountains and dawn light and my arms around him. But all my preparation went for nothing. I thought I knew the worst they had done to him, but I was wrong.

They've taken Martin and the others. They say they'll do

whatever is necessary to make them confess to treason. I can hear them screaming. . . . The voice in my head was as gray as the sea under storm clouds, as dead as a battlefield when even the gleaners have moved on, as joyless as the charred ruins of Xerema. Even on the worst nights of that terrible winter, Karon had not come so near despair. *They say they'll do the same to you. They say they've evidence you've done murder, and that you'll hang for it. Oh, gods, Seri—*

"They'll not touch me, Karon. Tomas has Evard's word." I gripped the raw wood frame of my bed until I thought the plank must bend. "Connor and I will be safe at Comigor. No one can harm us there."

The others won't understand what these people will do to them. They'll try to resist, thinking it will make some difference.

"They knew, Karon. They knew the risks as I did. You allowed us to choose our way. We were grown adults, and we made the choice to have you in our lives. It was not just words that night at Martin's."

I should have left Leire.

"Martin has known for years that the moment Evard's popularity waned, his life was not worth a copper penny. But even if that weren't so, we made the choice and no one of us would change it. It is life, Karon, the life we wanted, and you must let us embrace it as you do yours."

Which was, of course, exactly why I did not scream at him to use his sorcery to save us all, though in every corner of my soul I knew the horrors yet to come. How do you persuade the one you love to violate the very essence of his being? He had chosen, and I was his wife who had promised to sustain him in his life's path. But I could not think how I was to bear it.

CHAPTER 20

I awoke before dawn on the day of the trial and, as on most mornings, found Karon hovering on the edge of my dreams.

"I'll be close to you today," I said.

I wish you wouldn't come.

I understood why. He was afraid I would get myself into worse trouble when I saw what they'd done to him. He didn't realize that I already knew.

"You know I must have a chance to open my mouth. I'll tell them that if you're truly a sorcerer, then why did you not quiet your argumentative wife years ago? You will have abundant sympathy."

They've not stoppered my ears, so at least I'll be able to hear your voice.

"You see? They think that's the worst thing they can do."

I almost didn't recognize Karon when they brought him into the Hall of Judgment. In less than two months the strong, vigorous man I knew had become a bent, blind scarecrow, shackled so heavily he could scarcely drag himself into the prisoner's dock. How did they expect him to stand through the day's proceedings? They had covered the ragged remnants of his eyes with a strip of cloth so as not to offend the sensibilities of the onlookers, but the blackened, twisted claws that had once been a healer's hands were left visible as a comfort for the fearful. I could not bear to look at his ravaged body, yet could look nowhere else. As soon as he was in his place, I felt him with me.

Are you here?

I am. It was difficult to merely think the words, rather than speaking them aloud.

Where? I can't see you . . . with this blasted rag. . . .

Across the room to your left, surrounded by six stone-faced warriors, ready to defend me from your fiendish forays. Listen. . . . I coughed aloud quite vigorously and saw his head turn slightly toward me.

It's probably just as well you're that far away. If you thought I reeked of the barnyard in Threadinghall . . . well, my nose still functions properly, and I wish it didn't.

They've only let me see priests and inquisitors, and so my sensibility to foul stenches is perhaps not so refined as it was.

A nice way to put it.

It's so good to see you. I think you look quite dashing, you know, like some wicked pirate.

I don't think you can see any better than I can.

I see only what I know. My distress must have overflowed my words. There would be no miraculous escape that day. He could scarcely move.

Don't fret too much, Seri love. Things are not so bad as they must look.

But I can't help you.

Not so. You are life to me. Don't look at me at all. Look deep inside yourself, at the beauty you've stored there, the life you hold, the spark that is no other. They cannot touch it. It is where your love lies, that you can give and take as you please. You've let me in, for which I bless all spirits of earth and sky, and they cannot touch me while I live in you.

I tried very hard to believe him.

Karon was momentarily overcome by a wracking cough. Blood trickled from the corner of his mouth after it, and a young woman sitting behind me cried out, "The devil slavers blood!" Her companions fanned her, and a young nobleman demanded that the guards cover Karon's head so the ghoulish creature would not frighten the ladies. It took several moments to calm the crowd.

It's very hard to sort out what's going on. You must tell me who's here and what's all the commotion. I gather it has something to do with me.

And so instead of screaming or weeping, I set myself to provide him a commentary on those in attendance: a large crowd of courtiers, many of whom we knew, and an even larger group of commoners let in to witness the great events. Not one man or woman among the spectators would meet my eye. Interesting to inspire such terror, especially in ones who had shared our table such a short time ago.

Once Evard arrived in full regalia, and the Council of Lords was seated in the raised box to the side—Martin's place conspicuously empty—the proceedings moved quickly. The first witness brought forward was Maceron, the fish-eyed sheriff. He had dedicated his life to eradicating this greatest of evils from the world, so he said, and had relished his post in eastern Valleor, as rumors of sorcery had always been strong there. Tales of supernatural events had drawn him to Xerema: victims pulled from the ruins, alive beyond all reason, victims ready to be lured into the hellish legions. The devil was obviously recruiting himself an army of slave spirits from under the stones of the fallen city, servants of chaos who would challenge the Twins for control of the world.

To support this ridiculous contention, the prosecutor called the Vallorean singer. The girl was commanded to tell why she made obeisance to Karon in the very presence of her king. Not realizing what it was she did, Misara spoke eagerly of the rumors and stories that had circulated Xerema in the summer, of the blessed one who was said to bring life and hope beyond death. Her father had sworn to her that he had seen her mother, brothers, and sisters die, one by one, until the *Dispóre* had appeared in their living tomb and coaxed them back to life.

Had she seen her family recently, to judge of their moral bearing since the events?

No, she'd been brought to Leire to sing, but—

The prosecutor did not let her continue. I don't think the girl realized that the grotesque remnant of a man in the prisoner's dock was her family's savior.

The constant assumptions and speculation, the lack of any real evidence, the coloring and manipulation of events were beyond all rational belief. Surely the judges could see it.

The most telling witness was yet to come. Evard did not descend to the witness box, of course, but spoke from his gold-leaf chair on the dais to the left of the Council. With simple sincerity he described the episode in Sir Geoffrey's study. Lady Seriana was renowned for intelligence and honesty, so said the king. When aides brought him the dreadful suspicion that her husband was one of the demon sorcerers, he did not wish to believe it. She was the sister of the Duke of Comigor, his own sword champion, and she confirmed her opposition to sorcery in the very moment of his questioning. But then the demon had struck. He himself had not seen who stabbed the knife into the lady's back, but had seen the devil bring her back from death. A hundred honest witnesses could vouch that Lady Seriana had been irrational, hysterical, completely mesmerized since the event, spending all her energy defending the sorcerer beyond all reason. How could anything serve as more profound evidence of the prisoner's guilt?

Angry murmurs rose from the noble observers, and from the commoners standing at the back came cries of "Burn the devil!" The bailiffs did not quiet the clamor until Lord Hessia, the head of the Council, commanded it.

The king concluded his testimony with a dramatic recapitulation of the ill-fated Kerotean campaign, and, in an explosion of righteous anger, proclaimed that, as the protector of his people, he would allow no such sorcerous fiends ever again to torment the good soldiers of Leire. The place was in frenzy when he was done, and I thought the farce of a trial was to be halted. But calm was restored, and I was called to witness.

I could see now how it was supposed to read. The king had vigorously proclaimed my honesty, and now I was to demonstrate how thoroughly Karon had corrupted me by defending him in front of the assembly. Evard had unleashed such a tide of emotion that he believed no one would give me reasonable hearing, and he knew how easy it was for my spiteful tongue to get out of my control. Well, he would not get what he planned.

Vycasso, the Lord High Prosecutor, was a wrinkled old man who combed his long thin hair from left to right in an attempt to obscure his balding forehead and chewed anise seeds that failed to cover the smell of onions on his breath. He was also a wily prosecutor who had skewered many a witness. I would need to be careful. Once my guards had escorted me to the witness box, he began to skip around from topic to topic, while pacing, halting and turning abruptly, back and forth in front of me like a fencing master trying to keep his student off balance. "How long have you been under the influence of the beast in the prisoner's dock?"

"I think there are many people in this Hall of Judgment who will note that I am rarely under anyone's influence. My honored father, the late Gervaise, Duke of Comigor, was not the last to remark on my independent turn of mind." Amid the shocked murmurs at my levity, I glimpsed not a few nods and smiles. The Lord High Prosecutor had never jousted at Windham.

"Yet you have been enslaved to this creature in some degenerate parody of holy wedlock?"

"I met this gentleman, whom you have treated so despicably, some five years ago," I said. "After a seemly time, we became engaged. Two years ago last Seille, Pere Dejarier witnessed our marriage before at least fifty people who are in this room. If you remember, sir, that same good priest was a witness to His Majesty's marriage to our queen. I don't believe Pere Dejarier, a priest of Annadis since my father was a boy, presides at degenerate rites."

Vycasso halted a moment longer than usual, but then whirled about and poked a finger at my face. "Tell me, madam, who are this devil's friends?"

"Until these scurrilous accusations were brought forth, I don't think you could find anyone who knew my husband who would not claim him as a friend. He has been regarded as a gentleman of wisdom and scholarship by those of the royal household, as well as those in his employ. Several of you gentlemen on the Council have been guests in our home or have consulted with my husband on matters of his specialties, history and archaeology. His Majesty, whose judgment in friends is known to be impeccable, requests his advice on artifacts to display in the palace, and most generously invited us to dine with him at Seille. Several people in this room can attest to it."

Vycasso cast a sidelong glance at the king, but Evard wore no expression. "Yes, yes, we know the beast was a secret and sly devil," said the prosecutor, "hiding his vile craft behind a façade of respectability. But it is well known that he has practiced his depravity here in the heart of our beloved realm. Tell us, madam, of the evils he did perpetrate in your home."

"If you account eating, sleeping, studying, entertaining, and keeping company with one's wife to be evil, then the same evils as other men." A few snickers erupted in the crowd, quickly silenced by a glare from Lord Hessia.

The prosecutor forged onward, undeterred. "When did you learn this man was a sorcerer?"

"Tell me, Lord Prosecutor, what is your definition of a sorcerer? Explain it to me, and then I can tell you when I knew of it."

Smirking, he gestured toward the crowd. "Why, everyone knows that. A sorcerer is one who perverts nature, despicable filth who revels in the blood and death of human men and women and innocent children."

"Then my husband is not and has never been a sorcerer, my lord. Your own evidence contradicts such an accusation. You have accused him of healing my injuries and rescuing Misara's family from a dreadful death. Such acts, even if possible, could hardly be considered reveling in blood and death. Perhaps your definition of sorcery is flawed, for I'm sure you've no intention of slandering the honorable warriors of Leire who rejoice in the slaughter of our enemies. Do you accuse them of sorcery also?"

"Got you there, Lordship!" shouted someone from the back. Vycasso glared at a guard and jerked his head at the man, but before the soldier could move, those around him took care of the matter. A scuffle broke out amid murmurs of "Devil!" and "Devil's whore, accusing our own . . ."

I could not listen to them. I had to stay in control. My words were the only defense we were going to get. "Karon reveres life and cherishes nature, and the only perversion here is what you honorable men have done to him."

Careful, careful, echoed the soft words in my mind.

"Sorcerers have these exceptional abilities," piped up Lord Hessia, an intelligent and reasonable man who had done his best to make the Council a serious body. He was clearly disturbed. "Unlike those of ordinary men."

I held on to the edge of the witness box and leaned toward the lord, as if one hand's breadth less distance between us and I might convince him. "Like yourself, sir, who are accounted the finest swordsman ever to carry a blade? Or like my brother, who is said to be the only man in a generation to rival you? Like this young singer from Valleor, who had half the court in tears over a song that is hackneyed drivel? Are you a sorcerer, then, and my brother and Misara also?"

"No, no," burst out the prosecutor, brought to life once more by an impatient gesture from Evard. "Lord Hessia means abilities that are *against* nature. They claim for themselves powers reserved for the gods."

"Then tell me, my lords. What has Karon done that is against nature?"

The prosecutor exhaled his foul breath into my face again, nodding in satisfaction. "Clearly the beast has deafened you, my lady. Your very sovereign king has testified that this devil healed you from a knife wound that punctured your heart. If that is not against nature—"

"But there is Lord Dumont in the Council box, who has seen something quite the same." I pointed at a graying warrior who sat in serious contemplation, his mouth buried in one hand. "Lord Dumont, did not the respected physician, Ren Wesley, bring back your wife from the brink of death after your fine son was born last autumn? Her very heart had stopped beating, and you had closed her eyes with your own hand. How is it that nature rejoiced at your dear lady's recovery and is scandalized at my own?"

Dumont, the most respected of all the Counselors, waved his hand as if trying to shoo away such an association. "Such healing is natural. What was done to you is but a mockery." But his tone was thoughtful, almost a question of itself.

I directed my words as if he were the only judge. "Please explain to me, my lord, why the healing is ignoble, when the act of striking a knife to my heart is left unchallenged? Though His Majesty's sight was blocked, every other man in that room saw truer crime. The hand that wielded the knife was not the hand of my husband who was bound and restrained by the king's own guards—no weakling recruits—but rather that of this sheriff, Maceron, who sets himself above other men. Sober consideration will expose the truth of my words, for despite the wags' tales of spirit slaves and armies of the healed, Karon had nothing to gain by such an act. I had already defended him that night. And think of it—I had lived with him uncoerced for two years. What reason could compel him to strike me down and then heal me in front of the one witness who could be the most devastating? Monumental stupidity is not listed among the crimes of which he is accused." I turned back to the yellow-faced Vycasso. "No, my Lord Prosecutor, you must explain to all rational observers why Maceron's deed, the unprovoked act of attempted murder, rather than the undoing of it, was not the true perversion."

So it continued for an hour or more. I tried to answer every charge and insinuation with reason and logic. I had clearly won several of the Council lords, especially those who were friends with Martin and had frequented his salons; they likely knew why he was not in his place that morning. Yet their grim faces told me that every one of them would vote for condemnation. A verdict of sorcery had to be unanimous, and Evard would permit nothing else. He would appeal to greed, to fear, to patriotism, to blackmail, whatever was necessary to get his way. As this harsh truth sank in, my only defense against despair was the frail satisfaction that Karon would not die undefended.

A few more witnesses were questioned after me. A workman from the Antiquities Commission claimed to have watched from hiding while Karon made boxes and chests fly about the cellars, and to have hidden his eyes when the mummified remains of ancient Isker warriors pushed their way out of their caskets at Karon's command. A servant girl, whom I had dismissed for terrorizing a young chambermaid and stealing her wages, vowed that Karon had me thoroughly under his control, not allowing me to go out into society and forcing me to spend inordinate amounts of time reading and writing. "No great lady would do such things voluntarily," she said.

The lords looked embarrassed at this testimony, and the prosecutor moved quickly to his closing flourish. To gasps of shock and disbelief, he entered into evidence signed confessions from the would-be usurper, the Earl of Gault, and his chief counselor. The documents detailed the sorcerer's plot to murder the king and his young daughter, Princess Roxanne, to put the Earl of Gault on the throne as a vassal of the Priest-King of Kerotea. The prosecutor proposed that I be made to verify the handwriting, as the earl was my own cousin, and I was intimately acquainted with the accused.

It made no difference to claim the confessions were worthless when extracted by torture. King Evard permitted no torture, therefore, no torture was done. To allow the confessed traitors to speak before the court would only give them leave to denounce our king and give scandal to the good people of Leire.

I could not listen to these last absurdities. I fixed my eyes on Karon's back, blocking out every other voice, every other sound and face, the better to hear him and concentrate only on his words. *I could want no better counsel,* he said. *I wish—* He began coughing again and could not continue.

Less than an hour after the prosecutor's impassioned call for the final obliteration of the great heresy of sorcery, the Council of Lords filed back into the Hall of Judgment from the adjoining chamber where they had completed their deliberations. A red-faced Lord Hessia's lips were a thin line. Lord Dumont fixed his eyes on the ancient candlebeam above the witness box, the fifty thick candles lit by the servants and the beam raised against the early darkness. Just past the doorway through which they had returned, Darzid leaned against a pillar with easy grace, detached amusement flickering in his dark eyes. And so was my last spark of hope extinguished.

Things do not look promising, my love, I thought.

It will be well, whatever they say. I'm ready for it to be over. After another dreadful bout of coughing, Karon sagged against the wooden rail of the prisoner's dock. To make him stand up again his guards prodded him with spears until fresh bloodstains appeared on his filthy tunic. For the first time that day, I averted my eyes.

They said guilty, of course, but I had not prepared myself for the deadly precision of the words.

*   *   *

The sorcerer is to be taken to the command of Montevial at dawn on the first day of the week, there to be exhibited on public display. On that same day at one hour past midday he is to be set afire until the stain of his existence is removed from the paths of human history. His name is never again to be spoken in any of the Four Realms and is to be erased from any document or record in which it is written. He is to be forgotten as if he had never been.

Every possession of the sorcerer is to be destroyed by fire, including his place of residence, the furnishings and accouterments thereof, whether such possession is the rightful property of the sorcerer or the marriage portion or personal belonging of his wife, and any other object determined by the prosecutor or the priests to be polluted by his touch, especially any article of jewelry or stonework, or any artifact of writing, as sorcerers are known to store up wickedness in such things.

Because of the generous recommendation of His Most Gracious Majesty at the petition of her family, the sorcerer's wife is judged to be a wayward and deluded woman, rather than a conspirator. She will remain in the custody of the Crown until such time as she has done public penance according to the law. At that time she will be remanded to the physical and moral discipline of Tomas, Duke of Comigor, who will maintain sole sovereignty over her life, residence, property, and issue. She will remain on the life parole of His Majesty, King Evard, all rights of birth, rank, and grant to be removed from her until His Majesty may see fit to restore them.

Any person who has been judged by the Lord High Prosecutor to have condoned, had knowledge of, consented to, or failed to report any act of sorcery by this condemned prisoner is likewise judged guilty at this hour, and is to receive the maximum penalty of the law without further trial. Any other person who has, in any wise, been associated with the sorcerer, whether as servant, employee, or acquaintance, is required to report to a priest for purification within seven days' time. Failure to comply with this order will result in a charge of conspiracy to acts of sorcery, and punishment will be meted out accordingly without need for further trial. Thus speaks the law of Leire. All everlasting glory to Evard King!

*   *   *

"Without trial?" I leaped to my feet, the bleak brutality of the judgment destroying my composure. Karon's case was unsalvageable, but Martin, Julia, Tanager, and Tennice would not even be heard. "You can't do that! Lord Hessia . . . Lord Dumont . . ." I was shouting to be heard above the pandemonium. "To execute any Leiran without trial is a violation . . ." But no one of them would look at me, and a guard blocked my way lest I try to get any closer. "Karon, save them," I cried. How could he let them die?

But he could not have heard me. A troop of guards had dragged him from the dock by the chain around his neck. The shouting ruffians gathered outside the door battered him with fists and cudgels, pelted him with stones and refuse. The guards neither protected him from the blows nor shielded him from the spitting vehemence of the good people of Leire who laughed and jeered at his painful stumbling.

It was midweek. Four days. At least it would not be a long wait.

Martin and the others were executed that night. Karon was riven with grief. *I had to listen to them die, Seri, one after the other. I've tried . . . since they were taken, I've tried to help . . . to comfort them . . . but at the end . . .*

"Don't speak of it, if you don't want to. Just tell me how I can help you." I sat on my bed unmoving, staring dry-eyed at the coarse sheets as the weak daylight faded. I could not grieve. I had nothing left.

The only help is knowing that your brother will protect you and Connor. My blood and flesh grew hot with his outrage. *What kind of man is your brother? How can he let them do these things to you like public penance? Oh, Seri, it is so hard. . . .* Never had I known Karon so angry.

"The penance is nothing," I said, numbly, trying to ignore the fear that suddenly came tumbling over me like an icy waterfall. "As for the rest—whatever comes—I will survive it all. I swear to you I will." The Council's proclamation echoed in my ears. My brother was to have *sole right of sovereignty over her life, residence, property, and issue. . . .* Issue. My children.

*   *   *

In the next days, Karon was abandoned in his darkness and pain. I believed they gave him only enough sustenance to keep him alive until the day of execution. I prayed he would die before it, and in the same thought I would will time itself to stand still.

Lost in pain and sickness, his mind began to wander, but I could always bring him back by directing my thoughts to him. Often he would speak of the word and the images he believed were buried in him. *The images come clearer, the less there is of me. There is a bridge suspended over the chasm, and I see figures passing over it, some anxious or frightened, some joyful and full of wonder, some lost, looking for their way. The bridge is so fragile . . . made of ice, I think, for it's so cold . . . but glorious light . . . I think it sings.*

My blood burns, Seri. I feel such urgency. With everything that's happened, our closeness in these days—such a joy that has been—and all the rest of it, good and bad together, I've stored up so much power that I feel as if I might burst with it. Do you understand, love? Tell me that you understand why I can't . . .

"Of course I understand. You told me long ago how it would be."

But as Karon wandered in his dream world, I retreated more and more behind my private wall. I dared not tell him what I feared about our child's future. He had already demonstrated that his convictions were unshakable—and so I betrayed my son and betrayed my own soul and kept silent. It could be five or six years before a child showed signs of sorcery. Everything could change in that time. Tomas would never harm an infant.

Karon hurried time along. *I'm glad it isn't long. I think I can manage—how many days is it?*

"Two more," I told him.

Two more. That I can do, I think. Do they treat you decently? It must be so hard for you to be shut in for so long. You hate it so. I've been afraid to ask, and you've said so little of your situation . . . so little of anything these days. I've monopolized our time with madness. No one comes here any more, even to tell me lies about you.

"I'm as well as I can be. There's a mute woman named

Maddy who brings my meals and such. It doesn't break my heart that they ignore me." I prodded him to talk again. I was afraid of what I might say.

In the dark hours before dawn on the first day of the week, they took Karon to the broad commard in the heart of Montevial and chained him to the stake they had erected there. The weather was freezing, and they mounted a double row of guards around the pyre so that no misguided zealot could rob the people of their pleasure at his burning.

Stars of night, it's cold, he said to me, once they had him bound there. *But I don't think I'll make any wish to be warm. Not today.* That was the only reference he made to what was to come. He spoke of private things that morning while the guards came for me: of our meeting, of his family, of our talks about death and life and our speculations about gods who might exist somewhere behind the myths of the uncaring Twins. Two serving sisters removed my dress, and clothed me in a penitent's gown, a long robe of rough, undyed wool. Then they cut off my hair that had scarcely been touched since I was a little girl.

So passed our last time together. I let him talk, hoping it might shield him from the horror that seethed around him. He did not know I watched from the palace balcony there in the bright winter sun and freezing wind. The whole morning I stood with him, until an hour past midday when the bells tolled and drums rattled and the first wisps of smoke floated up from the pyre.

Only then did my fear and grief erupt into frenzied babbling—demanding that he save our child, begging him to free himself or to grab hold of me and take me with him, if he could do naught else. I called him cowardly and cruel and a hundred vile names. But my thoughts and words were in such chaos that he claimed he could not distinguish them. *Hush, Seri love. Please. There is too much. I can't understand you.* And when I forced myself silent, he tried to comfort me, who had to keep breathing while he suffered. *Live, my dearest love. You are the essence of life and beauty, and you will shine as a beacon to me long after I cross the Verges. Because of you, there are no demons in this darkness. No moment I've spent with you do I regret, not even this. And you must have no regrets either. This word I've found is a word of healing, Seri. I feel it. I know it. It's what I'm here for, and I think that if I wait until my power is at its greatest . . . from all that happens . . . then perhaps I'll do what I'm here on earth to do. It's a good thing to believe.*

But I could not answer. I did not believe. I closed off my mind and averted my eyes, and when the flames took him, I could not listen to his cry. Only much later, in my dreams, did I hear the word he shaped from his will, and the fire, and his destroyed flesh. "D'Arnath!"

CHAPTER 21

"D'Arnath!" I cried out, startling myself awake, the horror of the familiar dream swept away in the moment of revelation.

Baglos looked up from the tiny, smokeless fire that crackled in the hut's firepit. "What is it, woman?"

A few last golden arrows of the summer sunshine shot through the thick canopy of the trees and the unshuttered window of the charcoal burner's hut. I had fallen asleep in a dim corner after my return from Yurevan, only to dream of the fire yet again. But instead of desolation, bitterness, and self-hatred, the dream left me with a confusion of feeling so intense that the sunlight felt drab and lifeless.

"Ten years ago, my husband spoke that name. . . . How could he possibly have known it? He hadn't heard your stories. Your history. Buried . . . hidden . . . inside him. Your dead king's name. A word he could imbue with all his power as he died . . . hoping . . . believing . . . that something of meaning would come from it." I was on my feet, pacing the room, flexing my fingers, pulling at my hair, stretching my arms to feel the sunlight as if all my append-ages had been detached and were only now reconnected to my body, blood rushing into the dry, empty veins. "But I didn't believe. I couldn't hope, because I didn't have the words." D'Arnath. The king who had built the Bridge be-tween a land of magic and a land of exile. . . .

And as if I had pulled it from the weft of life's weaving, a thread lay in my hand, drawn from the tangle of the past. The thread that connected past and present. A thread of enchantment and fate and purpose. I halted in mid-stride and stared at the Dulcé and the Prince with new eyes. "Stars of heaven . . . I know what he did!"

D'Natheil was carving on his birchwood and glanced up curiously. He motioned Baglos to his side and never took his eyes from my face as the Dulcé translated everything I'd said. Tennice, who had been standing watch, walked into the hut just in time to hear my last outburst. "Who did what, Seri?"

"My dream. All these years I've dreamed about the day Karon died. No matter what I did, no matter how much I willed the past to be gone, I couldn't rid myself of that one horror. But I think it was because I never listened to what it told me, the comfort it offered if I but knew how to hear it."

"I don't understand."

"Nor did I until now. In all that pain and torment, Karon insisted on finding order and beauty. I never believed it. Or rather, I believed in what he found, but I never thought he accomplished anything. I heard no word of magic when he died. Our child was murdered. All of you were dead. I believed he failed, and I was so angry with him—oh, gods, for all these years I've been so angry with him—because he let it all happen for nothing. But I didn't know what to listen for. Today, when I dreamed it again, I heard him say the word."

"D'Arnath," said Baglos, reverently.

The memories of those last dreadful days came tumbling out of me. "He found images with the word: a great chasm and a bridge. He was almost mad with pain, and I couldn't tell what was real and what was delirium. I put it all out of my mind, because I was convinced it had no meaning and I couldn't bear the thought. But now I know. Baglos, Karon opened your Gates, didn't he?"

"It could very well be, woman. I wish I could tell you it was so."

"Tell me about the day the Gates were opened." For, of course, I had to know more. What result could possibly have been worth the price?

D'Natheil nodded to Baglos, and the Dulcé sat up straight, as he always did when telling stories of his land. "When the Gates are open, their fire burns white, and any may walk through without harm. But as they fail, the flame darkens, a fire that ravages first the spirit and then the flesh of any who attempt to pass. When the fire burns black— a fearsome sight—the Gate is impassable, and the dismal reflection of that dark fire permeates our hearts and every part of our land. And so it had been for hundreds of years.

"On that day the Zhid were attacking in a great fury, as if they thought that victory was only the next arrow away. In the fortress kitchens we were making hot soup to send out to those on the walls, for the cold winds were blowing off the Wastes. The runners thought their legs might fail from making so many trips, but they didn't complain. Too often they would go back for the empty pots and find the one to whom they had delivered it dead or his mind stripped away in the way of the Zhid that is worse than death."

The Dulcé transitioned smoothly from Leiran to his own language and back again. "But then came a peal of thunder, and we felt a surge of power, a storm of light and glory as if the Veils—the colored lights that grace the northern skies in summer—had descended on our hearts and infused us all with joy and hope. Though no one of us in Avonar had lived when last the Gates were open, we knew what the change signified, for there came a brilliance about every object from the most graceful tower of the palace to the least pebble underfoot, transforming the city with indescribable beauty. You could hear the warriors on the walls singing the Chant of Thanksgiving, so that your blood throbbed with it, and when night fell, no one could sleep for the singing and the talk of what the opening might mean. Would we wake to find the fire dark again? Would our young prince come to the Gate to walk the Bridge? With the strength and the light of the Gate infusing us, the Bridge strong, would we be able to push the Zhid back from the walls of the city? Would rain fall in the Wastes?" Baglos's voice cracked and stumbled with emotion.

"In his visions Karon saw brilliant light, and he thought the bridge was singing. How did you know it was the Exiles that opened the Gates?" *Prove it to me,* my skeptic's heart demanded. *Convince me.*

"Why, because even the Preceptors, as powerful as they are, cannot do it. Only D'Arnath's Heirs ever had power enough to reverse the darkening of the Gate fire, and since the Battle of Ghezir, where we lost half of the Vales of Eidolon and D'Arnath's sword, even they had not been capable. Prince D'Natheil was young and untrained and had shown no evidence of any power. We had seen no sign of the Exiles since well before the Battle of Ghezir. They had failed in their duty to walk the Bridge. But this *had* to be the Exiles for no one else could have accomplished it."

For a moment, all I could envision was Karon's Avonar and its forest of blackened pyres. Bitterness leaked into my heart. "All those years, Baglos, why didn't your people come here and find out what happened to the Exiles? They were being slaughtered. Perhaps everything would have been different if someone had come here to see what was happening."

"Because the Bridge was never meant to be crossed! It is not a roadway, but a link between our lands. It binds— Dar'Nethi power—It must remain open. To make things right. Your passions—Life flows—" All of a sudden the Dulcé was fumbling with words. A dozen false starts and disconnected phrases. Screwing his face in knots and tugging at his black hair with his short fingers. "I'm sorry I cannot explain better today. If only D'Natheil could—"

He bit his tongue and glanced uneasily at the Prince before grasping at some thought and plunging ahead more smoothly. "King D'Arnath could not allow the Zhid free passage to your lands. He sent J'Ettanne and his followers here to maintain the far Gate—the Exiles' Gate—and their part of the Bridge. Then he enchanted the Bridge with his strongest wards so that no one could use it to cross the

Breach. J'Ettanne and his people could never return to Avonar nor any come here to succor them. It took the Dar'Nethi hundreds of years to discover D'Arnath's secret way to make the passage. By that time, of course, the Gates were long closed. All was done for your mundane land's safety."

I puzzled at these spotty explanations, but no path of reason led me anywhere that made sense. We *had* to unlock D'Natheil's mind. If the Bridge was only an enchantment, then what did Baglos mean when he talked of people crossing it? What chasm was so wide that people could find no other way around it?

"It's near sundown, Seri." Tennice held out my cloak. "We have an appointment. Perhaps more of this mystery will come clear with it. The thought that some higher purpose was served by all that misery . . . I'd like to think it. But your evidence wouldn't stand in any court of law."

"He did it," I said. "Karon opened their Gates." No matter what the sense or nonsense of Baglos's explanations, my bones resonated with the truth of my dream. I had been adrift for so long. Now, perhaps, I had found an anchor.

The streets of Yurevan were full of people, hurrying through patterns of lamplight and shadow. I was afraid to expect too much from the meeting with Celine, but after the revelation of the dream, it was hard to keep myself in balance. What other truths might I discover, now that this one basic understanding was so changed? By the time the four of us entered the quiet, narrow street near the herb shop, my heart was racing.

The shop was closed and dark, shutters drawn, but Celine had instructed us to enter through her rear courtyard, where Kellea would meet us. Yellow lantern light and the heavy scents of herbs and flowers guided us through a dark alleyway, and we found Kellea waiting amid the crowded boxes and planters. But her greeting was not at all what we expected. In her hand was a battered, yet quite serious, sword. "Don't think that because I'm a woman, I'm incapable of using this. I practice, and I'm very good."

"Please believe me," I said. "We wish no harm to either of you."

"My grandmother took me to a sorcerer-burning when I was a child. She said it was 'necessary' for me to learn of it. And so I did. Nothing is worth the risk of such a death: not sorcery, not you, not princes who've lost their minds. I care only for my grandmother. If you mean what you say, then go away and leave her be."

"You say you care for her, but it's clear you don't care enough," I said. Kellea had not chosen her time well, not when the truth of the dream was so fresh in my mind. "You've chosen your own path. Good enough. But you deprive your grandmother of the same dignity. Is it because she's old? Is she incapable? You've listened to no lesson she's taught, if you set yourself up to make her choices for her."

"Ah yes, the holy 'Way of the J'Ettanne,' " said the girl, sneering. "Well, I despise their Way. I will not submit to my 'fate,' and I will not let you endanger my grandmother. You don't know. You didn't see it."

The arguments might have come from my own mouth. And only on this day did I have any reason to refute them. "But I *have* seen it. The one I saw burn was my husband whom I loved beyond anything on earth, and I had to let him do it."

Kellea shook her head. "You're a fool."

"Yes, I was a fool, but only because I didn't trust the choices he made. I could see only the horror and grief that would result from them. He believed there was more. I'm still not sure he was right—perhaps the universe does have some larger pattern that I just can't see—but it was not my place to judge."

"Kellea?" The dry voice floated from the window.

"One moment, Grandmother."

At Celine's call, Kellea's sword point drooped only a hair's breadth from its ready position, but it was enough for D'Natheil. In a motion as quick and fluid as a dancer's, he snatched the weapon and laid it on the brick paving stones beside Kellea's feet, bowing in mock courtesy. We left her fuming in the courtyard while the four of us walked into her kitchen and through a hallway to Celine's door.

"Come in, come in," said the old woman. The evening breeze carried the fragrances from the courtyard planters through the sitting-room window, and a white china lamp painted with pink flowers cast rosy shadows over the walls, leaving the boundaries of her little domain indistinct. "Forgive us. My granddaughter is headstrong."

"She loves you very much," I said.

"I wish—Well, perhaps someday she will find joy in her talent and her life. So this is our mysterious pair?"

The Dulcé and the Prince stood on either side of me, while Tennice crowded the passageway behind us. "Madame Celine, this is Baglos of the Dulcé"—Baglos bowed with great dignity, one arm behind his back, and Celine nodded graciously in return—"and this is D'Natheil, whom Baglos tells us is a prince of the royal house of Avonar." The Prince stood stiff and expressionless. Wary, I thought. Uncertain. I hoped the season stayed calm.

"Please excuse my lack of courtesy, Your Grace," said Celine, beckoning D'Natheil closer, deftly ignoring his rudeness. "Once I'm installed in my chair, not even royalty can dislodge me. And I've a serious lack of thrones here. You'll have to sit upon your own dignity." She tapped one slippered foot on the floor in front of her.

Baglos looked slightly shocked, but translated the old woman's words for D'Natheil. The young man listened gravely, then stepped out of the shadows, sat himself on the bare wood at Celine's feet, and bestowed upon the old Healer the gift of his smile.

"Oh, my," she said, raising her eyebrows and laying her dry fingers on his cheek. "What sorcery is this? I didn't doubt your words, Seri, but this . . . this is beyond your telling. Beyond wonder. Can you not see—?" She glanced sharply at me. "No, perhaps not. Kellea!"

The girl appeared in the doorway, her complexion an unflattering blotchy red.

"Kellea, dear one, I want you beside me tonight."

While I settled myself on a footstool beside the door, and Tennice folded his long limbs onto the floor beside me, Celine rocked gently in her chair, quietly staring at the not-at-all-self-conscious D'Natheil. Kellea took up a position beside the window, standing with her back pressed against the wall and her arms folded tightly across her breast.

"Do you know what I'm going to do?" Celine asked D'Natheil, when we were still.

Baglos, positioned immediately behind his master, translated quietly. The Prince kept his attention on Celine and nodded in response. The Dulcé managed this so smoothly, one could almost think that D'Natheil and Celine were speaking with each other directly.

"And you consent to it? You give me permission to enter your mind and relate to these people whatever I find there?"

D'Natheil nodded again.

"Seri has told you that this may help you regain your memory. That's possible. If some physical ailment is hindering your memory or your speech, I can almost warrant success. I am very good at such things. But what I feel in you . . . There is much *in* you that is not *of* you." She sipped from a porcelain teacup, and then returned it to the small table next her chair. "Well, we shall see. You will know whatever I find. I'll reflect each image I discover. Just nod your head if it's familiar, and we'll go on. When we find something that is new to you, I'll tell the others. If there comes a time when you wish me to stop—I understand you cannot speak, but just think your intent, form it clearly in your mind—and I'll hear you. Do you understand?"

Once more, the Prince agreed.

The old woman put a wrinkled hand on either side of D'Natheil's head. Interesting, I thought, as the familiar tension began to vibrate throughout the room, how those who feared sorcery believed it came through the eyes, while Celine, like Karon, closed hers to begin her work. After a while she blinked them open, and D'Natheil dipped his head. Another while and he nodded again. So it continued. Silently. Forever, it seemed, until Celine abruptly yanked her hands away. She shuddered, sat back in her cushioned chair, and dropped her hands into her lap, the wrinkles on her brow very deep indeed. "Powers of earth, what's happened to you?" Only the rosy light gave color to the old woman's soft wrinkles, and her eyes wrapped the Prince in an embrace of sympathy and concern.

"I've found no memory he does not recognize," she said. "The only images in his mind are those you've shared. Indeed, I can find no *person* here, no history, no hidden life. I sought out his earliest memory: fierce, biting cold and immense confusion, an overarching certainty of danger. The next thing he knows is your face, Seri, frightened, angry, in a forest near a stream—a stark, powerful image, as if a knife blade had pierced his head. But we know that was only a few weeks ago, and so I started again at the cold and reversed direction. But when I go backward, I find only darkness. A well of darkness. Terror, confusion, loss . . . holy goddess mother, such dreadful emptiness."

"But isn't this what you'd expect from one whose memory is damaged?" said Tonnice, voicing my own question.

"Not at all. With one whose memory is damaged, I would find traces, threads from the hidden life. I could follow them into the dark part of the mind and work to heal the injury. But not with this one. It's as if he were newborn from chaos at the time he met Seri. He is as you see him, unless"—she leaned forward again and laid two trembling fingers on D'Natheil's cheek—"unless this enchantment I sense is responsible. If I could unravel the enchantment, heal whatever damage it has done, then perhaps we could learn more."

D'Natheil listened carefully while Baglos repeated all of this, then motioned to the old woman to continue.

"This will be more difficult," Celine said to D'Natheil. "Once we start, we must go to the end of it. No stopping, no changing course." Her expression was drawn with worry, and, as if to soothe herself, she stroked his hair. I was surprised he allowed it, but indeed, he smiled for her again.

Celine's eyes widened. "Oh, my son, what miracle has brought you to us? Whatever I find in you, it will not be all of you, I think." She reached into the sewing basket that sat beside her chair and pulled out a tiny silver knife and a strip of white linen. "This is the way we'll have to do it, the only way I know to heal this deeper hurt."

Celine locked gazes with D'Natheil, and he held out his arm to her. Then she opened her arms wide, and my heart swelled as she began the J'Ettanni invocation. I whispered the words along with her. "Life, hold. Stay your hand. Halt your foot ere it lays another step along the Way. Grace your daughter once more with your voice that whispers in the deeps, with your spirit that sings in the wind, with the fire that blazes in your wondrous gifts of joy and sorrow. Fill my soul with light, and let the darkness make no stand in this place."

D'Natheil did not even blink when the old woman scored his muscled arm with her little knife. When she had done the same to her own left arm, so scarred that no bit of flesh remained untouched, she deftly bound her paper-skinned limb to the strong young one. "*J'den encour*, my son."

Celine might have been the only person in the Prince's universe. Curiosity and urgency defined every line of his body. Celine's eyes were closed, her only motion the constant, gentle nodding of her white head. About the time I came to the conclusion that this attempt, too, must come to nothing, the old woman's eyes popped open in astonishment, and in my head resonated a voice and a presence that belonged to no one in that room.

Let your ears be opened, D'Natheil, my honored prince, my beloved son. I trust this message finds you well and among friends. Know that it was never my desire to cause you the distress and confusion that cloud your mind, though it is the inevitable result of what I have done to you. Small comfort, I know, since you cannot remember me. If we succeed in our plan, then you will know my reasons; if we do not, then you will be beyond the Verges, and such trivial questions will be moot. I do not apologize, for I had no alternatives.

I had never heard such a voice, its timbre the image of thunder and wind, bearing within it a complexity of love, wisdom, and monumental pride. Everyone in the room heard the same, I judged. A pale Tennice slammed his hands to his ears. Kellea opened her mouth and stared at the Prince with revulsion. Baglos leaped to his feet, backing away from D'Natheil and Celine, hissing, "Dassine!"

To you, friends of D'Natheil, who have found a way to unlock this message, my gratitude and admiration. By your deeds you bolster our last hope. Some say it is unwise to trust any but our own with the knowledge I give you, but our days grow short. Now you have come this far, I must believe that you, whom I have entrusted with our future, are able and willing to do what must be done next. And so my words are meant for you as well as D'Natheil.

The man lived in my head as truly as did my own thoughts. . . . *a cool morning . . . a dove cooing mournfully from a garden beyond an open door . . . fat dripping into a cooking fire . . .* I would have sworn that I heard and smelled and felt his surroundings as truly as I smelled Celine's flowers and felt the shifting airs of the mild Vallorean evening.

My name is Dassine. I am a Preceptor of Gondai, and I dwell in the city of Avonar, from whence I have sent this D'Natheil and the Dulcé who is his Guide. With the release of this enchantment that I have buried inside you, my prince, you will know how to unlock the knowledge of the Dulcé. If you have not yet learned of our history, of the Catastrophe that we have wrought upon ourselves, of the war that threatens to throw the universe into chaos, or D'Arnath's Bridge that is your singular responsibility and our lasting hope for redemption, then you must ask these things of the good Dulcé.

Baglos stumbled backward over my knee, grabbing the door frame to steady himself. I paid him no mind, for I was mesmerized by the enchantment, especially when I believed . . . when I knew . . . the sorcerer's words were meant for me.

Our world is not the world you know. Gondai exists side by side with your own in much the same way that a reflection or a shadow exists side by side with its original, its subordinate nature only a matter of one's point of view. As the reflection completes the image, and the shadow defines the light, so do our two worlds create a balance in the universe—the power of enchantment that exists in Gondai and the exuberant passions that flourish in your world. When life's essence flows between us as it was meant to do, we are both immeasurably enriched.

"I knew it!" I murmured, though no one in the room had attention to spare for me. Another world—the mad idea I had not been able to articulate. The only answer to the puzzle of two Avonars . . . of gates and bridges and the exiled J'Ettanne.

For thousands of years our talents, so different from those of your people, were nourished by the glorious abundance and beauty of our world. We knew of your

world, too. We wandered into it freely through the many
gateways that joined us, but we were shy of the vigorous
life you lead, never revealing ourselves and never staying
too long.

After our Catastrophe—a disaster birthed of three sorcerers' pride—our world lay in ruins. Yet we believed that our
connection to your world would be enough to empower us,
even to repair such damage as had been done. But the Catastrophe left a Breach between us, a chasm of chaos that destroys the reason of any who attempt to cross it and blocks
this flow of sustenance that we need so desperately. Thus
our king, D'Arnath, conceived and built this Bridge—a link
of enchantment between the worlds—to be our salvation, to
restore the balance and allow life to flow between as it had
ever done. He and his beloved brother J'Ettanne pledged
their lives and those of their heirs to defend the Bridge and
the Gates that bounded it against any challenge. Once a year
they would pass through the Gates and walk their part of
the Bridge, using the link as a lifeline through the chaos and
spending their power to repair and strengthen and sustain it.
Their oath is a bulwark of the Bridge, a critical part of the
enchantment that sustains it.

The Dulcé can tell you how we have fought to keep their
oath for this thousand years, and how often we have failed.
We Dar'Nethi are much diminished since the days of D'Arnath and J'Ettanne, and stand at the verge of losing everything we value within ourselves, as well as without.

You children of that other world might well say, "What
has this to do with us? Why should we care that a foolish
and greedy people have destroyed themselves?" What you
must understand is that our doom is also yours. When the
Gates are closed, your world, too, falls out of balance, dis-
harmony and discord festering into wars and great wickedness. And the Lords of Zhev'Na—these three of our kind
who have created this disaster—rejoice, for the evils of your
world nourish their power and strength far beyond what our
lore can explain. D'Arnath and J'Ettanne knew that if the
Bridge were to fall, your world would follow Gondai into
everlasting ruin. Thus, they took upon themselves the responsibility for your safety, as well as ours.

For hundreds of years the Gates have been closed, the
Lords growing in power with every rising of the sun. We

fear the Bridge is near its end, either from the corrupting influence of the Breach it spans, or from the relentless assaults of the Lords on Avonar. Ten years ago, the Exiles gave us one last chance to repair it. We have come near squandering that chance. And so now, in our last hour, we have sent our prince, D'Arnath's last Heir, to walk the Bridge once more.

What I have done to you, D'Natheil, was necessary. I had counted on time enough to help you discover your way, to help you learn what you must do to make the Bridge strong and resilient. But our luck has run out. After a thousand years of trying, the Lords of Zhev'Na have at last discovered how to break the power of D'Arnath's oath, a secret that we ourselves do not know. You are all that stand in their way. I fear for your life, D'Natheil, and for your soul, and I fear for the Bridge. It must not fall. Our enemies don't know what I have done to you or how little we know about D'Arnath's enchantments, and so your task is even more difficult than they suspect.

This is a formidable burden, and in your darkness and confusion must seem impossible, but you must understand, my prince . . . my son . . . that there is no one more worthy of our trust than are you. As you learn of yourself, you will discover what must be done to save us. The glory of your fathers lives within you, and, given time, it will blaze forth as hope for the peoples of both worlds.

I thought perhaps the message was done, but anger rumbled in my belly, and I did not believe it was my own.

One last truth that even the Dulcé may not know. With shame I must tell you that not all of our enemies have the empty eyes of the Zhid. Some who wear our own likeness have become so lost in their despair that they've sold their souls to preserve this fragment of life we call Avonar. They think that the Lords will honor their word, and that they themselves can embrace life again once enough murder and betrayal has been done. The sword of D'Arnath is a mighty talisman. Tales say it can give our warriors strength to hold against the Zhid, perhaps to push them back. For more than four hundred years has the sword lain with the Lords in their stronghold of Zhev'Na, but now these traitors have made an unholy—

The crash of splintering wood and breaking glass shattered our trance, breaking off the message. Rhythmic pounding battered the front of the herb shop, as if someone were trying to kick in the door. Emitting a string of oaths that would make a soldier blanch, Kellea retrieved her sword. "Take care of my grandmother!" she cried, as she disappeared into the passage.

"Seri, get them away!" Tennice said, drawing his sword, and starting after her. "I'll meet you at the horses if I can. But don't wait for me."

Baglos charged into the room and dropped to his knees beside the Prince. "My lord D'Natheil! Come quickly!" But D'Natheil's gaze was locked on Celine.

"Madame Celine, we must go," I said, forcing my voice calm as I crouched beside the old woman's chair and snatched up her healer's knife. "I need to cut the binding. Please, can you hear me? I'll wait for your word."

"One moment," said the old woman softly. "I must look deeper. I must know what he is."

From the shop came a thundering crash, then shouts and the clash of swords. A man's cry of painful wounding. But around me enchantment surged, and in the midst of the clamor intruded a sound so at odds with all the rest, I almost could not name it: laughter.

Celine sat pale and fragile by her fragrant window, chuckling merrily. "Cut it now," she said, her voice soft and hoarse. "Oh, to meet this Dassine! What audacious conceit! And what power to do this thing. . . ."

I cut the bloodstained linen, and Celine's arm dropped limply into her lap. "Seri, come here," she whispered, falling breathless back into her cushions. "Come close." Even in my terrible anxiety, I could not refuse her. "You have to know," she whispered in my ear. "Look deep. It is a wonder, all—" The old woman took a breath and tried to speak again, but shook her head. Then her head fell back, and, still smiling, she closed her eyes.

The noise from the other room grew louder. We dared not leave the old woman here alone. I shook her shoulder. "Madam Celine, we must get the Prince to safety. You need to come with us, too. D'Natheil, you'll have to carry her." I tried to tell him with my stupid gestures and the smattering of words I knew in his tongue.

Though his face was beginning to reflect the desperate sounds from the other room, the Prince remained at Celine's feet. He took her dry, wrinkled hand and kissed it, and then he looked up at me, tears welling in his blue eyes. "It's no use to take her," he said hoarsely. "She's dead."

CHAPTER 22

"Ce'na davonet, sacer Vasrin," cried Baglos. The Dulcé praised his god, allowing himself only this moment's wonder at D'Natheil's recovery. In a succeeding babble of exhortation, he pushed and tugged his master to his feet, urging him toward the doorway, the courtyard, and escape. D'Natheil refused to move, his hungry gaze lingering on Celine's face.

She looked so peaceful. Her dry, pink cheeks were relaxed. I bent my cheek to her mouth that still bore the trace of her smile and felt no breath. Dead. Beasts of earth and sky, what had we done?

A monstrous crashing from the direction of the shop wrenched the Prince's attention from the old woman. He looked up, bewildered at first, shocked as if someone had struck him.

"Mie giro, bence . . ." Again, Baglos shoved him toward the kitchen and the outer door, but D'Natheil snarled, slammed him against the wall, and charged toward the front of the shop. *"Ne, ne, mie giro!"* I thought the Dulcé might tear out his beard. How could he imagine D'Natheil would avoid a fight? Baglos and I hurried after him.

The shop was in chaos. Tennice was wedged against one wall, trying to persuade a snarling assailant to loosen the grip on his throat by bringing down a shelf of jars and bottles on the man's head. Kellea was circling with two men at sword's point. As she parried one attacker's sword, she used her left hand to grasp for whatever missile she could find—a box, a tray, a bronze measuring weight—to hurl at the second man who was feinting at her with a dagger. The shop door hung in splinters, and a burning torch lay on the floor next to a sprawled stranger with a bleeding head.

Wasting no time, D'Natheil lifted Tennice's opponent and flung him against the far wall, causing another loaded shelf to crash down on him. Tennice slumped to the floor between two barrels, staring straight ahead, bleeding from a wound in his side. While I dropped to my knees and tried to revive him, wadding the tail of his shirt to press against the wound, D'Natheil turned to Kellea's fight.

"Get out of here," Kellea yelled. "If you care for my grandmother as you say, take her out."

The man by the doorway struggled to his feet and lunged for Kellea's back, while her other two foes moved in for the kill. D'Natheil, his handsome face transformed by rage, hoisted a table and slammed it into the wounded man, sending him back to his place on the floor. As Kellea battled the swordsman, the Prince pressed the dagger-wielding attacker away from her and into the wall. Grabbing the hand that held the weapon, he forced the dagger back on its owner, shoving it smoothly, inexorably into the wide-eyed man's throat.

Baglos shrieked and pointed toward the broken window; two more men were climbing into the shop. I grabbed a broken table leg, ready to defend Tennice with it if I could find no better weapon. But in the next instant the flames from the fallen torch ignited a barrel, nearly blinding me and pelting us with sparks and splinters. Fiery tendrils raced through the baskets, dried plants, and old wooden planks of the shop. Flame engulfed the front wall, quickly filling the room with acrid brown smoke. Kellea dropped her sword, grabbed a woven sack from a pile in the corner, and started beating at the flames. D'Natheil and Baglos did likewise. As far as I could tell through the murk, the attackers who yet lived had run away.

Raising one arm to shield my face from the heat and sparks, I tugged at Tennice's arm. "Come on," I said. "We need to get you out of here." He remained limp and unresponsive. It was all I could do to haul him upright to lean against my shoulder.

Heat burst the glass jars, showering us with shards of hot glass, and flames consumed their contents in sweet-scented geysers of green, blue, and orange. Baglos tugged at D'Natheil, who was still flailing at the fire. "My lord, the day is lost! Save yourself. Please, my lord!"

Kellea slapped at her smoldering tunic. "Damn you all," she cried. "Damn you bringing your troubles here. Where is my grandmother?"

Coughing, choking, breathless with the heat and the effort of dragging Tennice toward the back of the shop, I could only shake my head.

The girl stared at me in horror, then dropped her bags and ran past me toward Celine's room. No ear in Yurevan could have failed to hear her wail. "Murderers!"

Tennice's long, limp body kept sagging out of my arms. Flames licked at his boots, and I had to knock away a flaming bundle of dried burdock that fell from the ceiling, threatening to set our clothes and hair afire. *Come on, come on,* I begged silently. *I won't leave you.* My sweat-slicked hands slipped on his bare arms as I stumbled forward, no longer sure I was going in the right direction. His body slipped again, and my arms were empty. I spun around, peering through the smoke, panicked when I couldn't locate him. But a grunt just ahead of me came from D'Natheil who was dragging my old friend through the doorway ahead of me. A hand on my back was Baglos, pushing me after them.

The air in the back passage was slightly cooler. I caught a breath and wiped my watering eyes. Beyond the sitting room door, Kellea knelt beside her grandmother, her head in the old woman's lap, no tears softening her cold mask of grief. Smoke snaked through the doorway and the window.

"Kellea, come away. The roof has caught." I had to shout over the roar of the fire.

The girl did not acknowledge my presence.

"Listen to me. You're right that we've caused her life to end, though we had no such intent. But I want you to know that she laughed before she died. She was filled with joy at what we brought her. Don't ruin her life's ending by wasting yours."

"Go away. You speak of choices. Let me make my own." Her words were shaped of granite.

I joined the others who waited in the firelit courtyard. Ash drifted down on us like unholy snow.

"Where's the girl?" asked Baglos.

"She'll come," I said. "She's too afraid of burning to stay, but too angry to come with us."

We hurried through the alley, stopping where it met the street. The fire had attracted a crowd. A bald giant of a man was trying to organize water buckets and blankets and pails of dirt, anything to keep the fire from spreading to the adjoining houses. "You can't go in there," he yelled at someone in the crowd.

Outlined against the flaming shop front was a man trying to escape the hold of two onlookers. "Let me through, damn you! There's a woman inside." The furious voice slowed my steps; it was Graeme Rowan.

"Might be several women in there if Kellea and her granny didn't get out," bellowed the bald man. "Blink your eye and none of 'em will be alive. You will be neither if you go in."

I scanned the crowd for the priests. The Zhid were no-where to be seen, but I recognized another face—a face I didn't expect to see and could never forget. My gorge rose. Maceron, the fish-eyed sheriff, was leaning against a fence-post, arms folded, unruffled, observing the frenzied mob as if the burning were a jongler's play put on for his private amusement. Ducking my face, I backed away, only to bump into D'Natheil. "Quickly. Away," I said.

"A moment. I'll have to carry him," D'Natheil said in a hoarse whisper. He hoisted Tennice onto his shoulders, and we edged our way between the mass of onlookers and the dark shopfronts.

Occupants of the nearby houses were dragging trunks, bedding, and children into the street. A wagon filled with water barrels rumbled through the narrow lane, forcing the crowd to squeeze into doorways and alleys and on top of each other to keep from getting trampled. Despite the creeping dread that had me checking behind us every few

steps, no one paid us any attention as we made our way
through the crowded streets toward the city gates. Traffic
thinned as we hurried under the gate and turned into the
jumbled, stinking district of stables and stock pens outside
the walls. Baglos paid the hostler, while the Prince handed
me the reins of Tennice's horse and put Tennice up on his
own mount. "Lead us," he said, after he had gotten himself
into the saddle behind Tennice.

Where to go? Tennice needed warmth and care and time
for us to care for his injury. I dared not return to the charcoal burner's hut, lest we'd been followed from it, yet I
couldn't feel safe so long as we were in Yurevan. After the
disaster I had brought down on Ferrante, Celine, and Kellea, I couldn't seek out another friend, even if I had one.
But that consideration gave me sudden inspiration. I would
seek out the friend to whom I had already brought disaster.
"Back to Ferrante's house," I said. "They'll never look for
us there."

Neither D'Natheil nor Baglos questioned my judgment,
though I questioned myself often enough as we left Yurevan behind us and raced through the dark countryside. But
luck rode with us, for we saw no sign of pursuit. The parkland and orchard were silent as we slipped into Ferrante's
stableyard, the cherry trees as still and somber as grave-
stones in the night. D'Natheil carried the insensible Tennice
through the kitchen garden, back the way we had come
only one long day before. The house was dark and deserted. Still no sign of Ferrante's servants. I tried not to
think about the professor, frozen in his death terror just up
the stairs.

D'Natheil laid Tennice on the tidy white bed in the steward's bedchamber, neatly tucked away next to the kitchen,
while I collected candles, water, brandy, and clean towels.
Baglos set about lighting the stove, promising to put water
on to heat as soon as he had the fire going.

When I returned to the bedchamber, D'Natheil was sitting on the bed beside Tennice, studying him intently,
brushing the graying hair from Tennice's thin face. The
wavering candlelight revealed the burdens of the day written on D'Natheil as clearly as the bloodstains drying on his

shirt. "He's fevered." The young man's voice was hoarse and soft.

Fever . . . so soon. "Let's get his shirt off." Using Celine's little knife, crammed in my pocket and still bearing the blood of prince and healer, I cut away Tennice's shirt. The wound in his side was a ragged, ugly gash, the skin around it red and fiercely hot, very like the injury D'Natheil had had when he first came to me. As I sponged the wound with brandy and water to loosen the last stiff fragments of linen, Tennice moaned pitifully. Worrisome to remember how ill the young, strong D'Natheil had been. Tennice must be past fifty and had never been robust. I covered the gash with a clean towel and ripped another in half to tie the first in place.

"I need to see if they have medicines here," I said. "Stone-root or woundwort, willowbark for his fever. Ferrante's cook used herbs from Kellea's shop. Maybe they have other things."

Baglos hovered like a worried moth at his master's side. "I would seek out these things for you," he said, tapping his fingertips together rapidly, "but I have no knowledge of them today."

D'Natheil touched the Dulcé's shoulder. *"Detan detu,* Dulcé. Find the medicines for the lady."

Such a transformation came over Baglos in that instant that I could have been no more surprised if he had grown two heads taller. No longer hesitant, no longer unsure, the almond-eyed man bent his knee to D'Natheil and said with calm confidence, *"Detan eto, Giré D'Arnath."*

"You've remembered," I said, as Baglos left the room.

"Not precisely," said D'Natheil, as he watched me wipe Tennice's brow with a damp cloth. "I know the words to command the Dulcé, which I did not know this morning or yesterday, but I cannot say I remember. Nothing tells me that I ever knew how."

"But Baglos will bring what I want?"

"If any such thing is to be found here."

I spooned a few drops of brandy into Tennice's mouth, then shot another glance at D'Natheil, who had stepped away from the bedside, his hands clasped behind his back, and was examining the furnishings of the room. "Do you know other things that you didn't before?"

"No. Except for your language, as you see. Before to-night it was like the speech of animals—nothing recognizable. Only the words you taught me had meaning. Dassine's message was like a key inserted into a lock, all the tumblers falling into place about it. But that is not 'remembering.' "

"So you didn't learn the rest of his message or what made Celine laugh before she died and say . . . the words she said?"

"I know no more than you."

While I cleaned blood and soot from Tennice's face and hands, D'Natheil leaned against the wall, arms folded, watching me. I urged him to have some of the brandy for himself, so he would not lose what little voice he had regained, but he shook his head, indulging in the surer remedy of silence.

Soon Baglos returned and genuflected to his master. "It is done, my lord." Then he presented me with two paper packets. One held small heart-shaped leaves and was marked "for lacerations, scrapes, burns, festerings, mortifications." The other held strips of rough, gray bark.

"They're exactly what I wanted," I said. "Thank you. Both of you."

D'Natheil nodded. Baglos beamed, his delight dimmed only when Tennice moaned in his sleep.

"When your water is boiling, we need to soak the bark. . . ." I instructed Baglos on how to prepare willowbark tea and what I would need to make a poultice of stone-root leaves for the wound. An hour later the bark was steeping, and I was tying a bandage over the dressed wound.

"Is there anything else to do for him?" Baglos asked, fussing about the sheets and pillows as Tennice's breath came harsh and uneven.

"Someone needs to stay with him. Give him the willowbark tea, if he settles or wakes. Later, when he can take it, we'll need broth or gruel to sustain him. It's all I know to do."

We agreed that I would take the first watch. The Dulcé said he would find ingredients for broth and start it simmering, and then get some rest until I called him to take my place.

I glanced around the bedchamber, orderly and spare as one would expect for the room of the steward of a well-run household. A clothes chest with a stack of clean, folded linen set on top of it, a wooden chair and footstool in the corner and a candle table beside—now littered with cups and spoons—a small desk holding a crisp ledger, pens, paper, and stoppered ink bottle, a washing stand set with comb, razor knife, and a stack of small leather boxes of the type to hold collars and belts, buckles and fasteners.

Rummaging in the steward's clothes chest, I found a clean nightshirt, soft and thin from years of wearing. I asked D'Natheil to help me lift Tennice and get the shirt on him. The young man did as I directed. As I peeled the remains of Tennice's shirt from his back, D'Natheil's eyes narrowed. "What is this on the back of him? He is no warrior. Nor slave, nor servant either, by his manner."

On Tennice's back were the knotted, ugly telltales of my friend's captivity. Shy, scholarly, brilliant Tennice . . . My stomach clenched with anger and revulsion. "He was beaten," I said. "Cruelly beaten, put to the sword, and left for dead. Those in power wanted him to betray his friends, to tell our king that my husband and our friend were planning to steal his throne. Tennice didn't want to say anything that would make our fate worse. He tried very hard."

"But he did as this king wanted?"

"Yes."

"Betrayed his comrades—your husband, your friends?"

"Yes, but—"

"He should have died in silence. With honor." The Prince sounded as though he needed to scour his hands. "How is it you still care for him?" His scorn was hot on my own back.

After we settled Tennice on the pillows, I tied the loose neck of the nightshirt and drew up the blanket. "It wasn't Tennice's fault. Karon forgave it, and I know the others did, too."

"To forgive such a betrayal—"

"Forgiveness has nothing to do with the offense or its consequences, only with the heart. They needed no proof of Tennice's love, and they'd have done anything to spare him this. They were going to die anyway. There was no honor in any of it."

"You must hate the ones responsible for such deeds."

"For many years I hated them, but now . . . I don't know. Hatred won't undo what's been done."

D'Natheil gazed down at the sick man for a moment. Then he walked out of the room.

I watched Tennice long into that night, holding him as he thrashed and moaned in delirium, sponging his face and hands when he sank into a feverish stupor. While he was quiet, I occupied my thoughts with the incredible events of the evening. It was impossible to grieve for Celine. She had been so full of joy in her going. I could not regret bringing her purpose and laughter at the end of her life. Kellea was a different matter. To leave her loose with the knowledge and anger she bore—and so close to the Zhid—was a risk. But the girl was surely capable of defending herself. We couldn't take her prisoner.

And Dassine . . . such an incredible story. Two worlds, reflections of each other. What had made J'Ettanne's people forget their duty? Corruption? Fear? Perhaps simply living in a world that was not their own had dulled and destroyed their memory. I could understand that. Perhaps they had felt what was happening to them, and created their stories and traditions, Av'Kenat and all, in an attempt to remedy it. Whatever they had done, it seemed it had not been enough.

Storytelling had been such a part of Karon. How he would have relished this one. So much explained about his people. A tale of wonder, he would say, and his eyes would slip out of focus and he would lose himself in the imagining, building his power as he experienced every adventure for himself.

As the night slipped away, my thoughts lingered on Karon as they had not since the day I had walked out of Evard's palace. For all these years I had refused even to think his name, though reminders of him lurked everywhere like thorns waiting to draw blood: a dew-laden rose, the whisper of rain moving across the meadow, the morning sun at just the angle he had declared to be the most perfect—

The floor creaked. Startled from dreamy dozing, I almost leaped out of the chair I'd pulled up to Tennice's bedside. The candles had gone out, and someone stood poised at the edge of the shadows. "I came to see if all was well with you and your friend."

"Yes. Thank you, D'Natheil," I stammered, smoothing my tunic and pushing the hair out of my eyes. "Tennice is asleep. I must have fallen asleep, too. I need to fetch Baglos."

He was already gone again. As I walked into the kitchen to wake the Dulcé, I shuddered slightly. The scent of roses still lingered from my dreaming.

CHAPTER 23

For more than a week, Tennice hovered between life and death. Baglos and I got enough tea and broth into him to sustain him through the bouts of madness that battered him like waves in an ocean of terror. The wound itself should have been well on its way to healing in a week's time, but it swelled and seeped black fluid just as D'Natheil's had done. Baglos swore it was tainted by Zhid poison. He had seen such wounds often, he said, with exactly the same symptoms. Unfortunately his people knew no remedy except to seek out a Healer.

Baglos seemed to take Tennice's illness as a personal affront, and he expended hours of tender care on the sick man. Over and over, as he redressed the wound, I would hear him murmuring indignantly, "Why, why, why Zhid poison? Those men were not Zhid. They did not want him dead. . . ."

Not Zhid, no. The attackers had been ruffians with brawn enough to smash shop windows, but so little skill they could be outfought by one warrior, a girl of twenty, and an aging scholar with poor eyesight. True, Graeme Rowan, a man I knew to be a Zhid informant—still a puzzle in itself—had been in the street nearby. Yet, if the attackers were Graeme Rowan's men, then why was Rowan so ill prepared for our escape? Maceron was there, too. He had hunted Karon and betrayed him to Darzid . . . Darzid who had been hunting D'Natheil. But if the attackers were Maceron's men, out to destroy a den of sorcerers at Darzid's behest, then why Zhid poison on their blades? No arrangement of alliances and evidence made sense.

My companions were no help in clearing up my confusion. Though D'Natheil had found his voice, he was more aloof than ever, as if the breach in his wall of silence made companionship less necessary. He refused to be drawn into conversation with me beyond the plan for our current meal or setting the watch. Poor Baglos fared little better, despite his frequent attempts to engage his master in discussion of the future. D'Natheil would either interrupt him with a rude command or bolt outdoors. For either of us to see the Prince except at mealtime was an event worthy of remark. Strangely enough, Tennice's illness was the single thing that drew him into our company.

On our third night at Verdillon, Tennice became so violent in delirium that neither Baglos nor I could control him. We were struggling to keep him still, when his flailing hand sent Baglos sprawling. The loud crack when the Dulcé's head struck a table said nothing good about the his ability to come to my aid. I was desperately trying to prevent Tennice from kicking over the lamp when he cried out in mindless terror and one of his hands smashed into my eye. Temporarily blinded and losing my hold, I felt hands drag me away and thrust me firmly into a chair.

I pushed back my hair and wiped my watering eyes to see D'Natheil sitting on the bed behind Tennice, wrapping his arms around my friend's writhing body. One by one the Prince captured the flailing limbs, trapping them within the confines of his own long arms and legs. *"Tassaye, tassaye,"* he whispered. *Softly, softly.* Before very long Tennice gave a shudder and fell still, though his haunting moans and terror-glazed stare yet tore at my heart. I grabbed a damp cloth and blotted Tennice's face, using the opportunity to spoon willowbark tea between his dry lips. Soon it seemed the worst was past.

"You can lay him down now," I said. "I'll tend him."

D'Natheil shook his head. For another quarter of an hour he held the sick man. Only when the moaning and the racking shudders had stopped completely and Tennice slept did he untangle himself and slip the older man's body onto the sheets.

"That was well done," I said, noting several bloody scratches on his arm. "Let me take care—"

"Call me if he is in need again." D'Natheil hurried out of the room.

Though I chafed in frustration at D'Natheil's reticence, I hesitated to push him too much. It had been easy to patronize him when he was only a lost youth with an annoying temper. But now I had begun to think of him as a prince, and, though rank held no awe for me, his position as the last scion of a magical race from another world could not but separate him from the ordinary. He had a great deal to think about. As did I.

That Dassine meant for me to aid D'Natheil in his mysterious task seemed certain. Yet I was not sure I was willing. If Karon's dying and its mortal consequences had presented the Dar'Nethi with a chance to win their war, then I had already given all one woman could be expected to give. Perhaps it was time to get on with my own life and leave this brute of a prince to deal with his. Besides, he seemed uninterested in my help.

Baglos refused to enlighten me on any matter regarding the Prince's mind, claiming that a Dulcé Guide's bond with a Dar'Nethi precluded it. The link between them was of such an intimate nature that it demanded inordinate trust, he said. When a Dulcé participated in the madris, the rite of bonding, he permitted his knowledge, his actions, his very perception of the world to be shaped by his madrisson's command. And whenever the Dar'Nethi partner invoked his power to access his madrissé's store of information, he, in essence, left his own mind open and vulnerable to the Dulcé's insatiable craving for information. Thus, when the madris was performed, the Dar'Nethi madrisson swore never to misuse his power of command, while the Dulcé madrissé vowed never to betray his master's privacy. Because D'Natheil had not commanded Baglos to tell me anything of their discussions, the Dulcé could not and would not do so.

All right. I could understand such an arrangement, but the subject of the future must be broached, whether it suited His Grace or not. On the evening of the fifth day since the fire, I decided the time had come. Baglos was watching Tennice while D'Natheil and I ate the simple supper the Dulcé had prepared. Perhaps if I spoke before the Prince finished eating, he wouldn't bolt.

I set down my cup. "Do you believe the things this Dassine told us?" I began.

D'Natheil pushed a bit of turnip about his bowl with a chunk of bread. "I know very few things, but that I can say. Dassine did not lie."

"Have you decided what to do?"

"I must try to accomplish what's needed."

"Do you understand what that is?"

"I've had no magical insights." His curt response seemed nothing more than the rudeness I had come to expect. Yet, as I searched for some reason to keep on caring about him, I noted how tight his skin was stretched and how long and thin were the new lines about his eyes. The shifting candlelight made him look deathly tired.

"Have you been sleeping?"

"Some." This declaration was in no way convincing.

"What prevents you?"

"I watch." He tossed the half-eaten bread into his unfinished soup and shoved the bowl away.

"But we've all taken our turns watching. There's been no sign of anyone. Why—"

"The Seeking comes almost every night. Your friend's suffering draws it. I can . . . divert it . . . if I'm awake. They know we live, but they don't know where we are. It must stay that way."

"The Seeking . . ." I had taken my turns walking the

garden and the front courtyard. How could I have missed the insidious dread, the sensory horrors? But then I recalled D'Natheil staring into the fire back in Jonah's cottage, listening to things the rest of us could not hear. Perhaps the essence of the Zhid Seeking was not the alteration of light or the wafting stench. "You should have said something. We can share that watching as well as the other."

"You and the Dulcé care for your friend."

"We can do both. You don't have to bear these burdens alone."

He shrugged.

"All the more reason we must decide what to do next," I said. "If the Zhid are so close, we need to be away from here as soon as we can move Tennice."

"But I don't even know where to begin." He stood up abruptly, knocking over his chair. I expected him to storm out of the kitchen, but instead he began to circle the table, words pushing and crowding themselves past his reserve like a sudden cloudburst on a quiet afternoon. "A thousand times I've gone over it. This Bridge—I have no concept of its nature or form, no clue as to its location. No one knows anything of the Breach it spans, save that its horrors drive people to madness and 'unbalance the universe'—whatever that means. Baglos tells me that the Heir of D'Arnath walks upon the Bridge and performs some enchantment to prevent its corruption by the forces of the Breach. Clearly I am expected to do this 'walking,' but no one can tell me of the enchantment I must work, and my own people doubt that I am capable. Oh, yes, and these Zhid likely want me dead. The Dar'Nethi assume that my death upon the Bridge will destroy it."

Astonished at this outburst, I found myself searching for something to answer him. "The Gate. Start there."

He dropped into his chair again, leaned his forehead on the heel of one hand, and stared at the table. "The Dulcé says it is a wall of fire hidden in a chamber that only I am able to unlock . . . assuming I am who they claim. One passes through the wall of fire in one world, and after the perilous crossing of this Bridge which he cannot describe, one emerges in the other world—"

"—from the other Gate. They call the one in this world the Exiles' Gate."

"Evidently, that's the usual way. But he says the destination can be changed before or during the crossing, and that's likely why the Dulcé and I and the Zhid who followed us came out at different locations." This colorless recitation of facts could not obscure his doubts.

"Yes, Baglos says he was 'blown' from the Gate by what he calls the 'fracturing'—displaced abruptly from it *and you* by some enchantment. But if you are to perform some deed at the Bridge, then those who sent you would want to make sure you could find it." I spoke faster as I bent my mind to the mystery. "What if the destination was changed to protect you from the Zhid who had broken into the chamber? Perhaps only Baglos and the Zhid were removed from the Exiles' Gate, not you. So if you go to the place where you first set foot in this world—"

"But I remember nothing of it. You heard the old woman." Louder. Harder. His control was slipping again. But he wasn't going to learn anything if he wallowed in doubt.

"Think about it. Work at it. What was the terrain? The landforms? Were there towns or villages nearby?"

His lips formed a stubborn line as he shook his head. "I ran. Days and nights without stopping, as if I had been running forever."

"And so it appeared when you came to me. You were starving, exhausted, and sick. Baglos says he had been hunting for you for fourteen days when I found him. If you came straight to me from the Gate, then the Gate must lie ten days—ten days running—from Dunfarrie."

"You're guessing." His fingers traced the grain lines in the oak table with such intensity that I would not have been surprised to see smoking patterns etched into the wood. He had dropped these few bits of himself in my hands, but clearly he had no confidence that I could make sense of them.

Yet I was not discouraged—not with the most intriguing mystery of my life unfolding in front of me. I jumped up from my chair and began my own pacing. "Another conclusion we can make. It was cold. Baglos says he felt the 'icy breath' of the Zhid at the crossing. Celine said that your earliest memories were confusion—and bitter cold."

"Confusion, certainly."

Pieces snapped into position. "Ah, but you see, Karon told us, too. In his vision. When he found the word of healing buried inside him, he said he felt cold. The bridge he saw was made of ice."

"But it's summer." His rebuttal was more a question than a protest.

"Exactly. But if you were to travel ten hard days straight west of my cottage, where would you be? Deep in the heart of the Dorian Wall, the highest mountains in the Four Realms, mountains so high that the snow never melts."

"The royal city, Avonar, is in the mountains, so Baglos says," said D'Natheil softly. His hands fell still as he looked up at me. "And that's where the Gate exists in the other world, my world. Perhaps they built both ends of the Bridge in mountains."

"Yes. In the mountains. They would have wanted it hidden, hard to find, hard to stumble onto by accident. It would have to be safe . . . a special place . . . a fortress . . ." Stars in the highest heavens . . . the answer lay before me as clear as my name. "D'Natheil, I know where it is. Or at least where to find out. There's a map!"

"How so?"

"The J'Ettanne built a stronghold called Vittoir Eirit at a place that was sacred to their ancestors, although they had forgotten why. One of them left a map, telling how to find it. We'll have to decipher the map. . . ." I was afraid to let myself feel excitement. The evidence was so flimsy, the prospects so uncertain. Tennice had never seen the map, so his memory couldn't reproduce it. I would have to go to Montevial and gain admittance to the vaults. I could envision the exact place where the journal was hidden. No one would have disturbed it. I told D'Natheil about the journal, and the Writer, and Karon's and my futile attempts to interpret the map. ". . . but with you and Baglos, it's possible. When Tennice is well, we'll go get it."

On the next day Baglos called me into the sickroom. Tennice had wakened and would not quiet until he spoke with me. He was so weak that Baglos feared to deny him.

"Where is he?" Tennice's eyes blinked wide open as soon as I kissed his hot forehead. "Where's Karon?"

I sat on the side of his bed and stroked his thinning hair. "He's dead, Tennice. Ten years dead. You remember."

"He stayed with me. In my head." His eyes burned with more than fever. The pounding of his blood was visible through his pale skin.

"You were his friend, and he loved you. And it helped him, too, to be with you."

"Run away, Seri. Take him away from the darkness." Tennice clutched my hand with no more strength than a child. "The shadow will destroy him . . . enslave us all."

"We'll leave here as soon as you're better."

"You must get him away."

"Hush, Tennice. Karon is beyond the Verges. No one can harm him any more, and all the shadows have fled with your dreams." I took a cup from the Dulcé's hand. "Here, have some soup. Baglos is a cook without peer." After two swallows, Tennice fell asleep again.

Unsettled by Tennice's delirium, I wandered into Professor Ferrante's study. On the night of our return to Verdillon, Baglos and D'Natheil had come here to remove the professor's body, only to discover that someone had already done so. Baglos claimed it was not the way of the Zhid either to hide or bury their victims, so we assumed the household staff had done it. But we had seen no further sign of Ferrante's servants. In almost a week, neither friend nor foe had come to Verdillon. It was very strange.

The study was quiet and sunny, a lovely high-ceilinged room painted yellow and white. Leirans having no foolish notions about unquiet spirits, I was not uncomfortable in the room. Only my mind was tainted with the lingering aura of murder, not the place itself. Baglos and I had both spent a number of hours there in the past days, the insatiable Dulcé devouring the professor's books and maps while I poked through the records of Ferrante's teaching. On this afternoon I lost myself tracing students' names and studies, so that it seemed only a short time until the tall clock downstairs began to strike the hour. It struck slowly, reminding me both that I ought to wind it and that I was past due to relieve Baglos. As I left the library, a sunbeam glinted off something nestled in the thick carpet. I picked it up, a brass button of the type used on military coats. Guilty at having abandoned the Dulcé, I thought little of it and dropped it in my pocket.

On the next morning, just at dawn, the mystery of Ferrante's missing servants was solved. After turning my bedside duties over to Baglos, I went out to walk in the kitchen garden to get a breath of air. The nighttime coolness had yielded early to one of the few hot days of Vallorean summer.

My mind raced ahead of my feet that morning, as I considered the problem of getting into the storerooms of the royal antiquities collection. Habits from my years in Dunfarrie had me stopping every few steps to pull up a straggling clump of threadweed that threatened a healthy plant or to pick a precocious bean that had ripened earlier than its fellows. When I found a row of carrots whose tops bulged from the damp soil, I stooped to pull a few of them for our supper. The carrots were hidden behind a row of trellises draped with limp pea vines, and so it was through the leafy barrier that I came eye to eye with a small, smudge-faced girl. Both of us stepped backward in surprise. The child recovered quicker and streaked for the iron gate in the garden wall, but I had longer legs and grabbed the waif before she could make her escape.

"Let me go!" cried the child in Vallorean. She looked to be eight or nine years old, with stringy hair that might have been straw-colored had it been it clean. "We've leave to take bits from the garden. Master said. I'm not stealing." Tears rolled out of the child's long-lashed eyes, streaking her grimy cheeks.

"You can keep the vegetables." The child clutched an onion and a tiny cucumber tightly in her stained apron. "Just tell me who you are. Come on, what's your name?"

"Kat."

"Do you live nearby? On the grounds here perhaps?"

The child clamped her mouth shut.

"I promise—I wish you no harm. Was it Professor Ferrante who gave you permission to take things from the garden?"

Kat nodded, her lips quivering. "But he's dead now."

"Yes . . . I know." My surprise had me stumbling. "Please, Kat, can you tell me what happened here? Where are your mama and papa?"

"Mum's dead, just like Master." Kat nodded with a weary acceptance that had no place on the shoulders of a child. "Same ones as killed Master did it."

"Gracious gods . . . did . . . did they kill everyone?"

"Some ran off to the woods. But Mum fell and got tramped on by the horses. She didn't remember me before she died, nor even her name. I don't want those men to come back." Kat gave a big sniff and wiped her face on her sleeve, leaving the sleeve and the face equally smeared. "You're hurting my arm."

I loosened my grip, but did not release her. "I didn't mean to hurt you, Kat. It's just that I'm frightened of the wicked men, too. Are you hiding with your papa, then?"

She shook her head. "With Aunt Teriza. She was Chloe's helper in the kitchen."

"And the bad men didn't hurt her?"

"We was gone to market that day. As we come back through the fields, we saw everybody running and screaming. We've been hiding in the root cellar all these days for not knowing what else to do. Aunt Teriza's terrible afraid."

"Can you take me to your aunt? Or perhaps you could bring her here? You could get more vegetables, and I could talk to her." I laid my beans and carrots in the child's apron. "Tell her that my name is Seri and that I'm here with Master Tennice, the professor's friend."

"She's out by the gate."

"Could you bring her? Will you trust me?"

Kat nodded, and when I let her loose, she sped down the path. In only a few moments, a rumpled, grimy young woman approached timidly, holding the little girl's shoulders protectively.

"Please, don't be afraid—Teriza, is it? My name is Seri. I'm a friend of Master Tennice."

The young woman curtsied abruptly, cast her eyes down, and sat obediently on the bench I indicated, her hand gripping Kat's.

"Kat, there's a pot of soup on the stove. Go on and help yourself to all you want." Brightening considerably, the child ran off, leaving Teriza looking even more uncomfortable. "Kat tells me you were cook's helper here."

"Yes, ma'am."

"And Kat's mother worked here, too?"

"Yes, ma'am. Nan was chambermaid for ten years, since she was fifteen. She got me the place when it come up." The woman's eyes filled with tears.

"I'm so sorry about your sister, Teriza. Kat is lucky to have you to care for her."

"Kat's a good child. Nan and I thought she might get on as scullery in a year or so."

"Teriza, could you tell me of the ones who did these horrible things? Did you see them?"

I needn't have worried about prying the story out of her. She poured out the tale as if it were burning a hole in her stomach. "It was the awfullest sight, miss. We come through the fields, tripping along smartly, for the day had made out rainy, and Chloe was anxious for the goods for the master's birthday feast. When we come round the north paddock, we heard screaming so terrible it chilled my blood. I told Kat to get in the root cellar, for the commotion sounded like the war back when I was a girl. I thought maybe the Leiran soldiers had come back again." She glanced up at me, flushing a deep scarlet.

"I crept up behind the stable, and peeked around, and saw what I hope never to see again in my years on this earth. Chloe and Jasper were running through the stableyard wailing, their eyes orange and bright like you hear about demons' eyes. Chloe was tearing at her hair like it was burning her head, and it was all down flying wild, and her head was bloody from pulling at it. The two of them ran off into the woods. Then Loris come from the house, crying to Damien, the stable lad, 'Master's been murdered!' Damien stopped her and says, 'What do you mean?' And Loris was crying and said, 'The demons. The demons slit poor Master's throat.' And right then, two men—horrible men that I couldn't bear to look on—come out of the house and pointed their fingers at Loris and Damien, and the two of 'em screamed so's you thought their arms and legs was being pulled off. Then they ran into the woods too, and Damien pulled out his knife and started cutting his flesh to bits as hc ran."

Silent, dignified tears dribbled down Teriza's smudged cheeks. "All I could think of was to find Nan. Sure enough, she runs out of the house into the yard, wailing like a cat what's prowling. I was going to run grab her, but I feels Kat up close behind me. I lay on top of the child and shushed up her questions, and in no more time than a fingersnap, four riders come barreling from the front of the house, and they see Nan . . . and, oh, miss, they just trompled her down. When the riders was gone, we run to Nan, but she looked wild, and said, 'Who are you?' She didn't even know her own child or her own sister." A single sob escaped the young woman's control.

"Poor Nan." I put my arm around the girl's shoulders and released the flood.

"She died right there," the young woman snuffled into my shoulder. "Kat and I took her to a hole down by the stream where they dig out ice in the winter. We put her in, and closed up the hole, and tried to say a prayer for her, though I don't know my prayers as I should. But then I didn't know what to do, for I thought of Master murdered, and I'm the only one left to tell. No one'd believe me, and they might think I done it. But Master was fair and honest and I'd never . . ."

The stretching shadows took on a more ominous cast. I squeezed Teriza's shoulders as I gazed around the garden uneasily. "Of course you didn't do it. Master Tennice is ill just now, but we'll get him well, and he'll advise you. Until then, you and Kat must stay with us in the house. My friends and I are at least a little protection."

Teriza straightened her back and wiped her cheeks with the back of her hand. "I'd be most grateful, ma'am. And most willing to do my duties or whatever might be needful. It's a blessing to be sure to hear Master Tennice is alive. We didn't know but what the wicked men got him as well."

"Good. It's settled then. All I ask is that you keep private any of our conversation that might seem . . . strange. If Professor Ferrante trusted you to be discreet, I'm sure we can also."

"You can trust me, ma'am. I promise."

None of this made sense. Why were we still unchallenged? If the Zhid had killed Ferrante and the servants so easily . . . Perhaps D'Natheil's efforts were indeed shielding us. I considered Maceron and Rowan and the Zhid again, but I still could not get all the puzzle pieces to fit together.

Later, as a more cheerful Teriza washed up the dishes and wiped the table, I asked her again about a part of her tale. Tennice had said something similar and I hadn't thought to question it. "You said there were *four* men riding out."

"Aye, ma'am."

"Tell me about them. Three of them were priests, is that right?"

"Aye. Three of them wore robes such as priests do. And the Leiran wore a coat."

"A Leiran?"

"I believed him so, as he spoke only Leiran. Nan was teaching me, for Master had guests as was Leiran, and Nan said everyone in service should speak enough of it to do her duty. He wore a dark coat with shiny buttons."

"Shiny buttons . . ." I reached into my pocket for the brass button I'd found in Ferrante's library. Closer examination revealed what I hadn't noticed before. The design engraved upon the button's slightly tarnished surface was a dragon—the dragon of Leire.

"What was the Leiran like, Teriza? Did you get a look at him?"

"No, ma'am. They went by so fast. He wasn't so tall as the priests. Light hair. Looked strong. But I didn't see his face, as it was raining, and I was so scared."

Of course, I knew a light-haired Leiran who wore a dark jacket with Leiran dragons on it, someone who had done business with the Zhid once before—Graeme Rowan, the upright sheriff.

It was a great day when Tennice was able to sit up and eat a few shaking spoonfuls of soup for himself. We all made a fuss over him. Even D'Natheil smiled and said he was pleased our patient had improved so fairly.

"How long has it been?" Tennice asked.

"Nine days. We were thinking you were going to sleep until winter," I said.

"Thank you all. What can I say?"

"Say you're feeling better."

He smiled weakly. "No question of that." He fingered the thick bandage on his side. "I don't understand how a stupid knife wound could have such effects. Such nightmares. Vile. Strange."

"Baglos thinks it was Zhid poison. D'Natheil had a wound with similar effects."

Tennice looked at the Prince strangely. "You helped me a great deal, sir. Took me through the worst of it. It's difficult to remember exactly how"—his voice faded—"but I thank you."

D'Natheil tipped his head without speaking.

Kat made Tennice her special charge. She brought him food and clean linen, chattered to him when he was awake, and sat quietly at his side while he slept, solemnly feeling his brow for fever. She scolded him when he was up too long, demanding that D'Natheil or Baglos help him back to his bed, and she held his hand while he went to sleep, "so the master won't have wicked dreams." Tennice, for his part, was endlessly charmed and mystified by Kat's whimsical view of the world.

But with all his progress, I could not predict when Tennice would be well enough to travel. He must have felt my anxiety on the morning I told him of my belief that the path to the Exiles' Gate was the very same map Karon and I had puzzled over for a year.

"You must be off to get it then."

"As soon as—"

He laid a finger on my lips. "No. Much as I would like to have the resilience of a twenty-year-old, no amount of wishing will make it so. We had many a discussion of realism at Windham, and I remember a young woman declaring that she could never understand why people refused to see themselves as nature sees them. 'One should rejoice in the wisdom of years,' she would say, 'for it's of so much more value than youth's brute strength.'"

"Not fair to bring up a girl's silly prattle."

"She was right. While you are off adventuring, I will stay here. Teriza and Kat will spoil me unmercifully. I've food, wine, an abundance of books and paper, and immense quantities of ink. How could I lack? When you settle on a destination, leave a message with my father. This latest brush with mortality has convinced me that I must visit him. Once done, I'll find you again. No god or demon will prevent it.''

CHAPTER 24

''. . . dead these ten months. Our only boy. I've needs to tell my man. Please, Your Worship.''

''Your husband works in the armory, you say?'' The guard eyed the black ribbon tied around my sleeve and nodded knowingly. From the number of sleeves with black mourning bands I had seen, everyone in Montevial had lost a son or brother or father in the war.

''Aye, sir. Journeyman, he is. Honored to serve the king. And our Tevano was a legionnaire—no conscript.'' I moaned and pulled my apron up to cover my face, lest the young guardsman look too close and unmask my charade. One of his fellows, an older man with a thick red beard, had been staring at me from his post on the far side of the squat palace gate towers.

''All right. Go on then. But straight to the armory and straight out again.''

I dipped my knee and hurried through the dim passage under the gate defenses, taking care to avert my face from the red-bearded guard as I passed. Perhaps it had been foolish to enter the same gate Karon and I had used almost every day for two years.

Once across the outer ward, I angled away from the direction of the armory and headed for the workrooms Karon had taken over for the Antiquities Commission. For the first time in ten years, I approached the palace of the kings of Leire with anticipation rather than dread. Even the flying red banners that told me Evard was in residence could not slow my steps as I sped down the brick-paved roadway that separated the palace proper from the stone monoliths that were the royal storehouses.

The next task was to discover if anyone I knew was still employed at the Antiquities Commission. Everyone who had worked for Karon had respected and liked him, but they would have had to undergo the "purification" mandated at the trial, an expensive and humiliating ritual, so I couldn't summon much confidence that I would find someone familiar, much less sympathetic and unafraid. Matters looked even worse when I crossed a graveled yard to the Commission workrooms and found them occupied by a noisy, sweating army of leatherworkers.

"What's your business?" asked a bearded workman, dropping a daunting roll of hides about three paces from where I stood gawking in dismay. From this dark, stifling den of hammering, cutting, and stitching would come the mountains of saddlery, harness, and boots needed for the warriors who had carried Evard's war into Iskeran.

"I was to bring a message to the secretary at the Antiquities Commission," I said. "And I didn't think to ask where it was. Last time I had to deliver something, this was the place."

"It's been a while since you've carried a message then, girl, or you've got fair lost along your way. I've worked here eight years."

"Where is it moved then? My mistress will beat me sure if I don't deliver my message."

"Antiquities, you say?" The man scratched his greasy beard. "Don't sound familiar." His expression was vague. He had no idea what I was talking about.

"They work with old things dragged in from everywhere: statues, tablets, armor, tools, boxes, things used to decorate tombs, and such like."

"Oh. Like loot from the war?"

"Yes. Yes, exactly that."

"Maybe it's those fellows down to the pit."

"The pit?"

"Yeah. That's what we call it. Buried like moles, they are. Round behind this building you'll find a cellar stair. Go down, and in, and down some more, and give a shout. Those moles might be the ones you're looking for"—he gave me a good-natured, gap-toothed leer—"unless you decide you like us fellows better, up here where you can see and get a breath of air at the same time."

I smiled at the sweating man. "Not today. But if I find the man I'm looking for, you've saved my goose, and I'll not forget it."

"Good enough." The man hoisted his smelly bundle onto his broad shoulders and staggered into the noisy workshop.

When I found the cellar stair in the weed-choked alleyway behind the leatherworks, the steps were littered with leaves and twigs and chunks of broken paving, and the door at the bottom of the stair looked as if its hinges had been rusted shut since the Rebellion. I made my way carefully down the crumbling stair, wrenched open the heavy door, and stepped inside.

I felt hollow and sick at the sight of the dark and deserted passage. *No demons here,* I thought, but wasn't sure I believed it. The only sound besides the empty reflection of my steps was a quiet, regular tapping from the far end of the sloping way. I tiptoed past gaping blacknesses toward the source of the noise. A weak pool of lamplight spilled from a doorway on my left. The tapping stopped, and I peered cautiously through the opening.

A dark-haired man was bent over a table littered with tools and dust and broken chips of stone. The rest of the small room was crowded with stacks of crates and old books, heaps of rolled manuscripts, and shelves crammed with bottles and jars and rags, paint pots and boxes of every size and shape. A mangled oil painting lay on the floor beside a carved wooden horse that must be at least eight hundred years old. From Iskeran, I knew. Horses were sacred to the Isker gods. The man raised a small hammer and began tapping at something on the work table.

"Excuse me," I said.

The man jerked around, dropping his hammer with a clatter. He was small and dark-skinned with black, curly hair just beginning to show signs of gray. His nose, mouth, and chin came to a point in such a fashion as to be vaguely reminiscent of a rat.

"Racine!"

The man squinted at me, frowning. "Who's there? Step into the light, if you please. I can't see in the dark, though those who ration lamp oil must think it so."

I stepped into the room and had the disconcerting experience of having someone collapse in a dead faint at the sight of me. *Someday,* I thought, as I sniffed Racine's pots and jars to see if one contained water or wine, *someone will greet me with an ordinary, "Hello, Seri, how are you today?"* I satisfied myself that the contents of a fat green jug were not toxic and proceeded to dump them in Racine's face. I sat down beside him on the floor while he sputtered and shook his head like a pup, propping himself against the foot of his table.

"My lady! My apologies. I—It's just—I didn't—I thought—" The man's mouth opened and closed like a fish's.

"I'm sorry for startling you. You needn't be afraid. It's not unlawful to speak with me. I'm on the king's parole, not a fugitive."

"No. No. I just assumed . . ."

"I'm not a ghost either."

He pulled a handkerchief from his coat pocket and blotted the drips running down his face. "Just surprised. Amazed. It's so quiet down here. No one comes. And it's been so long. What's brought you here, my lady?"

"I'm visiting the city, and I was curious to see what had become of the collection. I'm happy to find it in your care."

His color deepened to scarlet. "Oh, my lady, to call this care! I'm the only one left, you see. There's no money to do the things we did. And the collection . . . *pffft.* Waging war in Iskeran is terribly expensive, I suppose. Anything that can be sold has been sold. All the bronzes melted down, and the silver. What gems were left in their settings dug out. Even the swords and armor taken away to use or to melt. Paper and stone are all that's left, and much of that was destroyed after—" His eyes darted toward me fearfully.

"Yes, they would have done that. But you're still employed. Who's the commissioner, then?"

He leaned close and dropped his voice. "No one. None dared show interest in the post. I'm still secretary, but to Commissioner Nobody. I'm not sorry for that. I can stay down here and do what I can. They just brought this lot from Kerotea. All rubbish save the horse and this box." Sitting on the workbench was a cube-shaped case of cracked and peeling leather, bound in corroded brass. "I'm working to get the hinge pins out so as to get it open, careful as Master Ka—the commissioner—taught me."

Heaving a great breath, Racine climbed to his feet, straightened his back, and gave me a gracious hand up off the floor. Though no longer rattled, he was not yet easy. He opened his mouth to begin several times, and then blurted out quite suddenly, "I never thought to see you again, my lady."

"I'm sure you didn't. I never thought to be here again." The unexpected encounter with Karon's old assistant made me hope the fanciful story I had concocted to get me into the vaults might be unnecessary. Racine clearly wanted to talk. I let him.

As he offered me his stool that was the only seating in the tiny room, he drew up his brow. "I've often thought—wished—I could go back and change some things."

"Who among us has not?" I perched awkwardly on the tall stool.

"I should have spoken." He paused, his eyes unfocused as if he were looking inside himself, before reaching out to meet my gaze. "No one but you spoke for him. I should have done. All Reagor's prattling, those stupid, impossible lies about flying boxes and living mummies, and no one said anything to dispute him. But I was afraid."

"For good reason. It would have made no difference, Racine. You would have died for it."

"But it wasn't right. At first"—he averted his eyes, his color deepening again—"I was glad he was found out, afraid that because I'd been close, he'd done something to me . . . and I hated him for that. I hated him for deceiving me and making me so afraid. But at the trial, I listened to what you said, and it made such plain sense. And I saw what they'd done to him, and I thought how he was a good man, just and fair, and teaching me, trusting me. I couldn't believe the wicked things they said about him. I thought someone should speak up, but I couldn't. All these years and I still haven't got my nerve up even to say his name here in the dark, where there's no one to hear it."

"Thank you for telling me, Racine. You mustn't feel guilty. The Holy Twins themselves could have spoken for him, and nothing would have been any different. But you've just made life very much easier for me!"

Racine screwed his features into such a morosely puzzled knot that I almost laughed. "I had another purpose for my visit. Regarding the collection. And I was afraid I'd find no one here that I knew. Or that if there was someone I knew, they'd spit on me and chase me away."

Racine put on his most businesslike face and bowed to me. "It has been quite a long time since I've had a request that was not in the vein of 'remove this useless refuse from my sight,' or 'don't you have anything of real value.' It would be a pleasure to assist you, madam. And I give you my most solemn word not to spit." He waved his hand to encompass his cramped domain. "What is your pleasure? A review of all we have left? Not much. An examination of your most efficient cataloging directories? Out of date, but still useful. Perhaps an extensive tour of our workrooms that extend from this wall here all the way to that one right there, a whole two paces longer than my armspan?"

"I wanted to find something. Something we catalogued that I would give a great deal to see. If I could get into the southwest vault . . ."

Racine's smile wilted, and my spirits with it. "The southwest vault? Would it were another. We had to abandon the southwest vault, as it was wanted for something else. I moved as much of the contents as I could, but they didn't give me much time. A good deal of it was burned. What was it you were looking for?"

"A leather trunk. Very old. It was in one corner, buried under a pile of rolled carpets."

He tapped his long fingers on his cheek. "I don't know. It doesn't sound familiar. You say it was catalogued? I've tried to mark all those things that came from the southwest vault with their new location."

"It had a number, but it would not have appeared on your list."

"Well, then, we must have a look. Most of the things I salvaged went into the northwest vault." Racine rummaged among the rubble on his table until he found a large ring of keys and a tired brown leather ledger. He took his lamp from its bracket on the wall and escorted me into the passageway, locking the door carefully behind him. He hesitated a moment, then said, "Would it suit you better if we were to be discreet about our journeying, my lady?"

"As a matter of fact, though everything I told you about my status is true, I would prefer that my visit be unnoticed. I promise you—"

He raised one hand. "No promises are necessary. This way."

He led me down the sloping passage into the labyrinth of tunnels. A quarter of an hour's brisk walking brought us to an iron gate, soon opened by one of Racine's keys. Faint rustling and murmuring floated from the yawning mouths of the side passages. I swallowed hard and kept my eyes on Racine's back. The lamp wasn't nearly bright enough. The path angled upward toward another gate and through a wooden door.

To stand in the midst of the jumbled vault was like going backward in time, yet a single glimpse told me how depleted the collection was. The paintings, stacked so carefully, were of poor quality, the statuary mostly broken. A primitive idol in the shape of a raven-headed man looked blindly on the rest, the jewels pried from its eye sockets, its splendid belt, collar, and staff pockmarked by gouges and gaps where silver inlay and even the tiniest chips of gems had been removed. Racine led me to the corner where he had stored those artifacts rescued from the southwest vault, and we rooted through stack after stack of boxes and crates. I couldn't think what I would do if the trunk wasn't here. After two futile hours, I concluded I might have to make those plans.

Racine ran his finger down the pages of his ledger. "I just don't know. If it wasn't in the original list . . . Where else could I have put it? You said it was under rolls of carpets." He thumbed through the wrinkled pages, slowly and deliberately, squinting at the crabbed writing that filled each one until I thought I might have to grab the book from him or scream. But then he tapped his finger on one page, and said, "One more possibility. I had them put a number of carpets in that niche behind the last row of pillars. It's a little drier there than most of the vault. If your trunk isn't there, then it must have been destroyed."

I held my breath as he hung the lamp on a bracket in the niche beyond the pillars. On a raised floor a stack of carpets rose higher than my head. I took one side and Racine took the other, and we pulled one after another off the stack. No irregularity in the stack indicated the presence of anything so awkward as a trunk. Foolish to expect that workmen would have installed it here in the same way as they had found it. But when we had were almost to the bottom of the pile, Racine gave a shout. "Ouch! Serpents' feet! Excuse me . . . what—? My lady, please come."

I clambered over the mountain of carpets to the other side. Racine sat on a dusty roll of wool, nursing a great bleeding gouge in his leg. "Look back there," he said, pointing into the dark corner of the niche. "I backed into something when we were shifting that last one out of the way."

I held the lamp high, and there in the corner, as if patiently awaiting my attention, was the trunk. "That's it!" Avoiding the sharp metal edge that had attracted Racine's notice so dramatically, I pulled the trunk from the corner. Holding my breath, I unlatched the hasp, opened the lid, and reached down into the dusty contents until I felt the smooth edge of the rosewood box. I looked up at Racine, my face hot with excitement.

I started to speak, but the man raised his hand in caution. "Perhaps it would be better if you say nothing. I think I'll go and stack up these carpets that have so carelessly fallen upon themselves, and when you are finished with your sentimental tour of the collection, we'll go. And, of course, there will be nothing in your hands when we depart."

I smiled at him. "You are wiser than you give yourself credit for, sir. I'll look around a bit while you stack your carpets, and then I will be ready to leave—with nothing in my hands."

While Racine turned his back, I opened the box and looked on the precious things I had last seen in Karon's hand. I removed the tattered journal, carefully wrapped it in a strip of gauzy fabric from the trunk, and slipped it into my pocket. Then I returned the box to the trunk and pushed the trunk back into the corner.

I found Racine diligently laboring to get the carpets back under his discipline, and I lifted one end of a heavy roll. "I've seen all I need to see. Whenever you're ready, I'd be happy to go."

Racine nodded and said, "Let's be off then. I remember that the dust caused you much distress in years gone by. I can finish this later."

The secretary led me along his underground paths, back to the door that led into the sunlight. I offered him my hand. "Thank you. I'll not forget."

"A small thing. Nice to have someone take an interest. Someday—"

"I'll come back and tell you all."

CHAPTER 25

If only the deciphering of the journal's secret could be as simple as its retrieval, I thought as I hurried toward the service gate. Surely D'Natheil or Baglos would have some insight into the puzzle of the map.

The day was warm and bright. The palace courtyards swarmed with servants and soldiers, carters and gardeners, bustling about to satisfy the needs and whims of the favored populace that resided within the walls. A few more steps and I would be out of the palace confines and on my way back to the small, hot room in the Street of Cloth Merchants, where the Prince and the Dulcé awaited me.

"Excuse me, madam."

I tried to ignore the well-dressed man who matched his steps to my gait. The journal tucked into my pocket felt heavy and obvious. My cheeks burned.

"A word, please, if you will."

A quick glance confirmed that he was addressing me. The gentleman who matched his pace to mine, trying to bow as he walked, appeared to be about my own age, the very model of a lesser courtier seeking to advance himself. His elegant attire was expensive, but in no way ostentatious, and his grooming was impeccable, though his light hair was precariously scant and the body squeezed into the dark blue breeches, ruffled shirt, and silk waistcoat precariously soft.

Cursing my ill luck, I dipped my knee and cast my eyes to the gravel path. "Is it me you want, my lord?"

"Indeed, my lady. Lady Seriana of Comigor, is it not?" A practiced eye assessed everything from my short ragged hair to my heavy, shapeless boots, even as he ducked his head.

"Do I look to be one with such a lofty title, sir?"

"You were recognized when you entered the gates, my lady, and I was sent to await your return here. Your brother would have a word with you."

"I make no claim to any brother."

"Please, please, madam"—he fluttered his eyelids and raised a deprecating hand—"I am acquainted with your reputation for verbal agility, and I will cheerfully concede you victory from the beginning. I dislike games of all kinds, almost as much as I dislike coercion. I would much rather you come freely. The duke would very much like to see you and will not permit me to accept a refusal." His eager courtesy set my teeth grinding.

I started toward the gates again. No point in further pretense. "To what method of coercion will you so regrettably resort when I say I have no intention of calling on the murderous son of my parents? Rope? Chains? Your oh-so-tastefully modest sword? Or perhaps you will just call for guards?"

The man kept pace with me, entirely unruffled, his hands clasped behind his back. We might have been conversing about an upcoming dinner party. "I make no claim to understand the depth of estrangement between you and the duke, madam. I am new to his service. But it is my impression that His Grace's request, though insistent, does not stem from animosity. He says that once you hear him out, you may be on your way. Will you not take a moment to alleviate your own curiosity, if not to satisfy His Grace's wish?"

An insightful gentleman indeed. Not at all like Tomas's usual associates. No sardonic glint in his eye as there would have been in Darzid's. Where was that snake?

My companion flicked a finger, and three guards in bright red livery appeared, hovering about us like bright hummingbirds around a particularly succulent flower. They kept a discreet distance, but they blocked every direction save the one in which my companion gestured. "This way, madam."

"So you choose the last of my scenarios. The cowardly one."

"Pragmatic. Better for all. My name, by the way, is Garlos."

When I stepped through the palace door, the years and the walls closed in on me. I wished fervently to close my eyes and transport myself to the hard, splintered bench in front of Jonah's cottage. How much better to breathe the sweet air of the valley, rather than the stifling, three-hundred-year-old deadness of this place.

Garlos led me through the echoing warren of bare walls, steep stairs, and creaking floorboards that were the servants' passages. A quarter of an hour later, we stepped through a discreetly placed door into long, wide gallery. The paneled walls were hung with weaponry: a shield of burnished bronze as tall as a man, blazoned with the rising sun of Annadis, a saber with a ruby-studded hilt, halberds, pikes, and a wicked-looking pick-like ax with a long head set square to the haft, curved and blunt on its top edge, pointed on its outer edge and sharp as a dagger on its lower. The lamplit alcoves sheltered heroic statuary and gem-studded armor. A turning led us into a portrait gallery in which twenty generations of princes and queens, kings and generals simpered, frowned, or stared from the walls, enough gold in each man-high frame to ransom a city. Thick red carpet muted the sound of our passing.

We stopped before an elaborately carved door, and while I cooled my heels beside the statue of a naked warrior, Garlos tapped quietly and slipped in. I pretended to study the statue. The stares of passing courtiers and servants were more intimately humiliating than my yearly appearance in the Great Hall. The interval until Garlos opened the door and summoned me inside seemed far longer than it was.

It was the custom for the king to present his champion with an expensive gift each time the swordsman took a challenge for him and returned victorious. From the look of it, Evard had not lacked for challenges, nor Tomas for victories.

Upon a hectare of priceless Isker carpet stood a wide desk of the rarest gaonwood, the sheen of its finish displaying the intricate perfection of its twisting grain. A mantelpiece of rosy Syllean marble was a fitting centerpiece to an impeccably selected collection of ancient swords. Fine leather chairs were grouped about the hearth. Another wall housed a library worthy of the University itself, the diamond paned doors of the bookcases displaying what must have been a thousand volumes bound in perfectly matched red leather, tooled with gold. Not one of the books looked as if it had ever been opened.

To complete the decor was the Duke of Comigor himself, a masterpiece of skin-tight, dark blue breeches and full-sleeved blue satin doublet, trimmed liberally in gold lace and belted with a jewel-studded green sash. He stood with his back to me, gazing out of the glass-paned doors that led onto his private balcony. So favored an apartment would surely overlook the royal family's private gardens.

The door closed behind my escorts, leaving the two of us alone, but Tomas did not acknowledge my presence. Well, two could play. I stood unspeaking just where Garlos had left me, my hands folded primly.

But when Tomas turned around at last, the face I saw was not the one I expected. Pride was there, but no hatred.

His eyes were not scornful, but cloudy and troubled. "What are you doing here?" he said.

Perhaps I was mistaken. "None of your business."

"Don't start this again, Seri."

"Pardon me, Your Grace. I am here because the Duke of Comigor, the Champion of Leire, has summoned me. I was given no choice in the matter."

He clenched his fists. "Hand of Annadis, why can we not hold a reasonable conversation? You pride yourself so on rational behavior."

"Tell me, Your Grace, how does one hold a rational conversation with a murderer? It's a behavior I was never taught. Must I curtsy or is complete obeisance proper?"

Tomas reddened. "I saved your life—" Before the words left his tongue, he tried to recall them. "Oh, confound it all. We can't get bogged down in the past. Let's start again and try to be civil." He took a breath. "Will you sit down? Can I send for wine? Something to eat?"

"I'll stand, if you please. And I'll take nothing from you."

"Fine." He fingered a pen that had been carelessly dropped onto the desk, disturbing its sterile order. "When I heard you were on the grounds, I decided it was time I spoke with you about this. It's been on my mind for a long time, but there's been no opportunity."

"You know where I live, Tomas, and you well know where I can be found on the first day of autumn in each and every year."

My brother clenched his jaw and snapped the pen, throwing it on the floor. I told myself to resist further goading for I was, indeed, immensely curious, and the J'Ettanni journal weighed heavy in my pocket. My brother stepped close, so stiff I wondered he could walk. I folded my arms. Feeble enough protection. But nothing would have prepared me for his words.

"Seri, I want you to come home." He rushed ahead, giving me no time to recover from my astonishment. "I've gotten you a full pardon from Evard. Your parole will be satisfied. You'll never have to do that . . . thing . . . again, if you'll come back to Comigor."

"You're mad." It was the only explanation.

"It's not right, your living the way you do."

"How dare you pass judgment on me! You know nothing of my life. You've never understood the least thing about me. Do you see my circumstances as yet another untidy blot upon your honor?"

"No! It's not that. Look at yourself, Seri. How long has it been since last you looked?" Before I could protest, he grabbed my shoulders and propelled me to an ornately framed glass that hung among his displays.

It had been a very long time. I had to blink and sort out the image at first, for I had never realized how much Tomas and I resembled each other. But there was a world of difference, too. I could still see traces of the girl I had been, but my red-brown hair was dull, my complexion roughened by years in sun and wind, and my eyes had lines at the corners and knowledge in their depths that had never been reflected in my mirror at Comigor. And I was very shabby. My white shift was frayed at the neck and wrists, my tunic threadbare, my brown skirt faded, wrinkled, and not terribly clean. I looked altogether straggly and tired, like a garden gone wild.

"Does it offend you more that I'm poor, Tomas, or that I'm thirty-five?"

He didn't answer, and I looked again at my brother's reflection, seeing in his brown eyes something I'd not seen in them for years. Sarcasm and anger lost their purpose, leaving only the dregs of years and bitterness and too much sorrow. "Why ever would you believe that I would care what you think of me, or how I live, or what I do? Is it shameful that I eat only what I can grow or barter for or that I wear the same skirt every day of the year? And do you think those things should bother me enough that I would share a roof with my son's murderer?"

He turned and walked away from me, rubbing the back of his neck with his long, powerful hand. "No. Those things have nothing to do with anything. So stupid to think I could do this without going back . . ." In a voice so soft I had to work to hear it, he said, "I dream, Seri. Bloody nightmares that have not left me since that day. Desolation and ruin. Fire. And sorcery. I see you with that knife in your back . . . and the child . . . oh, holy Annadis, the child . . . The dreams eat away at me until I feel I'm living in that horror, and my waking life is the dream." He spun about and held up his hand, his eyes closed. "Don't say anything yet."

He took a breath and continued. "You may never believe me, Seri, but I was convinced—absolutely—that what I did was right. That all of it was for the best . . . for the family . . . for you. I've thought that the dreams haunted me because I was weak, not because I did anything wrong. But in the last few days, my dreams have gone away, vanished as if they'd never been. A mercy it seemed. But instead . . . It's as if I've had no clear thought in fifteen years, and only now can I even begin to see what happened to us. To you. And now, if the dreams should return, I don't know what I'll do, for only the conviction that I was right kept them at bay. Then, on top of it all, I hear you're at the gates today, and it's like a madness in me that I can't let you leave."

I started to speak, but he interrupted again. "No. Not yet. Hear me out, for I don't know what's opened my eyes or loosened my tongue. I leave the city in three days. There's been a challenge, a serious one, from some rebel chieftain in the west. I'm to take care of it, of course. It's a strange and nasty situation, but I thought nothing of it until this other business came up. But now . . ."

His tongue would not form the words, but he was my brother . . . as close as a twin. I could read in him the thing he could not say. "You're afraid, Tomas. Why?"

"I have a son, ten years old. I'm often away from Comigor for months at a time, and I've never thought twice about it. It is my duty. But this time . . ." He paced the length of the room before he could go on. "Maybe this is what happens when a soldier's luck runs out—some say they know beforetime. The only thing that comes into my mind is to get you to Comigor to be with him, and then I could be easy." He ended his pacing by the balcony doors and slammed his fist into the lintel so hard that it rattled the glass. "Damnation! I'm a lunatic."

Magpies screeched in the invisible garden. A fountain splattered and gurgled. Fingering the telltale bulge in my pocket, I considered my brother's incredible confession. I did not believe that he was mad.

"Tomas, where is Darzid?"

My brother turned, gaping at me as if I had asked him the price of fish in the market. "Why?"

"Just answer me."

"He's gone off to Valleor on urgent business—family business—with some old friend, or cousin, or something."

"And did the change in your dreams happen before he left?"

"No. What are you getting at?"

"After he left, then."

"No—well, not exactly. It was only when I came back here from Comigor. Darzid had been down near Fensbridge shopping for a new horse when he got called away. He has nothing to do with any of this. He'd tell me I was a fool to speak with you."

Shopping for a new horse. Not hunting a missing groom. One by one I placed Tomas's words into the puzzle written in my head, but I could not yet read the answer. "Did he know you were coming to Montevial?"

"No. My business here came up suddenly. Seri—"

"Don't interrupt. Has he ever left you for so long before?"

"Perhaps once or twice. He is the most faithful and loyal of lieutenants."

"But would it be correct to say that, since Darzid was appointed as your aide, you have never, until this week, been in a place he didn't know you to be?"

"That's stupid."

"Am I right?"

"Most likely that's true, but—"

"Now answer me this. Who made the 'discovery' that Martin had sheltered a sorcerer? Who unearthed those incredibly ridiculous witnesses? It was Darzid, was it not?"

Tomas looked as if someone was twisting a knife in his belly. "It's the kind of thing I pay him to do. To gather information."

"And who first told you about Karon?"

"Darzid, of course, but he—"

"Who convinced you that only you, of all the bastards in Evard's multitudes, had to murder my son?"

"Seri—"

"Answer me!"

"Darzid said that—"

"Of course," I murmured. Darzid who had come to me with an improbable tale of old hatreds, who believed he was not living his own life, who felt that something had changed in the world when Karon died and had demanded . . . no, begged me to tell him of sorcery . . . "Turn over any slime-covered stone in this kingdom, and it is Darzid that slithers away."

"What do you mean?"

"Something a very wise man told me years ago. Perhaps it was truer than even he knew." Somehow I knew that Darzid was not just hunting sorcerers. "Tell me, Tomas, did you meet Darzid's friend, the one who accompanied him to Valleor?"

Tomas threw up his hands. "Clearly there's nothing more to discuss. You wanted to leave. I'll call Garlos, and you can take yourself to perdition as you will." He had closed himself off again.

"You may have your scribes record this momentous event, brother. For once in our lives we are in agreement. We have nothing more to discuss. And I'll not go to Comigor except as your prisoner."

"So be it." Tomas pulled the bell and turned his back.

I was not about to tell my brother of my own business, but as I watched his stiff back, I recalled what I had seen in the mirror. We were flesh and blood. I moved close behind him and said, quietly, "I understand what it took for you to speak to me in the way you have, Tomas. Unfortunately you've credited me with a more generous nature than I possess. But in return, I'll tell you this. I fear Darzid. I fear him more than I fear you and more than I fear Evard. If I were you, I would look into the eyes of Darzid's friend, and if they're as empty as I believe you'll find them, I would hide my wife and my son and tell no one in the world where they can be found."

He didn't answer. I didn't know if he had even heard.

Garlos led me back through the palace, looking pleased with himself. "You see? It was just as I predicted," he said. "You are free to be on your way."

"As you predicted," I said. "Tell me about yourself,

Garlos. Is our friend Captain Darzid so tired of playing nursemaid to a spoiled brat that he leaves you in charge of my brother now?"

The man's face lost its smiling aspect. "I am not privileged to be one of Captain Darzid's staff. His Grace decided to come to Montevial very suddenly. I'm a member of the administrative staff of the Guard, and was asked by His Grace to perform the duties of his aide while he is in residence here."

"I'm sure you understand that discretion is, above all, a virtue that my brother prizes."

The man was very eager. "I believe I have few rivals in that department."

"For example. this whole business with me . . . family business . . ."

"I've not been given leave to discuss it with anyone."

"And that would be anyone, no matter how close to the duke."

"Of course."

"Excellent. You'll go far."

As I disappeared into the crowds outside the service gates, I imagined Garlos staring after me, wondering at himself listening to political advice from one who looked as if she should be scrubbing the palace floors.

CHAPTER 26

Hot, sticky, my head jangling with the unaccustomed noise of the city, I shoved my way through the crowded Street of the Cloth Merchants. The sultry air was thick with the acrid stink of simmering dyepots, and everyone had moved out of the stifling shops in search of a breeze. Multicolored awnings stretched across the street like a paint-streaked sky. While sweating tradesmen tossed and stacked bags of fleece and bolts of cloth of every conceivable color and weave, hawkers screamed out the virtues of their threads and yarns, buttons and ribbons.

I wasn't sure what to make of Tomas's story. Guilt was known to haunt and terrify, and Tomas had earned his own particular nightmares. Now I was back in the daylight world, my creeping fancy that Darzid was somehow connected to the world called Gondai seemed ludicrous. He had been Tomas's aide for sixteen years and served Evard and King Gevron before that. I had no evidence that Darzid or his villainous henchman Maceron were guilty of anything but doing their sworn duty to exterminate sorcerers. Perhaps the Zhid were simply attracted to the most despicable residents of any world. But my brother's testimony had only strengthened my irrational conviction. Why would Tomas's dreams stop so abruptly with his separation from Darzid?

"Seri, girl!"

I whirled about to see a fluttering red kerchief waved by a white-haired man elbowing his way through the mob toward me. "Jaco, what are you doing here?"

He mopped his forehead with the kerchief. His grin seemed to wilt in the heat. "Barrels. You've heard me tell of my old friend Roger the Ox, the fish-seller? He sent word last week that he was short of barrels. I had the lot from the wreck of the *Mimi,* so . . ." He shrugged his wide shoulders. "But yourself, girl. What've you been about? Have you learned more about our young fool and his business? Has he found his tongue yet? Did you know that Graeme's in the city?"

"Rowan's here?" Though we had seen no evidence of pursuit on our journey from Valleor, D'Natheil had sensed that we were being followed. He wasn't sure whether it was the sheriff or the Zhid priests . . . or both together.

"Aye, he's about, and you'd best stay clear of him. He was like to split his gut when he came back from Grenatte and found you gone. Said you'd best be back before Sufferance Day, and how he'd a few things to ask you himself this year. He was after me to tell what you'd been up to."

"You mustn't tell him anything. That's why I can't let you—"

Jaco's face bloomed as red as his kerchief. "Don't say it! Dunfarrie has been wicked dull since you ran off. Made me see what an old fossil I've become. Dry-docked, I've been, but no more. I'll feed the horses or polish the boy's boots or whatever you like, but I'll not be left out of your adventure."

"This is far too dangerous, Jaco."

"I'm not doddering yet."

Would all of my words come back to haunt me? Tennice would have a good laugh. Mustn't Jacopo have the right to choose his danger, he'd ask, just like everyone else? "Of course you're not doddering. I never meant to imply it."

Jaco patted my arm and maneuvered me out of the way of a mule team pulling a wool cart much too fast through the crowded street. "Then tell me, where are you bound? What did you learn in Yurevan? Sailors have friends all over—people who could likely help you, if you'll just tell me what you need."

"Not now. I've an errand that can't wait, and we mustn't be seen together." With Rowan close, I dared not take Jaco near D'Natheil. But perhaps shutting him out *was* wrong. If the Dulcé and the Prince failed to translate the map, an experienced navigator or his friends who knew of maps might be valuable. "Tomorrow, Jaco. Get your business done. At midday tomorrow, I'll tell you everything. . . ."

We made plans to meet at an ale shop he knew of just inside the west gates. He seemed satisfied, and I waved as he hurried away. I began to make my way through the street again, wandering in and out of the shops and market stalls, watching for any sign of observers as I progressed toward the far end where Baglos and D'Natheil would be waiting.

I had just stepped into the shade of a bright blue awning when a bull of a man carrying two giant bags of fleece hurried past, forcing everyone to move aside. No sooner had I stepped closer to the shop front than I was knocked off balance by three small boys careening through the crowd, trailing a rainbow of shining ribbons pilfered from an outraged ribbon-seller. When a firm hand gripped my arm, I thought some kindly passerby was helping steady me. But instead of finding myself upright and on my way, I was dragged into a dark alleyway between two buildings.

And before I could utter a word of protest, a hand clamped over my mouth from behind.

"At last!" said a man's voice, not unfamiliar. "I thought I'd have to chase you across all of the Four Realms just to have a simple word with you."

So much for caution. I struggled and kicked, but Graeme Rowan was a good deal stronger than I and determined to hold on. He propelled me deep into the alley, deftly dodging the cats who snarled and raised their hackles at this invasion of their private feasting ground. I bit his fingers hard enough to draw blood. With a curse he yanked his hand away, and I spat out the blood, yelling as loud as I could, "Help me!"

Rowan immediately slapped his bleeding hand across my mouth and tightened his grip. "Curse it all, are you mad?" He shoved me into a corner of the gloomy alleyway and spun me around to face him. His grim face was flushed, his green eyes glittering. "Promise me you'll be quiet and listen, and I'll let go. Do you promise?"

I nodded, almost twisting my eyes in their sockets in an attempt to glimpse the brass buttons on his coat, wild to see if one was missing. But he stood too close. Tentatively he removed his hand, ready to clamp down again if I made a move to scream. When I stayed quiet, he relaxed his grip on my arm a bit, but not yet enough for me to break away. "I'm sorry if I frightened you," he said, "but after the miracle of finding you in this hellish city, I'll not let you get away again."

"How did you find me?"

"I have a friend with an extraordinary gift for following people."

Ah, yes. His friends. I could not allow myself to be deceived by his aggrieved sincerity. I was in no position to run, but I did wrench my arm from his grasp. "Are you going to arrest me? Where are your 'friends'?"

"I've no intention of arresting you. Now I've come out ahead on our little game of chase-the-cat, the only spoil of victory I ask is two moments without argument. Would that be at all possible?"

"I don't see that I have much choice in the matter." But I was certainly puzzled. He was a sheriff. No one would take him to task for questioning me. Why lurk in an alleyway?

He pulled a kerchief from his pocket and twisted it about his bleeding fingers. "You're acting the fool," he said in quiet vehemence. "You think you're so clever sneaking and hiding with your strange friends who do such extraordinary things. But you're not deceiving anyone. I'm not the only one after you."

My flip retort died unspoken as I watched the subtle changes in his features. The sheriff's unremarkable face with its weather lines and scar had never revealed much of his inner life. But on the few occasions I'd seen him express strong feeling—whether anger, disgust, anxiety, or anything else—his every action had proclaimed his face a true mirror of his sentiments. And on this hot afternoon, his face told me that he was worried and afraid.

"What do you want with me?" I said.

"This is about Jacopo."

My hackles rose, along with a rush of guilt at the thought of my recent promise to my old friend. "Jacopo is not involved in my business. Leave him be."

"I'm neither a fool nor blind," snapped the sheriff. "I saw him talking with you not a half-hour since. I just want to know if he understands what he's doing. Is this some kind of playacting like you did in Grenatte or is he in need of my help?"

Despite my efforts to dismiss Graeme Rowan and his worries, the day shifted uneasily. "Jaco is in Montevial to sell barrels," I said. "That's the truth." *Tell me if you know something more.* "Jaco often comes to Montevial to trade."

"Don't lie to me about this. You oughtn't put him in this kind of danger. As if his keeping such company wasn't bad enough . . ." Rowan stepped back a bit and rubbed one elbow. "I'm out of my depth, as you well know, but you'd best not be ignorant of the risks you take. It's naught of a secret that the odd little man was in Dunfarrie those weeks ago, seeking his servant with the bad temper. But do you know who else come hunting the two of them on that day, swearing me silent and claiming the whole business to be some matter of spies? It was your brother's man, my lady . . . and with him those damnable priests."

There it was! Darzid and the priests—the improbable connection, joined in the hunt for D'Natheil and Baglos. But if it were true . . . Dared I believe Rowan just because his tale matched my instincts?

"This doesn't surprise you?" he said, wrinkling his brow.

"Only that you would tell me . . ." But the evidence was stronger than Graeme Rowan's word or my instinct. Three riders had stayed back at the edge of the meadow when Darzid came hunting . . . and I felt again my inexplicable shudders when I'd noticed them. The priests . . . the Zhid . . .

Unimpeded by any argument from me, Rowan rushed onward. "They each went their own way after questioning me—the captain and the priests—but I saw them together again in Grenatte. And now the priests are after you and your friends . . . and I see Jacopo helping them along the way, first at your place and then at the house in Valleor. Blessed Annadis, do you have any idea what they did to your friend's servants?"

"Jaco help the devil priests? You're mad!" Why was I allowing Rowan to lure me into his snare? Gods, he was a sheriff! Our lives were forfeit if he uncovered proof of what D'Natheil was, and here I was with explanations on the edge of my tongue. Jaco, the kindest, dearest person on the blasted earth . . . Rowan's accusation made a lie of everything he'd said already, serving only to remind me of his other secrets and lies.

"How can I believe you, Sheriff? Perhaps your story might be more trustworthy if you had let me witness this great conspiracy for myself. You were quite anxious to get me out of Grenatte, as I recall. One might think you didn't want me to see the meetings that took place there."

A movement behind the sheriff caught my attention, but I quickly averted my gaze. Rowan had not sensed the tall figure gliding silently down the shadowed alley.

"I knew enough to guess that your presence in Grenatte was a violation of your parole," he said. "You couldn't afford to be anywhere near those people."

"And so you successfully defended the law from my depredations, while allowing Giano to go on his way—and yes, I heard what they did to the professor and his servants."

"Giano had committed no crime. Not then. You had. Or were about to."

"And so I'm to be grateful to the one who saves me from my own perverse wickedness and points the finger of blame everywhere but at himself." Anger consumed all my uncertainty, making my limbs and voice tremble—fury at a murderer who could come so near convincing me of his honesty and at myself for listening to him. "I'm to confess all my crimes to my generous savior, the upright servant of the law, one who protects us all by exterminating children and scholars. Who else have you murdered, Sheriff? Tell me the names of all your victims."

Graeme Rowan flushed the same scarlet as the flaming emblem on his coat, but before he could say more, something large and heavy crashed down on his head. I drew back into the corner of the wall as he toppled into the dirt. Even in the sudden quiet, the street noise seemed as remote as my own woodland, allowing my own doubts and accusations to scream warnings.

Expressionless, D'Natheil gazed down at the fallen sheriff. Slowly he pressed the tip of his sword into Rowan's neck, first dimpling, then pricking the tanned skin, blood quickly outlining the steel. I remembered the way he had pressed the dagger into the attacker at Kellea's shop—smoothly, inexorably, relishing his own lethal prowess. My stomach and spirit rebelled, and I laid my hand on his arm.

The startled Prince jerked his head around. After a long, defiant glare, he withdrew his blade and slammed it into its sheath.

I dropped to my knees and rolled the flaccid Rowan onto his back. Blood and dirt covered his left temple. Truth glared up at me from his blue coat. Third from the bottom was a wider space than between the other brass buttons and a dark thread broken off. The remaining buttons were identical to the one I drew from my pocket.

"Someone's coming." The Prince pulled me to my feet and gestured me deeper into the alley, glancing over his shoulder at the street. Rowan's "friend" was after us again, no doubt.

Shudders crept up and down my spine as we hurried through the shadowy maze of alleys, past stomach-curdling heaps of refuse, dodging a ragged, toothless woman tending a smoky fire, kicking aside chickens and feral dogs. D'Natheil halted abruptly where the lane opened into a small, weedy courtyard surrounded on all sides by tall warehouses. Beyond a clutter of stained dye vats, splintered crates of empty spools, and a skeletal apparatus that I realized was a broken loom standing on end, was a wooden stair, clinging precariously to one of the buildings. After a moment's watching, the Prince led me through the courtyard and up the stairs. He tapped three times on the darkpainted door at the top of the stair. A bolt slid, and the Dulcé let us in.

Mountains of mouse-chewed scraps of yarn and cloth lay about the huge, dim attic, layered thickly with gray dust and a century's worth of dead flies, moths, and beetles. An entire civilization of spiders had abandoned their webs under the rafters, especially in the low space where the steeply pitched roof met the front and back walls. This was not the same room where I'd left my friends that morning.

D'Natheil, crouching so as not to knock his head on the downsloping roof, positioned himself by a window with a broken shutter that looked out over the street below. Before I could say a word, he burst out, "You were gone a very long time. Very long."

"Well, it's been quite a day," I snapped. "But I would have eliminated a few of the more unpleasant encounters, if I'd known they would annoy you." I was too tired, too hot, and too disturbed to put up with a rude prince, however talented at rescuing he might be.

He glanced at me briefly, his expression cold, then turned his attention back to the street. "But you're well." He wasn't asking. He was telling me.

"Your arrival was timely. How did you happen to be there?"

"You were in need." He offered no more, and I looked at Baglos for further explanation.

The Dulcé had rebolted the door and was shoving a pile of broken crates up against it. "Earlier today, as we were returning from the market, we heard men making inquiries up and down the streets of this district, asking after a woman and two men, one man short and dark, one tall and strongly made. So we did not return to the other room, but found this place instead. I waited for you all morning by the palace gates, but you didn't come, so we met here to think how to find you. After only a short time, D'Natheil ran out the door, saying, 'She calls. She is taken!' "

"I was careless. Jacopo is in the city on business. He wants to help us, and, like an oaf, I stood in the middle of the street talking to him. The sheriff was watching. When he saw me with Jaco, he pounced." What game was Rowan playing? Why induce me to mistrust Jacopo? I thought they were friends. I rolled the brass button over in my palm, shock and anger tainted by profound unease. "Rowan wasn't dead?" I hadn't even checked.

"No." It was winter in the corner where the Prince sat peering out of the window. Was he angry that I'd kept him from killing the sheriff?

I chided myself for lack of resolution. Rowan had been a part of the horror at Ferrante's. In his blind adherence to the law he had allowed himself to be seduced and corrupted by the very thing he claimed to hate. He was our enemy and deserved to die. But for a moment, he had been very convincing. . . .

"Now that you are safely with us again, was fortune kind?" said Baglos. "Did you acquire the object of your search?"

I had almost forgotten the journal. "Yes, I found it." I pulled the bundle from my pocket and peeled away its threadbare covering. Even the Prince was drawn to see. The three of us gathered around an old crate, the only thing in the room that would serve for a table. All my irritation, all my fears, and all my questions fled in anticipation of revelation.

"My husband worked for over a year translating this. He got through most of it, though there were some entries he was never certain of, where the meaning of a few words could change the whole sense. We had to destroy his translation, but I suppose the two of you can read this easily."

D'Natheil ran his fingers down one page, but yanked his hand away as if it had burned him. "I cannot read the ancient tongue," he said, curtly, and stood up again.

Baglos turned a page, examining it closely. "If you command me so, my lord prince, I could translate the entire work."

D'Natheil looked at me. "Is that what you want?"

"The critical part is the map." Trying not to let anxiety make me heavy-handed, I thumbed through the fragile pages until I found the one where the Writer had sketched the elusive puzzle. D'Natheil returned to the makeshift table and crouched down beside Baglos. As the two of them examined the page, I studied their faces, eager to see the first sign of understanding. It did not come. First one and then the other shook his head.

"These symbols have no meaning for me," said D'Natheil.

"Nor for me," said Baglos, scratching his beard.

D'Natheil wandered back to the window. "*Detan detu Dulcé*," he said. "Translate the symbols in the diagram."

"*Detan eto, Giré D'Arnath.*" Baglos ducked his head in D'Natheil's direction and proceeded to study the crude drawing further.

As the sky over Montevial blazed orange, then cooled into evening blue, the clamor from the street quieted, and the odors of supper—frying fish, boiling cabbage, baking bread—hung on the air. D'Natheil sat with his back against the wall, his arms resting on his drawn-up knees as he stared through the irregular hole left by the broken shutter. I fidgeted. The Dulcé pored over the page, turning it this way and that, covering parts of it with his hand, scratching symbols and lines on the splintered crate with a rusted nail, until I thought that the only activity left for him was to stand on his head. Then he began to leaf through the journal, reading, it appeared, but at a pace ten times the ordinary. But at the last he carefully closed the journal, placed it in my hands, and bent his head to D'Natheil. "It is not in me, my lord."

"What conclusion do you draw from it?" The Prince spoke from his corner.

"Only this, my lord. It is not a map. Or better to say, it is not a map as we understand maps. The symbols do not match any set of landmarks or roads in the area of the Dorian Wall. There is some other meaning here to which I have not been given the key."

"Well done, Dulcé."

Baglos bent his head again.

"What do you mean, it's not a map?" I grumbled, staring at the dilapidated little volume. "The Writer says it on the page just previous. He was upset at how the local J'Ettanni lord had used Av'Kenat to terrorize his subjects, and so he's gotten the map to the stronghold. He didn't trust his memory, so he wrote it down. He wrote everything down."

"I cannot say what he did with what he learned, my lady," said Baglos. "But he did not draw a map."

"How can you know? I still don't understand why it is that D'Natheil can command you to read an ancient language and you can do it, but he can command you to translate this . . . diagram . . . and you cannot." These two and their magics and their moods and their condescending explanations pricked at my patience like woodpeckers at dawn.

D'Natheil stretched his legs out straight and deigned to look at me. "Master Dassine has given me this understanding. A Dulcé can know those things that have been instilled in him by his own study or experience or by transference from other minds. My command as his madrisson enables him to search through himself for anything related to my desire. If he has acquired sufficient knowledge then he can tell me what I wish to know or use what is in him to find it out. He knows enough to state that this is not a map, but he has not the necessary information to know what it might be instead. It is not a fault in him."

"It would have been helpful if he could have told us this an hour ago."

"This is the gift of the Dulcé . . . and their burden. To acquire knowledge and dispense it and to obey the commands of his joined madrisson to the very limits of his life—such is the service of a Dulcé who accepts the madris." He shifted his blue gaze to Baglos, quite serious. "To take a Dulcé as Guide must be a rare privilege, I think."

Baglos flushed and ducked his head.

I remembered the Dulcé's unceasing questions during our travels and how he had worked his way so voraciously through Ferrante's library. "So it must be that Baglos has encountered nothing in your world or ours that tells him where the Gate can be found or what the symbols in the Writer's journal might mean."

"To the best of my understanding, that is the case."

"So we've come to the end of another road." Disappointment hit me like a bludgeon, bringing with it the effects of constant worry and long traveling, lack of sleep, and the high emotions of the day. What in the name of sense were we going to do now? I could not even begin to consider it.

D'Natheil stretched out his long limbs on the filthy floor, yawned, and stuffed his cloak under his head for a pillow. "You'll think of something."

Before I could make a proper retort, he was snoring.

Baglos shared cheese and raspberries he'd bought in the market that morning, and then, before the light was completely gone, he curled up by the door and fell asleep as quickly as had his master. I, though still unsettled and confused, churning inside about Tomas's dreams and Graeme Rowan's accusations, was only a breath behind.

Shouts and screams and the shattering of glass yanked me from the depths of sleep. D'Natheil crouched beside the window, his back flattened against the wall. I hurried to join him, heeding his gesture of caution as I ducked under the sloping roof and dropped to my knees beside him. Baglos stood by the bolted door, his short sword drawn and ready.

I peered out onto a scene of chaos. The bright colored awnings were in shreds, and cloth, fleece, and spools of yarn were scattered and trampled in the muddy street. At least three people lay unmoving in the street muck, while foot soldiers flailed whips at the pressing, shouting crowd. Two soldiers dragged a young man from the dye shop across the lane toward a mounted troop of heavily armed soldiers guarding a roped cluster of men. A young woman clutching an infant ran out after them. A whip cut cruelly across her face, and she fell to her knees screaming. Several women surrounded the fallen girl and her child, restraining her while the soldiers kicked and slapped the struggling man, shoving him into the cluster of captives and fastening his roped hands to the others.

"A conscript gang," I said. I had known of forced military service all my life, believing it an unfortunate necessity of Leiran dominance. Karon had been the first to tell me of its cruelty and of the poverty and desperation left in its wake. I had never witnessed a conscription for myself. Soldiers didn't come for men in the streets where I had lived.

"They feed." D'Natheil was pale. Revolted. "This that we see. They feed on it, on the fear, on the wrongness of it."

It took me a moment to grasp his meaning. "The Zhid feed on it? Is that what you mean?"

"Not the Zhid. Their masters. I've felt the masters' hunger through all our travels—at the professor's house, and again on the night of the fire. I just didn't understand what it was. But seeing this, hearing it, feeling it, today I know. The masters devour the cries and the anger, the fear and the pain, and it makes them powerful. And their power creates and nurtures the Zhid." The Prince's voice overflowed with loathing.

The masters . . . the Lords of Zhev'Na, Baglos had called them. Merely thinking the name seemed to darken the day.

With the crack of a lash and the snarls and curses of the soldiers, the "recruits" were herded away. The wails of the bereaved echoed through the near-deserted street, mourning both the living and the dead. Little difference between the two—the living and the dead—I thought, for there was little chance the conscripts would ever come home. Even if the poor bastards survived their five years of service, they would likely be released somewhere hundreds of leagues from these streets where they'd spent their whole lives. They might spend the rest of their days trying to find their way home.

Never had I felt so small in the world, so alone in a hostile universe. *Home.* Somehow at that moment, the need to go home swept through me, a hollow craving so powerful, so physically real, that I had to press my hand tight across my mouth to keep from crying it aloud. For all the love and kindness that had blessed me there, Jonah's cottage was not home. I had never belonged there or in Dunfarrie. Nor was home the place of my childhood, the ancient keep where Tomas believed I could somehow protect his child from his nightmares. My home was in ashes, and I was alone, more even than the Writer, the itinerant Healer who always found his way home. . . .

"Home"—an idea flitted past like dandelion fluff on the wind of useless sentiment—"he always went home. . . ." I whirled about abruptly. "Tell me Baglos, where was the Writer when he drew the diagram?"

Baglos lowered his small sword, puzzling over the question. "It is my impression that he was at his residence. In this village called—"

"—Tryglevie," I said.

"Yes. In a very small house with a wife and six children—very noisy and undisciplined—and a pig, and a goat, and sixteen chickens, and a cat that wandered in from time to time."

"Karon and I looked at a number of maps of Leire and Valleor, but found no mention of Tryglevie. But doesn't it make sense that his route to the stronghold would begin at his home? Baglos, is it possible that you know something of Tryglevie?"

Baglos looked at D'Natheil, and the Prince gave him the proper command. After a moment of meditation, the Dulcé looked up in amazement. "Indeed, woman, I can guide you there!"

CHAPTER 27

"We must go south of this city, but north and far to the west of your home, to a countryside of rocks and hills and fields. No forest there, no trees." So Baglos described the way to Tryglevie. "The village has changed its name through the years and is now called Yennet. It is very small and appears on no map, but there is a ruin nearby—it was in a description of the ruin in the professor's library that I learned of this village. I can tell you no more at present."

We set off within the hour. I left a message at the ale shop by the west gate, telling Jacopo that we had found a lead and were off to chase it. I also warned him stay clear of Graeme Rowan, who had accused him of treachery. He was my friend. I could not leave him exposed.

Close onto midday, I rode into a village to buy supplies and fill our water flasks, leaving Baglos and D'Natheil waiting under a tree. When I returned, the road was deserted, the dust of my passing the only movement. But mingled with the buzz of locusts came a hiss from a blackberry thicket which led me to a cowering Baglos.

"We were followed," whispered the foolish Dulcé, as if any watcher would not have noticed me holding back the prickling vines to speak to him. "D'Natheil sensed the enchantment. He has led them south, away from our course, toward your village. We are to proceed on our way, and he'll meet us tonight west of the river at Fensbridge."

Baglos and I gave our horses free rein to gallop westward in the dusty heat, crossing the narrow arch of Fensbridge in late afternoon. The sunset had transformed the sluggish, weed-choked Dun into a river of molten gold. On the far side of the river we found a clearing where we could observe the bridge and the roads from the west, as well as the forest track that followed the river's west bank—the route we ourselves had taken up from Dunfarrie a month before. As we waited for D'Natheil, we built a small fire.

I sat, chin in hand, watching the day's last travelers straggle in from the western roads and cross the bridge into the town, seeking beds for the night. Without me or the Dulcé to slow him, the Prince should be able to evade any ordinary pursuit. The extraordinary, too, I hoped.

Baglos pulled the Writer's journal from his pack and sat down beside me. He had said he wanted to study it further, that he hoped to find some insight we had missed. He turned it over in his small hands several times. "Tell me, woman, what happened to the Exiles? You've said so little of them. Only that they were hunted and executed. Perhaps if I knew more, I could understand these writings better. Would you tell me of your husband?" His almond eyes glowed in the waning light. He was waiting to consume Karon's life as he had consumed Ferrante's maps.

No reason to refuse the Dulcé's request—to tell Karon's stories, to share the past that had spread itself so vividly across my mind's landscape since D'Natheil had invaded my life. I picked up a long stick and poked it in the fire, rearranging the coals as I cracked open the door of waking memory and peered backward. But a dull ache settled in my stomach and spread quickly to my chest. Even my new-found acceptance—this admission that some greater purpose might have been served by our personal horror—could not ease it. The fire popped, shooting sparks upward into the night. Suddenly nauseated, I threw down the stick and turned my back to the flames. "No, Baglos. Not tonight." Not ever. Some things were too difficult. I slammed the door shut once more.

Just at dusk a party of hunters, three young nobles decked out in velvet doublets with voluminous sleeves trailing silken ribbons, came dashing down the road toward the bridge. With great whoops and shouts, they paused at our clearing, circling on their quivering mounts. "Hey, you, woman," shouted a young man with an eagle feather in his cap. "Tell us where is the nearest public house. We have a thirst that is the desert."

"The desert in summer," chimed in one of the others.

"The most frightful noontime desert in summer," drawled a third, prompting the other two to break into giddy laughter entirely out of proportion to the wit displayed.

"Well, goodwife, speak up," demanded the man with the feather, his excited horse prancing closer to Baglos and me.

"Just over the bridge is a tavern that might suit," I said. "And I believe you'll find at least four more between the river and the Montevial road, so you needn't take a dry step."

Two of the men dashed off with raucous bellowing, but the man with the feather stayed behind. "Are we not a bit lacking in proper respect, woman? I hear no courtesy of address and see no attitude of humility before your betters."

Quickly and awkwardly I dipped my knee and cast my

eyes to the trampled grass. "My apologies, Your Honor, sir. My eyesight is none too good in the dark time."

The rider nudged his horse close enough that I could feel the beast's warm breath, and then he used the end of his riding crop to lift my chin. His long, straight nose, full lips, and receding chin reminded me of a number of young aristocrats I had known—the type it would be wise to approach with caution. "Why do I think your heart does not support your tongue, goodwife? You need a good beating. Is this your man who cowers so cravenly by the fire?" He rode closer to Baglos, his horse churning dust and ashes into our eyes. "And what's this? A book? Have our peasants got themselves learning? Here, give it over. Let me see what tract amuses you." His pale fingers were banded with jewels.

"This is certainly not my husband, sir," I said, crowding in between Baglos and the horse. How stupid of me to let things get so dangerously out of hand. "He is but my companion in service. Our master's fallen ill with plague and, as his wife is already dead and needs no service, he sends us to Montevial to serve out our bond in his brother's house. We left the town just before they sealed the gate. We're mortally afeared of highwaymen, sir. Perhaps we could join with your party and serve you on the way, so to earn your protection from thieves."

At the mention of plague, the rider backed away hastily, his voice but a thready echo of his sneering command. "We've no need of company or service. Our own servants follow us. You, man, tell your new master to beat this woman twice a day until she has a softer tongue."

"Aye, lordship," said Baglos, bowing and touching his forehead as I had told him was the custom when addressing a "better."

The man spurred his mount viciously and raced away after his friends.

"I did not like him," said Baglos, gravely, as he watched him go.

"Nor I," I said with a shivering laugh, vowing to bridle my shrewish tongue.

A short time later, a party of three heavily laden servants plodded into view. They asked after the hunting party, and

I directed them across the bridge. Trailing slightly behind them was a lone rider, his head drooped on his chest, his horse walking slowly as if he had all the time in the world. He seemed to melt into the gray light. One had to look twice to make sure he was not some mind's contrivance of limb and leaf and shadow. Only when his horse meandered into our clearing did I realize he was D'Natheil. The Prince dropped from the saddle.

"We should go at once," he said, as he drained a water-skin Baglos had ready for him.

"Are you still followed, then?"

D'Natheil wrinkled his brow, glancing over his shoulder toward the junction of the road and the dark path through the trees. "I shook off the two who trailed us from the city."

"They were Zhid?"

He shrugged. "They were constant, like a hound, but never close enough to identify. I was able to elude their enchantments a short way from your village."

"But something still worries you."

"I rode from the village up to your dwelling so I could find my way back to this path. Ever since, I've felt someone else following me. But I'm not sure. It's not so powerful a presence as the two—more like a flea than a hound. And no sorcery. We should go on. I'll catch him up."

The damnable sheriff, no doubt. I should have let D'Natheil kill him.

As we struck out west into the trees, the full moon beamed through the overhanging branches, transforming the road into a grillwork of light and shade. We rode fast and without conversation, as if now that the peripheral matters were taken care of, the true urgency of our mission could take hold.

Sometime near midnight, D'Natheil pulled up, motioning Baglos and me to ride on ahead. "The flea," he said softly, and then he melted into the dappled shadows at the side of the road. The Dulcé and I continued on our way without changing the cadence of our passing. After some quarter of an hour, we heard the brisk clop of hooves on the road behind us. Two horses. We reined in and held wary at the side of the road.

D'Natheil rode into view, leading a riderless horse. He halted beside us, and from a strange, elongated bundle thrown across the saddle in front of him issued a muffled string of curses that would have made Jacopo's sailor comrades blush. "The flea," he said, dismounting. He dragged the bundle off the chestnut and set it down on a pair of bare feet that protruded from one end. A tousled head popped out of the other end.

"Paulo!"

Most of the boy was lost in the folds of an enormous cloak. D'Natheil took a firm grip on Paulo's ear, transforming the boy's scowl of freckled ferocity itno a forlorn wince.

"Ow!"

Much to the consternation of both prisoner and captor, I started laughing, laughter such as only those who have lived at the edge of danger for days on end can produce.

"The most excellent ferocious boy!" said Baglos, and with only a momentary glance of apology at his grim master, broke into a lively chuckling that rang through the moonlit forest.

"Don't see what's so blasted funny," the boy mumbled.

D'Natheil had remained unremittingly somber since seeing the conscript gang. But as the disgruntled Paulo hitched up his oversized garment, a glint of amusement danced about the edges of the Prince's eyes. And then, as if the spark had touched fuel, he burst into a convulsion of merriment. I had never heard him laugh. Deep and musical, it seemed to come from the same deep-buried reservoir of joy as his rare smile. It might have been the sun piercing the clouds after a year of storms.

I could not keep my eyes from him, for somewhere in the resonance of his good humor was a note which made my blood burn as it had not in ages of the world. Thus even as I enjoyed the mournful resignation on Paulo's dirty face, I mocked myself for "widow's lust." I laughed until tears came.

"Oh, Paulo," I said, once I could articulate a word. "What in the stars are you doing here?"

"Nothin' better to be at," he said sullenly.

"Than running away from home again and chasing us

into the wilderness? Surely there are a thousand things better for you to be about. Your gram will be frantic."

"She's dead."

"Oh, no!" And so did the world swallow up our good humor.

"Put away one too many a tankard while I was off to Grenatte. Dead drunk she was. Then just dead."

"I'm sorry."

"Not as sorry as her, I guess."

"Who's to care for you, then?"

"Don't nobody want to. Well, Sheriff had said— But he's gone off and not come back. Dirk Crowley said as Loopy Lucy might take me, but I didn't want no part of an old crow like her. I can do for myself." D'Natheil had released the boy's ear, and Paulo squirmed a bit to untwist the voluminous cloak. "Gasso said he'd trade me this horse for my two silver pieces and whatever was in Gram's room, and I thought that was fine, so's I took the deal and rode up to your place. Thought I could watch it for you till Sheriff come back. Didn't steal nothin'. Just ate what was goin' to rot. And today I saw this'n come through and look about." He jerked his head toward D'Natheil.

"And you decided to follow him?"

"Nothin' better to be at. He's a sight more interesting than Loopy Lucy. Got a sword and all."

"You were welcome to the food. Was everything all right at the cottage?"

"Right enough. Those men—the priests what scragged the highwaymen—they searched right through it, but didn't take nothin' as I could see."

"You saw the three priests search the cottage?" . . . *they were up at your place* . . . The echo of Graeme Rowan's report sent a shiver through me.

"They left it all careful like, so's you couldn't tell nobody had been there."

"So they came to my house straight from Grenatte, then?"

"Nope." He hesitated for a moment. "Went to the village first."

"To Dunfarrie? Whatever for?"

"Talked to somebody. Askin' about you . . . who you

were and where'd you come from and was anyone with you."

"How did they find my cottage, Paulo? It's very important. How did they know where to go?"

The boy dug a toe into the dirt and kept his eyes away from me. "Somebody told 'em where it was when they first come from Grenatte. Somebody took 'em up there." With every answer, the words came slower and quieter. "It was the same person what told 'em everything about you, and about the Prince, and about where you'd gone with him— off to Valleor." The boy kicked a rock so hard it flew into the trees, flushing out three deer who leaped across the road through the moonlight.

I laid my hand on the boy's shoulder. "Paulo, sometimes we can be mistaken about people, and it hurts very much when we find out they're not as honorable as we believed. But the truth is important, especially when lives depend on knowing whom we can trust. Was it a friend of yours that told them?"

Paulo nodded, and he mumbled so softly I almost could not hear him. "Jacopo done it. Sheriff said they must've made him."

No. That wasn't right. Rowan was the betrayer, not Jacopo. The sheriff had met the Zhid in Grenatte, talked and laughed with them. They said he'd been of great service. And there was the button, of course, and Teriza's story of the Leiran in the dark jacket with shiny buttons, his pursuit through the forest, his presence in Yurevan . . .

"Who told them?" I grabbed Paulo's chin and forced him to look me in the eye, daring him to say it again, ready to yell at him that he was misguided at best, a tool of evildoers at worst, refusing to credit him, even as my heart and soul understood that he spoke truth.

"It was Jacopo." The boy's gaze did not waver, as if he knew that his best testimony was himself. His thin, freckled face displayed only sorrow and simple truth, forcing me to accept how dreadfully I had erred.

I had determinedly ignored ten years of observation that demonstrated nothing but Rowan's unremitting honesty. No strength of evidence had convinced me of his guilt—I could have come up with a hundred different explanations of buttons and light-haired Leirans. But I had listened only to my personal humiliation and seen only the hateful emblem on his coat. Even his "threat" to be wary of Paulo's and Jacopo's life was certainly a willfully misinterpreted warning.

Everything was so clear, now I was forced to look: the night of our feast in the meadow, the night the Seeking of the Zhid had come upon us like a summer hurricane. Jacopo's leg had been hurting him, and I could imagine him sitting and smoking a pipe on one of the stone fences between the edge of the forest and Dunfarrie. Away from the trees. Away from the house. It was on the next morning that he'd changed his mind about warning Graeme Rowan. He had denied the reality of our experiences on the ridge and insisted on knowing who I was going to see, even wanting the name—questions to which he had no need for answers. How had he known I was in Montevial? How had he come to be in the Street of the Cloth Merchants? I squeezed my eyes shut as if I could hide the truth again, but all I saw was Jacopo's old sea coat, dark blue with brass buttons—the jacket he'd worn every day since he'd come home from the sea.

D'Natheil led us to a clearing a safe distance from the road, and as we settled in for the rest of the night, I remembered the message I had sent to Jacopo earlier in the day. Not only had I revealed our departure from Montevial, but I had told him that Rowan had accused him of connection with the murderers. Would the Zhid have any use for Jacopo if he'd been discovered? Would they allow Rowan to roam freely with his knowledge of their wickedness? My detestable pride had likely murdered Jacopo and Rowan together.

Over our tea and bacon the next morning, Paulo, not Jacopo, was the first topic of conversation. Baglos told the boy that we had no use for him, and so he should take himself somewhere else.

I wouldn't hear of it. Fear and self-reproach and hard earth had made for a long restless night, leaving me snappish and out of patience. "We must either take him back to Dunfarrie where there are people who will see to his welfare, or we must keep him with us. A boy on the road alone . . ." While a mournful Paulo saddled the horses and strapped our loaded packs on them, I explained to D'Natheil and Baglos what happened to children who had no one to care what happened to them. An indenture agreement would be signed by a local magistrate, and it would stipulate that the child was to be given his keep in exchange for his labor until he turned sixteen. In other words, it was free labor for as long as you could squeeze out a day's work, and, as the master had no interest in the children after age sixteen, he could starve them or give them tasks that would cripple them. Most were dead by sixteen. A less than perfect boy like Paulo would have no chance at all.

"We've no time to take him back to his village," said Baglos. "We must find the Gate."

"No. Going back would be very dangerous." I wasn't yet ready to explain the extent of my rock-headed stupidity.

"Then the boy must stay with us," said D'Natheil simply, leaving Baglos with no argument and me relieved.

When I told Paulo that he was to accompany us on our travels until such time as we could return him to Dunfarrie, he stood at least a hand's breadth taller. "But you'll have to earn your keep," I said, "and obey any one of us without question."

"Whatever you want, miss. I promise."

"This won't be the safest road, but you've shown yourself resourceful in the past, and we'll expect nothing less of you now. And most importantly, you'll hear and see many things you can't tell anyone, now or ever. Our lives and yours will depend on your silence. I think you know what I mean. Are you willing?"

Paulo grinned and ducked his head, probably the nearest he'd ever come to saying thank you.

"To start," I said, "I think you'll have to care for the horses. Baglos dislikes it very much, and I know you're good at it."

While I told Baglos what I'd said to Paulo, the boy flung his arms about the neck of my little roan and buried his face in the beast's ruddy coat. Perhaps *some* good had resulted from all this.

*   *   *

By the time we were two days on the road to Tryglevie, the four animals were fast friends with Paulo. They nosed his neck and his pockets and his thin brown hands at every opportunity, and he had but to click his tongue and they stood ready for whatever he wished of them. I soon came to believe the boy was able to read the beasts' minds as clearly as any J'Ettanne. On the third morning of the journey, as the boy gave me a leg up, I grumbled that the roan didn't seem to be learning my commands very well. Paulo asked why I didn't use my horse's name, as that would make him listen better. When I said that I didn't know the beast's name and hadn't had the time to think of one, the boy stared at me in scornful disbelief. "Name's Firethorn," he said. "Don't know why you never figured it out."

"And what of the Prince's horse?"

"He don't want a name just yet. He's thinkin' on it." I wasn't sure whether Paulo meant D'Natheil or the horse. "The other one, now, he's Polestar." Appropriate for the horse of the Guide.

"And yours?"

Paulo flushed and gently stroked his horse's neck. "Molly. She's naught but a broke-down mare, you know. Just right for me."

We rode onward into the west.

CHAPTER 28

Three days' hard riding brought us out of the great forest and into the rocky foothills of western Leire. It was harsh country, afflicted with wild extremes of weather and dotted with poor settlements, suitable for little but grazing sheep. I could well believe such a place was the Writer's home.

In his journal he had forever lamented the unpredictable weather and rocky soil that made it so hard to feed his family, he was forced to sell the talent he would rather give freely.

As soon as we left the forest, we began to inquire at every house and village as to the whereabouts of Yennet and the ruins that lay nearby. Villages the size of Yennet rarely appeared on any map, and even those who had heard of the place were vague about its location. One said it was directly northwest. Another said it lay just east of the great bend where the Glenaven met the Dun. Another said it was no ruined castle, but a nobleman's quarry that adjoined the village. A traveling tinker we met at a roadside well seemed the most reliable source. He claimed to have visited Yennet. "Two years ago, that was. Wasn't hardly anyone living there. Folks too poor even to have a kettle needed mending." But he drew us a map showing Yennet about halfway in between something he marked as Pell's Hill and a ruined castle from the times before Leire had a king. Pell's Hill was likely an ancient barrow known as Pell's Mound, a site Karon had always hoped to excavate.

We set out on the tinker's route, still with no sign of pursuit. About twelve leagues west we were to watch for a fork in the road, the rightmost continuing west and north to join the main route that ran from Montevial all the way west to Vanesta. The less-traveled left fork, hardly a road at all, would bear slightly southeast to skirt Pell's Mound, then angle straight south to Yennet.

The second day from the tinker's well dawned overcast, and the thickening clouds glowered and grumbled as the morning progressed. Thunder rolled across the rocky fields, and at midmorning the black sky erupted into chaos.

Baglos was in the lead, hunched down in the saddle, his gray cloak pulled up tight against the lashing rain. Paulo on his Molly followed behind the Dulcé. Sometime near midday, the boy reversed direction and stopped, blocking the road and forcing me to stop in my turn. I yelled at him in irritation. "Keep moving, Paulo. We've no wish to be out in this any longer than need be."

The boy had his huge cloak draped over him and his horse, like Isker women who rode to war behind their husbands, forbidden to expose anything but their eyes. Without poking so much as his nose outside his shroud, Paulo gestured toward a muddy rut that led off to our left into the rain-swept meadows. The soggy landscape was dotted with sparse clumps of pine and birch trees, and massive, oddly shaped piles of granite poked out of the ground like the debris of a giant rock-boring mole. The rut was straight enough, one could imagine it might be a path.

"Good eyes, Paulo," I shouted over the roar of the storm. "Catch Baglos and tell him we've found the turning. I'll wait for the Prince."

D'Natheil had lagged behind us all day. Indeed, from our first night out of Montevial, he had withdrawn almost completely from our society. He rarely spoke, and when we camped, he ate little and slept less, patrolling the nearby ground while Baglos or I was on watch, and taking the late watches alone when the rest of us were asleep.

More than half an hour passed until he came into view. Irritated at having to wait so long in the cold rain, I didn't wait for him to join me, but waved and rode on up the muddy track, hurrying to catch up with Baglos and Paulo. With every step away from the main road, the track looked less like a road and more like a stream. The wind ripped and tangled my cloak, ensuring that no patch of clothing or skin stayed dry, and the gusts felt as if they'd come straight off of the snow-capped mountains to the southwest, making a mockery of my summer clothing. Soon the water and mud flowed from everywhere, and I was losing all sense of direction. As a girl I had delighted in watching storms rumble across the barren hills beyond Comigor. But turbulent weather lost a great deal of its charm when one had no three-foot-thick walls or six-hundred-year-old roof to keep it out.

Baglos halted in the middle of the open downs, Paulo beside him. Sheets of rain and lowering cloud obscured the view in every direction. "I can no longer assure you that we are on the path," said the Dulcé when I joined the two. "I don't know what to do."

My hair stuck to my face and dribbled cold rivulets into my eyes, and my teeth were chattering so I could hardly answer. "How far is it from the fork to the village?"

"The tinker said half a day, but that would be in fair weather. And if we've strayed . . ."

"I suppose we'll have to wait for D'Natheil and see if he can tell us more."

The Prince had fallen behind again. We had another long, wet wait until he came into view. About the time D'Natheil emerged from the curtain of rain, the hairs on my neck rose, and, not fifty paces from where we waited, a lightning bolt struck a pine tree, exploding it in thunderous fire. I had to haul sharply on the reins to control Firethorn, and Baglos clung to the neck of his mount.

"Can you not guide us, Dulcé?" asked the Prince as soon as our beasts were under control. His mount had stayed quiet under the simple pressure of his hand.

"No, my lord. To my devastation it is not possible just now. I have no reference in the storm."

"Then head for those boulders to our right. I'll be along." D'Natheil seemed agitated and distracted.

"Yes, my lord." Baglos turned his jittery horse.

The Dulcé led us toward a huge slab of granite that, in some long-past time, had split and shifted, leaving a great seam down its middle. The split was a boon for drenched travelers, for the two pieces leaned together at the top as if trying to rejoin, creating a deep, but narrow and blessedly dry niche at the base.

Paulo tethered the horses in the lee of the outcropping, and the three of us crowded into the niche. I huddled to one side, sinking to the damp ground and pulling my wet cloak about me tightly. Dribbles of water splattered from the edge of the rock onto the Dulcé's pinched face as he hunched beside the opening, peering into the gray downpour to watch for D'Natheil. Paulo curled up in the farthest recess of the crack and promptly fell asleep. The boy seemed capable of sleep in any circumstance. I envied him.

A bedraggled D'Natheil soon appeared from out of the storm, leading his horse. In his arms were sticks of soggy wood and some dripping brush. Baglos took the Prince's horse and settled it with the others, while D'Natheil threw his bundle down in front of me. Crouching down beside it, he blew softly across his palm and passed his hand over the sodden pile. This time the sensation was not lightning.

A tiny flame curled up from the pile, and, in moments, a sizable fire was blazing.

I crowded close and relished the moment that my bones began to thaw. "You did that very well," I said, as soon as my teeth stopped chattering. "I don't know what I'd have done without it."

D'Natheil stared into the growing flames. "Survived."

The word took me aback—he was so grimly serious. "Probably so. It never seems likely at the time, though. And this is far better."

"Would that the Preceptors could see it," Baglos mumbled to no one in particular, as he passed around his silver flask of sweet, potent wine that always seemed to appear when there was most need.

Thunder rumbled. The rain pounded harder, causing spits of moisture to bounce through the opening in the rock and hiss as they pelted the fire. "Baglos, tell us about the Preceptors . . . about this Dassine," I said. "Do you know him well?"

As always when I asked a question about the other world, Baglos deferred to the Prince. "Would you have me answer, my lord?"

"Have you learned nothing, fool of a Dulcé? Clearly this woman is inextricably entwined in our fate. Without her assistance and counsel, we would have been defeated long ago, and so whatever instruction you've been given about circumspection should not and will not apply to her. Is that clear?"

"As you will, *Giré D'Arnath*." Baglos quickly bowed his head, hunching his narrow shoulders.

But for once the Prince's annoyance bore no more weighty consequence than the reprimand. D'Natheil's mind was somewhere else altogether. Though his eyes were on Baglos, he was not truly looking at the dark head lowered so humbly before him. "You must follow her lead, Dulcé." His voice had fallen so quiet, I could scarcely hear him. "Answer her questions. Do as she commands you whatever the circumstance."

"Yes, my lord. As you say." As always when D'Natheil issued a command, the Dulcé's face went blank for an instant before resuming its normal animation. I wondered if that moment was when he retrieved his scattered knowledge and brought it to the fore, but the question seemed too intimate to ask.

And so, as D'Natheil's fire burned brightly, its enchanted fuel as inexhaustible as the dreary downpour, the Dulcé told us of the voice from the other world.

"The Preceptors are seven men and women who are considered the most wise and powerful among the Dar'Nethi, appointed by the Heir to aid him in his work of teaching and guiding the Dar'Nethi in the Way and opposing the Lords of Zhev'Na. They serve until they die or withdraw from service or are asked by the Heir to step down—this last a rare occasion. Master Dassine is a Healer, first named to the Preceptorate by D'Natheil's grandfather. He is frequently at odds with the other Preceptors, as I have told you, and often refuses to consult with them when he ought. He has studied the lore of the Bridge and championed our duty to preserve it at all costs, until many accuse him of being more concerned with mundanes and this world of yours than with our own."

"What is Dassine's disagreement with the other Preceptors? Was it only the decision to send D'Natheil onto the Bridge when he was twelve?" I asked.

"The conflict centers on the conduct of the war. Many years ago when D'Natheil was a child, Master Dassine was chosen to venture into the Wastes to learn more of the Lords and the Zhid. He was gone for three years. Everyone assumed he was slain or enslaved, which are much the same. But to our astonishment he returned to Avonar, crippled in one leg and asserting that he had escaped from slavery. No one has ever managed such a thing—the slave collars of Zhev'Na prevent any use of Dar'Nethi power—and Master Dassine refused to say how he had accomplished it. Even before he was fully recovered from his ordeal, he called a meeting of the Preceptorate that resulted in much argument and strife."

Baglos shifted closer to the fire, and his speech took on a greater urgency, as if the heat that warmed his flesh inflamed his story as well.

"You must understand our situation. The Catastrophe was an enchantment gone awry. It sucked our rivers dry, burned our meadows and forests, and left most of our world a reeking ruin. Those Dar'Nethi who stood in its path were likewise devastated, the fortunate killed outright, the others become Zhid. But in the years when the Heirs of D'Arnath and J'Ettanne preserved the Gates and walked the Bridge, the Wastes began to heal, and the power of the Lords and the Zhid declined. But when J'Ettanne's people failed us, no longer walking the Bridge as they were sworn to do, and D'Arnath's Heir tried to maintain the Bridge alone, this progress was reversed.

"As the Zhid grew stronger again, the Dar'Nethi were forced to become warriors, the Heir first among them, so as to uphold his oath to preserve and defend the Bridge. In his pronouncements to the Preceptorate, Dassine claimed that the Lords were more terrible and the Zhid more numerous than anyone had ever suspected, and that the Dar'Nethi must reverse their thinking on how to contain them. The argument was never explained to me, but many called Dassine a traitor. Master Dassine has often been heard saying he might not have gone to the trouble of his journey for all the good it did."

Baglos glanced at D'Natheil and reddened a little as he continued. "The matter of the young prince compounded their disagreements. It was while Master Dassine was away from Avonar that D'Natheil was named Heir and Master Exeget appointed as his mentor. Master Dassine proclaimed that Master Exeget was the greatest fool who was not Zhid and that he had done his best to destroy our last hope. He had no right to speak of Master Exeget so. Master Exeget is the head of the Preceptorate, a man of great talent and the highest influence. The terrible mistake of D'Natheil's too-early encounter with the Bridge grieved him greatly."

"You don't like Dassine," I said.

"The Dulcé serve all as our gifts permit."

"You were surprised when Celine released his message." He had stumbled out of the room when Dassine's message was unfolding in our heads.

"I was not told of Dassine's enchantment—his message, or the locking and unlocking of the Prince's voice, or this harm to his memory that Master Dassine must have caused as well. Master Exeget did not know of these things, or he would have told me." Baglos flushed. He took a hurried sip and stowed the silver flask away in his pack. "There are many things I wasn't told."

I could sympathize with that. "How could Dassine know me, Baglos? I've wondered about it since that day. How did he know to send D'Natheil to me?"

"I don't know," said the Dulcé. "My preparation was so hurried. I heard no mention of a mundane woman. Since his return from the Wastes, Master Dassine had speculated that the Exiles were all dead. He was proven wrong when they opened the Gates, as I have told you. But Master Exeget did not believe we could expect help from the Exiles on this journey. My master knew no one that could help . . . no one . . ." His voice trailed off.

"Your master . . . this Exeget was your master, then. You were *his* Guide?"

Baglos shifted uneasily, glancing up at D'Natheil, but the Prince was not listening any more. He stood in the opening of the niche with his back to us, staring out into the rain. So the Dulcé answered me as he had been commanded. "I was Master Exeget's madrissé for eight years. I accompanied him to D'Natheil's crossing. When Bendal was wounded by the Zhid, Master Exeget commanded me to take the madris with D'Natheil."

And so Baglos, sworn to obey his linked madrisson, had been given little choice in the matter of this journey.

Water poured from the heavy clouds. Baglos was reluctant to continue his story without the Prince's attention, and so our conversation moved back to the Writer's diagram. I didn't even have to look at the journal any more, but traced the familiar lines and symbols in the damp earth while we considered the land we traveled. Could Pell's Mound be one of the marks on the diagram? Or the ruined castle or the Glenaven River? Was there significance in the names? Baglos maintained his position that the diagram made no sense as a map. It was discouraging to feel we were on the brink of what we needed to know, yet were no closer to deciphering it than Karon and I had been ten years previous.

My head grew heavy, the warmth and smoke sapping my

energy and making it increasingly difficult to think. I had
the sleepy impression of the Dulcé snoring, and D'Natheil
disappearing through the cleft in the rock, back into the
storm. I wondered vaguely if the man ever slept.

When I woke to watery sunlight and birdsong, it took
me a moment to sort out where I was. So many different
sleeping accommodations in the past weeks, so many varieties of discomfort. The quiet was disconcerting until I realized it meant only that the storm was past. A small grove
of birch trees fronted our refuge, and a breeze rustled the
gold-rimmed leaves, sprinkling a last shower of sparkling
droplets on the grass. Baglos was snoring, slumped against
the rock. D'Natheil's fire still burned, its fuel not at all
diminished. Paulo sat close to the fire, his chin on his knees,
his eyes fixed on me intently, as if he were trying to will
me awake.

I stood up from the damp ground and stretched my
cramped muscles. Noting the hollow growl in my stomach,
I thought I might understand Paulo's unspoken message.
"Are you hungry?"

He nodded eagerly.

"Set some stones to hold our pot, and we'll make something hot. We'll surprise Baglos."

I wrestled with the sodden leather pack attached to my
saddle, pulling out pot and provisions. As I filled the pot
with water, Paulo was peering idly at the lines and symbols
I had drawn in the dirt.

"Paulo, if you can unravel that little puzzle, I'll keep
your stomach full until you're twenty," I said, as I crouched
by the fire and set the pot on the three stones the boy had
found to hold it.

"I was never no good at the riddle game," he said. "Everybody always I said was too stupid to play."

I almost poured the water into the fire. "What do you
mean—the riddle game?"

Paulo poked his bare toe at the diagram. "Looks like it.
You know."

"No, I don't. Tell me."

"Picture tells what riddle has to come first. What one
next. Stupid game."

I tried to contain my hopes. "I've never played. Could you tell me how?"

"Well, everybody makes up pictures, and one draws the lines in between to tell which picture comes first, which next. This foot means the one who plays first has got to tell a riddle about a foot. And if nobody guesses it right, then the same person gets to tell the next one about . . . well, whatever that thing is . . . and then about the face, and so on. If somebody gets it right, then that person gets to tell the next riddle. The one who fools the last, wins. I wasn't no good at riddling."

Riddles . . . Riddles that would tell us where to go. The Writer's children had played all sorts of games. He was always telling of them. One of his daughters had a special talent for riddling.

"Baglos! Baglos, wake up!" I shook the sleeping Dulcé, not caring if I frightened him out of a year of his life.

"What is it?"

"Get the journal, Baglos. Hurry! Paulo has solved the mystery."

Baglos shook off his sleep and dug deep in his pack to retrieve the book, mumbling to himself. "The boy solved the puzzle? Surely not."

I hovered at his shoulder, while Paulo gave me such a look as to say that adults were not quite sensible when they would abandon cooking for the riddle game.

"It's a children's game," I said, willing Baglos to hurry. "We must find where he writes of his daughter and her talent for riddles. The entry comes only a few days before he drew the diagram. We never had a reason to make the connection."

Baglos turned the pages to the familiar one, then leafed backwards until he found the passage I named. In his musical voice, he read the Writer's words.

Lilith hath taken herself to riddling, and a clever wit she is at it. Mori and I wonder if it be the girl will show herself a Word Winder or mayhap even a Speaker. I must inquire of Siddhe when next I work the fen country and have her tell me the signs. Mori says that Lilith yet be too young to show her gift, but JonThe and C'Netha of Isfan were no more than eleven, and C'Netha a Word Winder herself. Regretful, too, would I be, if the need for mentoring were to take my bright Lilith so far from her home, but such is the Way. Mori doth not prod the girls to show, as she doth for Tekko and Garnath. I must admonish her, for the girls must make their way in the world every bit as much as their brothers. Well should Mori know, for were not she the strong woman she is, how ever could I take this endless road that calls me?

But enough. Lilith riddling. Before I journeyed this day, we sat and played at it. I must record her tally for when she is a Speaker, to prove that she came forth when only ten.

Karon had not bothered to decipher the little girl's riddles, thinking the barriers of time, language, and culture would make the task impossible. We had prized the passage for its revelation of the Writer's life, and his love for his family and his calling, but never had we made the connection with the diagram.

I hung over Baglos's shoulder and pointed to the page. "Look. You see, he's added these lines. The pages are so worn, and he was forever adding notes, or marking things out, or changing them. You wouldn't notice, unless you knew to look. He would always leave space between his text, so he could go back and add things he had forgotten. See how close these lines are, and some were written with a pen having a wider tip. Paulo, you're marvelous. You've really done it."

There followed a whole page of short puzzles, but I had no trouble picking out the ones that had been added later. There were five of them, just as there were five symbols in the diagram, and a short additional passage written at the same time.

It is the lesser brother's portion that brings the greatest wealth, and the lesser passage that finds its destination.

Though he cannot see it, the hunter knows his prey, for it speaks to his heart whether he turns right or left.

When the wall births the flood, it is wiser to be the rabbit than the fish or the goat.

A journey begins on the road that never sleeps and whose travelers have no feet.

*When one ascends the ancient face that weeps, one sees
that it brings forth the fruits of youth from its decrepit pores.*

*Is the child not a marvel? The day will come when men
will cry out the name of our race, and it is my Lilith that
will shine in their memory.*

"So we might solve these puzzles to find our way?"
said Baglos.

"The Writer says that this diagram is his map to the
stronghold. Paulo says that the pictures in the riddle game
tell the player what the riddle must be about, and the lines
between tell the order in which to solve them. So if we can
match the riddles with the pictures in the diagram we
should have a list of clues to get us to the stronghold. Then
we just have to solve the riddles. First, the one about the
foot."

"A journey begins on the road that never sleeps and
whose travelers have no feet." Baglos crinkled his face as
if seeing only part of the words might make them clearer.
"That is the only one of the texts that talks about a foot.
I hope you're skilled at solving riddles, for this is as big a
mystery to me as the other."

"Oh, yes. I've done my share. I've been told I'm very
good at riddles. But I never played as a child, never this
way."

Paulo sat by the fire, mournfully watching the pot boil
dry, his hopes for supper drifting away on the vapors, not
even a good smell left behind. "Here is our hero starving,"
I said, "and I've promised to fill his stomach until he's
twenty."

"I will take on that duty proudly," said Baglos. "The
most excellent ferocious boy will not starve!"

While Baglos stirred up the pot, I wandered out past the
birch grove seeking D'Natheil to tell him the good news.
But the Prince was nowhere in sight, and the chestnut stallion was gone. By the time we ate the hot porridge and
packed up everything again, D'Natheil had not yet returned. Excitement faded into concern as the afternoon
hours waned. Baglos began to fidget. I told myself that
D'Natheil was scouting ahead, finding the direction to take
us back to the road, perhaps solving the mystery of Yennet.

I tried to concentrate on the riddles, but as the pale sun faded and night crept over the downs, I feared that something terrible had happened. And when D'Natheil's fire went out, I was convinced that the Heir of D'Arnath was not coming back.

CHAPTER 29

I was confounded. *Be rational, Seri,* I told myself. *Don't panic.* I stood outside the cleft in the rock and listened, but only the cry of a hunting owl interrupted the soft rustling of birch leaves in the moonless night. *Alternatives. Think.*

Had he been taken by the Zhid? If so, he was most likely dead by now—or victim to whatever they planned for him—and it didn't matter what we did. I looked down at the cold ashes of his fire. A last spark flared bright orange, then dulled to gray. That alternative was unacceptable.

What else then? Had he been injured in some ordinary mishap—a fall, an accident, bandits? If so, we'd not help him by hiding in the crevice of a rock. The rain had stopped about the same time as he had disappeared. As soon as there was daylight, we could follow his tracks.

Could he have decided that companions were unnecessary? That didn't seem likely. He had welcomed my help, expressed confidence in me, and he valued Baglos. Why would he leave us behind?

That left only the uncomfortable speculation that he had abandoned his mission altogether. Since the day of the fire he had carried the burden of two worlds on his shoulders, with very little to aid him. No memory. No understanding of himself. Asked to risk his life and what remained of his reason for a world he could not remember, for duty and loyalty he could not feel. Celine had said there was no person inside him. What must it be like to live with such emptiness? Many people would run away from such a burden. Yet even that could not be the whole of it, for when I'd managed to involve him in the investigation, he was willing, and he'd done what he could to keep us safe on our way.

The night passed slowly. Boiling clouds laced with pink and green lightning erased the midnight stars and doused us with a quick frenzy of rain. Even after I turned the watch over to Paulo in the midnight hour, I could not sleep. I stood by the entrance to the cleft, my damp blanket wrapped about my shoulders, and I fretted over the muddy hoofprints that would now be washed away.

Morning arrived. As I feared, the nighttime rain had erased any trace of D'Natheil's passing. A quick survey in the dawn light revealed that our refuge helped form the base of a grassy knob that dominated the rolling sea of grass and rocks—the mysterious Pell's Mound, I guessed, a matter that might have been of some interest were not our immediate concerns so critical. Karon had believed the hill to be a tribal holy place from which our ancestors—my ancestors—had worshipped the mountains. Indeed the peaks of the Dorian Wall loomed large, as if they had used the cover of the storm to creep up on us. And somewhere in the desolate country between the Wall and Pell's Mound lay the Glenaven River and the village of Yennet, once known as Tryglevie.

I could see no hint of D'Natheil's fate, no evidence of a mishap, no place that looked more worth searching than another. Baglos suggested that the three of us ride in different directions for an hour, then circle right and return to Pell's Mound by mid-morning. He sounded hopeless as he had not since he'd been reunited with his master. "The treacherous liars have taken him," he said. "They'll destroy him, shed his blood on the Bridge . . . Avonar is lost."

My search was fruitless. I saw more grassy undulations, one little different from the other, and more granite mono-liths protruding from the damp earth as if the roots of the mountains were beginning to sprout. When we came to-gether again at Pell's Mound, it took no words to share the result. Baglos led us silently to the road. We would go on to Yennet. If D'Natheil were able and willing, he would meet us there.

As the last of the morning haze burned away, we reached the outlying ruins of a dying village, piles of rubble that had once been neatly laid stone fences or low-roofed dwellings snug enough to hold back the bitter winter that would howl down from the Dorian Wall. The road was a sticky bog, with protruding islands of rock so exasperating to negotiate that we dismounted and led the horses rather than risk their injury in some unseen hole. What structures still remained in the village proper were cracked, crumbled, and overgrown with weeds. A pig rooted hungrily in the mud. The place was a squalid contrast to the mountain vista that lay so close behind it, as if set there solely to demonstrate that the works of man were but a corruption of the works of nature.

A hollow-cheeked man peered out of the door of a crumbling house. When I greeted him, he clucked to a dog that cowered between his legs and slammed the door. A little further along the way, a woman stood in the middle of a rock-bordered garden, watching our approach, three ragged children clinging to her skirts. Her garden, while not lush, was better tended than anything in sight. A slight move of her hand had the children scattering into the cluster of stone houses and broken walls.

I called out to her from a good distance. "Health and prosperity be yours this day, goodwife; may your hold flourish."

"And your road be smooth," said the woman. Her wispy braids were streaked with gray, her face lined, though she could well be younger than I. Her bare arms were ridged with sinew, and she gripped a rusty hoe, but did not lean on it.

"We're travelers from Montevial," I said.

"We see few strangers in Yennet. Why would you come here?"

The air was crisp and sweet, the sky a deep and brilliant blue behind the sheer white peaks. "To pay homage to the beauties of nature," I said, unable to think of any more plausible answer.

To my surprise, the woman nodded solemnly. " 'Tis the only reason to be sure. The Wall is worth a day's rising."

"Have you seen any other strangers about today? One of our company was separated from us in the storm. A young man of . . . some thirty years he appears. Tall. Clean-shaven. Blue eyes; light hair. Strongly made and riding a spirited chestnut of sixteen hands."

"I've seen no one like. Mayhap he took the road to Vanesta or got turned about and is halfway to Montevial once more. You'd best be after him." The woman's fingers shifted on her hoe.

"Perhaps." No other villagers had made an appearance. I saw only one other person, a slim young man sitting on a fence far down the road. Tales said that untaxed grain often found its way into Valleor through the foothills of the Dorian Wall. Smugglers were rightly shy of company. "Is there somewhere in your village where we could stay the night? We hope our friend will make his way here."

The woman's glance darted toward her house. "I don't know. We're but poor sheepherders. Most everyone is out with the flocks."

From the corner of my eye I caught a movement in the shadowed doorway. I stood my ground. No use to run. To move my hand toward the knife beneath my skirt was to invite unfortunate consequences. "We have our own provisions. We just need a roof and a dry floor. I promise you we're interested in naught but finding our friend."

"But"

A body separated itself from the shadows. "What Marika is trying not to say is that she has already sheltered a refugee from the storm. One who asked her to be discreet."

"Sheriff!"

Graeme Rowan looked about cautiously before approaching me. His left temple was mottled purple and green, swollen and marked by an ugly scab. In the center of his forehead was a faint gray smudge of earth. His god had sent him on another journey because of me.

How do you apologize to a man you despise? Honor demanded it, but my back bristled. Why couldn't it be enough that we hadn't killed him? "Sheriff, I—"

"Madam, I'd be grateful if we could leave off any talk of my profession. I've had to swear on my life that I am not here as a representative of the law. Perhaps that vow might ease your own worry."

My cheeks felt like a smith's furnace. "I'm glad to see we did no lasting damage."

It was his turn to be surprised.

"How did you find us here?" I said.

"It was my impression that you found me, but for the sake of avoiding an argument so early in our meeting, I'll tell you again, I have a new friend who is very good at tracking."

"But it's not Pere Giano?"

Rowan's quiet explosion of laughter was as unstudied as his manner. "Is that what you think? That I—? Holy Annadis, you believe that the one you've scorned for ten years as the willful scourge of a corrupt law—a man happy to murder children to prove his worth—is in league with these vile, sorcerous . . . whatever they are? How in perdition did you come to that fancy?"

I did not share his good humor. "Perhaps we could sit down and discuss this, rather than interrupting this good woman's work."

Paulo had sidled up to the sheriff with a crooked grin. "I'll show this young renegade where to put your horses," said Rowan, tugging at the boy's unkempt hair. "Perhaps then we might have a word."

Marika, appearing relieved at the amiable result of our confrontation, invited us inside. A large, well-swept hearth, its chimney blackened by countless years of burning fir and tar bush branches, was the heart of the single room. In the center of the floor stood a thick table and six stools. A pile of sheepskins in one corner were the family bedding, and two grain bins in another corner served for the pantry. A basket held a spindle and a pile of brown wool. A few pegs and a wooden shelf along one wall held the sum of their material wealth that was not sheep: five cups that Marika set out on her table, a chipped flask with a narrow neck that likely contained oil, some wooden bowls, and a few tins, one of which held dried herbs that the woman spooned sparingly into the cups before pouring hot water from the blackened pot hanging over her coals. An ax with a splinted handle hung by the fireplace along with a coiled rope, a fishing net, and two pair of snowshoes. This made my cottage look like a palace.

"You are very kind to have us, Marika."

"It's good to see a new face, perhaps to hear news of the world." A red-cheeked boy carried a crock to the table and then sped back outdoors. Marika spooned milk into the heavy cups.

"Not much news worth hearing, I'm afraid. War or the fruits of war."

"The tales we hear say mayhap our life is not so bad as one might think," said Marika, handing cups to Baglos and me, while pausing over the third and peering out the door. Her boy had joined the other children who stood in an admiring circle around Paulo, treating him with the awe due a bold adventurer, rather than Donkey, the stupid boy with the twisted leg.

"To make a life in such a place must be very difficult."

"Our families have been in Yennet for five generations. Once we sent wool carts by the dozen to Montevial, Vanesta, and Yurevan, but now we're lucky to send three a year. Our flocks have not flourished nor our people. But times will change if we work hard enough."

"I hope they will."

I hoped. What would happen if D'Natheil could not do what was needed? There was little enough hope in the world. Baglos was the very image of despair, leaning heavily on the table and staring into his cup, unspeaking. I likely could have pricked him with a needle and elicited no reaction.

Marika poured the third cup of tea, dropped a tiny pinch of sugar in it, added two spoons of milk, and then laid a rag on the top. "Rilia!" she called, and a tiny, curly haired girl ran to the doorway. "Take this to Old Ghouro and see he drinks it."

"Aye," said the child, in a whisper, her dark eyes fixed on Baglos and me.

"We have to watch the old man," said Marika. "He don't want to eat. Took his flock too far into the mountains two years ago. When he didn't come back before snowfall, we thought him dead. But didn't he wander into the village in the middle of winter, half starved and off his head? I hope your friend don't come to the same." She finished pouring and returned the tins of tea and sugar to the shelf. "I got to get back to my work now. You can spread your wet things out back if you want or poke up the fire."

"Thank you again for the tea."

Rowan joined us as Marika left. He picked up his cup of tea and drank, looking at me as if expecting another bash on the head. I didn't know what to say. He had fought at Avonar.

"So the mysterious 'servant' has gone missing again," he said, at last. "Have the priests taken him?"

"I don't know. He would not go willingly, but we've no evidence that he's been forced."

Rowan had left his laughter behind. "Why did you think me allied with the villains? I thought we understood the same thing about what they are."

So I detailed the case I had built up against him: his meeting with the Zhid in Grenatte after pretending not to know them, his appearance at Kellea's shop on the night of the fire, the brass button in the dead professor's library, and, of course, Teriza's testimony about the Leiran wearing a dark coat with shiny buttons. "You're right that I despise you," I said. "To my mind, you have willingly participated in acts that are beyond forgiveness. So I refused to believe you. Then, two days ago, Paulo very simply and innocently confirmed everything you'd said." I told him how I'd sent Jacopo a warning of Rowan's accusations. ". . . and so, because of me, they know you were trying to warn me. I'm afraid I've put both you and Jaco in more danger than before."

As the sheriff considered what I had told him, his fingers nudged the button I'd laid on the table. His response, when it came, was wholly without rancor. "If a petitioner had brought me such a case, I'd have needed no trial to pass judgment either, especially with what you know of . . . my past." His skin was as red as his hair. "I'm grateful to Paulo for being such a good witness. As for Jacopo—I don't think there's anything you could have done that would put him in more danger than he's in already."

I couldn't bear thinking of Jaco. My determination to spite Darzid had made me reckless, dragging my only friend into this horror and leaving him in the path of these murderous Zhid. And now I had given the Zhid reason to believe he was of no more use to them. Yet self-recrimination would not help him. Defeating the Zhid might. "Tell me what really happened, Sheriff. Why didn't you say you knew the priests? And how do you come to be here?"

"The reason I didn't say that those you'd seen in During Forest were the same who had come to Dunfarrie hunting for the two strangers was simply that, until I looked through the doorway into Bartolome's common room, I didn't know it. They weren't dressed as priests when Captain Darzid brought them to me, talking of Isker spies. I overheard the captain say he would meet them in Grenatte. It sounded as if the whole world was traveling to Grenatte, and I was damnably curious. When I saw you there, I knew the matter had nothing to do with spies. Only sorcery could have drawn you out. If Captain Darzid caught sight of you, you were going to be arrested."

And Graeme Rowan had saved me from it. A hard truth. "You rushed me away."

"When you confronted the priests so recklessly, I guessed you didn't know about the captain's dealings with them—"

"—and I wouldn't listen."

"To me? It's certainly not your custom." Grim amusement touched his features, fading as he continued. "Giano was full peeved that you three had escaped him, and when Jacopo told him that you'd taken the fugitives off to Yurevan, they were riding out after you before I could spit. I thought it odd they didn't capture your friends on the road. You were easy enough to track at the beginning, but I never saw the priests behind you. They must have ridden straight through to Yurevan. When I lost you after Glyenna, I did the same, hoping to intercept you before you ran into them. I must have reached the house just as your servant girl was watching from the other side. It was just as she said." His eyes clouded. "I've been a soldier. I've seen men do things . . . shared in things . . . no thinking creature should be capable of—as you well know—but that . . . There are no words to speak of it."

"Jaco was there?"

"Yes." Rowan cast a sidelong glance at me, grimaced,

and rubbed the back of his neck. "Before I could go into the house to see if anyone was left alive, your gentleman friend rode in. He appeared to belong in the place, so I left matters to him. It was only later that I discovered that he was a man the law of Leire believes to be dead."

Blood rushed to my face. "You won't—"

"Father Arot and his sons do not grant us life beyond death," he said without changing expression. "How could an ignorant village sheriff contradict the gods?"

I breathed again, and he continued. "I wandered in circles for half a day, hoping to warn you, but I ended up back at the house. When I let myself in, I found only the dead man. I couldn't leave him like that, so I buried him in the orchard. That's probably when I lost the button— the damning evidence."

And then he had followed us to Yurevan and tried to save us from the fire. "How did you know we survived the fire, and how did you follow us here?"

"You've not guessed it?" He stepped to the door and waved his hand. The slim young man I had seen sitting on the fence sauntered down the road toward us. Only it wasn't a young man; it was a young woman who could find any herb, no matter how rare—Rowan's friend with a knack for following people. Kellea.

"This must be worth a story," I said.

Kellea offered no greeting when she stepped through the door, nor would she sit when Rowan pulled out a stool for her. He remained standing as well.

Rowan glanced over at Baglos. The Dulcé had looked up when Kellea walked in and then quickly returned to his own thoughts, eyes fixed on his cup, though it was long drained. "I wasn't sure what was happening in that house," said the sheriff, "or even whether the ones who attacked were your friends or enemies, but I saw the girl creeping out of an alleyway down the road from the burning house, covered in soot and blood, and decided to ask her. She had no more use for me than you ever did. I foolishly tried to persuade her that I was a friend of yours."

"And that did you no good," I said. Kellea's sour look told me nothing had changed on that score.

"She insisted that she'd as soon kill you as look at you,

which pleased me in a way, since it told me you were still alive. She got away from me, and for a most of a week she led me a merry chase over half of Valleor. When I finally caught her, it took several days of disagreement for us to come to a truce. I told her what I'd seen, and why I thought we needed to help you fight these priests. She knew your friend, the professor. Eventually, she took pity on my ignorance and told me your guests' story, and something of the history her grandmother had taught her, and how it all fits together. I don't understand it all, but the business got stranger yet again when I tried to figure out where you'd got off to after the fire. She hadn't bothered to mention that she was herself one of . . . these sorcerers . . . and she let me spend three days chasing my own tail before telling me that she could find anyone if given enough to go on. She just needed to be in a place given where you'd been. So I took her to that charcoal burner's—"

"You knew about that?"

"I followed you there from Yurevan the afternoon before the fire. Your sturdy friend never left off his watch long enough for me to speak to you. I thought it odd he spent the whole night making fires and letting them go out again. It was several hours of watching before I realized he had no flint . . ." Rowan's expression was subtle as always. Awe might rob him of words, but it left only a crease in his brow and a slight shake of his head to reveal its depth.

Outside the open door children squealed with laughter. Something—a rock or a ball—thumped against the side of the house, and Marika's quiet command shooed the giggling group farther away. So much to consider. I mouthed some feeble apology for Rowan's injury and my misjudgment of his motives. To say more would be to acknowledge that somehow the honor of a man sworn to exterminate a race was worthy of respect. I could not yet bring myself to do that. But he had surely earned my gratitude. His dogged pursuit had brought me exactly what I needed.

"Kellea, we need your help."

"It seems a permanent condition. Who will die this time?" The girl dared me to make her care.

"Your grandmother and Professor Ferrante believed the stakes were worth the risk." I did not blink.

Kellea stood in the doorway, her shoulders square, her back as stiff and angular as the granite peaks outlined against the sky. "Go on."

"Yesterday in the storm, D'Natheil left our shelter and never returned. Can you find him?"

"Unless he's worked some sorcery, I can. I would need something of his, something personal. I've been following the group. Without something that belongs to him alone, I might lead you back on your own tracks."

Shirts, weapons, even his own cup . . . D'Natheil had taken everything with him. "I don't know. . . ."

"My lord's woodcarving." I was startled when Baglos spoke up. "He left it out two nights ago, and he's not wanted it these two days." Rummaging in the pack at his feet, he pulled out the chip of birchwood.

A sober grief had enveloped the Dulcé since D'Natheil had gone missing. All day his dark eyes had been luminous with unshed tears, his endless chatter and questioning stilled. And now his short, warm fingers spoke eloquently of his sorrow yet again, holding tight to the carving even as he laid it in my hand. I could not understand his reluctance to yield the wood . . . until I looked at it.

The face of the smooth square was half covered with a fine tracery of lines. Flowers—a veritable garden of miniature blooms of infinite variety and simple grace, delicately traced in the white wood. As I ran my finger over the fine work, the images took on new depth, subtle shadings, and a velvety texture. The scent that rose from them was not that of newly carved wood, but of a spring garden. Such enchantment. Such artistry. I glanced up at Baglos, but he had turned away. I held the piece a long while before offering it to Kellea. "What you do won't damage it?"

"What I do has nothing to do with its substance. I only look for him in it."

Kellea held the wood with both hands and closed her eyes. After a few moments she set the carving on the table and wandered across the room, arms folded. She stepped out of the door and stood alone for a long time, head bowed.

Rowan leaned across the table. "It takes a while for it to happen," he said, his voice quiet, filled with wonder.

"She says she's not very good at it." His eyes were fixed on the girl.

"She never had a mentor. A 'third parent' they called them, one who would teach her how to use her gift, and how to hide it, the ethics of it, how to bear its burdens."

"It's hard to get used to the idea."

"But you're not afraid?" Not ready to arrest her or bind her to a stake and set her afire . . .

"I've spent ten years learning not to fear those things I don't understand. Though the tutor had no such intent, I'm grateful for the lessons. But I can never go back—" He broke off, his lined face bleak and honest, speaking things a soldier was never taught to say.

I shoved our empty mugs to the center of the table. "Jaco always told me I should trust you."

The corner of his mouth turned up ever so slightly. "He always told me that you were pigheaded, but that eventually you'd see the error of your ways."

Before I could formulate a proper retort, Kellea reappeared in the doorway. "He's not far."

CHAPTER 30

We found him in the ruined castle, half a league south of Yennet. Kellea had led us down a narrow track that wandered across the green hills toward the mountains. The bronze sun was low over the western peaks when the crumbled ruin came into view at the crest of a rise. Kellea pulled up and waited for us, pointing at the hilltop.

"I'll go on alone," I said.

"I will go," said Baglos. "I am his Guide."

"He commanded you to follow my lead," I said. "You'll wait." The Dulcé, more like himself again, went into a pout, but I trusted it would last only until his worry got the best of him. He didn't hold tempers long.

Rowan didn't like the idea of my going alone, either, but I refused his company as well. "If I'm not back in an hour, you may ride to my rescue," I said. "But carefully, please." We had seen no signs of a fight. No guards. No hoofprints or corpses or blood to hint at hunters or sorcerer-priests. Whatever had brought D'Natheil to this place, I didn't think swords were going to repair it.

A warren of collapsed stone crowned the green hilltop. The exaggeration of evening shadows evoked a ghostly remembrance of the round towers and thick walls that had once dominated the countryside. Only one end of the ancient keep remained intact, three walls and a few sagging roof beams that created a shadowy shelter. The wind, heavy with the scents of damp earth and verdure, had picked up with the cooling hour and rustled the tall grass from behind me, and as I tethered Firethorn to a shrub that had sprung out of the rubble, an uneasy flock of sparrows swarmed upward in a fluttering mass. I picked my way carefully through the silent ruin. It didn't seem proper to call out in such a place.

A quick survey from atop a ruined wall told me that D'Natheil must be inside the keep if he was here. Neither he nor his horse was anywhere to be seen. I climbed over a fallen beam and up a crude staircase of stone blocks to a raised remnant of stone flooring. This would have been the great hall of the long-dead lord. Here had stood the huge hearth, back in the days when the fire would blaze through the night while the lord's soldiers and courtiers, children, cousins, and dogs ate, drank, and bedded down on the rush-strewn floor. Had I believed in ghosts I could have found them in the sun-drenched stones or, at the least, conjured the remnants of old songs and drunken jests and good fellowship.

The end of the keep where the roof still held seemed as deserted as the rest of the ruin. Disappointed, I was on the verge of turning back, when I caught a slight movement in the deepest shadows of the farthest corner. He was huddled against the wall like a child in disgrace, his head buried in his arms.

"D'Natheil," I called softly. "My lord prince."

He didn't move. I approached quietly and knelt beside him, relieved to feel the warmth of life still pulsing from him.

"D'Natheil, tell me that you live. We're afraid for you."

"Go away from here," he whispered. "Far away."

I released my breath. "Why should I?"

"Please." He spoke with his jaw clenched, as if to keep himself from screaming.

"I've never heard you say please in all these weeks, and if my going would encourage it, I might consider the matter. But I also do nothing without a reason. Why should I leave you?"

"I can't hold them back any longer." He drew in a shuddering breath.

"The Zhid, you mean? The Seeking? Are they after you again?"

"Unceasing." A wrenching groan slipped through his control, and he shrank further into his corner, as if driven by the lash of an invisible taskmaster.

Unceasing. "And you've been shielding us from it."

"They're coming for me." He raised his head. His eyes were pits of blackness, his skin stretched across the bones of his face. Exhausted. "You must be far away."

"We won't let them take you. Baglos would give his life for you. And we're two more now. Graeme Rowan and Kellea have offered their help. If we're together, we can protect each other, find a house, a forest—"

"Numbers, houses, forests. Those things don't matter if I invite them. They force me to look into my mind before the running, and I can't do it without madness. They've promised to give me back my life." He shook his head. "You mustn't be here when they come."

"They do not give life. You've known that since the beginning," I said. "You demonstrated it for me with two blades of grass. You're a warrior. So fight."

"There is nothing in me." The haunted ruins around us were not half so bleak as his words. No lingering ghosts of joy or pleasure walked D'Natheil's mind. No grace of evening sunlight bathed the stones of his being. His pain was palpable in the dimness.

Walk away, I told myself, rebellion prompting me to my feet. *Leading him on a journey is one thing. Using your intelligence and experience to set him on the road to his destiny is only right. But this* . . . To draw a soul from despair is such an intimate thing. I would need to know more of him than Baglos's meager tales. Something of his dreams or desires. Something of the person hidden behind the changing seasons. How could one forge such a link with something that didn't exist? *Impossible. Walk away.*

But irksome tethers of responsibility and caring bound my feet. Perhaps all I needed to do was wake him up. Make him think. I stood straight and raised my voice. "How dare you dismiss these weeks since you came to me? I've worked hard to teach you a thing or two. Perhaps it's not been a life a prince might expect. But you came to me a despicable bully, and now you give of yourself: to Tennice, to Paulo, to me, even to Baglos. That would not be possible if there were nothing in you. These voices of shadow fear you, D'Natheil, and despair is their ally. What kind of warrior would allow them to succeed with such a paltry weapon?"

He ground the heels of his hands into his eyes. "I tried. I'm still trying, but I am not enough."

"Didn't you hear Dassine? You told me he spoke only truth, and, if so, then you cannot discount the things he said of you nor the voice with which he said them. He loves you as a son and says you are worthy of our trust. Whatever he's done to you, I cannot believe he would send you forth with no resources to fight this battle."

"He sent me to you. . . ." His eyes were as stark as northern winter.

"So he did."

". . . but I cannot . . . will not . . . bring you harm. Go away." He was half pleading, half commanding.

The sunlight beckoned beyond the broken walls. I didn't want to be here. I had not asked for this. Why had Dassine sent D'Natheil to me? Was it only that I knew the words to understand his needs? Was it only that I had knowledge to help unravel the puzzle of his destination, to find what was left of the Exiles to unlock his message, to keep him safe in my world? D'Natheil had isolated himself to protect us, and his mind had become a prison in which his tormentors could do whatever they willed with him. Indeed I *should* leave him. I had no weapon to repel this kind of assault.

A prison . . . As I watched the Prince huddle alone in his anguish, harsh truth ripped my soul like the first blast of winter. I *had* been here before . . . and I *had* walked away. Had Karon felt me abandon him as he shivered alone in the cold wind, awaiting the first touch of flame? Had he heard my pleading and accusations and condemnation there at the end, only pretending confused hearing? He had believed his soul was the price of our safety, and I had cursed him for not paying it. And because I could not forgive him, I had turned my back on him, refusing the only thing he had ever asked of me. *Live, my dearest love. You are the essence of life.* . . . I had walled myself up in my own prison and allowed my life to wither away.

Forgiveness cannot change what has gone before. Were Karon standing in front of me in this ruin, he would hold to his conviction that he could not use his power in corrupt ways just to save us. And I would argue until my last breath that a man of honor, a man who loved, could not allow his child and his friends to be murdered. But forgiveness is not a matter of repayment or surrender or forgetting, of winning or losing. It is a transformation of the heart. Yes, I knew of prisons and torment. That was why my feet wanted so badly to walk away . . . and why, in the end, I could not. Not this time.

I sat down on the rough ground in front of D'Natheil, pushing aside the broken paving stones that poked through my skirt. "Listen to me"—he had buried his head again with another shuddering breath—"and look at me. I want to tell you a story. Baglos told us of your childhood, a childhood blighted by war in a city that should have known only peace, but I'm going to tell you of a childhood of peace, among people who fought a battle that was much the same as yours. It should have been your childhood, too, if your people had not forgotten how to make it so. . . ."

I told him Karon's stories of growing up in Avonar with the descendants of J'Ettanne, where the children always had an uncle or an aunt to listen to their troubles, where they waited anxiously for their talents to emerge, even though use of them brought only danger and risk, where they listened wide-eyed to the magical stories of Av'Kenat and dreamed of one day sharing in such a celebration. I told him of Celine, and all I could remember of the exploits of Eduardo the Horse Tamer, and Gaillard the Builder, who stayed late every night after his workmen went home and sang to his bricks until they nestled smooth in their mortar. When his workmen would return the next morning, Gaillard would laugh merrily as the men stood and marveled at their own prowess, boasting that nowhere in the Four Realms were there such skilled bridge builders as in Avonar.

For hour after hour I forced D'Natheil to listen and to look me in the eye as I spoke. I did not stop when I heard Rowan walk across the stone paving, stand behind me for a few moments, and then leave again when it became clear there was no rescuing to be done. And I did not stop when D'Natheil cried out in anguish as the light beyond the sagging roof failed, and it looked as if everything we had gained was lost again. Instead, I touched his cold hand and felt the quivering tension as he fought to hold back the darkness . . . and as I held fast, the darkness enveloped me as well. . . .

Come, Lord Prince, freedom and power await. . . . The whispers crawled up my back and between my shoulders, twining about my neck and ears, sending threads through my hair and wrapping cold fingers about my belly. . . . pricking my flesh and bone . . . pricks that became barbs that became spikes . . . *We can give you back what you have lost . . . come do us homage.* . . . Streaks of red, and green, and purple . . . mammoth dark-clad figures, seated on huge thrones of black stone . . . their massive heads turning to examine my soul . . . I was lost if they saw me. They had no faces . . . only streaks of light . . . ruby, emerald, amethyst . . . glittering facets . . . lurid light reflecting in a sea of black glass . . . nauseating light in a roiling, smoke-filled blackness . . . a storm of choking ash. . . . *else you are left as nothing, condemned to look back at all you are.* . . . And the void gaped before me like the maw of a monster, like the sky when the last star winks out. . . .

My head was cracking, my skin charring with a blazing heat, my stomach rebelling at the formless emptiness. "No!" I growled. Forcing my tongue to answer my command, forcing my eyes to stay open, I wrenched mind and tongue back to the stories . . . to life . . . to beauty. . . . The darkness receded, and it was only night, reality comprised of our linked hands and my voice, telling of laughter and sadness and courage and hope, like the tale of Errail the Gardener, who made his flowers bloom only one day longer each year, until after thirty years the other gardeners of Valleor feared their plants were failing, because they bloomed a full month less than those of Avonar. And so on through the night . . .

About the time I thought my voice and my supply of tales must fail, D'Natheil's hand grew warm, the suppressed trembling faded away, and his breath began to flow soft and even. Careful not to break his hold lest it wake him, I stretched my cramped legs and eased around to rest my aching back against the stone wall.

How many hours had I racked my brain for every scrap I could remember, so there would be no crack in the armor I built for him? The words could have been about things other than Avonar and the J'Ettanne, but I thought Karon's stories might have the most meaning.

The wind whispered about the hilltop. In the distance a night bird screeched. Impossible to sleep. I remembered my father returning to Comigor after a long campaign, day after day of riding, fighting, poor food, no sleep, so tired he couldn't even lift up my tiny mother and twirl her about as was his custom. My mother would urge him to go straight to bed and could never understand why he would sit up late in his study, drinking brandy and smoking his pipe and talking to any who would listen, saying he was too tired to sleep. Karon had been the same. Whenever he returned from one of his secret journeys, he would sit up late in the library or the garden, staring into the fire or the sky, saying he could not sleep until he had rested a while. Now I understood. I was beginning to understand so many things.

The sounds of horses and muted voices told me that Rowan had brought the others up the hill to be close. And before very long came footsteps and a quiet question. "Do you need anything?" It was Rowan.

"I would kiss the ground for a drink of anything," I whispered, "and my cloak or blanket would not be unacceptable. One for him, too."

"I've had to sit on the little fellow to keep him away. Should he come?"

"No. If you'll—"

"I'll take care of it." The sheriff soon returned with two blankets and a wineskin. I had rarely tasted anything quite so delicious as Rowan's sour wine.

"Thank you, Sheriff. Tell Baglos that the Prince sleeps and that I believe all will be well with him."

"Done."

When the morning sun penetrated the ruined keep, I woke hearing lingering echoes of Karon's voice from my dreams. *Seri love,* he had called, *let me in.* My arm had burned, and I had felt his life flow through my veins as it had on the terrible day of his arrest, filling me, enriching me, forgiving me as I had at last forgiven him. My response to the dream had been quite vivid. When I realized I still clung to the Prince's hand, my cheeks grew hot, as if, even in sleep, he might somehow have shared this most intimate of stories.

D'Natheil slept peacefully, sprawled under the blanket Graeme Rowan had thrown over him. I hated to wake him, but events could not wait. We could not know how long the road to the Bridge might remain open. And, of course, I had to see if what I'd done had been enough. I carefully extracted my hand and climbed to my feet. "Well, my lord prince, are you going to sleep all day? You've led us a merry chase."

He stirred slowly, and after a few moments, mumbled, "What? I didn't—" He sat up, rubbed his head, and peered about his desolate refuge. When his gaze came to me, it was filled with questions. "I don't remember coming here."

"What do you remember?"

"The rain. Fire. I don't know. A jumble of things. Nothing clear." His face was troubled.

"Come, let's find the others."

While we walked the length of the ancient hall, I told

him briefly what had happened. ". . . and so you left us during the storm in an attempt to draw the danger of the Zhid away from us. You thought you couldn't hold out against them, but you did."

"Because of you, I think."

"I've told you several times that such things are easier together. If your mentors taught you that in all of history there has been any battle won by one man alone, then they know no more of history than does Paulo. I suppose they taught you, too, that women are weak and must be constantly coddled and protected. Perhaps you should have taken lessons from your friends, the soldiers on the walls of Avonar. My father always said that a soldier's wife could make soup from sticks and swords from stones and could hold a citadel long after the warriors had given it up. Women make the . . ." But I never told him, because my voice trailed off into a prolonged coughing fit from the irritation of my throat.

"Perhaps you should give your voice a rest," said the Prince, as he gave me a hand over the fallen roof beam. "Or you'll find yourself being dragged about by argumentative, flame-haired women, unable to say a word to deter them from having their way with you."

I stopped and stared at him as he continued across the littered ruin toward the sounds of our friends. After a few steps he looked back and smiled at me as he had not smiled for many days. The beauty of his face brought joy to my heart, though in the morning light I could not fail to notice that he'd aged a good five years in the past two days. Strands of gray threaded his fair hair. The stubble on his face could not hide the deepening lines. Baglos would not be able to deny the change this time. What did it mean? Shoving aside a sudden disquiet, I hurried after him.

The others were camped just beyond the fallen guard tower. Baglos caught sight of us first, raced to D'Natheil, and bent his knee. "Oh, my lord, forgive me for my absence from your side. My duty called me, but these . . . our friends . . . called upon the command that you laid upon me to be led by"—he took a deep and wounded breath—"this mundane woman. And I did follow it. But I respectfully ask if that was your intent?"

"I redouble my command, Dulcé, and I've placed it on

myself as well. You are my madrissé, who can lead me on the proper road and answer whatever I ask of you. But the Lady Seriana is my counselor, who must tell me what road to take and what questions I must ask."

By the time I dealt with two more bouts of coughing, D'Natheil was eating his second bowl of Baglos's porridge. I wanted a drink of something hot to soothe my throat and was forced to resort to gestures to let the Dulcé know.

Graeme Rowan sat a short distance away on a remnant of a fallen wall, munching a hard biscuit. Kellea was sitting halfway down the hill with her back to the company. Gratefully, I took a cup of hot wine from Baglos and perched next to the sheriff.

"Good morning," I said, croaking a bit.

"Good morning, madam."

"Just Seri will do."

"As you wish." He cocked his head toward the Prince. "So, do I kneel to him?"

"He does not expect it."

"It was awkward enough with you for so long. To know who you were and what you were accused of. And then Kellea, a sorcerer in the flesh. But she tells me that this one is a prince, and that he and his odd friend come from a land—a world—that is not this one we walk. Is it true?"

"Yes."

"Hand of Annadis . . ." The hand that held his biscuit fell into his lap. For Rowan, I had learned, such a reaction was the equivalent of an earthquake.

"That realization was not much easier for me. Paulo is the only one who takes all of it in stride."

The sheriff grimaced. "Paulo's life is naught but irrational events. And he talks with horses. Why would anything amaze him? He tells me you chose to keep him, rather than shove him off to a magistrate. I thank you for that."

"You know I could never—"

"I thank you anyway. Folk busy saving the world ofttimes fail to note illiterate boys." He lifted the biscuit to his mouth again, pausing only long enough to add, "May I ask what was last night?"

My throat soothed with Baglos's wine, I told Rowan about the Seeking of the Zhid, and how D'Natheil thought he had to fight it alone so as not to endanger the rest of us. "What I did, just talking to him long enough, enabled him to grab an anchor in a world in which he was at sea. He used his own strength to deflect the attack. I thank you for your discretion."

"I vow never to interfere where this sorcery business is involved."

"You may find it less terrifying than you think."

"Hmmph." A skeptical grunt. "So, what now?"

"We must get him to the place they call the Gate, as Kellea told you, so he can do whatever he was sent here to do, avoiding the traps the Zhid and the traitors among his own people have set for him."

"And do you know the way?"

"We have clues." I told him of the journal, and the Writer, and the riddles.

"You're wagering the future of two worlds on four-hundred-fifty-year-old riddles written by a ten-year-old girl?" Rowan's sandy eyebrows looked to fly off his face.

"She only gave her father the idea. He wrote his clues interspersed with her riddles, then left the key to them in the form of a children's game."

"Still sounds like hunting a bear with a stick."

Rowan finished his biscuit and I my wine, watching Baglos bustling happily about with food and fire and pots. After a while Rowan said. "So the little one is his servant. He seems very devoted. Obedient . . . trustworthy."

"Their relationship is much deeper than master and servant—a magical link of the mind. Baglos would have difficulty disobeying his commands, even if he wanted to. What about it?"

"Mmm . . . no matter. I just wasn't sure. Back in Yurevan—" He waved his last bite of biscuit in dismissal. "Naught, then."

My cup empty, I was anxious to get on with the day. "Then let me introduce you, and we'll be off."

The Prince was still eating voraciously. Paulo was attempting to match him bite for bite, but was falling behind.

"D'Natheil, I must introduce you to one whose honesty I've much maligned. He was pursuing us with only good intent. This is Graeme Rowan, whom I induced you to bash on the head out of my mistaken interpretation of events."

The Prince looked up.

"Sheriff, this is D'Natheil—no, more properly His Grace D'Natheil, Prince of Avonar, Sovereign of Gondai, Heir of D'Arnath." D'Natheil was still dressed in the clothing of a dead farmer, the same shabby shirt and breeches I had rifled from Jacopo's bins, but when he nodded his head, Rowan bowed to him, though I believed he had come to the meeting with no such intent.

"You're not a wicked villain, then?" asked the Prince solemnly, as he motioned Baglos to empty the last dregs of breakfast into his bowl, even while scooping the last bite into his mouth. "Not a heinous, hide-bound slave of corruption that parades under the name of the law?"

"A servant of justice and order, but no slave, and neither heinous nor hide-bound, I trust," said Rowan, just as solemnly.

"But at least a surly, knavish rascal who cannot abide the possibility of rational discourse from a female, and who could likely not even recognize such a thing were it to pop up from a tankard of ale?"

Rowan shook his head emphatically. "I've learned my lesson on that score from several sources."

I looked from one to the other and felt my cheeks grow hot. "What is this conspiracy, gentlemen? I lead this expedition, and I'll have no pompous men having secret understandings and uncivil attitudes. You've just met. How can you be conspiring already?" I threw up my hands and busied myself with smothering the fire, pointedly ignoring the two who burst out laughing at my discomfiture. But I felt a smile bubble up from deep inside me . . . from a place I had believed barren.

Baglos packed the last of his pots and bags and went with Paulo to collect the horses. Moments later, Baglos came running to D'Natheil in great agitation. "My lord, we cannot find your horse! We've had no luck at all in summoning him. Unless you can do something . . ."

"He'll come." D'Natheil closed his eyes, flicked his fingers in a small gesture, and whispered a word I couldn't hear. But I felt it. Most definitely. The sheriff felt it, too, and watched the Prince intently. When I heard the distant pounding of hooves and saw the chestnut appear on the next hilltop, I was not surprised. D'Natheil looked satisfied as the graceful animal galloped into our camp and stopped within reach of his master's hand.

Paulo grinned. "You must've learned his name."

D'Natheil stroked the horse's head. "Indeed I did."

"And what is it, then?" I asked.

"He is called Sunlight."

A relieved Baglos finished the loading, while I pulled out the journal and showed Rowan and D'Natheil its secrets.

"The first riddle is obvious," I said, tapping lightly on the page. "A river is a road that never sleeps, and its travelers have no feet—boats and fish and such, of course. And we know we're going to the mountains, so we must head upriver. But how far? When do we look for the next clue? The chest is the next, and it must indicate this one, 'It is the lesser brother's portion that brings the greatest wealth and the lesser passage that finds its destination.'"

"It would imply a decision point," said D'Natheil. "A fork in the road or some such, and we would take the inferior way."

"We'll have to trust that we'll recognize it."

In a short time all was ready. The sheriff knelt at the top of the hill, raising a dirty thumb to his brow, as stubborn in his piety as in all else. And so we set off in the sparkling morning, leaving the mournful ruin to the wind and the sparrows. With six of us together, and D'Natheil yanked back from the brink of despair, I felt more confident than I had in many days. But after only an hour's riding on the little used path that paralleled the restless Glenaven, D'Natheil pulled up and looked back the way we had come. "We'd best ride hard," he said, taking a deep breath. "Someone's close behind."

CHAPTER 31

The day flew by in a blur of grass and rocks and scattered trees. As we galloped toward the soaring majesty of the Dorian Wall, the gently sloping hillsides to the east and west of the river yielded to rougher country. Craggy knobs appeared, at first one here, one there, and then on every side. The meandering Glenaven moved faster here, darting restlessly between the rocks that threatened to stay its progress. Nowhere did I see any choice to be made as to our course.

We stopped briefly at midday to rest the horses. The hills and knobs had finally formed a continuous barricade on either side of the river, creating a narrow valley sparsely scattered with pine and fir. The air was hot and sultry, the breezes of the open country blocked by the encroaching walls. Though it seemed a year since Midsummer's Day, little more than six weeks had passed. The land remained awash in summer.

We did not resume the morning's banter at our stop. D'Natheil's eyes flicked frequently back the way we had come. Half an hour and we were on our way again, Baglos in the lead. Rowan and Kellea rode side by side just behind the Dulcé. Paulo stayed close at their heels, and D'Natheil and I brought up the rear. I was not about to let the Prince lag behind as he had on the day of the storm.

"Do the Zhid still call to you?" I asked, as we wound our way up the narrowing gorge.

"Yes. But it's easier now. I try to concentrate on everything you told me, on your stories."

"The J'Ettanne were your people every bit as much as those in your Avonar. That's why I chose those things to talk about."

"You're an exceptional storyteller. They seem far more real than anything Baglos speaks of."

"Can you remember nothing of your years with Dassine? Ten years it would have been."

He shrugged. "I keep thinking that if I work at it hard enough, I'm bound to see. But the memories stay just out of reach."

"Why would Dassine have taken your memory and your voice before sending you? What circumstance could force him to do that? He said he had no alternative."

"Perhaps he thought I wouldn't do what was needed. Because of the person I am. It's likely I don't want to know what's hidden." Winter had touched his voice, and he dug his heels into Sunlight's flank. "Come, we must move faster."

The Prince rode ahead to where Graeme Rowan was picking his way across the swift water. The track ahead of us on the east side of the river was tangled with tree roots and underbrush, for the water had eaten away at the bank, leaving it narrow and steep-sided. The track on the west side of the river was still unobstructed. I considered briefly that the east side might be the "lesser passage" of the riddle, but a few moments' observation convinced me it had been more than four hundred and fifty years since the east bank had been passable.

I needn't have worried. The Writer had buried his instructions so cleverly that he hadn't felt the need to make them true riddles. The way was very clear.

Half an hour or so after the river crossing, we heard a considerable rush of water ahead—a swirling pool of icy blue-green, the turbulent confluence of two healthy streams that formed the Glenaven. The stream on the right flowed from a broad grassy valley that angled almost directly west, funneling the afternoon sunshine straight into our eyes. The stream leaped and bounded its way through thick grass, dotted with clumps of yellow, blue, and white flowers.

The left branch flowed from a passage of very different character, a gloomy, narrow slot that at first glance appeared to have no path at all. Everything in my nature beckoned me to follow the sunlit valley, but I assumed that the darker way was ours.

"The lesser brother?" asked Rowan.

"It's the first likely thing," I said. "If there's a path . . ."

"I'll take a look. If we go a little west where the water's slower, we can cross easily." In moments Rowan was on the spit of rocks and sand between the two forks. Then he splashed through the stream, rode into the shadowed mouth of the narrower passage, and disappeared.

D'Natheil kept glancing over his shoulder while we waited. After a time that likely seemed far longer than it was, the sheriff rejoined us. "There's a path. Narrow. But I went in fairly deep, and it continued as far as I could see."

"Hurry," said D'Natheil. "Choose."

"We go left," I said.

"Some will go left," said Rowan. "Kellea and I have decided that it's impossible for all of us to outrun a determined pursuer in these conditions. And it looks to get worse. But if the two of us were to go west, while the rest of you take the opposite way, then, unless the fellows on our tail have Kellea's talent, we might fool them. She says that it might be possible to mislead even one like her, if we take something with us that belongs to each of you. That may give you time enough."

"I hate splitting up," I said, though I knew that he was absolutely right.

"We'll loop back if we can. Kellea can find you."

I pulled off the scarf I used to tie back my hair. Baglos produced a kerchief of his own and D'Natheil's discarded sandals. Paulo had nothing to give, but Kellea startled him by riding up close and yanking a hair from his shaggy mop. "Ow!" Paulo slapped his hand to his head.

"We'll see you again before we're done!" called the sheriff. Kellea was already galloping into the sunlight, and Rowan's great black horse shot after her.

"Go with your gods, Graeme Rowan. And you, Kellea," I called.

D'Natheil and Baglos were almost halfway across the water, and I was right on their heels, glancing back to make sure Paulo followed. But the boy sat at the joining of the water, looking back and forth between the two parties. Before I could call out to him, he clucked at Molly and bolted westward after Graeme Rowan. I couldn't worry about his safety. There were no assurances along either route.

I disliked the eastern passage from my first step into it. The path Rowan had seen was scarcely worthy of the name—a narrow band of damp sand along the west side of the river. The walls of the gorge became steeper and rockier the farther we rode, and, in some places, the river widened until it reached almost from one wall to the other. Once, the track disappeared completely, and we had to ford the shallow water to pick it up again on the other side.

Another hour and the walls had become sheer rock faces, and the bottom of the rift grew darker, musty and close in the warm evening. Stomach in a knot, I glanced up frequently to prove to myself that there was no roof to cave in on me. The sky held the deep blue of evening, but in the flat-bottomed gorge it was already dusk, forcing us to slow our pace. The path varied a great deal in width, drips and trickles in every direction warning of side streams waiting to trip us up. And early spring waterfalls had bored out deep pools in the streambed, abandoning them as traps for the unwary traveler now that summer had quenched the falls. When the first stars winked into life overhead, we had found no spot suitable to stop for the night. I had to trust Firethorn to find safe footing.

We proceeded without incident until a soft word from the Prince signaled a halt. We dismounted, unsaddled the horses, and pulled out food and blankets, fumbling our way about in the dark. Baglos dragged brush from the steep banks and piled it up between us. "My lord, the only fuel hereabouts is damp and green. I'll never get it lit. Hot food and warmth would restore us all. If you could help, as you did in the storm . . ."

"I think not," said the Prince. "Since we split off from the others, I can't feel the pursuit behind us. Every time they've caught up with us again, I've just worked some sorcery. I'm beginning to think that the more I do such things, the easier I am to find."

His theory made sense. And as for me, I was too tired to regret the lack of comforts. I was long past hungry and could think of nothing but rolling up in my blanket and stretching my tired muscles on the damp earth. I told my companions to wake me when it was my turn to watch. ". . . or if there's need, I'll watch with you," I told D'Natheil.

"This night is not so dark as the last," he said from somewhere in the murk. "Nothing to fear."

As I drifted off to sleep, I felt vaguely as though I were forgetting something important, but I was much too tired to dredge it up.

Baglos woke me while the strip of sky above us was still crowded with stars. "There's been no disturbance," he said, as I tried to clear my groggy head. "When the Prince turned the watch to me, he said our pursuers have not yet discovered us. He sleeps."

It didn't take Baglos long to join D'Natheil. Soon I heard the soft snoring I'd come to recognize as his. I leaned against the cliff face behind me and to my disgust found my back soaked almost immediately. Groping about in the dark revealed no dry spot. It would be a mistake to lie down again and expect to stay awake, so I had either to sit up without support or try to walk a few steps here and there without stepping on my companions or falling into the river. The hours until dawn stretched very long.

Morning came to the sky much earlier than it came to the bottom of the gorge, but even in the gray light, I found both the source of the dripping noises and the reason I could find no dry spot to lean on. I'd never seen anything like it. Moisture was leaking from the pores of the rock wall. If the sky had not been cloudless, one might have thought rain was falling high above the cliff tops. Thick moss, tiny red flowers, and slender vines of deep green laden with miniature purple berries burrowed their roots into the wet rock face, creating a colorful vertical garden. The sight changed my whole perception of the rift.

"The ancient face that weeps."

I jumped. D'Natheil stood just behind me. "Of course! The third clue. 'When one ascends the ancient face that weeps . . .' " I peered into the blue-gray haze up the gorge. "But how does one ascend it? The walls go straight up and crumble in your hand. And why would they send us this way, if we needed to be on top? Surely there would be an easier path."

"I suppose it will come clear like the other clues."

Not half a league up the gorge, the river made good on the previous day's threat. The path vanished, and the water spanned the breadth of the rift. For a while the going was easy, the clear water only hoof-deep, the stony bottom easy to see. But then I followed D'Natheil around a sharp bend and saw the water lapping almost to his knees. "Stay to the right," he called back to me, as I felt the icy water seep into my boots. Repeating the warning over my shoulder for Baglos, I fixed one eye on the Prince and one eye on Firethorn's footing to make sure we followed his lead exactly.

For a long hour we had no relief from the frigid water that varied from ankle to knee in depth. My feet were numb, and I patted and soothed Firethorn, promising him a winter of dry oats and hay if he would carry me through safely. I did not see Polestar step into the pool or Baglos slip from his saddle into the water. I only heard a great splash and a cry for help behind me.

"D'Natheil!" I yelled, coaxing Firethorn back toward Baglos, who flailed the water in panic. The Prince was just disappearing beyond the next turn.

D'Natheil quickly reversed direction and dived into the river from the back of his horse, swimming with powerful strokes toward the floundering Dulcé. Catching him around his chest, D'Natheil dragged Baglos back across the pool, swimming until he could get a foothold and then wading through chest-high water until he could haul himself and his soggy servant across the saddle of the patiently waiting chestnut. The wild-eyed Polestar found his way back to the shallower water. I maneuvered myself so I could grab the jittery beast's reins before he could bolt back down the gorge. The incident was over in moments, and I was relieved to see the chestnut lunge out of the water onto a mostly dry shore after one more turning of the path.

Soon the three of us were pouring water from our boots and stretching the cramps from numb legs and feet. The drenched Baglos was shivering, for the morning shadows held none of the previous day's warmth. "I don't know what happened, my lord," he said. "My vision grew blurry, the beast stepped off into the deeps, and everything was topsy-turvy."

D'Natheil looked at me. "I should make a fire for him."

"No, look," I said, pointing to the rift wall. The timing of the rescue was perfect. The rays of the morning sun that had shone so tantalizingly on the west wall finally swept the shadows from the floor. "Go over by the rocks, Baglos. Wring yourself out and sit in the sun, and D'Natheil won't have to risk an enchantment to warm you."

The Dulcé was indignant. "I would never ask my lord to endanger himself for me," he said through chattering teeth.

"Of course not. I didn't mean to imply it."

As I tethered the horses to a willow sprouted from the weeping wall, I noticed Baglos's leather bag hung over Polestar's saddle. Thinking to make a peace offering for my ill-considered remark, I pulled out the Dulcé's silver wine flask and took it to him. "Might this help?"

Baglos snatched the flask from my hand and jumped up. "No, woman, not this one! This is not—This one is only for the most dire circumstances. The other is the one to use." He crammed the flask back in the leather bag and pulled out a different, plainer one. He took a sip and offered it around.

We wiped down the horse, wrung out our clothes and each found a spot in the sunbeams. D'Natheil groaned in pleasure as he stretched out next to the cliff wall and closed his eyes. I sat with my back propped against the wall and my face to the sun and watched the steam rise from my soggy boots. "One blessing of this experience," I said, "is its close resemblance to a bath. Just a bit warmer water, and I might have dived into it myself."

"Bathing!" said Baglos in disgust, as he dabbed at his damp tunic with the only dry corner of his blanket. "Immersion is an unhealthy habit. Just feel the chill. I cannot understand those who promote such practices. My uncle Balzir said that bathing can reduce one's height by a full measure. The Dulcé do not hold with it."

"Dassine must have approved of bathing," said D'Natheil drowsily. "Someone was forever hounding me about it."

Baglos and I looked at each other with eyebrows raised. The Prince did not even seem to realize what he was saying.

"He most likely hounded you about many things if you were the wicked boy Baglos describes," I said.

"Many things: don't run, don't argue, don't fight me, don't tell. Be careful. Let me show you. Read . . . think . . . fifty generations. We're wrong . . . the answer is there to be found. Our enemies do not sleep. Look deep, beyond the surface. . . ."

I motioned the excited Baglos to silence and said, softly, "But he was kind to you. He didn't beat you like the other Preceptor—Exeget—did?"

"Yes and no. His voice was kindness. And wisdom . . . like my father. Wicked humor, but so hard . . . unrelenting. Always it was 'someday' "—D'Natheil's mumbling slowed—"someday all will be clear. Someday, your gift . . . make all the difference. But it was so long waiting"—the words were a long sigh—"so long in the dark. Why so long, Dassine? Let me go. For the love of heaven, let me . . . ah . . ."

D'Natheil jerked upright, startled awake by his own cry. A flush of embarrassment suffused his face. "I must have fallen asleep. Fires of night . . ." He rubbed his head vigorously. "Have you dried out, Dulcé? We must get on."

"I am ready at your command, my lord."

The lingering echoes of D'Natheil's anguish made ordinary conversation seem too trivial to pursue. I wondered if his memory was truly returning or if his rambling had been some dream-wrought confusion of all he'd heard from me and Baglos and Dassine. What did you dream when you had no person within you?

The next bend in the river shoved all thought of D'Natheil's memories out of mind, for the Writer's third clue lay revealed in awesome clarity. The path we traveled extended into the haze as far as we could see, but not fifty paces from the bend, another track branched off from it and angled steeply up the eastern wall. From somewhere in the distance, beyond our farthest view, we heard a muted rumbling of wind or water.

"Ascend the ancient face that weeps," said Baglos in wonder.

I took a deep breath. Heights did not terrify me as did confinement in the dark, but I'd never done anything quite like this. I wondered if there would be room to dismount if we had need. "I'll have to trust you once more," I whispered to Firethorn, stroking his neck.

We took it slowly, speaking calmly and continually to our horses. The trail, a great seam in the tilted strata of the rock, was wider than it looked from below—in a few spots even enough to turn the horse around—but not so wide as to tempt me to linger one moment more than necessary. I would not have been surprised to find it dwindle away into nothing at the first angle in the cliff. Truly, I believed my worst fears confirmed when we approached a jutting corner where a huge boulder hung out over the trail, only air visible beyond it.

D'Natheil went first, crouching low in the saddle to clear the overhang, then disappearing on the other side. I was next. I huddled down into Firethorn's ruddy mane and prayed the beast had sense enough to stay as close to the wall as the jutting boulder would permit.

Once I rounded the corner, the rumbling that had grown louder at each step of the ascent became a roar, and even the fearsome aspect of the ledge path faded into insignificance when I beheld the source of the noise. At the end of the gorge was a towering cliff of red and gray, the granite base of the ice pinnacles that stretched as far as I could see in every direction, so close that I felt I could reach out and grab a handful of snow from each one of them. From a seam in the cliff sprang a waterfall that dived in thundering splendor to the valley floor so far below us that the river was but a narrow ribbon. The afternoon sun sparkled on the spray that wreathed the falls, bridging the end of the gorge with a perfect double rainbow.

D'Natheil was stopped a few paces ahead of me. "It has to be there, does it not?"

"I believe so," I said. His words eerily reflected my own thoughts. No J'Ettanne could have resisted the call of such beauty.

"Perhaps I was sent just for this. I've never seen the like." Behind his wonder echoed such lonely sadness as would soften stone.

"Demon-spirited beast! Black-hearted wretch!" The cries came from behind us. Baglos stood just on our side of the overhang, looking back through the treacherous corner and waving his hands. Polestar was nowhere to be seen.

"Baglos, what's happened?" I called.

"The wicked son of a Zhid is most likely halfway back to Yennet." The Dulcé trudged up the steep path toward us. "The turning at the boulder was fearsome. I dismounted so as to walk, and the beast shied. Pulled the reins right out of my hand. Oh, my lord prince, what an incompetent fool they have sent you as Guide."

I could not disagree. One look at the long, steep track that lay in front of us told how near impossible was our position. Even if D'Natheil or I were to take Baglos up to ride double, almost all of our food was on its way to Yennet. Right into the arms of the Zhid. Everything . . . "Baglos, was the journal still in your pack?"

The Dulcé looked as if he were going to be sick.

"Most unfortunate," said D'Natheil.

"More than unfortunate," I said. "I can remember the clues and the map, but what if there's more we need from it? What if we've made the wrong interpretation and must begin again?" The stupid, clumsy fool.

"I know only one way to get it back quickly," said D'Natheil.

Sorcery, of course. Calling Polestar back to us. "I can't tell you to take such a risk."

"The journal must not fall into the hands of those behind us. Even if by some chance what I do doesn't bring them down on us, they would eventually decipher it. It might tell them what we would not."

Baglos was silent and anxious through all of this, clutching his hands to his breast, his dark eyes flicking from the Prince to me.

As he had on the hillside next to the ruined castle, D'Natheil closed his eyes, made a small movement of his fingers, and whispered the horse's name. Then he sat down on the trail to wait, drinking from his waterskin and dangling his feet over the stomach-churning drop to the rift floor. I was more comfortable close by the cliff wall and was too unsettled to sit down anyway.

Before very long, the black horse emerged sedately from the shadowed overhang, as if sauntering from the pasture into the stable for his evening oats. As we mounted up to be on our way, D'Natheil's shoulders sagged.

"Are you well?" I asked.

He shook his head, leaning on the horse for a moment before wearily pulling himself into the saddle. "We're being followed again."

Though D'Natheil laid no word of reproach on him, Baglos said very little. He rode stiffly, eyes forward, his volatile emotions for once held close.

As the afternoon sun baked the weeping cliff wall, it was difficult to recall our shivering of the morning. The ascent seemed painfully slow, especially now the enemy was on our trail again.

Late in the afternoon we came to the waterfall, the last steep ascent leveling off into a wide shelf that extended to the very brink of the thundering cascade. I slumped down in the shade, reveling in the cold spray. Baglos, his black hair and beard dusted with the droplets, shouted to be heard above the roar. "What now? Have we come the wrong way? I see no further path."

"It must be that way," said D'Natheil, pointing to a rocky chute that led to the cliff tops far above us. The chute was even steeper than the last bit we had just done and was slick with the spray of the falls. In no wise could the horses negotiate it. It would be treacherous enough for human hands and feet.

"Should not the next clue point our way?" asked Baglos. *When the wall births the flood, it is wiser to be the rabbit than the fish or the goat.* "What could it mean? It seems to fit—at least the part about the wall birthing the flood."

"I see no choice of directions here," said D'Natheil. "The divided way must be above us, where we would have the opportunity to cross the river like a fish, or climb again like a goat, or take some other way. The 'rabbit' way, whatever that is."

I could not imagine the J'Ettanne using the path up that steep chute. They would have wanted the fortress approaches secure, yes. Secret, yes. Secluded, yes. But not impossible. Examination of the shelf revealed no evidence of a bridge to the other side of the gorge, where there looked to be easier ways up.

Baglos was already fussing about the packs and mumbling to himself about what we would need to carry, and what must be left behind with the horses, and was it not ironic that so soon after bringing on danger by recalling Polestar, we must abandon the beasts and send them back down the path. When he pulled out the journal, I snatched it from his small hand and stuffed it in my pocket. I would not risk losing it again.

Discouraged, I sat by the wall munching a piece of dry bread. D'Natheil sat beside me, his gaze following an eagle that soared on the warm updrafts over the falls. "Perhaps it's time I went on alone," he said quietly.

"Don't you dare—"

"Foolish, I know, to think you'd allow it. You'd throw your horse at me before riding him down that hill, wouldn't you?"

The flicker of amusement in the Prince's face rapidly doused my indignation. "Exactly right."

"I most sincerely do not like dragging you into this . . . whatever it is that will happen. And not because you are female or incompetent. On the contrary"—his eyes traced the lines of my face—"I think this world would lose much of its richness if you were not a part of it." He reddened a little and shifted his gaze back to the waterfall.

"Thank you," I said. A stupid, priggish response, but I could think of none other. I should laugh and dismiss it by teasing him—and teasing myself even more. Only a few weeks had passed since I was trying to decide how to be rid of him. Only days since I had admitted that anything about him sparked feelings beyond annoyance or pity. He changed so rapidly, as if every day the previous day's persona was sloughed off like an unwanted skin to reveal a new character and manner.

As we sat there, D'Natheil in embarrassment and I in confusion, a rock-mouse scurried from some unseen crevice near the edge of the falls and picked up a crumb that had fallen from my bread. When I shifted my leg to let it come closer, it skittered off to the brink of the falls and disappeared into the spray. I berated myself for my clumsy movement, sure the tiny creature had been swept away in its hasty flight, but in moments it was back, damp but undaunted, searching for another treasure to add to its horde.

"Where did you come from?" I said, as it scuttered back the way it had come. Curious, I crawled toward the curtain of water.

"Have a care, woman," said Baglos, an anxious edge to his voice.

But I needed no warning. The shelf did not end abruptly at the edge of the falls as it appeared, but extended well past it. As I peered closer, the rock-mouse zipped between my feet and into the shower of droplets. "If you can go there, can we?" Hugging the wall, I stood up and stepped into the spray. Beyond a thin curtain of water was a sheltered overhang, as dry and calm as the eye of a storm. And at the center of the dry niche was a hole in the wall, twice the height of a man and almost as wide. A hole. A rabbit hole.

CHAPTER 32

After all that had happened in my life, how could walking into a hole in a wall be so excruciatingly difficult? Every hardship of our journey paled in comparison to the first step into the cave behind the falls, but I told myself I'd be Evard's whore before I'd give D'Natheil an excuse to leave me behind. "Have we anything to use for a light?" I asked, taking pride in my matter-of-fact demeanor.

"I think I can provide that," said the Prince, snugging the ties that held our waterskins to the saddles.

"No, you mustn't—"

"It makes no difference now. They're coming, and we'll be able to go faster." He peered into the mouth of the cave. "I have no love for darkness."

I did let D'Natheil go in first. I wasn't a fool. A pale yellow light took flickering shape from his left hand, and then settled into a steady white glow. I took a deep breath and stepped through the opening after him. *There's plenty of air,* I told myself. *Plenty of room. Annadis preserve D'Natheil and his light.* I was not in the habit of invoking the Twin who controlled fire and lightning with his sword, but if he was interested, I would not turn down his help.

We had to lead our horses, as the ceiling soon became too low for riding. Baglos, who had been unusually quiet since the near disasters of the day, followed Firethorn. The path tilted slightly upwards, and the damp walls and floors were worn smooth by uncounted years of flowing water. The rumble of the waterfall was deadened by the mountain's foundation, soon fading away into heavy silence, broken only by the ring of hooves on stone. Occasionally we walked past pockets of cooler air, unrelieved blackness where the soft light made no inroads. I tried not to look at them; they made my chest hurt.

Rather I focused my eyes on D'Natheil's light, wondering what was the source of the radiance—fingers, palm? Anything to take my mind off of the oppressive stone, and its associated images of tombs . . . dungeons . . . Xerema collapsing around its people after the earthquake. I tried to start a conversation with Baglos, but the three of us were separated by the bulk of the horses. And whenever I managed to get the Prince's attention, his light would fade. So I stayed quiet. How far could it be to travel under a mountain? *Keep breathing, Seri. There's plenty of air.*

We walked, stopped to rest, and walked more. Hours passed.

"Hold!" D'Natheil's voice echoed through the stone passage.

"What is it?" I asked, squeezing past the chestnut to where D'Natheil stood frowning. He held up his hand, and my stomach constricted. Our way was blocked by a pile of rubble. "Oh."

"I think I went wrong back where the path bent to the right. It was hard to guess which was the side passage and which the main. We don't have a clue to tell us, I suppose?"

I tried to keep my breathing steady. "We've only one more riddle. I've assumed that it tells the final destination."

Somewhere water dripped slowly. The soles of my feet throbbed.

"We'll have to go back then. Only a few hundred paces. I can switch places with the Dulcé." The Prince smiled at me in the glow of his enchantment. "Baglos and I will find our way, will we not, Dulcé?" Baglos did not answer. As we got the horses turned around, it was quite obvious why. Neither Baglos nor Polestar was anywhere in sight.

"Baglos!"

"Dulcé!"

We called out together. Only our own echoes answered.

"I don't think I quite believe this horrid day," I said. "How could they have sent you such a dolt for a Guide?"

The Prince peered into the blackness beyond his circle of light. "When did you last mark him?"

"I've not been paying attention. It must have been when we stopped to adjust his boot."

"Fires of night, that was half a league back!" D'Natheil shook his head. "Baglos has a good heart. But I'll confess, I don't understand him at all."

We tied the chestnut's halter to Firethorn's saddle and started back the way we had come, a task easier set than accomplished. We'd had few choices of direction along the way, but looking backward was a different matter. There seemed to be passages everywhere and no distinction to be made between them.

"This is where I went wrong," said D'Natheil, pointing around a sharp corner. "When we find the Dulcé and return here, we'll need to go left. Easy to see now that it's the main passage."

"We should mark it," I said. "I should have thought of that from the beginning." *Stupid. Stupid. Perhaps the dark would be less fearsome if you kept hold of some sense.*

I pulled out my knife to scratch a mark on the stone, but the Prince stayed my hand. "Perhaps there's an easier way." He let out a slow breath, as if to settle himself, and then he rubbed a finger on the stone. A glowing green mark appeared. "I've no idea if it will last as long as we need. I hope so."

"This is an immensely opportune time for your talents to manifest themselves. I don't suppose you can search for Baglos as Kellea does?"

He laughed a bit. "Unfortunately not. We'll have to hunt for him in the usual way."

Carefully, always marking our path before losing sight of the previous mark, we picked our way back through the warren. At every opening we called for Baglos, but heard no reply save our own voices bouncing around in the hollow spaces. One hour, two hours we searched. D'Natheil's light faded to a sickly yellow.

When we reached the place we'd last seen the Dulcé, I leaned my back against the wall and massaged one tired ankle. "Perhaps he stayed on the main route after we went wrong. He's most likely on the other side by now, worrying about *us*."

"I hope you're right," said the Prince. "I don't think it would be wise to search beyond the main passage."

He got no argument from me. I eyed his hand and the shrinking circle of light radiating from it. "Perhaps we should go all the way back to the ledge to spend the night. Try the passage again in the morning . . . when we're rested."

"Better not. The ledge will be closer to our pursuers, and the tunnel will be safer in the dark."

"Probably so."

We reversed direction and started up the path, proceeding slowly through the closing blackness toward the green mark, taking turns calling out for Baglos. Soon the Prince's light encompassed no more than a single footstep. I dared not blink lest I lose sight of his hand.

"I'm sorry I can't hold the light for you," he said, as the last glimmer faded. "I'm not practiced at the art. We'll follow the marks as long as we can manage, and then rest for a while. Tell me when you can no longer bear the dark, and I'll try the light again."

"I'll be all right," I said. Despite this boastful claim, doubts gnawed at me.

We passed the first green mark. "I should remove it," said the Prince, pausing for a moment. "It will aid our pursuers. But if the Dulcé is lost . . ." He left it.

I was not so gracious. I would have abandoned the incompetent little fool to fend for himself.

To my surprise, I endured the next few hours quite readily. We returned to our missed turning with no sign of the Dulcé, but by that time I had to stop for other reasons. One blistered heel was raw, my ankles were wobbly, and my neck felt as if someone had hung me from a meat hook. "This isn't a place I'd choose to spend a night," I said, "but my feet will not move another step."

We unsaddled the horses, pulled out our blankets, and shared some bits of cheese. The horses whuffled softly as the Prince gave them each a handful of oats from our emergency stores. "I'll take these two and go a little farther down the passage," he said.

"Please stay close," I said. "Proprieties are long past."

"As you wish." His voice was clear and comforting in the darkness.

It never came morning, of course. The absolute blackness was only relieved when D'Natheil spoke his word of magic. With his other hand he passed me a hard biscuit. "We must hurry," he said. Even with no light to reveal the strain on his face, I could have felt the tension in him. "I don't think our pursuers slept."

I hadn't slept much either. The stone passage was hard and cold, and my tangled thoughts and worries would not stop spinning and permit any decent rest. We were off in moments, on a tedious repetition of the previous day's journey. After two hours we stopped to rest and drink. Fortune was with us, for if we hadn't stopped in just that place, the sound of the horses' hooves might have masked the faint moaning. We heard it at the same time, and D'Natheil strengthened his light so we could see into the side passage.

Baglos lay in a crumpled heap at the base of a sizable step down from the main passageway. The Prince jumped down and knelt beside him, listening for breath, examining the Dulcé's limbs. Soon he rolled the Dulcé to his back, revealing a bloody scrape on his forehead. "Seems he's only knocked his head a bit."

I tossed the Prince a wineskin and a rag to clean the injury, and then clambered down beside him. No sooner had I knelt beside Baglos and dribbled a little wine on his lips than his dark eyes popped open, darting quickly from my face to that of the Prince.

"What have you done to yourself, Dulcé?" said D'Natheil.

I poured a little wine on the rag and began sponging the wound.

"Ah, my lord . . ." Baglos snatched the cloth from me, pressing it to his head as he pushed himself up to sitting. "Please, woman, I can take care of this. I am good for little else, it seems, but causing delay."

"We feared you were lost," said the Prince.

"I . . . was feeling ill. The incident of the morning in the river, the long climb in the heat. Ah, my lord, I was shamed and I could not—Well, I wished to maintain some dignity before you. So I held back until I had recovered, believing there would be no divided way until we emerged from the tunnel. I assumed I could follow your light, but I could not catch up with you no matter how fast I traveled. I came dizzy once more and thought to myself that I ought to wait until I had more sense about me before proceeding. But like the fool I am, I stumbled down this step. . . ."

"You're fortunate that it wasn't one of the pits we've seen in some of these side passages," said D'Natheil. "And we're fortunate also," he added, before the Dulcé could reply.

"Bless you, my lord. You should leave me. I've caused nothing but difficulty."

"I don't think the Heir can proceed without his Guide." D'Natheil displayed remarkable patience. "You will fulfill your mission, Dulcé."

Baglos bowed his head, but not before I noted that his expression was quite at odds with his demeanor. His shame and apology sounded quite sincere, but he was not at all flustered. His almond-shaped eyes were sharp, and his face filled with determination and sorrow. I had always considered the Dulcé a simple, shallow man who wore his feelings and beliefs quite openly, one whose oddly constrained intelligence obscured nothing but a good heart. Yet in that moment his expression carried such conflicting stories that I began to think that perhaps he was more complex than he seemed. Though determined to continue this journey, he was afraid of its ending.

Well, so was I, I thought, as I watched the Prince help Baglos to his feet and boost him over the tall step in the rock. More so by the day. How could a man change so rapidly as D'Natheil? I could no more envision the Prince striking Baglos as he had once done than I could imagine myself embracing Evard.

Polestar was nowhere to be found. The Prince tried to summon him as he had the previous day, but after a quarter of an hour with no sign of the beast, we dared wait no longer. He insisted that Baglos ride the chestnut. Baglos protested, vowing unending humiliation. After what I'd seen of his private feelings, I wondered at his true sentiments.

Two more hours of slow progress and I felt a slight movement in the dead air. I lifted my face and hurried my steps. In a few moments more, the Prince allowed his light to die, and ten steps later we stood on the southern door-step of Mount Kassarain, inhaling cool, thin air. We laughed and made jests about adventurers who feared caves or made wrong turns or stumbled off steps. Pursuit and uncertain destiny were momentarily forgotten in our delight at being in the open.

We stood high on the mountainside, overlooking a lush meadow of rocks and flowers, laced with tumbling streams, a green gem set into the harsh framework of the mountains. At the meadow's eastern end the streams converged into fretting rapids that vanished into a bottomless, blue-white vista of gentle forested hillsides. To the west a faint track traversed a grassy slope and led deeper into the heart of the rugged peaks. But on every other side the grass yielded to boulder-strewn slopes and barren cliffs that offered no passage. We let the horses graze for a while.

Soon, D'Natheil was ready to press on. Urgency and excitement burned in his eyes as he peered into the west. "It's there, ahead of us. I feel it."

I climbed onto Firethorn. Baglos mounted the chestnut behind D'Natheil. The path led us from our high perch down through the flowered meadow, where blue, yellow and white blooms stood higher than the horses' knees, and then across the velvet slope that funneled us into a narrow, grass-floored valley. Though easy and pleasant at first, the valley trail quickly became so steep and rocky it was difficult to pick out a good path.

Banners of wind-driven snow flew from the highest mountaintops, filmy white trailers against the intense blue of the sky. The air grew colder and thinner. By early afternoon the cold wind gusting in our faces made it impossible to distinguish the swirling banners from the clouds gathering over the icy peaks.

Another hour and D'Natheil halted in front of a short wall of massive boulders that stretched the width of the gorge. "We'll have to leave the horses," he said. "A foot trail hugs the wall on the right, but the beasts won't be able to manage it."

I didn't ask him how he knew. His movements and words were abrupt, and I found myself looking over my shoulder, expecting to see our empty-eyed pursuers bearing down on us. If Baglos and I didn't hurry, the Prince would go on without us. I dismounted, pulled my cloak tight about me, and made sure the journal was in my pocket.

"What should we carry with us, my lord?" asked Baglos. He, too, was anxious.

"Don't burden yourself heavily, Dulcé. Food and drink for a day. I don't think it will be a concern beyond that."

The Prince rubbed Sunlight's head and spoke to him softly. When I declared myself ready and Baglos had shouldered a small pack, D'Natheil slapped the horse's rump and the beast trotted back the way we'd come, Firethorn close behind. "They'll go back to the grass and wait for you," said D'Natheil.

"Paulo isn't the only one who communicates with horses," I mumbled as we started up the steep rock stair. I couldn't say why I felt so resentful.

An hour's difficult walking brought us out of the gorge onto open, gently sloping tundra, surrounded by spires of ice and rock. It was as if we had stepped back a season. Everything was huddled to the windswept earth. No trees. No growth of any kind stood taller than a finger's height. The afternoon had turned gray and bitterly cold. We came to the crest of the modestly rising ground, and before us lay an ice-bound lake, ringed with sheer cliffs. There was no going any farther.

A gust of wind billowed D'Natheil's cloak as he looked out over the gray lake. He said only, "I think we have arrived."

CHAPTER 33

No hint of green could be seen in that ice-bound vale. Rather a thousand shades of gray and white lay one upon the other, as if the artist who had painted that particular canvas had forgotten to dip his brush in any other region of his palette. Massive stones lay jumbled about the water's edge, and behind them steep, ice-clad slopes of crumbled rock footed jagged cliffs that soared straight into the iron-hued sky. A faint tread wound from where we stood through soggy tussocks to the lake shore, skirting granite slabs that stood two and three times D'Natheil's height. It was hard to imagine anyone, man or beast, coming willingly to such a desolate spot. How could it be the refuge of the J'Ettanne? No life existed here, only rock and ice, dead water and silence.

The fifth clue was the most obscure of all. *Though he cannot see it, the hunter knows his prey, for it speaks to his heart whether he turns right or left.*

Nothing in that landscape spoke to the heart; nothing beckoned or charmed or seduced. The wind off the lake whined through the boulders, nosing at our cloaks like a mournful dog. I wrapped the scratchy wool close about my face and tried to remember it was summer.

Willing my blistered feet to take a few more steps, I joined D'Natheil and Baglos on the rubble-strewn edge of the lake. There was nowhere else to go. No passage, no trail. Nothing but cliffs and rocks. Journey's end. I was so tired that I could not rejoice in the stopping, and so uncertain that I could take no satisfaction in the accomplishment. "Where could we have gone wrong?"

"We're not wrong," said D'Natheil, his voice hungry. "Can't you feel it? It's like the heat shimmer that rises from the desert."

I felt nothing but my feet. "Are you saying that what we see isn't real?"

"Not at all. It's just there's much more than substance here—layer upon layer hidden behind what we see. I've never felt such a concentration of life." Was it anticipation or dread that dropped his voice to a whisper and colored his skin like burnished copper?

I wrenched my eyes away, sank to the ground in the lee of a rock, and wrapped the damp tail of my cloak about my freezing ankles. "I still don't understand the fifth clue."

"It's doesn't matter. The Gate is here."

He was right, of course. And the fifth clue was no more obscure than the others. From somewhere high in the encircling crags a white-tailed hawk screeched the doom of an unlucky rock-mouse, the lonely call reflected once, and then again, and then again from the rocks, a perfect triple echo. Then, from somewhere beyond the three reflections of the hawk's cry, a thousand other birdsongs teased at the edge of our hearing, the songs of birds that had never known this pocket of ice and snow, flamboyant birds of deserts and jungles, sweet singing birds of deep forests, majestic birds of the ocean's edge, larks and pipits and magpies and loons. Indeed, enchantment existed here. And abundant life.

Hardly had the eerie music faded when I discovered the tiny yellow and white flowers, each no bigger than the head of a pin, packed together tightly in a rocky crevice just beside my hand. When I rubbed a finger across the miniature garden, I was enveloped by the scent of lilacs, roses, jasmine, and a hundred varieties of flowers that could no more live in the thin, cold air than those tiny jewels could live in lowland heat.

I was going to call D'Natheil to come and see, when I was startled by a booming, "Hello!" rolling across the lake.

He was standing on the lake shore, and he turned to me, his eyes piercingly bright. "Do you hear them?"

"Hello . . . hello . . . hello," rang through the air, accompanied by a chorus of innumerable voices: cries of greeting, of joy, of farewell. Voices without bodies. Memories of life.

"Yes. Yes, I hear them."

"The Gate must be somewhere beside the lake," he said. "Come on." He set off along the narrow shoreline, his steps as vigorous as if he were just beginning the journey.

"What of pursuers, my lord?" asked Baglos anxiously, hurrying to match his short steps with D'Natheil's long stride.

"They're holding back. They should have been on us by mid-morning."

Waiting, I thought, as I hobbled after them. *They're waiting for you to show them the Gate.* The Zhid didn't know the way. I shivered, but not from the frigid wind. These Zhid were not heedless, hotheaded bullies, rushing after us ready to pounce and fight. I thought back to Montevial, to the forest, to Tryglevie. Even back to Ferrante's house. They had stayed just close enough to follow, to prevent our escape, pushing us . . . herding us . . . to the ending. Much more dangerous. And yet we could not stop. Not now.

We examined every slab and boulder around the lake shore for a passage or entrance. Hundreds of people would have lived in the stronghold during the Rebellion: women, children, old people. No matter what destruction had overtaken them, there had to be some remnant of the space where they had slept and sheltered from the harsh winter that would settle here for all but a few weeks of the year. But in many places the ice extended right down to the water, leaving treacherous footing, or the way was blocked by boulders from ancient landslides and we had to clamber over them or slog through the icy water. Halfway around the lake from our observation spot was a long, narrow strip of sand fronting an expanse of barren cliff face, but we found no breach in the rock.

When we returned to our starting point, D'Natheil picked up a rock and slung it into the water, breaking the gray wind-ripples. "We're missing something."

"Four hundred and fifty years," said Baglos. "Perhaps there's nothing left."

"No, it's here. I'm sure of it. I've been here before. . . ." D'Natheil's voice trailed off, as if he weren't quite sure what he was saying. "As far as this wooden head of mine can tell me, I was born on the shores of this lake. Here I began running, from terror and confusion and because I was so cold, I thought I would die before I had a clear thought. My clothes had been torn off me in a violent storm . . . darkness, lightning, fire, screaming . . . and I had only the knife in my hand. I dared not stop"—he dragged the words out of himself—"and then sometime, though not at first as we believed, but later, in the lowlands, past the end of the meadow with the flowers, I knew I was pursued by servants of . . . I didn't know what it was . . . this shadow that wants me. I believed that if the pursuers caught me, I'd never find what I was looking for." His bleak face yearned for answers. "I was looking for you."

I wanted very much to give him what he needed. But I was a plodding mundane, as Baglos had told me so often. "Let's look at the journal again. As you said, we're missing something." I pulled the fragile volume from my pocket, trying to shelter it from the blustering wind. Baglos huddled beside me, while D'Natheil leaned against a boulder and stared at the lake. The page with the diagram held nothing new, and the following entry was a long description of the Writer's difficulties with spring planting.

"Turn back to the riddles," I said. "Maybe we missed one." Baglos and I pored over the page in the gray light, searching for any that might have been written later than the original description of the little girl's game. The later entries were written with a pen slightly wider at the tip than the originals. Still only five, plus the additional phrase the Writer had inserted with the telltale pen. Not phrased as a riddle, it had never seemed significant. "What is this again, Baglos? He asks if his daughter is not a marvel, but I don't remember the exact words."

The Dulcé read, "The day will come when men proudly cry out the name of our race, and it is my Lilith that will shine in their memory."

"Cry out the name of our race . . ." My gaze met D'Natheil's. With a trace of a smile, he bowed and returned to the edge of the lake.

Baglos whispered to me anxiously. "Will the name of the Dar'Nethi show us the Gate, then?"

"No. Not *Dar'Nethi*. . . ." Would D'Natheil think of it?

The Prince stood for a moment, eyes closed, the wind ruffling his light hair and the shabby cloak that could not obscure the truth of him. Then he opened his arms wide and cried out in a voice that thundered through the desolation, "J'Ettanne!" And as his voice called back to him through the thin, cold air, I felt a great release, as if the very stones had let go a monumental sigh at the command to share their long-held secret. Whispers and murmurings were all about us just beyond the range of hearing, quiet laughter, tears, whispers of pleasure, of love, of sorrow and grief and prayerful wonder, buzzing unseen like tiny insects about our ears, chaos existing in tandem with the wintry silence. But any expression of amazement was stilled in deeper awe of the doorway that now stood open in the stone cliff across the lake, an opening no less than fifty paces wide and three stories in height.

Without speaking, we repeated our journey around the lake, never taking our eyes from the incredible sight, never giving thought to pursuit or danger or anything beyond our moment's wonder. The twin columns supporting the massive stone lintel were covered with the most graceful and intricate carvings: birds, beasts, flowers, all so perfectly worked that one could feel the life of them as they crowded the white stone. In the center of the rectangular lintel was carved an arched triangle, with a floweret in each sector it scribed.

The Prince stepped first through the gaping expanse. It was only right. The stronghold was part of his realm, marked with the emblem of his family. Baglos and I followed close behind. It was dark inside, but the Prince whispered the word *illudié* and torches blazed on every wall. I caught my breath as the great cavern came to life. Never had I seen a space of such beauty.

The cavern was so enormous, we could not see the roof of it. It was as if the whole mountain had been hollowed out and the stone walls polished smooth, displaying the mountain's embedded treasury of tourmaline and jasper and lapis as magnificent waves of rich blues and greens, dazzling murals no human artist could replicate. Shining veins of quartz glittered in the torchlight like faceted gems, and a wide staircase with no visible supports twisted its way up through the center of the gleaming air to reach at least four levels of columned galleries carved from the cavern walls. The stairway and the galleries were connected to each other with a series of arched bridges, so delicate and graceful they could have been spun by a magical spider. And the bitter wind of the iron-gray lake was left behind, the air inside the cavern fresh and pleasantly warm.

A raw and desperate longing scribed D'Natheil's face, even as he turned to the task in hand. "I need to explore the place a bit. A wall of fire shouldn't be difficult to find."

"I'll stand guard, my lord," said the somber Dulcé, drawing his sword and taking a position near the gaping doorway to the outside. "Do as you need." With his ferocious glower, he looked quite small and foolish.

The Prince nodded graciously. "Thank you, Dulcé. We shouldn't need your warding for long," he said. "If I can't do what I've come for within the hour, I don't think it will matter."

Then, like a desert-bred child visiting his first garden, he began to wander. All my own weariness was forgotten as I trailed after him into room after room of marvels: an amphitheater whose dark-painted ceiling was inlaid with bits of faceted quartz, so that the flickering torchlight gave the illusion one stood under star-scattered skies; an immense refectory, its gigantic wooden tables perfectly free of dust, crockery bowls and neatly laid spoons awaiting the next feast; the kitchens, huge stone hearths and chimneys bored into the mountain's heart. We explored workrooms, granaries, storerooms of all kinds, sewing rooms, map rooms, a library with so many shelves of books and scrolls that wooden-railed walkways spiraled up six men's height or more in front of us—everything needed to support a population of many hundreds.

Climbing the wide staircase took us to rooms of all sizes, sleeping chambers, I guessed, though all were empty of furnishings. On the uppermost level, the gallery that overlooked the central cavern did not make a full circuit of the walls as did those at the lower levels, but instead opened into a long, narrow passage that delved deep into the back wall of the cavern. The torches were smaller there, and the walls rough-hewn and very much older. Promising. While D'Natheil was still opening doors off the main gallery, I explored the narrow passage. A hundred paces in, the passage ended in a wall of rock.

Disappointed, I started back, only to find D'Natheil just coming into the passage. "Nothing here," I said.

But he shook his head, and I followed his gaze over my shoulder back toward the aborted way. The light flickered and the rock . . . shifted . . . and a pair of massive wooden doors stood in the center of the wall that had appeared to be solid stone only moments before. The doors were smooth and undecorated and dark with age. I could easily believe that no one had touched them since the days of J'Ettanne himself. No handle or latch was visible, but at the Prince's first touch they swung open, silently and easily as if the hinges had been oiled just the previous day.

The passageway beyond the doors was chilly, and the light emanating from the arched opening at the far end was an odd bluish-gray. Another hundred paces and we entered an immense chamber, its walls, ceiling, and floor colorless and obscured by swirling, icy fog. A constant low-pitched rumble, unlike anything I'd ever heard, caused my hands to clench and my jaw to tighten. And so instantly confused were my senses of perspective and direction, only the stone beneath my feet gave me anchor. I felt as if I had stepped off the edge of the world.

But the moment's sensory uncertainty vanished when we walked a few steps farther into the chamber and saw the curtain of flame that reached from the colorless floor all the way to the murky heights. Flame was the only name I could put to it, though its color was a bruised blue, darker than the coldest heart of a dying hearthfire.

"The Gate," I said, raising my voice a little so as to be heard over the deep-pitched rumble.

"Yes." D'Natheil's voice was scarcely audible.

"And the Bridge?"

"Just beyond the wall of light."

"Then we've truly reached the end of our journey."

The Prince gazed upwards, face shadowed by the dark

magnificence. "When we first entered the cavern, the image
of a city passed through my mind—a glorious city of graceful towers, of gardens and forested parkland, encircled by
mountains sculpted of green and gold light. Here will that
city, that world, and all that exists in it live or die."

"So what must you do?"

"I don't know." His grief was wrenching. "Were you to
offer me the entire wealth of the universe or a thousand
lives to fill my empty head, I could not tell you."

"That's why it's time for those who know such things to
take charge of this most delicate venture, is it not?"

We whirled about, as five men with drawn swords
stepped out of the fog and quickly surrounded us. Three
were brawny, well-armed fighters. The fourth, the sneering
speaker, was Maceron, the fish-eyed sheriff. But it was the
fifth, the one who held an unwavering swordpoint at my
belly, that caused my soul to freeze. The fifth was Baglos.

"Dulcé?" D'Natheil's query was quiet.

"I am most abjectly sorry, my lord Prince. There is no
other way."

"Did you never learn to look under your bed for snakes
or in your boots for spiders, oh, Prince of Fools?" said the
gloating Maceron.

The fish-eyed man might not have existed for all the
notice D'Natheil paid him. "What means this, Dulcé?" No
anger marred the Prince's speech, only questioning and
sorrow.

"It means the salvation of Avonar, my lord. If you could
remember its beauties, you would agree."

"How do betrayal and treachery become the salvation
of beauty?"

"A bargain has been made, my lord. You'll see. You are
to be given exactly what you desire—the chance to save
your people with honor and grace."

"Do you understand who these people are, Baglos?" I
asked, dismay swelling to outrage at his choice of conspira-
tors. "This devil has done his best to exterminate the descendants of J'Ettanne. And now he's serving the Zhid."
Giano, Darzid, Maceron . . . my certainties were unproven,
but certainties nonetheless.

Maceron bowed mockingly to me. "Not at all a polite

introduction, my lady, but what can we expect from one who has such a dangerous habit of involving herself with perverse wickedness? I thought you'd learned your lesson ten years ago."

"You made the mistake of leaving me alive. Were you working for these same soulless villains even then?"

"My master is no devil sorcerer, but a noble warrior who works to rid this world of these perverted creatures who would enslave us and the traitorous scum like you who welcome them. He works with the priests of Annadis. That's good enough for me."

His master . . . dared I say the name I was so sure of? My tongue stubbornly refused to pronounce it, as if the very word were some evil incantation that would precipitate our doom. And the priests . . . "You're a fool," I said.

Baglos frowned, looking from me to Maceron. "How is it you know this woman?"

"It's many years past and has nothing to do with our present transaction. You've done well, ensuring the priests kept on your trail. Now, we must ensure that your prince will not disrupt the smooth completion of our business."

The three men moved in, and D'Natheil at last paid them a full measure of attention. The Prince grabbed one of the brutes by his sword arm and neck and slammed him into a second man. The two crashed to the floor in a tangle as D'Natheil tried to wrest the weapon from his remaining attacker. He spun the man about and pressed him to his chest, the screaming villain's arm bent into an unmaintainable angle.

When Maceron raised his sword above the Prince's head, I yelled and reached for the sheriff's arm. But one of the fallen men stumbled up from the floor and crushed me to the wall. While I fought to get a breath, he shoved Baglos and his sword at me. The Dulcé's sword tip pricked the flesh under my breast. I dared not move. His small face was frightened, but his hand was steady. Determined.

Maceron slammed the hilt of his wide, heavy blade into the Prince's head. D'Natheil staggered, tightening his grip on his opponent, but the disputed sword clattered to the floor. Seizing their opportunity, Maceron's two shaken henchmen pounced and wrestled the Prince to the floor, freeing their fellow and pinning D'Natheil on his face. Roaring in pain and fury as he clutched one arm to his side, the Prince's freed opponent ground his thick boot into D'Natheil's neck. A comrade stomped on the Prince's right forearm and stabbed the point of his sword into the Prince's outflung wrist, pushing down slowly until blood flowed freely from the wound. D'Natheil continued to writhe, lashing out with his feet and twisting his torso to get free. But the third ruffian kicked him in the side, leaving him flat and gasping.

Maccron grabbed my arm so tightly that his fingers bruised the bone, and he growled into my ear. "I would recommend, my lady, that you inform your testy friend of what we do to sorcerers. I've heard he can't do much in the way of sorcerer's magics, but I'll cut off his hands if he so much as waggles a finger and remove his tongue if he utters a whisper. You remember. The priests prefer him undamaged, but they do most certainly want him. I'll take no chance—no chance at all—of his escape. We're going to destroy all of this." He jerked his head toward the fiery Gate.

"You see, Baglos," I said bitterly, as the men continued to kick the Prince in the side and the legs and the head. "This is the devil with whom you've made your bargain."

"It is necessary," said the Dulcé, refusing to look at what was going on behind him, even as he flinched with every thudding blow. "I do not wish it to be this way."

When D'Natheil at last lay still, Maccron put me in the custody of the man with the damaged arm, a snarling brute with a drooping mustache and broken teeth. "You and the little vermin take the woman, while we get the sorcerer properly restrained. Have Kivor make sure she is secure."

Disappointment and self-recrimination were lead weights in my boots as Maccron's thug shoved me down the passageway toward the cavern. I stumbled and Baglos reached out as if to steady me. I jerked my arm away.

"You cannot understand, my lady."

"I thought you loved him. I thought you were sworn to his service. The honor of the Dulcé and all that. Where's the honor in betraying him to his enemies—*your* enemies?" We started down the circular stair, the ruffian's knife pricking my back. Baglos walked beside me, his short legs hurrying to keep up.

"D'Natheil does not know the things necessary to save Avonar," said the Dulcé. "It is not his fault. He was never meant to be the Heir and was not suited to it, especially after his injury. But on this day he will accomplish that duty anyway, because those who are wiser than we have devised this plan. His duty is more important than anything. He must understand that. We have no other hope."

"You've given him to the Zhid . . . you're risking the destruction of the Bridge . . . for what?"

"Just before we stepped through the Gate, our Preceptors took possession of D'Arnath's sword and knife, held by the Lords in Zhev'Na since the Battle of Ghezir. As long as the Dar'Nethi hold the sword, Avonar cannot be defeated. The knife should have remained with the Preceptors, too, but the sword alone is enough. I was commanded by my bound master to complete the bargain by delivering D'Natheil as soon as we came to the Gate."

"You're not stupid, Baglos. They're going to kill your prince and destroy the Bridge. How can good come from that?"

Baglos averted his eyes. "Avonar will live. If D'Natheil is to die, then that is his destiny." He hurried down the steps ahead of me.

And he *would* die. I was complicit in the murder. In my confidence, in my everlasting pride, I had ignored every warning, sure that no evil would befall because I willed it so, sure that we would unravel the puzzle successfully because my intelligence and determination would allow no other outcome—unlike the last time. And now, for a paltry piece of sharpened steel, D'Natheil was to be given to the Zhid. He would be dead. My reawakened soul shriveled at the understanding. My veins felt parched. Who would ever have believed that I would care so much?

We descended into the main cavern. The enchanted flares had gone out, leaving a few mundane torches as the only light. The yellow flames illuminated a circle of cracked stone flooring, tracked with mud and littered with packs and saddles. The lovely walls and bridges and staircase were lost in the darkness.

Maceron's men bound me to a slender column just beyond the pool of torchlight. A sallow-faced young man with a shaven head, bright, darting eyes, and bloodless lips ran his bony fingers over my arms to check my bindings. I shuddered at his touch. He grinned, making his head look even more like a skull. But even his presence was benign beside the three robed figures who now walked into the circle of yellow light. Giano's voice was an icy claw scraping steel. "You have what we want?"

Maceron had arrived at the same time. "We've got him. You are quite trusting of this little vermin."

"You needn't worry. A Dulcé's bound service is quite reliable. We can afford to be trusting."

Giano strolled over to Baglos standing stiffly between two of Maceron's men. The Dulcé would not look at the Zhid, who stared at him with his empty, unblinking eyes. "Though we still have a portion of our contract to fulfill. Somehow the lesser talisman was left with the Prince. The Dulcé will have to risk the Bridge passage to return it to his masters," said Giano. "Who would ever have thought these little oddities would take such a large part in great affairs?"

Baglos flushed. "But the Preceptors have the sword."

"Indeed, D'Arnath's holy weapon will likely serve the sad Dar'Nethi better than D'Arnath's Heir ever did. We have no objection to the pitiful little city continuing to exist for a while, if the talisman holds the power you believe. We may even find it amusing. The prize is ours. The victory is ours." Giano spun on his heel. "It's time I examined our prize. I've heard his mind is damaged, and I'll not be generous if it's too much." His cool manner failed to disguise his lust.

Maceron snapped his fingers, and the sallow-faced young man disappeared into the gloom. "I was told that some damage was done 'at the crossing,' whatever that means. But he's all of a piece, more or less."

"And the woman?" asked the Zhid.

Maceron swept his hand toward me. "The lady awaits your pleasure."

The cool smile fell away from Giano's face as he sought me out in my shadowy niche. The Zhid stood close enough to breathe on me, and quicker than I could see, his murderous knife appeared in his hand. Ever so delicately, he traced a line across my neck with the knife point. I shrank back against the cold pillar. "Oh, madam, it is most tempting to make a permanent end to your meddling. Rarely have I been thwarted in so blatant a fashion, and I do not care for it. . . ."

His gray eyes seemed to grow larger, sucking away reason and breath. The stench of decay, of burning flesh, of hot blood on stone filled my senses. I was drowning, suffocating in horror. It took every bit of will I possessed to pull my eyes away from his, and even as I accomplished it, I was not sure whether it was my own act or Giano's consent that released me.

" . . . but your life is of interest to someone of importance. I'll have to be content that your interference is at an end, as is that of your rustic allies. I've brought you a fond remembrance of one of them." He motioned to one of his gray-robed companions, who brought him a dark-stained bag of burlap. With a mirthless grin, Giano reached into the bag and pulled out a severed human head. The hair was white and wispy, the wide brown eyes staring. Terrified. Jacopo.

I closed my eyes and bit my lip until I tasted the salty blood, withholding the cry of grief and horror and outrage that would feed Giano's pleasure.

The Zhid's thin lips widened into a grin. "The other three who led us astray so briefly have met a similar fate. A pitiful crew they were."

"No," I moaned, as the chill of death crept from my feet to my wobbling knees to my hollow belly, paralyzing my heart. Not all of them. Not again.

The torchlight glittered on Giano's gold earring, and his cold fingers stroked my jaw, as he whispered his morbid litany. "Oh, yes, we left them quite dead on the rocks of Mount Kassarain. The vultures have most likely picked their bones clean by now. Unfortunate in a way. The Dar'-Nethi girl could have been amusing. But the noble sheriff had become annoying, and the cripple is no loss to anyone." The cold fingers on my face then brushed my mind, galling . . . filthy . . .. detestable . . .. depraved . . . No matter how I twisted in my bonds, I could not escape his touch.

"Well, enough of that," he said, removing his touch abruptly, leaving me limp and numb, sagging in my bindings. "We've a few surprises yet in store. I hope you enjoy the culmination of your adventure." He leaned toward me, so close I could not escape him, and pressed his cold lips to mine, his tongue licking away the blood where I had bitten them. I fought not to vomit.

Giano's attention was diverted by the return of the sallow-faced man and another guard, pushing D'Natheil ahead of them into the circle of light. The Prince was gagged and blindfolded, his feet close-hobbled, his arms and hands twisted awkwardly behind his back, wrists fastened so tightly to a loop of rope about his neck that lowering either head or arms would strangle him. His shoulders bulged with the strain. The left side of his face was mottled with blood and bruises.

Maceron gestured to Giano. "You may inspect the merchandise."

"Remove its coverings," said Giano harshly. "All of them. I will see what lives in this body."

One of the gray-robed Zhid removed the Prince's blindfold and gag, warning him not to speak unless he wanted a knife in his tongue. D'Natheil coughed and shuddered when the wadded cloth was yanked from his mouth. While one guard held the knife point to his neck, another cut away his clothes, until the Prince stood bound and naked, his body covered with darkening bruises. I stared at his face. The light was so poor. The brow, the jaw. What was it that made me tremble so? He could not have seen me in the shadows, for his eyes were only slits, blinded by his captors' torches.

Giano walked around D'Natheil, inspecting him like a prize horse. "So, it's come at last. After a thousand years, the Heir of D'Arnath confronts his enemies face to face. Did you ever think it would be you, or that you would be the last of them? Has the little seed of doubt begun to sprout in your starveling brain, the most minute scrap of understanding that the faith your wretched kingdom has lavished on your family is soon to be put to the test, and that you are quite inadequate?" He stroked the Prince's straining arm, and as D'Natheil tried to jerk away, growling in fury, the guards tightened their hold. "What a pitiful end to a line of such great promise, no better than any other naked slave. And yet"—he stopped and stared into the Prince's face, cold and haughty even in his captivity—"something is distinctly odd about you. Dassine, the wily bastard, what has he done? You have so little mind as it is, why would he bother to mask it? It's made you very difficult to follow; I'll give him that. You are not the same as you were half a year ago and not even as you were when you made the crossing." Giano put his hands on the sides of D'Natheil's head. "So, one closer look to be sure, then we can send these bloodthirsty mundanes on their way."

The light of the torches dimmed, and a cold wind swept through the cavern, bearing a hideous certainty of death and desolation, cruelty and loathing, unending pain without hope. Even the impassive Maceron looked wan and sickly. His men held their heads and moaned. I shivered uncontrollably.

All color drained from D'Natheil's face, sweat beading his forehead. His stance wobbled briefly, but he clenched his jaw and held . . . and in a moment's breath, the shadow was gone, the air clear again. Giano snatched his hands from D'Natheil as if they'd been burnt, his smirk erased. The Prince's eyes flew open, bright and disdainful.

"He is the one," snapped Giano. "Let us proceed. You have his knife?"

Maceron handed D'Natheil's silver dagger to Giano. The Zhid held it to the light and examined its markings. "The lesser talisman," he said. "With this and the sword, the Dar'Nethi believe they have ensured their future, abandoning this useless prince and this Bridge that has brought them nothing but grief." He tossed the knife into the air and caught the spinning weapon by its hilt. "With the return of this dagger is our bargain done. The Gate fire yet burns, and, now, before we quench it forever, we will allow you to venture its dangers and return to your masters. Is that your wish, Dulcé?" He presented the knife, laid across his palms, as if he were a servant delivering a favored dish to his master.

"It is." Baglos, his hands trembling, his complexion jaundiced, took the weapon, quickly bundled it in a cloth, and shoved it into the pack he carried on his shoulder. "The bargain is complete."

"Do you recognize these bindings, my lord?" Giano ran a finger along the silvery cord that circled the Prince's neck. "Dolemar is far stronger than rope or chains. As you may have noticed already, it gets tighter as you struggle, and the least touch of sorcery will cause it to burn. Too much and your flesh will turn black, and you will beg us to sever your limbs."

He hissed a word that made the firelight dim and tweaked the cord that attached the Prince's wrists to his neck. Though he made no sound, D'Natheil arched his back as if the binding had been pulled tighter.

Giano smiled. "Happily, you'll wear your bonds only a short time. At dawn tomorrow the line of D'Arnath will end. The Bridge was created with D'Arnath's blood and sweat, and the last of D'Arnath's blood will destroy it. Simple, is it not? Ridiculous that it took a thousand years to discover that it takes only your life's essence—the blood of D'Arnath's anointed Heir—sprinkled in the Gate fire to finish this matter." There could have been no words more filled with hate since the world began.

Giano beckoned his two Zhid companions. "Put him away until morning."

As two Zhid grabbed D'Natheil's strained arms, Baglos turned to Giano and bowed stiffly. "Before I go," he said, "I would request one consideration. My master has neither eaten nor drunk anything for near a full day. It was part of the agreement that, although confined, he would not be cruelly treated before he discharged his duty. May I, as a last service, offer him food and drink?"

Giano laughed. "If you think he'll take anything from you, Dulcé, then by all means proceed. We must wait until morning for the last chapter in this saga, and I'd not wish his strength compromised. D'Arnath's Heir must champion his people with his full capabilities. I would have him know what it is he does."

Baglos reached into his leather bag, genuflected before the naked prince, and extended his silver wine flask. "I beg your forgiveness, my lord prince. I did not know you when we began. In these past days . . . your kindness . . . You are not the person of whom I was told. Though it has not shaken my belief in the necessity of my course, our companionship has made my grief the weightier. Would that it could be different." Tears rolled down the Dulcé's round cheeks. *"Ce'na davonet, Giré D'Arnath."*

I understood the words, as I had not when Baglos first greeted D'Natheil with them. *All honor to you, Heir of D'Arnath.* And I remembered D'Natheil inspecting the scars on Tennice's back, struggling to comprehend the relationships of honor and treachery and forgiveness. Perhaps the Prince believed Baglos had been given no more choice in his treachery than had Tennice, for in a movement that was scarcely more than a blink of his eye, he nodded. Baglos stood and raised the flask to his master's lips. The silver glinted in the yellow torchlight.

The flask . . . What was it? It was not the same as the Dulcé had shared with us along the journey. This was the other one, the ornate one that was only for dire circumstances, and yet the Dulcé's own near drowning had not been dire enough. Baglos's duplicity was so hard to accept. Now that I knew, I could recognize so many signs I'd missed. Yet, Baglos honored D'Natheil—loved him. I could not doubt that, for I had seen his grieving when he didn't know I watched. I looked at the weeping Dulcé and the flask in his shaking hands, and in an instant I was filled with horrific certainty.

"No!" I screamed. "D'Natheil! My lord prince! Don't! Oh, gods, don't drink it!"

D'Natheil looked up in shock. He couldn't have even known I was there, hidden in the shadows.

Baglos did not turn, but held the flask to the Prince's lips. "Please, master, I beg you . . . before it is too late . . ."

But the silver flask clattered to the paving when Giano yanked Baglos away from D'Natheil. Giano shoved the Dulcé to the ground, then motioned to the gray-robed Zhid to take the Prince away. The two Zhid quickly wrapped the blindfold about D'Natheil's straining eyes and dragged him into the darkness.

"Foolish, mundane woman!" cried Baglos. "Now they will use him to destroy the Bridge. We could have prevented it. You've ruined it all. I am forever cursed."

"Oh, Baglos, was betrayal not enough?" I said. No matter how hopeless the day, I could not keep silent and watch murder done.

Baglos could not reply. Giano had turned his impassive gaze on him, and with no more feeling than a man crushing a gnat, flicked his knife across the Dulcé's throat. The blood of the Guide soaked quickly into the dry stones.

CHAPTER 34

Once Giano had followed his prisoner into the darkness, Maceron and his men settled for the night in the cavern, rolling out blankets, passing food around, and setting the watch. The sallow-faced young man who had been charged with my security loosened my bonds enough for me to sit on the floor. An eager smile played over his bony face; his tongue licked his full lips. As he refastened the ropes and knots, his tight little fingers brushed my arms, and soon his hands were wandering freely. I almost wept in relief when Maceron called him away.

I told myself to sleep. There was nothing else to do but mourn, and too much of that even to begin. Rowan, Kellea, Paulo, Jacopo . . . I could not bear thinking of them. And the cursed, foolish Baglos. Earth and sky, how blind I had been. Bound by his Dulcé's vows to a master who, by Baglos's own account, had come near destroying the Prince once before. Loyal to Dar'Nethi traitors willing to sacrifice the prince they had damaged—and my own "mundane" world—in a scheme to save their precious city. Baglos must have been terrified that Dassine's message would expose him. Had he called in Maceron's henchmen to attack the herb shop, causing Celine's death and Tennice's injury? He had run out of the room during Dassine's message and been dismayed at finding Zhid poison in Tennice's wound. I grieved that Baglos was dead, for I wanted to rip out his traitorous heart.

But my anger waned quickly. What was the point? Perhaps I should have allowed Baglos to carry out his plot. Perhaps D'Natheil would be better dead at the hand of his servant than at the hand of his enemy. This time tomorrow none of it would matter. And the Bridge would fall.

Beyond grief and mystery lay the tale of enchantment and corruption from another world. Did I believe the disembodied voice that swore the doom of Gondai was the doom of my world, too? And if I believed it, did I care? For so long, I had cared about nothing and no one on this earth. But when I closed my eyes I saw Paulo embracing a nuzzling horse, and Kellea's head on her dead grandmother's lap, and Graeme Rowan's eyes opening in wonder while grieving for his past, and Jacopo laughing as he helped me tend my garden and paying too much for people's bits and pieces because they needed his silver more than he did himself . . . so much goodness in this world . . . and I knew I did care. Only now it was too late.

At some time in the night, torchlight, voices, and the bustling of horses and men announced another party of travelers. The activity took place far across the cavern mouth from where I sat, and the oppressive darkness swallowed up the new arrivals before I saw or heard anything to identify them. Baglos's body lay in a forlorn heap not ten paces from me until two of Maceron's men decided it was in the way, dragged it off, and dumped it under the colonnade.

The horrid night dragged on.

An hour had passed since the last change of the watch, and most of the torches had burned out. Rumbling snores echoed through the cavern, but sleep eluded me. When I closed my eyes, I would see Jacopo's staring head, and Baglos weeping, and D'Natheil straining to catch sight of me as he was dragged into the darkness. My arms and shoulders were cramped from their awkward position bent backward and wrapped around the stone column, and the muscles in my stomach and chest ached and burned so that it was hard to get a decent breath. My fingers had gone numb, too, so when someone started fumbling at the ropes that bound my hands, it took me a few moments to notice it.

Certain that it was the sallow-faced man come to continue his loathsome caresses, I tried to scream, but a thin, cold hand clamped over my mouth. When my hands fell loose, I twisted around, grabbing and scratching the hands that kept such firm hold of me. All my anger and grief was channeled into that battle, but my cramped limbs had no strength, and my small and wiry captor seemed to have four hands. Soon I realized there were two of the bastards, one wrapping a bony arm about my throat and grasping a painful handful of my hair, the accomplice capturing my flailing hands and helping to drag me through the darkness and down a dark flight of steps.

"Would you stop?" The angry whisper hissed in my ear. "You're going to bring the whole place down on us! If you promise to be quiet, we'll let you go. Will you promise?" I nodded my head vigorously. But the attacker was no fool. I had barely opened my mouth to yell, when the hand smothered my mouth again, and the villain twisted one arm behind my back until I thought my shoulder would pop out of its socket. I was shoved through a stone passageway and into a room that smelled faintly of horses. A door fell shut behind me, and I spun about and backed away from it into the dark.

"Give us a light, boy," said the person just in front of me—a woman, breathing rapidly. "She'd best see who's here before she sets up a holler."

The darkness parted to reveal a yellowish light . . . a sputtering lantern with a dark cloth being pulled off it. A flushed Kellea leaned against the wall in front of me, casually brushed her disheveled hair from her face, and massaged the hand that I had bitten three times over. Paulo squatted by the lantern, grinning despite an angry scratch on one cheek. And slumped in the corner on a pile of ancient straw was a wan, smiling Graeme Rowan. His shirt dangled from one shoulder, and blood-soaked rags were tied about his middle.

I was without words.

"She was determined not to be helped," said Kellea. "I thought I might have to stick her a bit to shut her up. A good thing the boy was with me."

"But I thought—" I felt a thorough fool. "One of the men up there—You were all—"

"I think I'm altogether more cooperative when being rescued." The girl ignored my stammering.

"Indeed you are," said Rowan in a whisper. "The best thing I ever did." He shifted his position uncomfortably, and Paulo scrambled to support his shoulders.

"They told me you were dead," I said. Forcing aside the first tears I'd shed in a lifetime, I squeezed Kellea's small, hard hand, and then hurried across the room and ruffled a blushing Paulo's hair. Then I knelt beside Graeme Rowan and gripped his hand and pressed it to my brow, giddy with relief that the three were not illusions. "How did you get here?" I said. "What happened to you?"

"We were going to be dead, but she—"

"I'll tell the story, if you don't mind," said Kellea, interrupting Rowan. "You'll never get yourself together again if you don't shut your mouth and be still. I can do only so much."

Rowan smiled weakly, shrugged his shoulders, and began coughing. Paulo grabbed a waterskin and helped the sheriff to a drink.

"We felt them coming up behind us just at nightfall," said the girl. "Wicked, creeping—I thought I had spiders in my head. The boy told us what the little man had said, and we stuck to the trees as much as we could. But the valley narrowed and the going was slow in the dark, so we decided to go up the side of the valley where the way was easier. Well, *I* decided. Graeme thought it was risky, but we climbed up. Straight into their arms. The boy was clever and ducked into the rocks before they noticed him, but I got myself royally captured. Graeme was a fool and tried to fight them off alone. Got himself skewered for his trouble. They believed he was dead, and I did, too,"—Kellea looked at Rowan with fire in her eyes—"but he was stubborn and prideful and refused to die as any sensible man would. Just before dawn, when the villain priests finally left off trying to crack my skull from the inside out, he and Paulo came rescuing. Graeme could scarcely sit his horse."

Kellea twined the string ties of a palm-sized cloth bag about her fingers. "We couldn't go far with him so hurt, so we hid in the rocks. The devils were so anxious to find your prince that I thought we might be left alone. At first light I went off looking for herbs to dress Graeme's wound, but didn't I see them scouring the hillside for us. And so . . . There's a plant I know of—astemia. If you chew its roots, it slows the heart enough to simulate death. Wouldn't have thought of it, except I'd seen the plant while hunting the others I needed. So I made Graeme and the boy take the astemia, smeared Graeme's blood over us all, and then chewed some of it myself. By the time it wore off, the cursed priests were gone, and we were still alive."

"And so you followed us here. You might better have gone another direction."

"That man out there—that sheriff—he's the one that fired the shop and killed my grandmother. And Graeme told me he'd seen this Baglos talking to him just before the attack. Since you'd said he was bound to obey the Prince, Graeme figured the Prince must know of it. But seeing the sheriff coming after you with the priests, we decided that the little bastard was up to no good, and we'd best come warn you. I guess we were too late for that. Is the Prince dead?"

"Captive," I said. "The Zhid are planning something for the morning."

Rowan leaned his head against the wall and closed his eyes. "Sorry I'm not much help tonight," he said, gasping. His halting breathing—holding every breath and releasing it only when he had no choice—hinted at the severity of his injury. "A few hours sleep, and Kellea will have me up. We'll get him free."

Kellea crouched in front of the sheriff and slapped his cheek lightly—enough to force his eyes back open. "Don't you dare go to sleep until I give you more of this." She took three or four small leaves from her little bag and crushed them in her fingers, telling Paulo to pour a sip of wine into a cup. She stirred the leaves into the wine and made Rowan drink it. He dozed off almost immediately.

"He's not doing well," I said. Rowan's hands were cool and clammy.

"I told him he'd be no help to anybody if he was dead." Kellea doused a rag with water and blotted Rowan's brow. "But he thought you might have need of us, and he'll not keep sensible where you're concerned. And he believes I have some stupid sentiment about saving my people."

"Dassine said the consequences would be dreadful if we

let the Bridge be destroyed. Do you think that's true?" I badly needed Kellea's help.

"I just want to get out of here and be left alone." The girl stuffed the herb bag back into the pocket of her leather breeches. She nodded her head at Paulo, and the two of them carefully lowered Rowan to the straw. Paulo pushed a rolled-up cloak under the man's head.

"We've got to free him, Kellea. They're going to kill him. Even if you don't care about that, he might be able to help Rowan. I don't know what all his talents are, but he's a sorcerer who's growing more powerful by the day. We should—"

"I'll help you, no matter," said the girl, standing up and adjusting her sword belt. "We've come this far and are like to get no farther if we're not smart about it. Pardon me if I don't trust our safety to you."

"All right, then." I climbed to my feet, weariness forgotten. "We'll need to take him some clothes, and whatever weapons we can get together. . . ."

We set out with three knives, two swords, and Rowan's black cloak. Kellea left her bag of herbs with Paulo and told him what to do if the sheriff woke in pain or fever. "I'll bet the Prince can fix him," said the boy.

"We'll take care of him," said Kellea, laying her own cloak over the sleeping man. "Douse the light now, until we're off."

Once our eyes had adjusted to the darkness, Kellea and I slipped out of the storeroom and up the steps that led back to the cavern.

"Finding the Prince would be easier if I had something of his, you know," Kellea whispered.

"If no one's taken it, I've got something. . . ." We crept through the dark colonnade until we encountered Baglos's body. The Dulcé's leather pack had been thrown on top of him. I rummaged inside. No one had bothered to retrieve D'Arnath's silver dagger.

I gave Kellea the weapon, chewing my lip as she worked her magic with it. When she handed the knife back to me and pointed toward the winding stair, I shoved it into my knife sheath, keeping Rowan's more ordinary knife in my hand. The Zhid had confiscated my own blade.

Kellea glided through the dark cavern and up the stairway. At each landing, she paused for a moment before continuing upward. I followed close. A faint steady light shone from one end of the third-level walkway. Quiet voices came from the nearby shadows. Kellea drew me toward the opposite end of the span, and we approached the light by skirting the cavern wall through the gallery. One man sat on the floor beside the lantern; two darker forms stood on either side of a closed door. We crept close and crouched in a shadowed doorway, a few rooms away from the men.

". . . don't trust nobody won't show his face," murmured a man with a gravelly voice.

"Orders is orders," snapped a second. "We've been in stranger company."

"Don't know when. This place gives me the cold sweats. Did you look at that priest, the one that does show his face? I thought I was a dead man when he looked at me— or maybe he was."

"Me, too," said a third voice, younger, jittery. The soft lantern glow outlined a youthful profile. "And I keep hearing things. Like voices, but nobody's there. When we come past that lake . . . all the birds. I never liked birds, specially ones you can't see. Did *you* see any birds, Dirk?"

"Just do your duty, both of you," said the second man. "Mouth shut, eyes open, and opinions to yourself. I don't trust those animals downstairs any farther than I can spit."

So these were the newcomers. Not Maceron's men.

"Who is this prisoner that's got everybody so wrought up?" asked the gravel-voiced man.

"It's not ours to know. His lordship says they've got him fair trussed. If we keep him tight, we'll be out of here tomorrow."

His lordship . . .

Kellea pulled my ear to her mouth. "He's in the chamber just past these three. I'll get the bastards away. If you can't free him in a quarter of an hour, leave him be, and we'll think of something else."

I squeezed her arm in acknowledgment, and she slipped away into the darkness. Whispers and murmurings floated through the air. I flattened myself into the niche. Moments later, a faint green light twirled and streaked through the air above the walkway.

"Cripes, what's that?" said the gravel-voiced man.

"Go check it out."

Scarcely had the running footsteps disappeared along with the green light when a new voice rang out in the darkness. "Dirk! Downstairs at once! His lordship's orders." The voice was male, but it was impossible to tell from what direction it came. I had underestimated Kellea's talents.

The leader spewed out curses. "You'll have to hold here, Rigo. Don't budge now. Anything happens to this prisoner, we're maggot fodder." He hurried across the walkway and galloped unevenly down the stairs.

The edgy young soldier didn't have a chance. A handful of pebbles bounced across the gallery floor, then his shrouded lantern was snuffed out by a gust of wind.

"Who's there?" said the shaking voice. He sounded no older than Paulo.

A faint laugh, another shower of pebbles, then light footsteps tripped down the gallery. The young soldier hesitated only briefly before running after them.

The moment he was away, I jumped up and pushed open the heavy door. The walls of the barren chamber gleamed faintly of their own light. Against the far wall hung the Prince, his feet spread apart and fastened with the silver cord to bolts newly set into the stone. His hands were lashed to a wooden beam high above his head, leaving him to support his weight on the balls of his feet. The silver loop about his neck was tethered securely to another hook in the wall. He was very still, scarcely even breathing. Only a slight tremor in his legs hinted he was alive.

Seri . . .

I could have sworn I heard someone say my name. But the rag was still in place about the Prince's mouth. "Stay quiet," I whispered. "I've come to get you." I freed his mouth, untied the blindfold, and slipped the loop at the end of his neck tether from its hook. While he was still blinking and swallowing, I bent to examine the bonds on his ankles.

Stifling a cough, he whispered hoarsely, "Don't you get tired of riding to my rescue?"

"We've come this far. If we can get you away, you'll have time to think about what you need to do here. You can come back when you're ready." I could not look at his face. I told myself that I didn't want to shame him because of his nakedness, and that it was only fear of someone catching us that made my hands shake so wretchedly as I worked. But there was more. Enchantment was all about him, stronger than I'd ever felt before.

"Can I cut this cord?" I asked. The silver cord had bitten deep into his flesh, leaving oozing blisters and raw, ugly patches. His legs, stretched so awkwardly, were trembling with the strain of his position as he tried not to make things worse by moving.

"As long as it's an ordinary knife, not enchanted. I tried several ways to get loose, with sorcery and not, and wished I hadn't."

It was nearly impossible to wedge Rowan's heavy blade under the bindings, and I knew the pain must be excruciating as I sawed away at the cord. "I'm sorry to hurt you."

"I'll not complain. Honestly." But his voice was very tight, and he mumbled a curse when I had sliced through the first one and peeled the cord away, a strip of blackened skin attached. With a grunt, he drew his freed foot under him, supporting his weight less precariously.

The other ankle was even more difficult. His foot was dark and swollen, and I could feel the cord tightening as I worked at it. This was taking too long, and his hands were still bound. *Stupid, why didn't you do his hands first?* Where were the guards? *There! Ankles free.*

I could scarcely reach his hands. They'd put five turns of cord around his wrists and the beam. Five knots, so that each turn had to be cut individually. I jerked violently, almost slicing his flesh, when I thought I heard someone outside the door. But the pounding was only my heart. Three turns done. A quarter of an hour, Kellea had said. Who could tell how long it had been? Another layer cut. Then the last.

After we wrestled the loop of silver cord from his neck, I gave him Rowan's cloak, unbuckled the sheriff's heavy sword belt from around my waist, and held it ready. "Maybe this time you'll keep your clothes on," I said.

"I promise I won't throw them back at you tonight," he said, shaking the blood back into his hands. He stuck his arms through the side-slits in the cloak, pulled the garment tight around his middle, and buckled the sword belt over it. Then I gave him his own dagger—D'Arnath's blade.

As we slipped into the deserted gallery I felt fortunate, and when we reached the stairway unchallenged, I allowed myself the beginnings of hope. But as I took the first step downward, the Prince caught my hands and stopped me.

"I can't go with you," he said. The darkness hid his face. "Though everything in me wants to follow you, I must go up instead."

"No. Surely, you need—"

He put a finger on my lips. "There are no words to thank you for all you've done. You've fed me, clothed me, nursed and healed me in countless ways, taught me of this world and how to live in it, and given me a part of yourself that I'll carry with me always. But now it's time for me to stand on my own. I had time to think tonight. Once I figured out that I'd best not even move if I valued my limbs, I—I don't know how to explain it—my mind took itself away from my body—"

My neck prickled. "You don't have to explain it."

"Giano has said over and over that my death on the Bridge will destroy it, but I think perhaps it's only if I let them bind and slaughter me like some stupid sheep. The answer is so simple, I can't think why it seemed so difficult. Someone's come to fight me, set me a challenge. If I fail to meet a challenge to the Bridge, D'Arnath's oath is violated—so the Zhid want me captive . . . or to run away. It's not my death will cause the Bridge to fall, I think, but my failure. No one thinks I'm capable or willing or clever enough to see their trick. I have to be there, and I have to fight. That has to be enough. It's all I know how to do."

"So you're going to the Gate to wait for them."

"You've given me the chance."

Nothing more could be said. It was his Bridge, his battle, his choice. Berating him that he needed more than some wild supposition before tangling himself in mortal enchantments would only bring the others down on us. I had done all I could to bring him to this point, and the fact that I could not bear the thought of leaving him had no relevance to the matter at all. "Have a care, D'Natheil." I could scarcely form the words.

"And you, my lady." And then he kissed my hand, there in the midnight of Vittoir Eirit. "There are no demons in this darkness," he said. "No need to be afraid. Such beauty lies within you, such light. You've pushed away the shadows and given me life."

I didn't hear him walk away. But my hand stung with fire, and his words hung in the air like the tail of a comet. *. . . no demons in this darkness . . .* Where had he found those words? Words extraordinary only in their familiar composition and the fact that they'd been spoken in another time, by another voice, comforting me when I was afraid. How did he know of my terror of dark places? I'd never told him of it, and yet, in the tunnels under Mount Kassarain, in the darkness of the rift valley . . .

My boots moved downward to the next step of the curving staircase. It was as if the burning of my hand and the tale of his words had penetrated the barriers of reason and uncovered a jumble of questions I'd stored away there as too odd, too difficult, too inexplicable to think about.

What did Celine mean when she asked what miracle had brought this man to me? What had made the old Healer laugh with delight at the moment of her death? What had made Tennice cling to D'Natheil in the madness of his fever? Why had the Prince come to me . . . as a storm-wracked ship will follow a beacon to safe and familiar harbor?

You will shine as a beacon to me. . . .

My body trembled with the thoughts that blossomed within it like bonfires at a midsummer's fair. My mind refused to give credence to the absurd speculation taking shape from its confusion. *Impossible. Inconceivable. Lunacy.*

A heavy hand fell on my shoulder. "Are you mad?" Kellea whispered fiercely in my ear. "You're a fool. Any one of these bastards could see you standing here. Let's go some place safer, if you don't mind."

I let Kellea lead me. I couldn't have said where we were. "Did the soldiers come back before you got him loose?

Is he still prisoner?" Kellea asked, when we reached the second-level gallery.

"No, it worked wonderfully well." I could not focus on Kellea's words for the chaos inside me and the fire that lingered on my hand.

"Where is he then?"

"The Gate. He went to the Gate to wait for them. . . ." I crushed her hands in mine, knowing what I had to do. "Kellea, you've got to put me back." Now I dragged *her* down the stairs.

We reached the next turn of the stair, and she balked. "What are you saying?"

"They've not discovered I'm gone. The ropes are still there. Put me back."

I tugged at her again, but she held her ground. "In the name of reason, why?"

"Because I have to know. I can't explain. I must be at the Gate in the morning, and there's nowhere to hide in the chamber. So, Giano wants an audience for his triumph. He'll take me. Please, Kellea. Put me back."

"You're mad."

I yanked free of her and glided downward on airborne feet. Kellea followed me around the dark perimeter of the cavern until we reached the column where I had been held prisoner. A few moments fumbling and I found the lengths of rope. I pressed the bindings into Kellea's hands.

"Are you sure?"

"Absolutely sure. Perhaps this will keep you three safe, too. If you stay hidden until we win or lose, they won't suspect you're here. Do it quickly. Please."

I stretched my arms around the column, paying no attention to the ache of my shoulders or the pull of the bindings or the scratch of the ropes about my abraded wrists. *Oh, holy, blessed gods . . .*

"I hope you know what you're doing," whispered Kellea as she tied the last knot.

"Be safe, Kellea."

The Dar'Nethi girl laid a hand on my shoulder, and then slipped silently into the darkness.

In the next hours, I relived every moment that had passed since Midsummer's Day. When had I first felt it?

At Ferrante's when he came out of the shadows to check that all was well with me? I had caught the scent of roses and thought I was dreaming. In the forest out of Fensbridge, when his laughter set my blood afire? I had called myself a lustful fool. As far back as the day he threw the knife at the rock and I felt the touch of enchantment? Tennice had seen it in his illness, and I had called it delirium. Stars of heaven, he had even named the great chestnut Sunlight. The Vallorean word for sunlight was *karylis*, and only one horse in my memory shared the name of the Vallorean mountain that sheltered the lost city of Avonar.

No wonder the stories I'd told him in the ruined castle seemed more like his own memories than any Baglos had provided. I could not shake the implausible, impossible, lunatic conviction that they *were* his own memories. In some way beyond all rational understanding, the man who had appeared out of nowhere on Poacher's Ridge, the man who sat upstairs in the chamber of fire, setting himself ready to prevent the doom of the world, was Karon.

CHAPTER 35

Dawn crept over the lake outside the cavern. Muddled with unchecked speculations, incoherent plotting, and unsettling half-dreams of disembodied faces, I scrabbled my way out of the long night. I had not wanted to sleep. I had wanted to do nothing but ponder on how it was possible that Karon could live. Only a madwoman could even consider it.

Baglos still lay under the colonnade like a discarded boot. As I shifted my cramped shoulders and stiff neck, I wondered if the Dulcé had known anything of what had been done to D'Natheil. D'Natheil . . . If this inconceivable fantasy were true, then what had become of the true prince? The man who had come to me in the woods on Poacher's Ridge did not know himself. His body and spirit were alien to each other. I had seen that from the first, but hadn't understood it. How did a soul exist in a body that was not its own? A constant struggle of emotion and instinct, untempered by experience or memory. Even his appearance had been in flux. Was that, too, the result of this inner combat? Dassine said that D'Natheil's clouded mind was the inevitable result of what he had done to the Prince. What had he done? What I wouldn't give for a few moments' conversation with Dassine!

With the daylight came doubts about all that had been so convincing in the darkness. And even if my mad beliefs were true, his circumstances were so desperate that I might not see him again. Yet somehow my spirits were no longer bound by rational thinking or the limits of possibility.

As the pearly preamble to the day gave way to bold pinks and reds, Maceron's men stirred and began the usual rituals of morning: rummaging in packs for food, relieving themselves under the colonnade, saddling horses, grumbling, bawling orders, curses, and insults. An hour passed and Giano did not come. Had he already found the Prince by the Gate? I craned my neck in a futile attempt to see. Where were they?

Maceron strolled across the mud-tracked paving. He gnawed on a leathery piece of jack, wiping the grease from his unshaven face with the back of one hand. "So you're still here," he said, grinning.

"And where else would I be?" I snapped, finding it easy to reclaim a combative spirit on this singular morning. "Why would I wish to be anywhere but here with my arms bent so charmingly about this stone tree? Have the villains finished their murderous doings?" I didn't have to force the tremor into my speech.

He tweaked the rope binding my hands. "It seems our prisoner has escaped his guards."

"Escaped?"

"You needn't get your hopes up. He'll not evade the priest. Can't say I'd be sorry to see this Giano humbled. Though if I thought the devil sorcerer had the least chance to escape, I'd hunt him down myself and to perdition with all business arrangements. But the priest hates him more than I do." He drew his knife and twirled it through his fingers as soldiers will do to amaze small boys.

I shrank back against the pillar, away from the flashing edge. "You claim to hate sorcerers, and then you help them with their murders. It makes no sense."

Maceron shrugged. "The priests say our world will be free of sorcerers when they're done. My master believes them, and who am I to question?" He sliced through my bonds, yanked me to my feet, and propelled me through the cavern, relinquishing custody to the gray-hooded Zhid waiting at the foot of the stairway. "Don't think I'll lose track of you, madam," he called, as the hooded Zhid herded me up the steps. "You will reap your proper reward!"

On another day, I would have devised a proper retort for the vile sheriff, but my mind was far ahead of my feet, reaching into the chamber of blue fire. *Is it you? Tell me. Give me a sign.*

Giano awaited us at the first landing. His usually colorless face was flushed and his empty eyes gleamed hungrily in the torchlight. "I almost came to visit you last night," he said, smiling. "But I wonder if I would have found you where I left you?"

"I am very proficient at releasing myself from captivity and reattaching myself to stone pillars," I said. "It's always such a lark."

"Mmm . . . I wonder." The Zhid wagged a dark-stained fragment of silver cord. "This doesn't look like sorcery to me, and I don't think the Dulcé has waked from his slumbers to perform yet another service for his prince."

"Don't blame me for your incompetence," I said. "I might have thought of something better to do with a knife than freeing this infantile prince. The whole lot of you—Dar'Nethi, J'Ettanne, Dulcé, whatever you are—should leap off of this ledge and good riddance to you."

Giano laid cold fingertips on my cheek, and I was almost sick with the dead feel of them. "Words are worth nothing. You are a mistress of words, but look at where they've gotten you: your friends dead, yourself on the way to your long-delayed execution, your grand mission in shambles.

No matter what your activities of the night, my lady, I cannot find myself unhappy with you." Indeed the Zhid seemed almost serene, not at all like a man whose prized prisoner has gotten the upper hand. "I especially want you to witness the precision of well-laid plans coming to fruition." The Zhid waved me up the stairs. "Come, now, my lady. Great events to witness this day. A thousand years of history will come to an end. In truth, all of history will be made obsolete. Your little world will at last have its umbilical severed."

"And, of course, as the good Maceron believes, none of your kind will remain in the Four Realms," I said. "But you've no need to stay, have you? The Lords of Zhev'Na feed on our sorrows all the way from their wasteland—"

"Do not speak of those you cannot comprehend," snapped Giano. "If you mundanes rip each other's flesh, that is your own doing, not ours."

Just outside the doors into the passageway, Giano and his companions discarded their priest's robes. All three were attired in long, belted shirts of purple or gray, tight black hose, and supple black boots that reached above their knees. Each wore a single gold earring and carried a quite serious-looking sword. One of Giano's henchmen was a burly man with reddish hair, thick forearms, and a gray cast to his skin. To my astonishment the other was a woman, tall, angular, and severe, arms like a plowman and iron-gray hair twisted into a knot atop her head. Her eyes held no more human feeling than did those of her companions.

"And now, madam . . ." said Giano, motioning me to precede him.

The blue-gray frostlight of the Gate flooded the passage. As I walked into the chamber, flanked by the two Zhid, my breath was visible in the frigid air. It took me a heart-searing moment to find the one that waited. He sat by the fiery wall, his arms wrapped about his knees, his head bowed as if he were asleep. I tried to shout a warning, but my tongue would not obey, no matter how I tried. Even so, the Prince's head came up quickly, his face awash with unhappy surprise.

It's all right, I thought. *I chose to be here. To stay with you.* Gods, how I wished he could hear me. Indeed, no answering words sounded in my mind, but on his face blossomed a smile of such brilliance, one might think all the beauty and joy of the universe had been gathered into his soul. Karon's smile. I was right. Oh, holy gods, how was it possible?

A quick movement to my left was Giano, his gaze snapping from the Prince to me and back again. The Zhid's eyes narrowed briefly, picking at my soul before he moved on to his business. "We stand at this artifice of enslavement called D'Arnath's Bridge," he said, focusing sober attention on the man seated in front of him. "Who speaks for the dead despot?"

And so the challenge was opened.

"I speak for D'Arnath, the father of my fathers," answered the Prince, remaining seated, though shifting his full attention to the Zhid. "Who intrudes on this holy place?"

"Those who deny D'Arnath and his whelps any place in the worlds that have repudiated them. We refute your claim to these objects you so pompously declare to be holy. This bridge and its devices unlawfully bind the power of your own people. And the residents of this sad world"—he swept his hand wide—"have long declared they want no part of Dar'Nethi magics."

"I'll take on any challenge. I'll not lie down and die for you, Zhid."

Giano smiled. "I never intended you should."

The Prince sat relaxed. Waiting. "Who has appointed you champion for this world, Giano?"

"Much as I desire to be the sole bearer of this challenge, D'Natheil, and to lick the last drops of D'Arnath's blood from my sword, this battle is properly fought by all concerned." He snapped his fingers, and the Zhid woman left the room. "It is time for your family's unique brand of slavery to end. Unlike your self-important ancestors, we do not assume the right to speak for these mundanes or declare what's best for their future. We've only shown them how D'Arnath and J'Ettanne have contrived to keep their world in bondage to Avonar, that dying crone who sucks the lifeblood of a child to extend her life one moment longer. No. This world has provided its own proper opponent, one who carries the honor of these lands and their sovereign on his sword."

I caught my breath. The connection I hadn't seen. Giano

did not need to name his champion, the lord who had arrived in the middle of the night, the same lord who had been sent to answer the challenge of a "rebel chieftain" in the west. The burly Zhid had pulled me to the fog-shrouded periphery of the chamber, so Tomas did not see me as he strode through the doorway behind the Zhid woman. How magnificent he looked, dressed in red silk, fine leather, and the ruby-studded tabard that was only worn by the king's defender, carrying the ancient sword of the Champion of Leire. Perfectly balanced, exactingly forged and tempered, there was no finer blade in the Four Realms. Now, where was his companion, Maceron's master, the sardonic snake who slithered out from under every vile stone in the Four Realms? For the moment, at least, Tomas stood alone.

My brother seemed scarcely to note his strange surroundings, but saved his attention for the Prince. He snorted when D'Natheil rose to face him. "This is my opponent, my liege's challenger?"

Though the two were equal in stature, the Prince looked shabby in comparison: barefoot, his face bruised, wrists and ankles raw and ringed with dried blood, Rowan's tired black cloak held about him with the sword belt. D'Natheil looked puzzled as he examined Tomas, and only after a long scrutiny of my brother's face and red-brown hair did understanding dawn. "Is this some jest, Zhid? I've no dispute with this man."

Tomas interrupted the smirking Giano before the Zhid could answer. "I am no one's jest. I stand champion for Evard, King of Leire and Valleor, Protector of Kerotea and Iskeran. No one challenges the sovereignty of my liege without answer from me."

"I make no challenge to your king," said the Prince. "My argument is with this Giano and his masters who have laid waste to my own land, who have devastated my people beyond your understanding, who have murdered my father and my brothers, and whose intent is to slay me before I can remedy the wickedness they've done."

"I care nothing for your personal disputes," spat Tomas. "But sorcerers of your race have lived in Leire uninvited, defying our laws and customs. You proclaim yourself sovereign of a neighboring realm, yet you do not treat with our king as would a legitimate brother. Instead you sneak about the Four Realms, committing murder and spying out our defenses. And this strange portal—do you not claim it as your rightful property, and is it not possible for your warriors to invade our lands through some secret avenue that lurks behind it?"

Someone had tutored him very well.

"You don't understand what you've been brought into," said D'Natheil. "I'll not fight you. I honor your house, and I acknowledge your king."

Tomas drew his longsword—the light, flexible, perfectly edged blade of the Champion of Leire, rubies glittering in its hilt. "I understand enough. Fail to fight, and you'll die at my hand. By our law, you should rightly burn. But because you've come from another land, I offer you a warrior's death." He stepped closer to the Prince. D'Natheil stood motionless, hands loose and relaxed at his sides, sword sheathed. I tried again to call out, to stop the wickedness that was about to happen. But Giano smiled at my struggle. His binding on my tongue was as firm as the Zhid warrior's hold on my arm. I could not make a sound, and my brother could not see me.

With the wickedly tapered tip of his sword, Tomas ripped a long slit in D'Natheil's collar.

The Prince did not move. "I have no dispute with you, sir."

Another tweak at his breast left a ragged tear in the black cloak. Tomas was proud and preferred a fight, but he took his duty to Evard very seriously. If he was convinced of the danger D'Natheil posed, he would take off the Prince's head without compunction. A third move left a bloody scratch on D'Natheil's cheek, and with a movement so swift as to be unseen, Rowan's sword, heavy and old-fashioned, scratched and nicked in a hundred places, appeared in the Prince's hand. Giano licked his lips. Was he still expecting the Prince to run?

With no further hesitation, Tomas attacked. I had not seen my brother fight since he'd come into his prime. He was a master of fluid power, the flash and speed of his youth replaced by intelligence and perception. It was as if he knew to an exactitude where D'Natheil's blade would be at any moment, and he scarcely had to shift his position to counter any move the Prince made. His king did not deserve such perfection.

D'Natheil began slowly, as if he were reluctant, or the weapon were too heavy, or he couldn't remember the moves. But as Tomas lunged and struck, the ringing swords sending blue-white sparks flying through the icy fog, the Prince shed his hesitation. Thrust, parry, counter, attack . . . spinning, circling . . . faster, smoother, more powerful by the moment, a new level of skill demonstrated with every closure.

Tomas's jaw was sculpted in iron, his lips a thin line. As far as I knew he had not lost a match since he was seventeen. A barrage of slashing blows from the Prince had Tomas almost in my lap, but my brother ducked and spun and twisted away, and then his weapon was slicing downward toward D'Natheil's shoulder. But the Prince spun, too, and his blade halted Tomas's stroke with a bone-shattering block.

After a while I wondered if D'Natheil even knew whom he fought or why. His face had settled into an expressionless mask. Every step, every stroke, every attack, slash, spin, and parry seemed to take him farther away from himself, as if there were no real dispute with rights or wrongs or consequences, no war, no meaning outside his actions, only the unthinking, unending, glorious abstraction of combat. He was lost in passionless exaltation, his grace making Tomas look heavy-footed, his speed and strength making Tomas look old. Whatever the truth of his soul, the body that battled my brother that day was D'Natheil, the Heir of D'Arnath.

A ringing blow and the Champion's sword clattered across the colorless paving stones. Tomas was on one knee, flushed, panting, and bleeding from a deep gash in his thigh.

D'Natheil held Rowan's blade high over his shoulder, its edge on a line for Tomas's neck. The Prince's face was cold and deadly, and I felt that the very universe must be weeping silent tears.

No. No. No. I ached to cry out, to alter D'Natheil's expression of uncaring inevitability. Tomas was my brother. Flesh of my flesh. I could not forget his eyes reflected in the glass back in his palace chambers—bewildered, guilt-wracked—craving forgiveness that he could not ask, knowing that I could not give.

Moments passed. The Prince did not strike. Slowly, he lowered his weapon and said, huskily, "Go. This is not your fight."

"Do not dismiss me!" Tomas's face was scarlet. "Finish me with honor or give me back my sword."

The Prince shook his head. "I'll not fight you. Those who chose you chose well, but I will not slay the Duke of Comigor, son of the Lord Gervaise." He stuck his sword tip under Tomas's blade and with a twist of his wrist flipped the gleaming weapon into the air, so that it came down hilt-first into its owner's hand.

Tomas's anger was supplanted by surprise and curiosity. "How do you know me?" D'Natheil glanced over my brother's shoulder and tipped his head. Tomas's eyes followed his. "Seri!"

The world paused in its turning.

"Yes, your traitorous sister is here, Lord Tomas," said Giano, breaking his long silence and drawing Tomas's gaze away from me. "She has betrayed you once again, Your Grace, betrayed your king, violated the sacred honor of your house by consorting with this sorcerer prince. She exemplifies the corruption he brings, mocking you, and prostituting your son's heritage. I'm prepared to turn her over to you as soon as you discharge your duty to your king."

Tomas stood up slowly and waved his sword point from Giano to me. "Let her go."

"The sorcerer disdains you," said Giano. "Can you not see the scorn in which he holds your king, your people? He thinks to make you impotent by flaunting his rape of your sister's mind, this ultimate violation begun by that other of his kind. You remember . . . the one you so prudently removed from this world, the one who sought to pollute your very bloodlines with his foul seed."

"You were right, Seri," said my brother, staring at Giano. "Until this moment, I'd forgotten your warning about the one with the empty eyes." He sheathed his sword and folded his arms across his breast. "I'll fight no more until I understand what's happening here." Without taking his eyes from the Zhid, he said, "This is his friend. Darzid's friend."

But in the moment he uttered Darzid's name, Tomas was lost. A leaden shutter dropped across his face, and like a wooden doll jerked onto the stage by its puppetmaster, he snarled and whirled to face D'Natheil. And before I could connect his altered behavior with Giano's upraised fist, my brother drew his sword, roared a curse, and attacked. The startled Prince could do nothing but counter, and Tomas, in his madness, could not adjust to his opponent's lightning response. D'Natheil's sword was driven deep by the force of Tomas's charge.

Tomas sagged, and when the Prince withdrew his blade, my brother slumped to the floor. Then the Zhid warrior released me and, together with the Zhid woman, drew his weapon and fell upon the Prince before D'Natheil could even see what he'd done.

I ran to Tomas and dragged him away from the combat. Blood poured from the gaping wound in his side. With his knife, I hacked a strip from my skirt and bound the folded rag in place around him with my cloth belt. *Not fair. Not fair.* Did the saving of the world require this blood, too? I clutched my brother in my arms and wished that I could pray.

A sword skittered across the paving, coming to rest beside the curtain of fire. The burly Zhid was down, leaving a smeared trail of blood as he crawled toward his dropped weapon. The woman was fading fast under D'Natheil's relentless assault. I assumed Giano would be the next to attack, but the smiling Zhid commander leaned his shoulder against the wall and watched.

The fallen Zhid reached for his sword, but the battle raged close, and D'Natheil kicked the weapon past the Gate fire. The Zhid warrior lurched after it, reaching through the curtain of dark flame, then screamed murderously as he pulled back, half his body blackened and smoldering.

When would Giano move? The Prince's victory seemed close. Tremors shook the foundation of the chamber, and the cold gnawed at my bones. The Gate fire burned blueblack. I should be rejoicing in D'Nathcil's skill, yet I was foundering in a sea of dread. The Prince was furious and determined, his face void of everything but battle. The Zhid woman was staggering, bleeding from uncountable wounds. Then she was down, D'Natheil kneeling beside her with a knife in his hand, his own silver dagger with the emblem of D'Arnath engraved upon it.

What was the horror that filled me as I watched him, so grim and implacable, raising his dagger to finish his enemy? Giano smiled and did nothing. The Gate fire was the same bruised color as the storm that had driven us to Pell's Mound.

This was wrong. All wrong.

Dassine's message of love and trust resounded in my memory. He believed Karon should be here, not D'Natheil. Why? There had to be a reason. *There is that in D'Natheil that will tell him what must be done.* But Dassine had meant in the D'Natheil he had sent, not in the prince who had grown up in Avonar, the one who knew only of fighting and death. Why Karon?

As the Prince's dagger fell through the pregnant air, I lunged for his arm, deflecting his blow. D'Natheil shoved me away in cold fury. "Why? Why must I stop? What do you mean, this is not the way?"

Though I had uttered no sound, clearly he had heard the plea I was screaming in my thoughts. As a snarling Giano grabbed my shoulder and wrenched me backward, I tried desperately to focus my words. *Look at the Gate fire, how dark. Dassine took your memories because you had been trained in the wrong way. All these years, the Dar'Nethi have fought and lost. You must find a different way to accomplish your task.*

Giano shoved me against the wall. "Interfering whore. Do you think I can't hear your maudlin pleas? I should have disposed of you long ago." His hatred bored into my head like a hot poker, but I would not allow him in. I had not forgotten how to create a barrier in my mind.

The Prince's silver dagger was again raised to finish the Zhid. I closed my eyes and fought to keep my head clear of everything but what was most important. When I looked again the dagger had not fallen, and D'Natheil's gaze shifted frantically from one to the other of his victims.

"Giano has planned all this," I told him, surprised to find the torrent of words bursting free of Giano's silencing. "It's why we were able to free you so easily last night. He let us do it. Just as he let us go at Ferrante's, and in Yurevan, and again in Montevial. They never wanted to capture you. I was so stupid to think we had outsmarted them again and again. It was always too easy. Did you hear him? When you said you wouldn't lie down and die for him, he said he never intended that you should. He brought Tomas, knowing well he could never defeat you. Giano wants you to kill them all."

"Then tell me what I must do!" said the Prince, throwing his knife to the floor, his mouth tight with anger.

I had to follow Dassine's lead. Instruction could not give the Prince the power he needed. "You must find the answer inside yourself. Dassine believed you could. I believe it. I know you, D'Natheil. You are worthy . . . so very worthy . . . of our trust."

"So the Prince of Fools has become a slave to a woman," said Giano, stepping forward. Perhaps I only imagined the note of anxiety in his sneering. "Ironic, is it not, that by sending you to this woman, Dassine has robbed you of your only virtue? The Dulcé was right. She is a curse."

But the Prince was not listening to Giano. He took up his knife again, brushing his fingers along the blade and staring at the burned Zhid who lay moaning in wordless agony. D'Natheil's stony visage softened to puzzled curiosity as he touched the dying warrior's mutilated arm.

Giano stiffened and hissed, and without warning he wrapped his arms about me and yanked me to his breast. The dagger that had taken Baglos's life and that of the highwaymen in During Forest was poised at my heart, and one by one my senses burst into flame, until I believed that the Gate fire must be burning beneath my very skin. But the Prince did not look up, and I refused to cry out. He needed time to see his way.

My captor dragged me toward the wall of fire, the blue-black curtain soaring in vicious exhilaration into the murky heights, and the Zhid began to laugh with such triumphant wickedness that D'Natheil was drawn to look. When the Prince saw what was happening, all softness fled from his face. He leaped up, grabbing his sword, and my heart shriveled. Giano's fire had grown so fierce that I could not bear it, and I began to sob.

"Let go of the woman," said the Prince, cold and angry. "I am the one you want."

"So you are, but I will have you on my terms. We must rid ourselves of this meddlesome female before she saps all your resolve." And with wicked laughter that rang through the stone chamber, Giano shoved me through the wall of black fire.

CHAPTER 36

I was not dead. Either the Zhid was wrong that the passage of the barrier would destroy me or he didn't truly want me dead. But the place where I existed had no relationship to any world I knew. Bolts of lightning slashed through purple-gray clouds above a desolation of skeletal trees and naked crags. Though lurid and grotesque, such a view would have been almost comprehensible if it had been the entirety of the landscape. But from the corners of my eyes I glimpsed entirely different scenes: on one side a field of garishly colored flowers that budded and bloomed and withered in moments under a livid sun, and, on the other, a slow-moving river of filth that was a crush of emaciated men and women, clawing and trampling each other so as to drink from a lake of blood. When I turned my head to either hand, the scene would vanish, and only the alien landscape remain. A bitter wind lacerated my skin, leaving bloody tracks, and the tumultuous roar of the Gate fire— now deafening in its volume—was riven with a hideous, howling chorus of despair. Hellish pandemonium.

My flesh did not burn like that of the Zhid who had

touched the fire. But my being vibrated like a violin string
out of tune, and great cracks exploded through my reason
so that I could not hold the fragments of myself together.
Visions . . . or memories . . . yet not memories . . . nothing
of beauty or sweetness . . . displayed themselves against
the mad backdrop: my drunken father vomiting over Tomas's dying body, Martin laughing as he stripped the skin
from a screaming Tennice's back, and my mother, my
lovely, delicate mother, mating in a sweating frenzy with
Evard. One after the other, such twisted visions supplanted
each memory I treasured, severing every link to love, joy,
pride, or accomplishment until only horror was real.

*Perhaps this is death, after all. If so, then let it be done
with.* The dark void proclaimed by Leiran priests, the absolute ending I had always dreaded, would be far better.

Though my mind was chaos, my feet stood on solid
ground. I was no longer held captive by the hand that had
plunged me into the tumult, but he was close, a solid, ma-
levolent companion to the monstrous apparitions assailing
me from every side. He laughed as a pair of green, slaver-
ing jaws gaped before me in the darkness, and when I
turned away in panic, a river of molten lava blocked my
path. Another turn and a hideous beast with two heads and
razor-sharp claws the size of my arm loomed over me out
of the murk.

*Cry out to him all you wish, woman. His nature betrays
him. You've led him to his doom.*

The words meant nothing to me.

"Seri!" Ever so faintly I heard the call through the thunder, but I could pay it no heed. Something was approaching
from behind me, something more awful than anything I'd
yet seen. It had no name, but I had to run before it showed
itself, and the only path open led away from the beckoning voice.

Move, fool! I cried. Ignore the hissing cobra the size of
a tree that raises its hood, wrapping you in a gaze so malev-
olent it could steal your soul away. A rotting cadaver extended its bony fingers, leaving great smudges of
unnamable disgust on your arms. *Concentrate on the path
beneath your feet.*

"Seri!" The insistent call came again. But it was only

another voice in the cacophony of lamentation, the growls and wails and screams—screams that might be my own for all I knew.

I ran. But chaos has no direction, and my flight brought me only to the place I had been before. The two that battled in that place, swords glinting with the lightnings from the raging storm, were not apparitions. Both were in black, the one with thin lips and pale eyes that reflected nothing, and the other with broad shoulders and blue eyes that flashed with fire and steel. Real blood flowed from their wounds, and I should care. I should speak a name, but I could not bring it to my lips.

Frantic, I backed away from the combatants and fled once more. I ran along a perilous track so narrow I could not put my feet side by side. If I stopped, I would topple into the bottomless nightmare that gaped on either side of me. My throat burned. My blood pounded. The nameless thing was close behind.

"Seri!" The summoning rang out once more, and like a thread pulled from the weft, I was drawn inexorably to the place of battle. The two combatants were bathed in blood and sweat, so that one might think it was the battle for the doom of the world. But I cackled in my madness, for I knew the doom of the world was just behind me, and whatever the result of this duel, it could make no difference.

I had to get away. My path led through mud that sucked at my feet and rain that scalded my face. I could not run in the mud, only slog through it, pushing aside the half-rotted corpses that rose to the surface like flotsam in a morbid sea. My heart pounded with the effort, but soon the mud was up to my knees. The path led into a cave. *Beasts of heaven, not a cave!* Even the ghastly lightnings were swallowed by that pit. No glimmer, no spark, no dim ray, no pale reflection relieved the nightmare darkness. The hot mud was to my waist, but I could see nothing, and I dared not reach out for the walls lest I find them closing in on me. And the demons, too, were waiting . . .

"Seri! Stay close!" Weaker, yet enough to pull me back again. Next time. Next time I would escape his tether, leave him to his bloody combat, to his ending.

The two who battled were on the ground now, weapons

thrown aside. Grunting, twisting until the blue-eyed one lay atop the other. The pale one's arm outstretched was all that stayed the deadly stroke of the shining dagger.

Now, woman, witness the changing of the world. And as I watched, the pale one, the one with the empty eyes, broke into wild laughter and with a crow of triumph snatched his hand away. All the force of the battle was focused in the silver dagger that plunged into his own heart. So much blood! A fountain of it, washed into a red river by the scalding rain. The pale one's bestial exultation did not fade with his surrender. His echoing laughter was the essence of horror, and the evil thing was upon me.

"No!" I sobbed, and I crouched down in the river of blood and covered my head so I could not see the end of the world. The wind howled and the thunder roared; the hot rain fell on my back. The ground beneath me writhed and groaned. When I felt hands on my arms, I flinched and cried out.

But the hands that gathered me in were not the hands of a monster, nor of madness, but were gentle and strong. The voice that spoke in my mind was not foul, but comforting and dear. *Go back through the Gate. I cannot protect you any longer and do what I must do. I understand now, but there's little time, and I'll need everything I can muster. Do you understand?*

I looked up at the blue eyes, but I could not comprehend his meaning and could not answer.

The strong hands guided me to a veil of pulsing blackness. *Step through and wait for me, beloved. Wait for me.*

He gave me a gentle push, and I stumbled into a circular chamber of stone filled with clouds of ice and the stench of blood and death. Three lives were leaking away on the stone floor, two men and a woman. I could not say who they were.

My cold, wet knuckles pressed to my mouth, I sank to the floor among the fallen, no less wounded than they, though I did not bleed. Beyond the black veil of fire, my rescuer knelt by the empty-eyed one he had slain and yanked the dagger from the dead man's chest. But he did not sheath the bloody weapon as I expected, or wipe it clean, or plunge it in again to make sure of his evil opponent as I wanted him to do. Instead he turned the knife on himself.

"Don't! Please don't!" I needed someone left living to tell me my name.

He did not answer, but neither did he slay himself. Rather he drew the dagger across his muscled left arm with a sure and steady hand. Then he did the same to the fallen warrior, took a worn belt of woven string from his waist, and bound his arm to that of the dead man.

Numb, understanding nothing of what was happening, I whispered an echo of the words that rang clearly through the wall of fire. "Life, hold! Stay your hand. Halt your foot ere it lays another step along the Way. Grace your son once more with your voice that whispers in the deeps, with your spirit that sings in the wind, with the fire that blazes in your wondrous gifts of joy and sorrow. Fill my soul with light, and let the darkness make no stand in this place." The words became my anchor. *Wait for me*, he had said.

It seemed an eternity that I shivered in the chamber of the Gate, watching the strange drama play out, but I had nowhere to go and could not think what else to do. Beside me lay a man grievously wounded. He was ashen and sweating, each breath an agony. The rag bound to his side was soaked in blood, and I felt a great swell of grief as I gazed on him. *Tomas. My brother, Tomas.* I hugged my knees and rocked back and forth.

At last my rescuer untied the binding and stood up, lifting the pale man in his arms. He stepped through the veil of fire and laid the man on the stone paving, next to the others. The hot rain must have washed away the blood, for there was none to be seen on the one who slept so peacefully, chest rising and falling easily, rhythmically. Then the blue-eyed one came to me and laid his warm hand on my cold, wet face in a touch of such sweetness that I cried out when he took it away. He knelt beside my wounded brother and drew his silver knife across his arm once more, leaving a great bloody gash just next to a scar that shone pale against his tanned flesh. He did the same to Tomas's arm, and bound them together, and again spoke the words. "Life, hold . . . *j'den encour,* my brother."

For a long time he knelt there, eyes closed, head bowed.

When he finally loosened the woven belt, it was slowly, and his hands trembled a bit. "I've done all I can do for him," he whispered. "Not enough. I'm sorry." Then he moved to the moaning woman in black, the Zhid woman, and began again.

The clouds of terror and madness drifted away in the soft breath of healing, and before very long I understood what it was I saw. Tears rolled down my face, and I eased my brother's head into my lap, while the blue-eyed sorcerer worked to heal the two Zhid warriors.

"Seri." The word was more like a sigh than speech. Tomas's eyes had fluttered open. His breathing was easier, but he was still very pale, and his hands were like ice.

"I'm here, Tomas."

"What happened?"

"You've been wounded in a match."

"More than a match, I think, but I can't remember." His voice was so very weak.

"Don't try. It can come later." I stroked his damp hair.

"There will be no later. He told me when he was inside me. Too much damage to heal."

"You'll be fine, Tomas. I'll take you home."

He wrinkled his brow. "No, it must be now. Your pardon . . . Garlos has it. Find him and you'll be free. I'm so sorry, Seri, sorry for all of—"

"It wasn't your fault." I kissed his cold hand and held it to my breast.

His eyes were heavy, but I felt his urgency. "My son . . . he's fair. Has our looks. Intelligent like you. Stubborn. Opinionated." A faint smile graced his colorless lips. "I wanted to tell him—" His words stopped, and, for that moment, his hand crushed my fingers, as if he were grasping life itself.

"What, Tomas? What did you want to tell him?"

"—what a fine lad he is. A fine son. . . . so proud . . ."

"He'll hear it. I swear to you he will. And he'll know of his father's honor and the glory of his house."

Tomas allowed his eyelids to close and nodded his head slightly. His hand relaxed as he drifted away, his last breath soft and easy.

"Be at peace, brother," I whispered, gathering him to

my breast and rocking him gently as one would a sleeping child. The Prince had bound himself to the last of his fallen enemies, the Gate fire burned white, and the very air sang.

Once the last of the wounded Zhid lay in peaceful sleep, the Prince did not move again. He remained huddled over his knees in the center of the chamber, silhouetted against the brilliance of the Gate fire. I could not think of what to say. After a long while, he raised his head, his eyes glazed with exhaustion, and said, "I know you."

"Yes."

"When I can think again . . ."

"There's no hurry."

His chin drooped onto his chest. I could not see if he was asleep.

The white fire had burned away the shadows. The frost clouds sparkled with the brilliance of diamonds, as if the sun played hide-and-seek behind them. The walls of the Gate chamber no longer appeared somber gray, but displayed polished veins of rose quartz and green malachite, and the floor was tiled with intricate patterns of rose and pearl.

I laid Tomas out with the dignity the Champion of Leire deserved, straightening his limbs, smoothing his hair, and arranging his fine clothes to hide the terrible bloodstains. No wound was visible anywhere on his body. I placed the Champion's sword on his breast and folded his hands across the ruby-studded hilt. My father had been laid out so a lifetime ago, the gentle windings of death masking the ravages of drunken grief in the same way they now erased the remnants of Tomas's madness. From the passage I fetched the gray robes discarded by the Zhid and covered him.

These duties done, I was at a loss. I dared not leave the Prince. In his current state, a child with a wooden sword could take him down, and death and dangers still threatened from every side. That something marvelous had happened in this place was indisputable, but it seemed a fragile victory.

"Blast and perdition, what's gone on here?" Kellea stood in the arched doorway, staring at the white fire, the four prostrate forms, the unmoving Prince, and the bloodstains that streaked the lovely tiles like some macabre child's artwork. "Seri, are you all right?"

I must have looked wretched: soggy, bedraggled, and spattered with mud and blood. "I don't know." I had experienced every possible emotion in the past hours and could no longer tell one from the other.

"I felt . . . well, I could tell something had happened, so I had to come up." Kellea moved from one body to the next, peering into their still faces. A longer look at the Prince. "Where's the boy? He was determined to help. I couldn't keep him back."

"Paulo . . ." I peered through the fog, the knot in my belly eased almost as quickly as it formed. A slight body was huddled against the outer wall. The mist drifted by, revealing a thin, freckled face, a portrait of wonder as the boy stared up at the fiery Gate.

"You're all right, boy?" Kellea and I both breathed easier at his wordless nod.

"What happened here?" She turned her attention to the still forms around us. "Are they dead?"

I tried to gather words. "This one"—I laid my hand on Tomas's still form—"is the champion brought by the Zhid to be slain—my brother. They drove him to madness. To his death. The Prince couldn't save him. The three who were Zhid live, and I believe that when they wake they'll no longer be Zhid." The soaring fire filled my heart and dried my tears. "He healed them. And somehow the power of his enchantment—his healing gift—turned the Gate fire white . . . so he must have strengthened the Bridge, too, I think. He gave everything . . . and I don't know what the consequence of that might be. He may not have enough life left in him to wake again."

"He will awaken if I have anything to say in the matter. And if there is a breath of life left in him, he will remember you, Lady Seriana."

I would not have wagered an empty box that I had enough strength left to move, but when the voice boomed at us from the direction of the Gate, I grabbed the Prince's abandoned dagger and leaped up from the floor, standing between the unmoving D'Natheil and the intruder who limped out of the curtain of white fire, leaning on a wooden staff. He was a short, muscular man dressed in a shabby brown robe that gaped open to reveal a wrinkled white tunic belted over scuffed brown breeches. His curly hair and beard were brown, streaked with gray, but a youthful visage made his age quite unguessable. Nothing was at all remarkable about the man, save for his intensely blue eyes and the incredible voice that rang with wind, thunder, poetry, and wickedly prideful self-confidence. I dropped my weapon. No mistaking him. "Dassine."

CHAPTER 37

"Indeed, I am he that you name," said the man who walked out of the wall of fire. He bowed to Kellea and me, but his eyes were only for D'Natheil. "If you will excuse me . . ." He limped across the chamber and tenderly lifted the Prince's haggard face, examining it intensely. D'Natheil's eyes were open, but whatever he saw was far distant from that room. He demonstrated no awareness of Dassine, or me, or anything around us. "Oh, my dear son," murmured the sorcerer. "All I believed of you . . . How right I was." He pulled off his brown robe and laid it around the Prince's shoulders. "Rest now, and we'll care for you as you deserve."

He stood up slowly and leaned on his staff. "It will be some time before he can do anything but maintain his own existence, but I believe he will be fine."

"And he will know who he is?" I said.

"Not today"—Dassine heaved a great sigh—"nor tomorrow. Not for a goodly time. But he'll know. One day he will laugh, and ride his great horse, and grow enchanted roses for you in the middle of winter. As I told you."

"Then I'm right. He is . . . ." I could not pronounce the

name aloud, lest by the single word my hope would shatter itself on the bulwark of impossibility.

"Oh, yes. In this body lives the soul you know as Karon Lifegiver. It is neither dream nor self-delusion."

I could not speak.

"Some remnant of D'Natheil will always remain with him, but eventually it will seem neither strange nor uncomfortable. He will never look like himself, of course. His body is D'Natheil's and that will not change though it appears he has taken on something closer to his own span of years." Dassine laid a hand on the fair hair threaded with gray.

"How is this possible?"

"Mostly because of Karon himself—his strength and will and unparalleled love for life. His is a prodigious gift. Luck, too, has played its part, as have I—and you."

"Tell me."

"It's a long story."

"I can't stay for stories," said Kellea, who stood stiffly next the doorway. "Graeme—"

"Heaven and earth, the sheriff!" I said, guilty that my own desire had displaced thoughts of the injured Graeme Rowan. "Master Dassine, our good friend lies injured downstairs. . . ."

"And what has that to do with me?"

"You're a Healer, are you not?"

"I'm the most gifted Healer that lives, but I do not spend my talent lightly."

His arrogance pricked like a thorn in the shoe. "I'm well aware of the cost of healing," I said. "And I don't ask lightly. A friend is dying from fighting your war."

"Hmmph." The sorcerer wrinkled his brow. "I suppose I must look at him."

"He'll want no help given unwilling," said Kellea, snarling. "I'll care for him myself."

"No, no, you misunderstand." Dassine waved one hand dismissively. "I don't begrudge the man. But it's been my practice never to spend my power on minor matters, and I've no strength to spare today. But if your friend is so desperate a case, I'm quite willing to see to him. I'll warn you, though, young woman, that this cursed leg makes me damnably bad at dodging pursuers."

"I think I can get you there safely," said Kellea, choking on her fury. "There are only three frightened Leiran soldiers wandering about the cavern."

"I'll go then. You'll watch over him?" said Dassine to me.

"I will."

With every moment I spent near the Gate fire, I felt stronger, as if my blood drew sustenance from its glory. It was good that Karon was here.

At least an hour had passed by the time Dassine limped back into the room. "The good sheriff is resting. He will be healthier than he ever was and will very likely never appreciate it properly. The girl has stayed with him, and the ragamuffin boy." With tenderness that belied his grumbling pomposity, he felt the Prince's wrist, laid a hand on his temple, and peered into his vacant eyes. "It will still be a while until he can move. You want to know how it was done, I suppose."

"I want to know everything."

Dassine traced a circle in the air with his walking stick, and then, astonishingly, unfolded the ordinary looking limb of wood into a stool with a woven seat. He plopped himself onto it with a sigh. He didn't explain his bit of magic nor offer me any comparable accommodation.

"I was in the Chamber of the Gate on the day your husband died," he began. "The glory of that day was unimaginable, beyond hope, and the monstrous stupidity that followed was nearly our undoing. I think Exeget sent young D'Natheil to the Bridge early to destroy the evidence of his own monumental failure.

"The boy had been wild and incorrigible from the day of his birth, but intelligent, certainly, and strong-willed and courageous beyond his years. When his father and brothers died, he suddenly had demands on him: to act like a prince, to understand the war, to do those things you call magic. In their blind stupidity, the Preceptors could not see the worth of him and use his strength to encourage his best nature. As a result, D'Natheil excelled at swordplay and hand combat, but no heart developed alongside them. No wisdom or grace. Humility is a virtue we prize in our princes; Exeget, the pompous traitor, tried to beat it into him as if it was his fault he had received no teaching. When I first saw D'Natheil after my return from the Wastes, he had been forced to live out of doors for three days, unclothed in the most terrible winter weather, for refusing to bow to Exeget." Dassine's discourse was very like the spring storms that roll one after the other across the northern marches, each phrase a roiling intensity of disgust or bitterness or sorrow.

He glanced at me sharply. "You know of Exeget?"

I nodded.

"The boy preferred to shiver in his nakedness than to grovel before a fool. He hungered for war. By the time he was ten, some on the Council believed he was already a tool of the Zhid. Whatever the truth of that, the Bridge destroyed D'Natheil. When I carried him away from it, there was no soul left in him. An hour's examination told me that the last Heir of D'Arnath was never going to save his people."

"But if this was after Karon died, then how—?"

"Patience, madam!" said Dassine, rapping his staff on the floor in front of me. "The people were not told what their foolish Preceptors had done. While Avonar yet sang the triumph of the Exiles and the opening of the Gates, I sat by D'Natheil's bedside and mourned the noble line of D'Arnath, and with him, our future and yours. You see, as a result of the long years of war, we Dar'Nethi had lost ourselves. Our princes had been trained more and more strenuously in the art of war, yet the Gates had remained closed and the Bridge had grown weaker. If only the Heir was like the one who had opened the Gate, I thought. All of us had felt the power of his enchantment—the will, the glory of his life's essence. As I gazed on the deadness in D'Natheil's eyes, I wondered how those eyes would appear if the light of such a life was reflected there."

"Karon had not yet crossed the Verges," I said, dragging at the traces of the old man's story.

Dassine smiled crookedly. "It had only been three hours, three hours from exultation to despair. I was beside myself with anger, and so, there in my study, with D'Natheil half dead and the brave songs still echoing through the falling darkness, I sought through the ether for the one who had given everything to save us. Such souls do not cross the Verges quickly."

"And you found him." The wonder of it was almost unbearable.

"It wasn't difficult to identify his among the souls that traveled that night. I summoned him and told him what I wanted—to return him to life in our prince. He refused. As long as there was life in the boy, he could not supplant it, he said. And L'Ticre beckoned, as it will for any who have left their physical being behind. But I bound him to an artifact of power and told him that I would do my best to heal D'Natheil. If I was successful, then I would release Karon to go beyond the Verges. But if the Heir had been irreparably damaged as I feared, then he, Karon, must live again as the Heir of D'Arnath."

Dassine's eyes glistened with tears, and he drew a clenched fist to his breast, lost in his storytelling. "At first he would beg me to let him go. The agony of his death was real to him at every moment of every day. I chided myself that in prolonging his torment, I had come to be no better than our enemies. But I could not release him; we had no one else. And so we waited. Ten years—"

I was overwhelmed with horror. "Ten years? You made him wait for ten years between life and death?" Ten years with no body—no light, no scent, no sound, no touch of wind or rain or human hand. Only the fire. How could any man do such a thing to another?

Dassine reached out his hand for me. I recoiled, but his piercing blue eyes held me, insisting I accept his truth. "You must believe that he came to accept this half-life I gave him. As we grew to know each other, he became involved in my work and the pain of his existence receded. Karon became an extension of my mind, and, had I not come to love him as my own son, I could have been tempted to enslave him in such a way forever. We could have rivaled the Lords of Zhev'Na in our combined power. But, instead, I learned of this world and of you, and in the plan that evolved in my head, I knew you had to play a part.

"I was ready to bring him into D'Natheil after only a year. The boy could eat, and speak, and fight as he always had, but there was no thought in his speech, no moral grounding to his combat. Even so, Karon would not consider it while D'Natheil yet lived, though it would have meant release from his own captivity."

Dassine was no longer telling the story, but reliving it: the challenge, the awe at his own audacity and skill. "To pour the life essence of one man into the body of another is a deed of tremendous complexity, with immense risks and unfathomable implications. As the years passed, I devised the plan to take away all memory, so that the minimal functioning mind and the physical body could learn to work together. Over a period of months, I would carefully awaken each memory and do whatever was necessary to guide him through the difficulties of the joining. Karon consented, though I think the prospect of giving up his memories frightened him more than anything. It was you, you see. With all his being he desired to carry his memory of you beyond the Verges, and if I failed, he would be left with nothing. I promised that if we ever made the attempt, the first memory I returned would be something of you."

Dassine dropped his voice, and I had to lean closer to hear him over the flames. "Six weeks ago events caught us up. Avonar was nearing its end. D'Natheil raged at the wards that bound him to my house. Given his freedom, he would not fail to be in the thick of battle. So I released the boy to his war. I stayed close, watched, and knew I was right. He stood tall and beautiful and soulless, and he slew fifty Zhid without thought, risking death without care. He turned the tide of that night's battle, but not until he met a crafty Zhid who used a mind-destroying poison on his knife and left D'Natheil among the dying. I knew that poison . . . as I knew the Zhid who wielded it."

"You murdered him!"

Dassine did not flinch at the word. "Some would say it. But I would not change the choice I made. Karon could refuse me no longer. Had he known what I'd done . . . well, I didn't tell him. At the moment D'Natheil breathed his last, I brought Karon back in his place, erasing every memory of both minds at the same moment. Then did I receive due retribution for my sin. On that same morning of new hope, a Dulcé named Bendal came to me with the

story of the traitors' bargain with the Lords of Zhev'Na—
to trade the Heir for D'Arnath's lost weapons. They had
decided that your world was not worth saving, and that
ours could survive even without the Bridge, if we but had
a royal talisman to protect Avonar. Traitorous fools."

"So you sent him onto the Bridge before he was ready,
before he even knew who he was."

"I *had* to send him. Not to do so was to concede defeat.
The Zhid were on the verge of closing the Gates, and I
had no assurance we would ever be able to open them
again. I could not accompany him, for if he failed, the last
battle would be fought in Avonar, and my duty lay there.
But I did not believe he would fail. You still lived. Karon
taught me that the gift of the Dar'Nethi . . . the power for
sorcery that lives in us . . . is life itself. He said that you
were . . . are . . . and ever will be . . . the very essence of
his magic."

"That's why you said the answer was in him."

"That had to be it. How else could he have opened the
Gates as he did? We needed a Healer to restore the Bridge,
one who would give everything. Look at what he's
done. . . ." He waved at the three Zhid sleeping quietly on
the floor beside the curtain of white fire. "These three have
souls again."

"Why didn't you tell us what you'd done and why? If
I'd known it was Karon—"

"What would you have done differently? I know you
better than anyone in the two worlds, better even than
Karon who is blinded by his affection for you. Though I
trusted you to do all you could do, you had parted from
him in bitterness—yes, I recognized it in his story. And
Karon's tasks were difficult enough without knowing he
had two missing lives instead of only one and an angry wife
he couldn't remember."

"Will he ever remember all of it?"

Dassine stood, picked up his stool, and, with a twist of
his wrist, transformed it into his walking stick again. "It's
why he must come back with me now. I will take him back
to the beginning again and help him open the doors to his
missing lives. He must understand that D'Natheil will always be a part of him and what that might mean. He must

know that he was dead and that the longing he feels for L'Tiere is natural and not some morbid perversion. And, too, he is truly the Heir of D'Arnath, as well as the man you know. He must learn his place in both worlds. Zhid have crossed D'Arnath's Bridge for the first time in a thousand years. Our battles are not over, and whatever life he chooses, he must be a part of our struggle. We have no one else to walk the Bridge.''

Dassine brushed the fair hair from Karon's forehead and unbuckled the sword belt from his waist.

"How long?"

"A few months, a year . . . I cannot say. But he will come back to you, my lady, and he will know everything of the life you shared. I promised him.''

"I don't know whether to bless you or curse you, Dassine."

"He lives. You will bless me." He handed me Rowan's sword belt.

"Can I come with you?"

Dassine shook his head. "Impossible. Even in the presence of the Heir, the passage of the Bridge is fraught with peril. To protect Karon as he is now will take everything I can muster, and once we are in Avonar, I'll not dare leave him." The old man paused for a moment, looking at Karon with sympathy. "And too . . . these coming days will be difficult. I must lay him open like a gutted fish as I give him back himself. He will have no defenses, and I'll not expose him so completely to anyone, not even you. But from time to time when I think he's able, I'll bring him to you. If you follow my instructions, I think you could be of some assistance in his recovery."

"I suppose I must entrust him to you, then."

"As I entrusted him—and everything—to you." Dassine took my hand in his, and when he let it go again, I held a polished bit of rose quartz about the size and shape of a robin's egg. The stone was unnaturally cold. "Keep this with you. When it grows warm and glows of its own light, we will come with the next day's sunrise to whatever place you are. You will make sure the place is secure. If it's not, throw the stone into a fire, and I'll be warned."

"I'll be waiting."

"I have no doubt of it." He gestured toward my lap and held out his hand, and I relinquished the Heir's dagger that still lay in the folds of my skirt. Sticking the weapon in his own belt, he turned back to Karon who still knelt on the cold stone paving, unmoving and unseeing. "Come, my friend. It's time we took you home." Dassine placed his hand under Karon's arm, lifting him easily. Karon towered over the sorcerer, but any observer could see which one supported the other. "Farewell, Lady Seriana. You've done well."

"Take care of him."

Dassine nodded and led Karon through the veil of fire.

"J'den encour, my love," I whispered as the dark outlines faded into the white flame. I fingered the cold, pale stone. I would wait and be ready.

CHAPTER 38

As Karon and Dassine disappeared beyond the curtain of fire, I felt as if I had fallen into a well of solitude. The wall of flame still rumbled, but no other sound intruded. It was a time suspended, a time between worlds, between lives. For that moment, I had no past and no future, no place to go, no puzzle to decipher, no question to ask, no thought, no memory, no joy, no pain, nothing to hear but the quiet pulse of life that remains when the world's tide has fallen beyond its lowest ebb.

"Madam, if you please," whispered a man's voice. The tide roared back again with the hesitant pluck of my sleeve.

My heart shriveled when I turned to see the narrow face, thin lips, and gray eyes so close behind me. Though Giano's face now displayed confusion, fear, and unending curiosity instead of inhuman malice, I stepped backward. My hand slipped through my pocket and fumbled at my empty knife sheath. Dassine would not have left me in danger. He'd said these people were no longer Zhid. But that was very difficult to comprehend.

"I profoundly apologize for your discomforting, madam." His voice was soft and tentative. "These other two and I— What place is this? And what season? I cannot remember past seedling time, and the others say they lost their way in high summer, but our skin tells us that winter rules here."

"The story is very complicated"—revulsion left my tones frosty—"and I don't know how long is your part of it. It's unlikely the seasons are quite the same in our countries. You're a long way from home."

The man's long face drooped mournfully. "We guessed as much."

Had Karon truly returned this man's soul? "What is your true name?"

"Marcus. Swordmaster and Thane of Sillimar." My skin crawled as the long fingers that had murdered so deftly twisted themselves together in agitation. "Can you tell us then, madam . . . what has happened to us?"

I could summon no delicacy of feeling. "Marcus, do you know of the Zhid?"

"Aye. Of course, we all know of the Lords' demon warriors. They slaughtered my cousin and my wife's brother and left my own dear mother a madwoman, she who guarded all of Sillimar with her weavings."

"You were taken by the Zhid, Marcus. You and the others. Only in this hour has the Heir of D'Arnath freed you from your enslavement."

"Taken . . . freed . . . You mean I have been Zhid? Soulless?" I thought the man was going to be sick. I tried not to feel pleasure at his shock and horror. Pale as ivory, he reached to his right ear and felt the gold earring and then stretched his thin hands in front of him as if to judge for himself the evidence of their works. "By the stars, can it be true? No one ever returns to themselves after being Zhid, yet truly I feel myself, though strangely confused. To be freed, restored by our Prince . . . such unimportant ones as we: a swordwoman, a blacksmith, and a thane of such a small hold as Sillimar. Such a blessing and a marvel. Surely it means we've done no lasting evil." His gray eyes looked up at me, asking . . . begging . . .

His poignant hope pried open a corner of my heart. Nothing could witness more clearly to his Dar'Nethi heritage. "It is indeed a blessing and a wonder, Marcus. Unfortunately, I don't know what we're to do with you now. The Prince cannot help you for a while, and I've no idea how to get you home." Why hadn't I asked Dassine what to do with them?

"Aye. That would be a boon. To go home, that is. My wife must be a pot fearful, left for who knows how long. If she thinks me Zhid . . . ah, Vasrin, guide me on this path. . . ." The man closed his eyes and buried his face in his hands for one moment. When he had composed himself, he dropped his hands to his sides and bowed respectfully. "If it please, madam, I must tell my companions of your words."

I watched the same range of emotions play out on the faces of the bewildered man and woman as Marcus spoke to them. A short time later Marcus returned, his face gray and his fingers knotted again. His speech stumbled and faltered. "One more question, madam, if you please. The Heir—we think we must be confused. Please to tell me what is the name and lineage of the Heir who has saved us?"

"D'Natheil, third son of D'Marte, sixty-third Heir of D'Arnath."

Marcus expelled a sharp breath, then ducked his head and returned to his companions. A moment later, they all came to me.

"These are Nemyra and T'Sero," said Marcus, a thin layer of composure regained, as he presented the tall angular woman and the broad-shouldered man. "Is there aught we can do for you, madam? If your facts be true, then the matter of our return to our homes is not important. Those who would welcome us have long ago made their way to L'Tiere. I was taken in the time of Z'Ander, the twenty-seventh Heir, and these two in the time of Nikasto, the thirty-fourth Heir. Our time is long past. But if we could aid you in some way, or some other who serves our blessed prince . . ."

What to do with them? Their lives were irretrievable. But I, of all people, should understand their need to give their loss some meaning. "I suppose . . . you must learn the ways of this world, so you can be ready to serve the Prince when he's able to return. I await him, also. I can teach you what you need to know. But, for now . . . I've things to do. Come along. You might want to look around the place. See a part of your history."

As I smoothed Tomas's covering, the three removed their gold earrings and threw them into the fire, each small missile causing an eruption of gold flame as it vanished beyond the Gate. Then they helped me carry my brother out of the chamber of the Gate. The wooden doors swung shut behind us and vanished into the stone.

I broke the news of Tomas's death to his three anxious soldiers, telling them that, because of the intervention of the mysterious prisoner and the strange conversion of the three priests, the challenge to Leire and King Evard had been successfully countered anyway. Thanks to my family resemblance to Tomas, they accepted what I said. Or perhaps they would have accepted anything to remove themselves from the haunting quiet of the cavern. But they were kind and offered Marcus and the others a share in their provisions. Then I enlisted their help in the sad duties that remained.

While the soldiers set to digging at the place I selected by the lake, I sought out Kellea, Paulo, and Graeme Rowan. The sheriff was awake with easy breath and good color, and no sign of his wounds save his bloody clothing. Even the scar from D'Natheil's ill-judged blow to his head had vanished.

At sunset we laid Tomas in the frozen tundra by the lake. Before we covered him over, I took his signet ring and a lock of his hair, and I replaced his sword with a lesser one, wrapping the Champion's sword in a cloth so it could be returned to its proper owner. Tomas's soldiers built a cairn over the shallow grave so that wolves could not disturb it. At his feet we buried Baglos, face down as was the custom for traitors. In a small third grave, I placed the dark-stained burlap bag that had been tossed aside by the Zhid. The soldiers were curious, but I had used the last of my strength to bring the grisly bundle and lay it in the ground. I wept for my dear old friend, but I could not speak of him.

On the next morning we set out on the long journey home. I was the last to leave the cavern. The enchanted torches faded behind me, and when I reached the far side of the lake and turned for a final look, only a bare cliff face stood where the doorway had been. I followed the others past Tomas's resting place and down the sloping tundra.

Three days after leaving Vittoir Eirit, we camped at the ruined castle south of Yennet. On that night Dirk, the older man who commanded Tomas's soldiers, said that he and his men would leave us on the next morning. They planned to report the tragic result of the "chieftain's" challenge to the duke's aide, Captain Darzid, and give him the Champion's sword so it could be returned to King Evard.

In the quiet travel of the preceding days, I had thought a great deal about Darzid, the mysterious spider lurking at the edge of my life's web. Was he a pawn like Maceron, a victim like Jacopo, or some vile transformation more like these three poor Dar'Nethi had been? Was he pursuing sorcerers to rid our lands of them, as Maceron claimed, or was he an ally of the Zhid? None of those things seemed to fit. My instincts told me he was something different yet.

"I'll return my brother's sword to the king myself," I told Dirk. "Your duty is at Comigor. The young duke must be protected when word goes out of his father's death, and it is the faithful Comigor retainers like you, not the . . . outsiders . . . who must see to his safety. Inform the Lady Philomena that I shall come to pay my respects to her and her son as soon as I've spoken to King Evard."

The old soldier touched his forelock, approving my concern for Tomas's son. When I awoke the next morning, he and his men were gone.

At Fensbridge, Graeme Rowan, Kellea, and Paulo turned south, accompanied by Marcus, T'Sero, and Nemyra. The three Dar'Nethi would stay in my cottage until someone came to take them back across the Bridge to Avonar. Rowan and Kellea promised to see to their welfare.

Graeme Rowan hung back for a moment as the others

rode away. "You're not coming back to Dunfarrie, are you?"

"I don't belong there."

"For ten years you did. You made a place for yourself."

"That wasn't me."

"Where then?"

"I'm not sure. It depends on the pardon. If it's real, there are several possibilities. I once had dreams of the University. I might be able to live better on my knowledge of history, philosophy, and languages than I ever could on my skills at farming."

Rowan laughed with me, but we soon fell silent, thinking of Jacopo, who had made it possible for me to live in Dunfarrie.

"I'll send word of my plans," I said, then clasped his hand briefly and rode north toward Montevial.

A fortnight after the opening of the Gate, I sat in the royal palace in Montevial, awaiting word that the king would see me. My hair was clean, my fingernails free of dirt, and I was dressed in a new gown of dark green, simple but well made, bought with silver from Baglos's purse. I felt more myself than I had in ten years. The guards had demanded to see what was wrapped in the long bundle of red silk I carried, but I told them it belonged to His Majesty, and none could look on it without his leave. The king would either give his permission for me to enter with the wrapped bundle, or I would await a time when he would.

Eventually a footman escorted me into a gaudy little sitting room. Evard sat by a blazing fire despite the warmth of the late summer day. On a footstool beside him perched a dainty, fair-haired girl of eleven or twelve in a heavily embroidered red satin gown with a white ruff about the neck. As I made my curtsy, she looked up at Evard and closed her book. But he laid a hand on the child's shoulder. "This won't take long, my treasure." His eyes rested on me. "Lady Seriana, my daughter, the Princess Roxanne."

I understood the trace of gloating in the introduction. His daughter was a princess, and she could have been mine. Yet of far more importance to me was the fact that he had a living daughter, whereas I had no living son. Perhaps he understood that, too, and that's why his eyes darted away so quickly. I curtsied to the girl, who condescended to tip her head.

"Now what is it that my guards are not allowed to view? You would not slay me before my child, I think." His laugh had a decidedly anxious edge.

"I've brought you that which properly belongs to the King of Leire. Since there is no other king, it must be returned to you. I trust you will find meaning beyond the artifact itself." I laid the bundle on a polished table and unwrapped the red silk. With reverence and care, I lifted the sword in my hands and presented it to Evard.

Slowly, reluctantly, he took it from me, scanning my face for the whole of my ill tidings. When he finally spoke, his voice was quietly harsh. "How did you come by this, lady? I know of no challenge to me, and who would dare challenge him directly?"

So he didn't know. And his grief for Tomas was real. I had believed it would be so. Evard possessed little enough of love or grace, but I had never doubted his affection for my brother. My multitude of offenses had never altered it. It had produced the unconditional pardon that Tomas had requested in his desire to have me return to Comigor and that I had carried in my sleeve since my meeting with a curious Garlos an hour before. It had preserved my life, for which I had never been grateful until I saw the reflection of Karon's soul in D'Natheil's eyes.

"If Your Majesty please, I'll tell you a story," I said. "It's quite a long story, and much of it will defy reason. You may accept it or dismiss it as the fantasy of a deluded woman, as you have judged me. But if you accept it as truth, then you will learn of a danger to your kingdom that is more insidious than any Isker spy, and you will learn how your friend and champion was used and then murdered in an attempt to destroy us all. . . ."

Three hours later I left the king's chambers. I could not tell whether or not Evard gave credence to anything I'd told him. My tale was alien to everything he believed of the world. But he had neither ridiculed me nor had me arrested. My voice had always carried weight with him. That was the reason for his unrelenting fury at my rejection of him. Evard would never stop hating me, but he might listen and be wary.

On that same evening, it was proclaimed throughout the kingdom that the Duke of Comigor, the Champion of Leire, was dead, having been lured into an ambush by unknown traitors. He had died as he had lived, with honor, defending his king with his mighty sword. A day of mourning was set.

Two notes were added to the proclamation, though rarely were they announced publicly, being minor matters as they were. In gratitude for the late duke's long service to the crown, his sister, the Lady Seriana Marguerite, was restored to full citizenship, all rights and privileges of rank restored to her under a full pardon for all crimes with which she had been charged. The second note stated that an investigation into the slaying was to be carried out by His Grace's military aide, Captain Darzid of the Royal Guard. The captain was to produce an explanation of the death of the Champion six months from this day. The appointment had been my suggestion, and Evard had promised to inform me of whatever story Darzid might produce.

Our world lay mired in misery; my husband had been brutalized, my child murdered, and my brother's life twisted into horror and ended too early. Somewhere in a desert fortress, three corrupted sorcerers who called themselves the Lords of Zhev'Na sat on thrones of black stone and feasted on our grieving, and I prayed that fate or gods or destiny would give me a role to play in their ruin.

One more duty awaited me before I could settle myself to listen for Dassine's call. I bore a message for my ten-year-old nephew. And so, a few days later, my carriage rattled over the ancient cobbles that fronted sprawling, thick-walled Comigor Keep.

Midsummer was three months gone. The angle of the morning sun and the touches of gold on the barren green hills that stretched in every direction from the windswept hilltop already spoke the waning of the year. The morning air bit sharply through my light cloak, whispering of storm and blizzard and the elemental purity of northern winter.

Thirteen years had gone by since I had left Comigor to

attend Martin's judgment before the Council of Lords, thirteen years since Karon had revealed his secret in the study at Windham and I had chosen the course that had barred me from the home of my childhood and led me into love and mystery and grief. The seasons pass. As my driver rang the bell and waited for someone to answer it, I rubbed the rose-colored stone that lay cool and secret in my pocket, and I breathed deep of the sweet morning.

About the Author

Though **Carol Berg** calls Colorado her home, her roots are in Texas, in a family of teachers, musicians, and railroad men. She has a degree in mathematics from Rice University and one in computer science from the University of Colorado, but managed to squeeze in minors in English and art history along the way. She has combined a career as a software engineer with her writing, while also raising three sons. She lives with her husband at the foot of the Colorado mountains.